WRONG WAY TO HEAVEN

WRONG WAY TO HEAVEN

THE WRONG WAY SERIES

KEVIN PETTWAY

<u>Anthology</u>

Last Night at the Jolly Chicken

<u>Misplaced Mercenaries</u> by Kevin Pettway

A Good Running Away

Blow Out the Candle When You Leave

Big Damn Magic

Illusions of Decency

Heroes Kill Everyone

<u>Hettie Stormheart series</u> by Jen Bair

One Good Eye

<u>Huntress and Harvester series</u> by Jessica Raney

A Seed Once Sown

<u>Wrong Way series</u> by Kevin Pettway

Wrong Way to Heaven

Gullhome
Oldam's Temple
Icebite
Norrik
Raiders Sea
Spum Oyster River
Vikkan
Summervatn
Krysuvik
The
Badiron
Dism
Mayloc
Summer Trades
Tyrran
Knarrax
Mirrik
Gradson
Pippin
Green
Sheaf
Low
Bramland River
Wood
Rousea
Watchpost
Rousland
The Arlean
Dalm
Arlea
Steed
Sejent
N
W
E
S
Sedrios
Southen
Whique
Langit
The Paradisals
Rumfish
Port Placid
Balf

Full-color map at KevinPettway.com

As ever, I dedicate all my efforts and writing to my eternally patient and supportive wife, Lena. She is there for me when I can't be there for myself and lifts me up every day. Without her, there is no me.

CHAPTER

ONE

Accounts of the beginning vary not just between the pantheons of Andos, but within them as well. If one were to winnow away the contradictory information and distill the event to what could be agreed upon among all the mythology presented, the only thing one might be certain of is that the beginning of time was very, very loud.

Probably.

Volume One of *Thank Gods* by Kohmose Oburn

Stars salted the deepening blue while a lazy ocean breeze picked at the more stubborn city odors and lifted them away. Street sweeps wound their way through Magda's Cross, filling sacks and single-wheeled carts with horse dung. Just a half-hour prior, the roads had been filled with running, shuffling, shouting, or laughing citizens of Treaty Hill, capital city of the nation of Greenshade.

Masika straightened the gold and red linen long coat over her kaftan and made a great effort not to appear impatient. Rainn and Heron had been through a tough couple of weeks, and that wouldn't be improved by her rushing them off to the Forest Castle, last home of the Hill Fury, even if the woman was Masika's all-time most favorite hero ever.

Beside her, moody Rainn lifted his pale, tattooed face to gaze up at the raven-sized waterfowl with the soft gray feathers, faint blue swirls that matched Rainn's tattoos glowing beneath. The bird perched on the statue shoulder of the goddess Magda in the center of the five-way convergence of cobbled streets. Masika was confident that if she just kept at it, she could wear away his crabby exterior and find the shining soul beneath.

"Well, *that* certainly didn't make our lives any easier," Rainn said, as if trying to prove her thoughts wrong. "May as well lay down in front of a team of horses and end my misery now. Though it'd probably just run over my crotch and leave me alive and cockless."

Heron squawked at him, raising her black crest with a firm shake of her head.

"No, I don't think he'll be there." Rainn narrowed his eyes. "Is that why you want to do this?"

The bird lowered her head and gave Rainn a sidelong glance.

Listening to the pair bicker had yet to teach Masika how to understand Heron's squawks and purrs. Though her body language required no such advanced knowledge.

"You know," Masika offered, "we could get to the castle now and avoid having to talk our way past the guard. They're probably going to close the gate soon, and I know you hate having to talk with anyone."

"What I know is that the imp we just made a deal with is gonna murder all of us." He looked at the sky again, his expression one of profoundest disappointment. Rainn preferred less perfect weather, and the skies had been clear as cut crystal for the last week. Unfortunately for Masika, he preferred them loudly and often.

There was no way Masika was going to sleep in the city tonight with the Hill Fury's home in plain sight. "He can't murder us if we're all comfy in our castle-beds."

"What makes you think they'll let us in anyway?" Rainn grabbed the front of his dark blue vest and held it out. "I'm dressed like a

Tyrranean, Heron's likely to end up inna cage or stewpot, and in case you haven't noticed the looks you're getting, these people don't seem to have forgiven the Darrish occupation over the last four months."

In truth, Masika had noticed. Her dark Darrish skin stood out here, even at night. She stood out at home because of her status, but here it felt creepy.

"All the more reason to get to the castle." At an interested glance from a couple of dirty street toughs, Masika pulled aside her coat and rested her hand on the pommel of her slim desert sword.

The pair lowered their heads and moved on.

She let the coat fall closed again. "Egren and Greenshade parted ways on good enough terms, and we're much more likely to find friends inside than out. *And* they'll let me in because I'm the niece of Egren's Holy Emperor."

Brows knit, Rainn's reply was more growl than statement. "I'm not here to visit some shrine to the fucking Hill Fury." The blue tattoos above his hairline drew together, thunderheads colliding at his irritation.

A smile broke out across Masika's face, intensifying Rainn's glower. "Look, Sir God, if everything is really as hopeless as you seem to think it is, then there's no reason *not* to go to the castle, right? Come on. We're not getting paid by the frown, you know."

"We're not getting paid at all."

In response, Masika's sunny smile spread further, and she batted her eyelashes. "You and Heron are. Or don't you still want to go home?"

Rainn blew out a long-suffering sigh. "If I go, will you at least shut up about it?"

Looping her arm through Rainn's, Masika pulled the Andosh god of Doing Things Out-of-Doors-in-Poor-Weather along beside her. Heron spread her similarly divine wings and followed, with no more noise than a shadow in a shuttered room.

EVEN AT NIGHT, traffic around the Forest Castle grew thicker and louder. Conversely, fewer and fewer people paid them any heed. Masika entered the outer wall through a massive gatehouse and stepped into the Quarters, the two gods following. To the right of their broad thoroughfare stood the massive longhouse embassies of the Norrik kingdoms, while to their left the famous Thirteen Markets shouted and bargained amongst the intense smells of an entire world's worth of late-night cuisine. All of the Quarters rose up on a wide, rounded hill, more embassies and markets visible on all sides.

The trio, well-lit by torch and lamplight, continued west up Coach Street and up the hill to the Forest Castle itself, perched on its summit. Even at night, she could make out the greenish tint of the stonework. A thrill ran through her. She knew from books the castle walls were built of green-tinted granite, but to actually see it!

Inside the smaller castle gate soldiers stomped and drilled, ran and yelled . . . and loosed dozens of arrows into a flying water dragon, its shining and suspicious feathers glowing as if aflame. With a ground-shaking roar, the mortally injured creature popped, a soap bubble of curving claws, teeth, and anger.

The soldiers cheered, Masika stopped in her tracks, and Heron dived into the hood of Masika's coat, filling it and pushing Masika's head out the front. The size of a fully grown raven with longer legs, Heron's comfort as a roommate in Masika's clothes topped out at zero.

"You still gonna tell me we're safer here?" Rainn asked.

Eyes wide in disbelief, Masika pointed at the soldiers in green tabards with yellow trim, the opposite of the typical soldiery of Green-shade. "We couldn't be safer. Those are King Keane's Rune Swords. Like the regular Swords, but they've been taught the runecrafting magic of Morholt the Red."

"Stop dancing." Rainn crossed his arms. "They gonna give us a room and a pot or . . ."

Masika lost the rest of Rainn's question as she took off running for the two women leading the drills.

Wings flapping, Heron fluttered back to Rainn.

"Hang on there, little missy." A strapping young man in a fancier version of the Rune Swords' uniform stepped in front of Masika, one hand raised. Despite the smile on his handsome features and genial tone, his other hand stayed near his sword hilt. "You got business here?"

The grin would not come off Masika's face. "I'm Masika Oburn, niece to the Holy Emperor Khasek the Fifth, and princess of my father's house." She rocked from one foot to the other. "Are those the wives of Morholt the Red? Can I talk to them?"

His eyes roved over her weapons, noting the slim sword at her hip and the poniard affixed to her boot, as well as the hunting bow over her shoulder. He shrugged. "Sure. I'll be watching you, Masika Oburn, but just so you're aware, cause any trouble and that lot'll have you in a thousand pieces way before I can get to you to kill you myself." All this was said with a sort of amused candor that indicated this man expected no such trouble from the sixteen-year-old girl.

Masika squeaked and rushed past. The wives of Morholt the Red actually *knew* the Hill Fury. She ran over and stuck out her hand. "Uh."

Once in front of the two women in charge, Masika found herself uncharacteristically at a loss for words. She stood to one side, mouth open, feeling the heat climb up her neck and into her cheeks. What if she said something stupid and disappointed the two women before they even knew who she was?

One of the two—older, thinner, and a bit more weathered—pushed a wide-brimmed straw hat back over sun-streaked hair and studied Masika. "What?" She was Darrish, but with the olive complexion of Kos.

"Um," Masika supplied, not at all helpfully.

She waited for a full second before turning to her counterpart, a pretty Pavinn woman with black curly hair and large eyes. "You handle this? I'm gonna rip some new assholes out there and send 'em to bed without their binkies." So saying, the taller woman stalked into the midst of the Rune Swords and threw corrections and deprecations in equal measure all about her.

Masika was certain the woman was enjoying herself.

"What do you need, dear?" The second woman wore a long, dun-colored dress and a flowered brocade vest, very much in contrast to the loose linen shirt and very tight leather pants of the first.

"I—that is—did you ever meet the Hill Fury? I mean, I'm Masika. What's your name?" Masika cringed. How had she not planned for this moment with something less idiotic to say than that?

"Hello, Masika." The woman spoke low, and Masika strained to hear her words. "I'm Catlia, and that"—she pointed at the taller woman who was smacking an enormous man in the side of the head to illustrate some point—"is Romi. We have a very important job to do here, Masika, and there are too many people who want to know about the Hill Fury for us to talk to all of them. Try the library. I understand there have been quite a few books written about her over the past decade or so."

"Yes, ma'am." Masika felt herself wilt. She wondered if Rainn was watching. She hated proving him right.

"What's the kid want?" Romi returned from berating the Rune Swords and put a hand on Catlia's shoulder. "Another Hill Fury chaser?"

"Yes." Catlia's response was even more muted, a dim light struggling to be seen in Romi's brash and bright presence.

A loud thump shoved Masika forward as Romi whacked her on the back. "That works. C'mon, kid. I'll tell ya about the Fury. You're buying dinner though."

ROMI AND CATLIA sat with Masika and Rainn on the rooftop of a whitewashed wooden restaurant called the Sundown, eating a heavily spiced lamb, grain, and tomato dish with even spicier dark green leaves fried and laced throughout. The flavor was amazing, but every bit of it made Masika's eyes water and sent her sniffling into her napkin.

In the dimly lit nighttime space, occasional glints of glowing blue shone from the runic tattoos on both Rainn and Heron. Despite what the glows represented, Masika found them pretty.

"Do all Sedrians eat this way?" Masika peered at the Sedrian embassy around them. The buildings that made up the embassy compound were all white and grand, with broad patios that ran all the way around them. To the immediate north the greenish wall of the Forest Castle blocked all other view, save for the narrowest and tallest of the castle towers. A light twinkled orange on the distant top.

"Nope." Romi took a long swig of an orange drink in a tall wooden cup with an angry face carved into the side of it. Masika had one too, but the overwhelming smell of alcohol got into her nose and made her cough.

Rainn had finished his own and was working on hers now.

"Sedrians eat a lot of fish and roots. *Gotcha.*" Stabbing with her knife, Romi speared a piece of lamb and shoved it into her mouth. "Mf. Good. Lizards too. That sorta thing. Course, what I really wanna know is where the bastard that runs this place gets these drinks from. I know he don't make 'em up himself."

"How do you come to us, Masika Oburn?" After a bit of angry orange drink, Catlia found her voice. Masika no longer had to strain at all to hear her.

"Rainn and Heron are gods of the Alir," Masika answered. "I found them beneath the Fell Citadel in Tyrrane."

From her perch on the rooftop railing, Heron started, fretting and clacking her beak at Masika. For his part, Rainn merely stared into his drink, oblivious.

Catlia's eyes widened, though Romi displayed no reaction.

"Catlia and Romi are friends." Masika leaned her head toward the jittery bird and whispered, "And what's more, they were friends of the Hill Fury. We can trust them."

"I don't trust anybody," Rainn said to the face on his cup before glancing up at Masika. "Especially not *you.*"

"They're trying to get back to the Alir, but High King Oldam won't let them pass through to their home." This time Masika angled her face so she couldn't directly see Heron's distress. The goddess was afraid of everything.

"You sure they're really gods?" Romi dropped her knife on her plate and picked up her cup, waggling it in the serving boy's direction. "Mebbe the king of all the fucking Alir just don't like drop-ins."

"Do you have any idea why Oldam wouldn't let them in, Masika?" Catlia's voice held a nervous edge, much like what Masika thought Heron might sound like if she were human again. "Is that why you've come to us?"

"Not exactly." Masika organized her thoughts before continuing, "After we left the Bitter Heights, where the Alireon is, we came to Greenshade and to Treaty Hill. Rainn felt a power here that we thought might be able to help us."

"And because Li'l Masika here wants to see where the Hill Fury took her shits," Rainn added.

As grumpy as he typically was in good weather, he was even worse drunk.

"Was it us you—he—felt?" Catlia asked.

"No. It was a tiny creature painted on a pasteboard card." Masika noticed Romi and Catlia staring at each other, neither speaking. Catlia's eyes were round and scared, while Romi's mouth turned down and her gaze narrowed. What did that look mean?

She knew it sounded ridiculous, but Masika kept speaking regardless. "It was with a troll, and it wanted us to go to the Undergates and bring its maker back from the dead in return for helping us persuade High King Oldam to let Rainn and Heron return home."

When Catlia opened her mouth to speak, Romi grabbed her hand, silencing her. She turned to Masika. "And just who did this creature say created it?"

"A woman named Glauth."

The two runecrafters exchanged another glance, this time resulting in a grin from Catlia and a tight-lipped smile from Romi.

"It's not April," Catlia whispered, looking around for anyone listening in. Romi nodded.

Who was April?

"That imp only wants us to bring this Glauth woman back so he can kill her again himself." Rainn's empty wooden cup scraped across the planked surface of the table as he pushed it away from himself. "In case that makes a difference."

The smiles fell off the two runecasters' faces.

"Thought so." Having nothing left to drink, Rainn poked through the food on the table without eating anything.

"Didn't know Glauth had the heft to make herself a little friend like that." Romi chewed the inside of her lip. "But it don't look like she had the personality to keep it on her side. Least it ain't April."

April? Who was that? Was there another imp like Ild somewhere?

Catlia put a tentative hand on Romi's forearm. "But we could help them. We could get Glauth back and then we could protect her from the imp."

"Glauth is already dead." This was tenuous moral ground at the very best, but Masika had worked it through to her own satisfaction— as long as she didn't think about it too hard. "Bringing her back from the Undergates for a short visit does her no real harm, and genuine good comes of it. If we betray Ild—that's the imp's name—then Rainn and Heron are stuck here and the imp will be looking to kill us."

From the other side of the castle, a low roar rumbled through the night, followed by a soulful honk and the sounds of birds. It was the King's Menagerie, and Masika desperately wanted to see the exhibit where the Hill Fury had avoided assassination. There were *slinks*.

"You can't bring her back just to be murdered again. That's monstrous."

"No, Catlia, it ain't. From their point o' view it makes perfect sense." Romi leaned back in her chair, plucked an olive out of the bowl text to her plate, and rolled it back and forth in her fingers. "And before you ask, yeah, I could make up a fake, but this Ild is made outta the real Glauth. It'd know we were playing it soon's we walked in the damn door."

This caught Rainn's attention. "Make up a fake?"

Voice low, Catlia answered him, "It's what she does. She makes people."

"And what do you do?" Rainn gazed with unreadable intent at Catlia, who shrank away from his regard.

Romi dropped the olive back in the bowl. "She makes you forget. Works great on normal folk, kinda untested on bitty devils painted on playing cards. I wouldn't rely on it." She frowned at the table and put both hands flat in front of her.

"Right. So, here's what we're gonna do. Me and Catlia're gonna help you however we can from here, with an eye to hoodwinking the paper rat at the end of alla this. I don't know how exactly, not yet, but we'll be thinking on it while you're running around the Undergates. Bring Glauth back to us first. If whatever we come up with don't work, we're none the worse for it. But maybe we'll figger something out."

Although Rainn was silent, he did not need to speak for Masika to know he did not approve of this. She was not certain what it meant either, except she was glad to have any help she could. On the nearby railing, Heron preened her feathers, apparently satisfied with the direction of the discussion.

"Where you staying the night?" Romi asked.

"Oh, uh . . ." Masika had forgotten about that. "I don't know? I was hoping to impose on the king and queen for a room in the castle, but it's so late. Maybe we'd be better off asking at the Egren embassy."

"Horseshit." A chuckle escaped Romi. "We can do that much for you. We get done here, I'll set you up with Roland. He's the castle chamberlain. He'll get you sorted."

Masika was afraid to ask the next question, but Romi had promised. "You said you were going to tell us about the Hill Fury?"

A snort came from Rainn as he returned to his food.

"Sure." Romi opened a hand and spun it outward in invitation to Masika's questions. "Whaddya wanna know?"

"I keep hearing she was a murderer, but I can't believe that. How many people did the Hill Fury really kill?"

Romi's brows drew together, but it was Catlia who answered, "I've heard rumors of millions, but it wasn't that many. Still, it was a lot.

Like, a *lot,* a lot. But she wasn't really a killer, except in the most technical sense."

"I'd say the technical sense is the important one when you're talking about killing folk," Romi said. "Least for the folk what got killed."

Catlia flashed a brief frown at Romi, her smooth forehead wrinkling slightly. "What I mean is, every one of those deaths weighed on her. She felt them. She didn't kill unless she had to."

"I knew she was a good person." Masika spoke through a satisfied smile. The murderous intent of the Hill Fury was constant fodder for argument within her own family.

"Maybe." Romi tilted her chair back on its rear legs and gripped the table in front of her. The woman fidgeted constantly. "But she sure had need of killing a lot more people than most. That's all I'm saying. Guess that makes her a real hero."

"Not to interrupt the Followers of the Genocidal Maniac meeting" —Rainn pushed his untouched plate away—"but we still need passage to the Undergates. I heard everyone's ex-husband, Morholt, knew of a place?" A blue glow shone from the tattoos on his wrist where the shirtsleeve rode up. He pulled it back down with a gloved hand.

"What I know," Romi said with a sharp glance down at Rainn's wrist, "is that Morholt could travel to the right spot, use a particular runecrafting ritual while there, and travel between worlds. Don't know where, and don't know how. I never wanted to go to hell, so it didn't really come up."

Rainn's irritation burned Masika's cheek, and she made an effort not to look at him. It seemed as if they had made no progress here, but was that true?

"That's good information to know." She raised a fist and began ticking items off on her fingers. "We know there are passages to the Undergates, and we know there are spells to activate them. We even know runecrafters willing to help if we can find either thing." Masika ignored the darkening glower from Rainn. "We'll be staying in the Forest Castle, and someone there'll know what we should do if anyone does." Masika was not certain on this last point, but it would be so *amazing* if she could talk to the king, the actual best friend of the Hill Fury.

"I'd add that we don't really know that little demon you made the deal with'll be able to keep up his end and get your two gods back home." Romi looked uncharacteristically apologetic. "All of this might be for shit."

No, Masika was not going down that road. As crazy as it all sounded, this was going to work. She knew it. "I'm not going to sit here and do nothing just because I might fail if I try. I made a promise to Heron and Rainn, and I'm going to see it through. One thing we all can say for certain is that we will fail if we never make the effort." And Masika would not be known as the one who reunited the Alir with their wayward children if that happened.

Sadness replaced irritation on Rainn's features. "You make me *so* tired."

CHAPTER
TWO

Because Mother Love is responsible for all that is, was, and ever shall be, she is much too busy to ever be appealed to directly. Instead, the Darrish people give their pleas to the other P'tak gods, who act as intermediaries for their worshippers. This has the dual advantage of adding a personal touch from the intermediate god to any request that reaches Mother's Love's perfect ears, as well as safety. The Mother can be short-tempered at times, and a beloved family member is much less likely to be murdered for asking something stupid.

Bless Mother Love's perfect mercy.

Volume One of *Thank Gods* by Kohmose Oburn

The suite of rooms granted to Masika and her "diplomatic delegation" from Egren would have—save for the greenish walls and exotic animal sounds coming in the window—been entirely at home in the Holy Emperor's own palace. Sheer curtains drifted over dark windows and an eight-foot-wide stylized representation of Mount P'takkin, a small golden dome perched on its left shoulder, adorned the wall opposite the main entrance. Even the sheets were Egren silk, which made Masika think of home more than anything else when she flopped onto her back on the wide bed.

Eyes closed, she smiled into the darkness of her own mind. This was the reason that the capital of Greenshade was named Treaty Hill. The Rances, historically the ruling family until Princess Megan Rance became queen and married the mercenary Keane, really worked to make their diplomatic guests feel welcome.

"I hate this place."

Of course you do. Masika did not open her eyes, but her smile felt more forced than it had seconds ago. "Have you checked your room, Rainn? I asked for a basin for you so you could pour water over your head and pretend it's raining."

After a moment of silence, Masika heard Rainn's footfalls retreating to his room. Her smile widened again when she heard the tinkle of water pouring. She really was good at making others feel better about themselves.

"Doesn't work!" Rainn shouted from the adjoining room. "What's the ribbon coming out of the wall for?"

"Pull it if you want anything." The floors and interior walls were mostly wooden, though the plastering had been tinted to match the stone. "A servant will come."

The sound of Rainn pulling the silk cord and a shifting weight in the wall came next. Somewhere nearby, a bell would be ringing to alert the castle staff.

"Beer!" Rainn's shout made Masika jump. "And cheese. I'm hungry."

"They can't hear you." She moved her fingers closer to her ears. Not being able to hear Rainn sounded like an excellent idea. It was getting late, and she was exhausted from the day's events. What did he think dinner had been for?

"Then what's the point?"

Masika was saved having to answer by Heron, who flew in through the open window and landed on a bedpost. She smelled faintly of fish.

"Squawk!"

"No, I don't." Rainn's footsteps brought him back into Masika's room. "I've got beer and cheese coming. Maybe she does."

"Squawk?"

"Heron wants to know if you'd like her to throw up any fish for you."

"Allz's wounds!" Masika sat up on the bed and tried not to gag. "No! Under no circumstances is anyone to throw up anything. Why would you even ask that?"

Heron answered with a nattering of chippy, frustrated-sounding squawks.

"She says she was just being nice," Rainn said. "You don't have to get all . . ."

Turning her head away from Rainn, Masika deliberately stared into the corner of the ceiling.

"What's wrong now?" he asked.

"Why are you naked?" She didn't want to, and she felt bad for thinking it, but she couldn't help calculating in her mind how long it would take her to get to the sword belt slung over the bedpost Heron stood on, and whether she should grab it and draw or grab it, dash away, and then draw.

"Because I'm tired and there's a bed in my room?" He seemed uncomprehending of her distress. "Don't you have naked humans where you come from? Can't Darrish take off their clothes?"

Without looking, she pointed into Rainn's room. "Please stop being naked. It's inappropriate." Maybe the gods did not wear clothes in the Alireon.

A sigh was the only evidence of his irritation as he walked back around the intervening wall and clothed himself. "So explain how you got so good with that sword of yours." He was making small talk. Good. That was good. "When you took down that Host sergeant? You said your uncle trained you. Is that right?"

Masika peeked through one eye. Rainn was in his own room, and Heron stared down from her perch, judging. "My uncle Mahu trained me to use a sword."

"That's the uncle in the Veiled Breath?"

She was surprised Rainn remembered that detail. "Yes. He and his partner Sabni. Sabni is great. Uncle Mahu can be kinda grumpy, but Sabni is sweet and really knows how to use a bow."

"He teach you to hunt?"

Those were fun days. She learned relentlessly, absorbing the lessons the two men taught her as the ocean absorbs the river. Until her mother learned of it, anyway.

"He did. Mahu and Sabni are wonderful. Maybe someday you'll get to meet them."

"Hope not." Rainn reappeared in the doorway, wearing his pants but no shirt. "I can only assume that if I'm meeting warrior uncles something important's fallen off a cliff and we're totally off track." He glanced at Masika's face. "Because your uncles won't be in the Alireon. Where I wanna be. Uh, I'm sure they're great."

Was Rainn being supportive? That hardly seemed like him.

No sooner had the thought entered Masika's mind than she heard Romi's words once more. All of this would be for shit if Ild couldn't aid Rainn and Heron past the stone form of High King Oldam on the road to the Alireon. But no. Rainn sensed the imp's power. He'd know if the creature were lying.

A knock came at the door. Polite and short.

"Beer and cheese." Rainn moved around Masika's bed and opened the dark wood door.

"Ah, Rainn. So good to . . . see . . . you?"

Tennat Oburn, youngest brother to the Holy Emperor of Egren and Masika's papa stood in the doorway, taking in the half-dressed god and his daughter sitting on the bed. Mouth open, he looked from one to the other unable to land on the correct way to respond.

"Um, yes. Good." Tennat put a hand to one side of his face, smoothing the black-and-gray beard. His golden robes of state, light and airy, fluttered with his movements. "Well, Lahamila, we received your message from the Host soldiers you spoke to on your way out of Tyrrane and made haste to meet you here in case you needed any help." His glance roved the room, never lighting anywhere for long, as though fearful of being burned by anything he might see. "Do you? Need any help?"

His calling her *Lahamila*, her papa's childhood nickname for her, calmed Masika's anxiety at his reaction to Rainn. Boots thumping to the floor, Masika slid from the bed and hugged her papa hard. "I always need you, Papa."

A slender hand pushed Tennat aside, and Masika's perfect sister, Meritities, stalked into the room. "Good evening, sister. Is this how you dress for company? We're not here to join your hiking expedition." She flicked a glance at Heron, who ruffled her gray and blue-tinted feathers, before turning her attention to Rainn. "And you need to put your clothes on. Father Rain's tears may water the world, but you are not him. You're making no one damp."

Excitement at seeing her papa turned to bitterness at Meritities's appearance. She claimed to want to return home, so why was she here? Defensive anger knotted itself into a tight ball in Masika's stomach.

In the face of Meritities's cascade, Rainn blinked, stared at his feet, and shuffled back to his own room.

Meritities drifted elegantly around the room, straightening everything Masika had touched.

"The shirt enough or you offended by feet too?" Rainn reentered buttoning his gray shirt, his pale feet glowing white against the dark red rug at the entryway.

"It may be meaningless to you," Meritities stated, leaning her beautiful neck backward to look down her nose at the taller god, "but deflowered my sister's value to the empire is negligible. Unless you intend to marry her?"

"Deflowered?" Rainn's face alternated between Meritities cool disdain and Masika's flaring embarrassment. "Her?" He pointed to Masika, and his face screwed up as if discovering a mass of pubic hair stuck to the inside of his favorite beer cup. "Don't be ridiculous. She's *human*."

Heron's squawk came across both haughty and amused.

Despite feeling insulted, Masika's opinion mirrored Rainn's. A god he might be, with the right amount of muscles and a ruggedly handsome face, but the instant he opened his mouth Rainn became the least attractive individual Masika knew. Except for her sister.

Before Meritities could contemplate a reply, a second knock came at the door. Rainn returned to the entrance and opened it, taking a pair of silver trays and leaving instructions for his beer and cheese.

"Here," he said, handing one of the trays to Masika. "I guess when you ring at night you get hot washcloths and these little cakes. We gotta keep our energy up for all the deflowering."

"Is there any way we can stop talking about this?" Masika set the tray on the bed and stood next to her papa. "Papa?"

"Meritities, stop being cruel to your sister. It's unbecoming."

Eyes flashing, Meritities's head snapped around to glare at her papa. For an instant, Masika saw her sister's infamous poise fracture, red-hot resentment shining through the cracks before she reasserted control over herself.

"*Shadows of the Alir*! Have you tried this cake? Does everyone get to eat like this or only your gods?" Rainn finished shoving the small dome-shaped cake into his face and waited an entire second before snatching its mate from Masika's tray.

"What have I missed? Why did your journey to the Alireon not work?" asked Tennat Oburn.

"After he and Heron were turned away by High King Oldam," answered Masika, "Rainn detected a power in Treaty Hill that could send him home. It was an imp looking for heroes to journey to the Undergates and return its former master. We impressed it enough to receive the job in exchange for a promise of aid at its completion, and now we are searching for a passageway between here and the Undergates, like the one used by Morholt the Red and his sister."

"These gods should be returned to the Andosh people." Cool and elegant once again, Meritities's words sounded seductively reasonable, and blew right past everything Masika had just said. "The Andosh are theirs, and they will help them more than we can hope to. This *mission* is frivolous and distracting. Masika has duties back home that are being left unfulfilled."

Her papa's hand slid over Masika's shoulder and gripped it, smothering her acidic reply. A screaming match with a bitter Meritities would do no one any good.

Punching her in the face might though.

"I have another thought," Tennat answered. "We already know the Alir's response. The Andosh can do no better than Rainn and Heron themselves. Instead, we will do as the penitent always have. We shall conduct a pilgrimage to Mount P'takkin."

"*Papa.*" Meritities clutched the chest of drawers' countertop, though it was unclear if she was holding herself up or holding herself back. "You're discussing blasphemy. The feet of the Alir are a desecration in the House of the Gods."

But it made perfect sense. Masika felt a trill of excitement run through her, her previous exhaustion long forgotten. "You said it yourself, Meri. We can't hope to persuade the Alir because they aren't our gods. So, we go to our gods instead. No one is more likely to know how to travel to the Undergates than Egren the Judge or Denari Clear-Eyed."

"I think the girl with the pole up her butt might be right here." Rainn indicated a thunderously scowling Meritities. He bowed ever so slightly. "No offense. I'm sure it's a nice pole. But the Alir and the P'tak have never been friendly."

"I disagree." Tennat lifted his hand from Masika's shoulder to his own bearded chin and slowly paced the room. "We cannot set foot in the House of the Gods if they do not wish it; therefore, if it happens, it must be with their blessing. It would require a miracle to get there at all, given that the peak is unscalable." He scrutinized Masika. "Miracles will be your job, clever daughter."

Her excitement thudded into her gut, a falling bird made of lead. As if it were not enough to set the responsibility of impossible feats solely on Masika's shoulders, her papa had to call her the clever one right in front of Meritities, who prized her own cleverness above all others.

As if reading her mind, Merities's heated gaze slid from Rainn to Masika, settling in one place and scorching Masika's cheek.

"Papa," Merities said, her voice utterly sensible despite the enraged tempest Masika knew swirled and crashed behind it, "even if you succeed, you will be an outcast at best and executed at worst. The family will be ruined, and you will be dead. Is that what you want?"

Of course. Merities *would* be the most fretful for how this might make the family look.

"Not if we're successful, child. Do you think the Holy Emperor would condemn those whom Mother Love had just blessed?" Tennat cupped his oldest daughter's jaw in one hand. "Meri, your concern is a blessing too. But consider how we might appear if we are not all dashed to the rocks. We will have rendered great service to all the Andosh kingdoms at no real cost to ourselves, the very definition of a diplomatic coup. The Holy Emperor will be free to ask anything he wishes in return."

"And the rivalry between the gods of the north and the gods of the east?" Masika did not really want to ask the question, but she also didn't want to have to lead the climb up an unclimbable mountain.

Tennat flashed a canny grin, his pointed black and white beard lending him a devilish air. "I'm counting on it. What better inducement for the P'tak to give us aid than that the Alir do not wish it?"

"Then that's what we'll do." Masika put her hands on her hips and tried to stand as if she were not jittery at all. "We'll head to Mount P'takkin and petition the gods to help us return Rainn and Heron to the Alireon."

"I cannot be a part of this nonsense." In a perfectly dignified and serene boil, Merities stalked to the door of the chamber and opened it. "Papa, you are an old man. Youthful idiocy does not become you. I'll arrange a room for you with Chamberlain Roland to give you a place to rest from your more foolish daughter's conniving. Good evening."

She shut the door behind her.

"I'm not old," Tennat said.

"That one's a ray of sunshine." Rainn frowned while he searched both trays for cake crumbs. "And I mean that in the worst possible way."

"Papa." A new idea formed, and Masika brightened. "I imagine it would be rude for the youngest brother to the Holy Emperor, and his chief diplomat besides, to visit the castle of the king of Greenshade without at least saying hello."

"It would indeed. Why do you ask, my dear?"

"Please introduce me to King Keane. Papa, please. He was the Hilly Fury's best friend! I won't be a pest. He can tell me anything he wants. I'll barely talk at all." Masika's jitters had turned to thrilled trembling. She could not have asked for a more perfect circumstance than this.

"Hmph." Rainn slouched dispiritedly back to his own room. "Two weeks of Hill Fury talk was enough for me. Come get me when my tray shows up."

For a moment Tennat appeared as if he might argue. But Masika knew just how to melt the man's heart with a soulful look and a wistful turn of her head, and in the end, he lifted his arms in defeat and blew out a sigh, having never even mounted a defense.

"Very well, my Lahamila. Tomorrow will be for diplomacy, and the following morning will be for adventure."

She stood on her tiptoes and threw her arms around him. Surmounting an unassailable mountainside to defile the gods' house with the presence of rival deities no longer seemed so impossible. Or rather, it did, but it no longer seemed quite as *important*.

She was going to meet the Hill Fury's actual friend.

For the third time, a knock sounded from the door.

Rainn ran through, bulling past Masika and her papa. He stopped in front of the door, composed himself, and opened it. On the other side, a young kitchen maid lifted a tray with a large wedge of orange-yellow cheese, a similarly sized loaf of black bread, and a perspiring clay jug of beer.

"Your refreshments, sir?"

The tray whisked out of her hands, and Rainn retreated back to his room. "Good night! Everyone can shut the hell up now and let a god enjoy his meal without talk of dead murderer-women."

The maid's brow rose, betraying her apprehension.

"Fear not, young one." Tennat smiled and the creases at his eyes crinkled warmly. "I've only met the unfortunate fellow twice, but I can assure you his comments have nothing to do with you. He is simply a bit of an asshole."

CHAPTER

THREE

Everyone knows the story of Ahmen and Dedi, the twin sons of Immortal Queen Nefret and Egren the Judge, who together ruled as the nation of Egren's first Emperors. The common belief is that when Dedi transformed a woman both brothers were pursuing into a housecat to prevent either brother suffering jealousy for the other, that this was the end of the disagreement. My research shows this was not the case. In fact, the more hotheaded Ahmen spent the next several years tracking down every chef in the country who made Dedi's favorite dessert, (a chocolate-orange tart made of a very specific strain of red citrus) and putting them all to the sword as revenge. For good measure he burned all the red citrus trees as well.

To date, Ahmen and Dedi have enjoyed the most harmonious relationship of any imperial siblings in Egren's history.

Volume One of *Thank Gods* by Kohmose Oburn

Struggling for control, Merietities stalked away from her sister's room in the Forest Castle. This could not be happening. All her life Masika's thoughtless collisions with the love, fulfillments, and plans that Merietities worked so hard to achieve collectively made her life a continuous uphill struggle. And now that she finally rounded the bend, her final objective in sight, Masika threatened to crash into her once more and bring it all down.

Mother Love endure.

Thankfully most of the staff were abed by now, and the castle halls stretched, voiceless and lonely, with nothing more than the occasional torch and whispering breeze to bear witness to her misery.

No. Such reactions were the refuge of children and simpletons. Meritities straightened her back and stiffened her resolve. At twenty-three no woman in the empire held greater favor with the holy emperor or his son the divine prince than Meritities. True, Empress Khadiga stared down her nose with distaste every time Meritities entered a room, but the empress's long life dimmed just as did her elderly husband's, and her opinion mattered less than his anyway.

Divine Prince Majada was only twelve years old. He would require a steady wife upon the imminent death of his dottering parents, and who was better placed with the family than she?

Unless, that was, Masika brought eternal and crushing shame to the Oburn family name with her idiotic plan and destroyed Meritities's dreams forever.

Think. Meritities went nowhere without resources. What did she have here?

Ambassador Pahnout presided over the Egren embassy in Treaty Hill. Meritities met him two years ago at a diplomatic dinner hosted by the ruler of Greenshade, War King Keane Rance. Ambassador Pahnout boasted most of a century behind his overtight belt and was of the generation that did not believe that women belonged in politics. While this alone might prevent him from helping Meritities, he held a reputation as a court gossip, and this made him vulnerable to her particular brand of charm.

Though charm might not be exactly the right word for it.

Meritities collected Nebet, her hulking bodyguard, from the foreign military billet outside the castle wall and headed through the lamplit streets for the Egren embassy, almost opposite the main gate. At night the collected embassies along Diplomatic Way brooded, shadowy and sinister, watching each other—and watching her.

No one approached Mer012ities as she strode, fast paced and stiff, along the cobbled path. Likely that had something to do with the unseen aura of menace radiating from Nebet that pushed people from the street in front of them. His fists curled up reflexively whenever anyone got too close, though that never lasted long.

With a short sword strapped to either thigh and a dull golden breastplate over thick layered muscles, the man looked more like a professional killer than a bodyguard. He looked like death.

He could not be more perfect if she had bred him on a battlefield.

"Nebet, how would you handle Masika if she were about to destroy your family and dash your chances of ruling the empire?"

The huge man furrowed his brow, but never took his eyes from the people ahead of them, a wolf among rabbits, searching for threats.

Or prey.

"I would cut off her head while she slept." The answer was delivered matter-of-factly, with no more consideration than one might have given to stepping on an ant in the larder.

"Really?" Meritities made a mental note never to leave the brute alone with her sister. "In her sleep?"

Nebet grunted affirmative. "Mahu taught her the sword. I would defeat her, but a smart soldier only fights when he must."

Amused, Meritities watched a young couple stumble drunkenly off the cobbles ahead of Nebet, their eyes wide and steps shaking. "I suppose you would know best. But she's still my sister. Killing her isn't really an option."

"What help do you expect to find from Ambassador Pahnout?" As he spoke, Nebet jutted a square jaw at the couple, whom he appeared to think were not moving fast enough.

"I'm not certain." Meritities pondered the question. "Perhaps a way to ship Masika home without her Alir charges? That seems like a thing he would be able to do."

With a shrug, Nebet grunted again.

Meritities's stride gained length and grace as she passed the

Verranese embassy. A pair of duty guards observed her and scowled at Nebet. Her slender skirted gown of expensive silks and short, red and gold jacket marked her as a noble of Egren. By displaying her superiority to the rabble of Verran, she represented all Egren as well. She barely thought about it, her control and poise came as naturally as her scorn, which her mother said she mastered before breathing.

Common Verranese soldiery should not be permitted to look upon her at all, though, other than letting Nebet off his chain, her imagination failed to devise a proper resolution to the problem. It probably was not worth a war with Verran.

Diplomatic Way led between the embassy of Kos and a recreation of the Colossus of Ippo, glaring down on the street as if it could burn the cobbles with its loathing. The towering statue's eyes glowed with the firelight kept ablaze in its head. Behind it, Imperial Park provided a place for the indolent nobles of Treaty Hill to picnic by day, and a public toilet for the drunkest of the same by night.

"Oh, thank the hounds." Meritities felt the anxiety fall away when she rounded the great statue and finally saw Egren's embassy. Constructed in an identical style to the Holy Palace of Egren, where Meritities spent much of her time, just the sight of it was enough to calm her nerves.

"Wait in the Landed Halls." Meritities held an arm out to the right toward the nobles' portion of the building, much smaller than the Holy Palace back home. Though he hardly looked it, Nebet's official station allowed him such amenities. "Get something to eat but be quick. There may be more stops after this one."

Suspicious eyes narrowed at the embassy guards, Nebet skulked off with obvious reluctance. As far as enormous murderous thugs went, Nebet was in a class all his own.

Ambassador Pahnout kept her waiting exactly two minutes, as tradition dictated. Any less would have conveyed servility, and word of Pahnout's pride stretched even further than his voluminous shadow. Any longer conveyed disrespect, an unhealthy attitude to take with a niece of the Holy Emperor. And being ousted from bed could not have improved his mood—or alacrity.

She would teach him better.

"Princess Meritities. My humble offices shine in the light of your presence." The honeyed words dripped from Pahnout's jowly face without pleasure. He reclined further into the gleaming mahogany chair at the end of what could easily be mistaken for a throne room, a hint of a scowl on his face. "What brings this honor on my person?"

A pair of functionaries scribbled away under elaborate candlesticks in one corner of the ostentatious room. Gold and red cloth covered the walls and leant the space a further regal air, while long windows, three feet long but no more than four inches high, lined the north and south walls, providing a breeze but no means of entry.

"My business here requires privacy, Ambassador." Meritities stood straight and held Pahnout's gaze.

The two functionaries continued to take notes, unconcerned that a princess of Egren requested their dismissal.

"All proceedings here are the purview of the government of Egren, princess. They may remain." His tone was that of a starving man roused from his meal by a blood-covered dog running across the dinner table and squatting in his plate.

Not that he looked as if he had ever been hungry before.

"Very well." Inwardly Meritities sighed. Pahnout's attitude wearied her. Not only did he judge her for being a woman, he also presumed his superiority over her privileged upbringing. Better men than he had learned the folly of that mistake. "But given that the situation involves the family of the Holy Emperor, and your life should be forfeit if word of it got out—"

Pahnout snapped his fingers, cutting Meritities off midsentence. The two functionaries rolled up their papers, rose, and quitted the room without a sound.

"And your listener, as well." Though ridiculous that this man forced her to specify hidden ears as well as present ones, Meritities welcomed the opportunity to display her knowledge of Pahnout's private workings to his face. Her papa taught her well on the obvious and the secret workings of Egren embassies.

A grimace accompanied Pahnout's gesture toward a wall covered in a golden relief of the Sermon of Kohoc and the Boy from the Mountain. After a moment, Merities heard the faint sound of a door closing through the wall.

"This is what comes of children playing at adult games." Pahnout punctuated his statement with a small sigh, all pretense of civility gone. "Say your piece and leave, that I may get on with actual matters of state."

Rather than rising in anger, Merities settled into a cool thoughtfulness. Despite his smug self-assuredness, Pahnout had unknowingly stepped into her arena. She studied him, made a few decisions, and plotted her strategy.

"There is a citizen of Egren in Treaty Hill I would have taken custody of and sent back home. Could you aid me in this?" While almost certain to result in a refusal, by starting straight with Pahnout, Merities showed him respect and removed his first brick of defense —umbrage—from his wall of obstinacy.

"No. Shall I call someone to show you out?" The pig smiled as he spoke. "I am aware unfamiliar corridors can become taxing to a young woman's brain."

Merities smothered a smile of her own. "I see. I was aware of your lack of authority, but I'd hoped experience and creativity would make up for it. Must have been my woman's brain leaving me short."

A red flush crept up around the folds of Pahnout's neck, and his eyes narrowed dangerously. "In point of fact, I have no authority to take anyone into custody outside of these walls. Good news for your quarry but less so for you." He gripped the arms of his oversized chair in a manner that might have appeared threatening in a younger and fitter man. "Does the Sarach know what you're up to, I wonder?"

"Papa?" Merities purred. "In fact, I am here at the request of Prince Tennat, Sarach of the Divine Grainlands and brother to the Holy Emperor himself. As the request is delicate, I had intended to leave him out of it, in that the knowledge of his involvement increases your exposure to harm both here and at home immeasurably."

The thick brow furrowed.

Merities continued, "But then, your needless disrespect to a *member of the imperial family* gives me little reason to except you from danger after I have had my use of you. Woman though I may be, I am favored in my uncle's court, and he will not find this encounter as amusing as you seem to believe he will. You have been away from the palace too long." Merities paused a moment, savoring her next words. "But then this is what comes of puffed-up has-beens playing at the games of their betters."

Pahnout opened his mouth to shout and closed it again. His jaw worked back and forth as Merities let him consider his options. A too-quick smile replaced his previous scowl, and she knew she had won.

"But of course. No need to say more. *Please* don't say more." The change in Pahnout from arrogant snob to sycophantic lickspittle brought a genuine smile to Merities's lips. "I cannot do as you ask myself, but I know how it can be accomplished."

"Of course, Ambassador." Merities let her gaze linger on the golden relief where the listener recently hid. "Your reputation must be maintained. It is, after all, the best part of you."

"I have allies on the Great Council of Greenshade." Ambassador Pahnout's hands dithered in his lap and sweat broke out across his round face. "Important allies. They can have this enemy of the state taken into hand and held until an official ship of Egren can be dispatched to return them home in two days, three at the most. This incident never need return on me"—his eyes flashed up to Merities's —"or anyone else."

What an ass.

"That will be sufficient, Ambassador Pahnout. I'll provide sealed instructions for your ally, and you should work to ensure that they are followed to the letter." Merities let her countenance grow cold. "If this person is harmed in any way, I'll hold you personally responsible, as will the empire."

Pahnout tried to smile and released a nervous titter. "Of course, of course. Let me fetch you paper and quill. Would you like a glass of wine?"

CHAPTER

FOUR

Owing to her excessive wheedling the night before, Masika's papa agreed to allow her to sit in on his audience with the king. She found herself thrilled beyond reasoning to actually meet, or even see across the room, the best friend of the Hill Fury. Unfortunately, the meeting between Tennat Oburn, Egren's top diplomat, and King Keane of Greenshade was bound to be considered highly secure by policy, and no one who did not need to be in the room was allowed. After a bit of discussion, a reasonable compromise was found and Masika found herself in Queen Megan's personal audience hall, meeting privately with not just the queen, but Royal Officer Baroness Roselle Stonewall as well. This was so much better than just watching her papa talk to the king.

"Your Grace, Lady Stonewall, I present Princess Masika Oburn of Egren, daughter of Prince Tennat Oburn and niece to Holy Emperor Khasek the fifth."

After making introductions, the tall and serious chamberlain bowed and backed out of the small room, closing the carved wooden door shut behind him.

Tall arched windows spilled light into the cozy chamber and set the flowers beneath them aglow in brilliant blues and yellows. A cool breeze from well above the city filled the space with clean ocean air.

Masika curtsied in the Andosh tradition, holding herself at its nadir, her eyes downcast.

"I am pleased to meet an ally to Greenshade from the land of ancient wisdoms." The queen smiled down on Masika from a cushioned chair carved from a single piece of silvery-white marble. "Was your stay restful?"

"I slept as if in the house of Mother Love herself," Masika answered. She straightened and clasped her hands in front of herself, as her papa had instructed. Holding her own hands also helped prevent her from flying apart from excitement.

"Well-mannered and pretty. I can see why my son-in-law insisted you be allowed an audience." Baroness Stonewall inclined her head toward Masika.

Of course. Baroness Stonewall was previously Baroness Tralgar, but had married the current chamberlain's father, Secreed Stonewall. Roland, Secreed's son and the current chamberlain, was both the man who introduced her and the one her papa made the arrangements with.

"I thought Roland had set his cap for Lady Whitforth." Queen

Megan cut a knowing glance at the baroness and tucked a wavey tress behind one delicate ear. "Or am I behind on my royal gossip?"

"Honestly, Your Grace, I can't keep up." Baroness Stonewall extended her hands and sighed. "At his age you'd think he'd be showing signs of slowing down. Or possibly settling down."

"I'm beginning to think the man is actually your child, Roselle, and not Secreed's." Megan's lip curled up on one side.

"Ah-*hem*." The baroness indicated Masika with her eyes.

"Goodness!" Queen Megan stood from her chair and stepped off the small dais to the floor. She went to Masika and took both her hands. "How thoughtless of us. Nattering on while you stand and wait. What can Greenshade do for the daughter of Tennat Oburn?"

The queen's hands were soft and warm. There was a strength underlying them, as of any mother who had kept her children fed, clothed, and alive by force of arm and will. Except in Queen Megan's case, that extended past her family to all Greenshade, and she had not had an easy time of it.

Masika looked down into the queen's large brown eyes and giggled, turning her head. The woman was too real, too important, too *beautiful* to stare at this close. Masika's head filled with the scent of flowers.

"Um, I'm . . . um." Her face burned. She had precious little experience with shyness. Even her uncle the Holy Emperor elicited no such reactions from her. As a rule Masika never found herself afraid of anything, except the possibility of disappointing someone important to her.

Glances crossed the air between the queen and the baroness. Queen Megan released Masika's hands, and Baroness Roselle guided the young woman by the shoulders around the gleaming stone chair and through an open archway behind. The smaller room jutted from the tower, one half of it covered with tiny paned windows behind a cushioned bench that followed the wall's circuit.

"Sit down, dear," the baroness instructed, pressing down on Masika's shoulders until she sat at one end of the curved bench. Roselle settled next to her, while the queen sat opposite and leaned over a glossy oval table and poured—no. The Queen of Greenshade was pouring tea for the three of them.

For Masika.

She giggled again.

The baroness conjured a flask from her fitted dark blue dress and tipped its contents into Masika's cup. A smell of sweet fire rode the tea's steam.

"Drink this"—the baroness stirred the cup and handed it to Masika—"and we'll start again."

The tea tasted of rich alcohol, honey, and lemon with a mild earthy bitterness beneath it all. If she had known drinking could be this wonderful, Masika might have taken it up ages ago.

Emptied, the artfully decorated teacup clicked against the saucer when Masika set it down. While her cheeks still burned, the embarrassed shyness had evaporated.

"That was delicious." Masika could feel a grin spreading across her face of its own accord. "Did the Hill Fury drink that too?"

"No." The queen gave a curious little smile and sat, back straight with her own cup in both hands in front of her. "She was more for tavern ales and cheap wine. This would have been too fussy for her."

Masika grinned and inclined her head to Baroness Roselle. "I'm in the castle, drinking with the queen, talking about the Hill Fury." The best day in the world continued to unfold before her, rolling out vast expanses of possibility, green hills of camaraderie and belonging. Before she left here, she would know the Hill Fury as well as any of her best friends.

She might even consider herself to be one of those friends.

"Is that why you're here?" Suspicion crept into Baroness Roselle's voice. "Did you seek an audience with royalty to satisfy your curiosity about a dead woman?"

Barred doors clanged shut in Masika's brain, and terror that she had already squandered her opportunity froze it in place. The worst day in the world dropped her into darkness, where the Hill Fury, who certainly would have hated her had she been alive, could now forget she ever existed.

Through the glass, the call of a hoop gull filtered into the silent room. Tears filled Masika's eyes. She had never felt so out of control of her own emotions. What was in that flask?

"I'm sorry." Masika stared down at the red whorls in the glossy table. "I didn't mean to make anyone angry. I just . . . The Hill Fury is my hero. She was so amazing, I wanted to know about her. I wanted to be like her. And you actually *knew* her. I didn't think. Please don't tell my dad I insulted you."

"Young lady"—Baroness Roselle set her own cup down and spoke out of sight of Masika's downward gaze—"the queen is not here to answer your questions. You have a responsibility as a family member of the Holy Emperor to conduct yourself with respect and—"

"Oh, Roselle, what could it hurt?" Queen Megan reached over and patted Baroness Roselle on the knee. "And before you start, I already know what you're going to say: The world is filled with silly children worshipping Sarah. If we bend to this one, we'll have to bend to them all."

"No, Your Grace. I was going to say—"

"But we don't." The queen continued as if the older baroness had said nothing. "I am the queen, and I am allowed to play favorites. Who knows? This child may yet grow up to become the next hero of the land. We've both seen far more improbable things happen in our lifetimes."

Baroness Roselle rolled her eyes and smiled, then focused on Masika. "What would you like to know?"

Although Masika's brain continued to flail in its awestruck mire, her mouth fully disengaged and ran away with the baroness's opening.

"How old was the Hill Fury the first time she saved Greenshade? Was she the daughter of a powerful sorcerer and a god? When did the Anger Under the Mountain first become scared of her? Did she have to battle challengers all the time to prove she was the best swordswoman in the world? Was she destroying the Temple of the Sky from the inside when they named her the Pilgrim Handmaiden? Do you think she would've liked me?"

"Stop." Queen Megan held up a hand and cut her eyes at the

smirking baroness. "First, she hated all that Hill Fury, Pilgrim Handmaiden nonsense. She would have wanted you to call her Sarah."

The next few things Queen Megan said were lost to Masika. Only those closest to the Hill Fury could have called her by her name. Only the very closest of all.

Sarah.

". . . who her parents might have been."

Masika found the queen's voice again and listened, enraptured. She needed to pay perfect attention. Every detail would be important if Masika wanted to truly follow in Sarah's footsteps.

"Was Angrim ever afraid of her? I suppose he was at the end." Queen Megan's attention left the room, sifting back through time. "He tried several times to recruit her to his side, as he had Queen Jasmayre. But Sarah was a tougher sell than that."

Queen Jasmayre of Tyrrane had treated Masika with respect and kindness when they met a month ago. That was when Masika discovered Heron and Rainn in Angrim's chambers below the Fell Citadel. It was hard to imagine that poised, thoughtful woman battling the Hill— battling *Sarah* with steel and magic.

"As for challengers . . . Roselle, do you recall anyone ever challenging Sarah to a duel?"

The baroness shifted and tapped her chin. "No, I don't think so. The king told me about a mercenary who provoked her once, but by the time she got to us, most everyone was already afraid of her."

"That's how I remember it as well." Queen Megan nodded her agreement. "What was the other question?"

"Was she a secret saboteur in the Temple of the Sky," Baroness Roselle provided.

"Oh. Well, sort of." The queen tapped her chin. "She took their help until she realized they were sort of crazy, then she smashed them. The king's been dismantling the temple ever since, but they never really recovered from their earthly representative flinging their general and all his knights to their doom." Queen Megan put her hands in her lap and tilted her head to one side.

"And yes. I believe she would have liked you very much."

Another giggle bubbled up from Masika's throat.

"But now you must return the favor." The queen's intensity changed as she leaned in ever so slightly. "Tell me how Mahu and Sabni are doing. I haven't seen them since Prince Volker's wedding."

The request caught Masika unawares. "You know Uncle Mahu?"

"The queen knows your uncle and his partner quite well, my dear." Baroness Roselle refilled the teacups as she spoke, neglecting the flask this go-round. "While she was already an accomplished archer on the pitch, Sabni taught her grace to use a bow in actual combat. My queen is quite the formidable adversary herself."

Masika's mouth fell open as she stared at the queen. That had never been part of the stories.

"Are they still traveling with the young witch?" Queen Megan asked. "Ameli?"

While Masika had never met Ameli, she had heard of the heartbroken sorceress from the pirate islands of the far west. "I believe the three of them are living in a village somewhere in the south of Egren. Uncle Mahu has taken up farming, and Sabni is the local priest."

Queen Megan laughed. "That sounds about right. Now, we are aware of your mission to restore two of the Alir to their home," Queen Megan said. "What do you intend to do next?"

Masika considered how much she should reveal. Whether or not the queen and baroness were actual allies was uncertain, but they were not enemies. In the end Masika went with her gut.

"There is a being who has volunteered to help us if we can fetch its master from the Undergates. We'll go to Mount P'takkin and petition the Darrish gods for help traveling there and back. There's no greater source of wisdom in all the world. If the P'tak cannot help us, we cannot be helped."

Queen Megan shifted her stare to the baroness, who returned it before shrugging.

"It's your decision, ma'am, but I suppose I agree." The hint of a smile played around the baroness's mouth. "As if it would matter. I'm clearly outvoted by both you and the apparent wishes of Sarah."

What was this about? The meeting had so far been a stormwater event for Masika, joyfully cresting the tallest waves before falling back into the anxiety of their troughs. She could fight and run and climb as well as any man she knew, but this was going to kill her.

The noise of a lock being opened in a lacquered wooden box on the queen's lap reclaimed Masika's jittery attention. Where had that even come from?

"Romi visited us this morning"—Queen Megan said as she opened the long and narrow lid—"and dropped off a couple of things for me to give to you if I approved. She seems to think that your mission to Mount P'takkin is important enough for this."

In Masika's estimation, Romi and Catlia had not given a fig about returning Heron and Rainn to their home, but they *had* been extremely interested in the return of their friend Glauth from the Undergates. Masika's interest in what might be in that box outweighed any consideration of speaking to that, however.

"Apparently the queen's schedule is open reading to anyone with an interest." Baroness Roselle shook her head and frowned. "I think I'll have a conversation with Roland about that."

"Let it go, Roselle." The queen lifted a newly forged sword out of the box. "You know you can't keep anything secret in a castle." She handed the blade to Masika. "I believe Romi intended this for your god-friend."

The blade was long and a bit heavy for Masika's liking, though the balance was exceptional. It would turn like a dream. The fuller was covered with runes impressed into the shining steel, and she noticed that there were more, set into bronze rings that divided the grip into man-sized fingerholds.

"According to Romi, this sword is called Forbryttan, and cannot be broken or dulled. It was made recently by one of the king's own Rune Swords." The queen reached back into the box.

"That means it's worth more than all the swords in Egren," Baroness Roselle said. "So take care of it, and mention it the next time you talk to your holy uncle."

"And this"—Queen Megan reached out with a piece of jewelry that dangled with a bit of fine chain—"is for you. Put the bracelet on your wrist and the rings on your second and third fingers. The chains connect everything together."

Runes ran in circles around both the bangle and the two rings, some of which moved. She put them on, and her vision went swimmy. Masika put a calloused hand on the window behind her.

"It only takes a moment to get used to." Already Masika's vision was returning enough to see the queen's warm smile. "I tried it on earlier. It's called Inlittan, and it's supposed to help you see? Or see things you couldn't before? Maybe read small print? I'm not sure, but Romi assured me it would be helpful."

The inside of the room threatened the contents of Masika's stomach, so she stared out the windowpanes instead. It helped. She could, in fact, make out more of the distant citizenry going about their lives far below than she should have. The glare of the sun did not hurt, and everything looked closer the longer she studied it.

A pair of Swords meandered down a busy street, waving and laughing to a street vendor selling roasted fowl. A dirty child cried and held up its arms to its equally dusty mother, who lifted it up and hugged it tight. A trio of washerwomen shooed away a young man who smiled back wickedly—though one of the three could not stop giggling.

"I think it works." The baroness snapped her fingers in front of Masika. "Don't lose them, make sure the Holy Emperor knows we helped you, and good luck."

CHAPTER

FIVE

When the world was yet young, well before humans first toddled across its surface, the Andosh goddess Lorrianna peered into the future and Foresaw a thing which frightened her. In response she dropped the river krait into the mouth of every waterway that leads from the land to the sea, to keep the freshwaters safe from the things that swim and slither in the deeper ocean depths.

In theory. The kraits grew, with Lorrianna's blessing, as much as two hundred feet in length, and many new sailors on Andos's rivers now find it very difficult to be comforted by their presence. Even veterans on the waterways acknowledge the potential dangers of—having spotted a river krait's looping coils on a river's bottom—trying to guess where the head is.

For this reason, the river krait is often used as a symbol in works of fiction for an unseen villain, or an already present character with unknown motivations.

Not this work, obviously. This is a history.

Volume Two of *Thank Gods* by Kohmose Oburn

Masika stood to leave the queen's private chamber. Back through the adjoining audience hall where their meeting began, a knock came from the outer door.

"Open it, please," said Queen Megan.

Masika backed out of the smaller room and went to the door.

On the other side stood a fidgety page flanked by a pair of castle guards. His eyes widened when he spotted Masika, and he leaped sideways out of the doorway.

"That's her!"

The two guards flowed through the doorway to either side of Masika and gripped her by the arms. What was happening? How could anyone here be after her? One of the guards twisted her wrist behind her back and yanked Forbryttan out of her hands.

"Ow!"

"What's this about?" Queen Megan rushed into the room, a tiny hurricane of intensity and power. "And I warn you the explanation had best be a compelling one. This woman is my personal guest, and I am not inclined to set precedent now for arresting guests in my own chambers."

Confusion halted Masika's reactions. She forced her eyes away from the guards' exposed throats, no matter how much she wanted to kick them there. Her words, bitter and hot, slid back down her throat. What would her papa think? The why of her arrest dwindled away before the disappointment he would feel in her.

The page, a small thin man in his early twenties, gulped, his glances flitting between Masika, Baroness Roselle, and Queen Megan.

"I have no explanation, My Grace. I was ordered to take Princess Masika Oburn of Egren into custody under the general authority of the Great Council. I was advised she would cause trouble and was instructed to detain her immediately to the castle dungeons before she harmed anyone else."

"What?" The guard holding Masika's wrist twisted harder when she spoke, and she grit her teeth around the word. "Ow!"

"Else?" One eyebrow went up on the queen's forehead. "Who has been harmed?"

"I, uh . . ." The page took a step back and looked at his feet. "I wasn't told, ma'am. Maybe someone important?"

"Stop that immediately." Baroness Roselle stepped forward to stand at Queen Megan's elbow. "The girl is obviously hurting no one, and we do not require your guesses. Were you told to break her wrists?"

"Yes, Baroness. I mean, no, Baroness. We aren't to harm her, that was very clear, but we were also told not to take chances, as she is extremely dangerous."

"This smells to me." The queen stepped forward and glared up at the two guards until they released Masika, though they did not move away from her. "Do you have any enemies at court, young lady?"

Masika rubbed at her wrist. "None that I know of, Your Grace." Her thoughts locked in on Meritities. Unlikely, but even if her sister were somehow behind this, she couldn't admit that here. She could never bring a family squabble into the queen's chambers.

Lips pursed, the queen nodded. "All right. You're going to have to go along with this for now. By using the Great Council, whoever is behind this has ensured that neither the king nor I can countermand the order without an investigation. It also probably hides the specific councilmember for a few days." She nodded to the baroness, who returned the gesture. "Roselle, I want you to figure this out. If the girl has done something and is lying to us now, we'll still need to prove it to her uncle and ship her back to him. If it's horseshit . . ."

The baroness smiled, and Queen Megan closed her eyes and shook her head.

"Sorry," the queen continued. "I've been married to him for too long. Anyway, if this is some political maneuver, I want to know who's behind it and why."

As the queen shouted for her staff, Masika found herself being led away by the page. The two guards flanked her, though they no longer tried to touch her. Masika's face burned with shame every time a curious eye turned to her in the wide, descending hallways. Her papa would be so disheartened to see her being led away like this.

"Masika? Where are you . . ." Meritities stood in Masika's path, arms crossed and beautiful face stern. "What's going on here?"

What was going on was that Meritities now stood witness to Masika's being dragged away to the dungeons in Sarah's home. Because *of course* she was.

The procession halted on one of the grand stairs that led into the Welcome Hall. They were intentionally parading her through the most densely populated areas of the castle.

"We were warned against interference." The page drew himself to his full height, still a good two inches shorter than Meritities. "If you do not stand aside, I am authorized to remove you by force and take you with us to the dungeons."

A few gasps escaped the crowd, and the volume of the surrounding nobles and merchants dropped precipitously. Further into the massive hall, the stone backs of Greenshade's historical kings showed Masika their opinions of her plight.

Even the statues were hostile and uncaring.

Wait. What was Meritities doing here?

"Do you know who this woman is?" Scorn dripped from Meritities and ate away at the jittery page's resolve. "Do you understand the consequences of what you are doing?" She wore a white gown with golden jewelry and looked every inch the niece of an emperor.

Her sister was rescuing her? Denari clear the fog, Meritities was helping!

"Thank the—"

Meritities raised a finger to Masika, who shut her mouth with a snap. Let these people watch. They would see how a daughter of the empire dealt with those who threatened their family.

A roll of blotchy paper shook as the page handed it to Meritities. The circle of quiet continued to spread across the opulent hall. Meritities uncurled the page and read, her noble brow coming together as she did so.

"On whose authority was this writ delivered?" Meritities's glare withered the page, and he stumbled a backward step up the stair.

"The Great Council, milady. It's not, um, specific." He glanced around at the amused persons on the stair, not one of whom considered him more than a moment's entertainment. "I have to take her. And anyone else who tries to stop me."

Meritities spared a look for the two less impressed guards and rerolled the paper. She whipped it back to the page, who jumped before taking it from her. "Go with them, Masika, but don't say anything. I'll go find Papa, and we'll get this worked out." She reached forward and gripped Masika's shoulder, whispering into her ear. "I'm the only one who is allowed to treat you badly."

The next few minutes were a blur, as Masika was whisked down yet more stairs and into the dark. Not knowing why she was here or what sort of charges were being levied against her was worrying, but the thought that Meritities had rallied to her side made the entire experience worth it.

Assuming she didn't die down here.

Her cell door slammed shut with a jarring metallic clang. Masika went to the lantern on the cell's small desk and lit it.

Her dungeon room was large, as such things were reckoned, and in addition to the desk, there was a curved wooden chair, a bed with an actual mattress, a brass chamber pot, and most extravagantly, a bookcase filled with bound volumes of all sizes and colors. A fresh scrubbed smell attempted to cover a low-hanging sour note in the air. While they wanted to lock her away, it appeared no one wanted to insult her too badly. She doubted many of the other prisoners beneath the castle found themselves this well cared for.

On a whim, Masika tried reading the book titles from where she stood. The shadows in the room shifted, and the titles stood out as if printed in sunlight: *Older Sisters: Book One of the Pirate Witches, Bounty Hunters of the Thirteen Kingdoms, Lost Civilizations of the Yellow Sea, Jungle Mixology, The Kith and the Kin, Thank Gods: Volume Eight.*

Her brother Kohmose's textbooks on the religions of the world were here? She had to escape. They truly did intend to torture her.

What would Kohmose think of her spending time in a dungeon? Allz's wounds. Her mother would just die.

Resigned and having little better to do, Masika crossed the smooth stone floor and picked a volume at random. Almost random. She didn't pick the book her brother had written.

She was not suicidal or anything.

THE FIRST NIGHT Masika found herself scandalized by the presence of a large, round khef-tet on her dining plate. The dinner breads were an Egren favorite among the worker classes, but no self-respecting member of the nobility would be caught dead eating one. Reluctantly she sat at the desk and assayed her meal.

She pushed at it. It was crisp, in the Egren style, instead of softer and chewier as they were in other Darrish nations. Or so she had heard. Masika had never actually touched a khef-tet before.

Fruited mead greeted her nose from a small wooden goblet, with more in an accompanying pitcher, slim and gently rounded. She picked at an edge of her bread and broke it off. There was a hallway that ran the full length of her cell outside the bars and ended with a locked door at either end. No one would see her eat, and she was very hungry.

Masika watched the doors as she slipped the first bit of the khef-tet in her mouth: emmer and cornmeal, cooked until crunchy, just as tradition dictated. She broke off another bite and chewed it. Shavings of salty cheeses melded with thin curls of dried meats and tangy fruits. It was infuriatingly delicious.

Her papa would watch over Rainn and Heron until this situation could be sorted out, although no explanation jumped into Masika's mind for when she eventually saw him. The daughter of a diplomat ought not find herself in the dungeon of a foreign castle.

No help for it now.

As she finished off the last bite, washed down with the flavored mead, a terrible thought came to Masika. The khef-tet had been prepared perfectly in the Egren style, which meant the cook knew enough to follow the rules. But that implied they also knew better than to serve one to a noble unless it was a deliberate insult. Even worse, the most likely source for a properly cooked khef-tet was the Egren embassy, and if they knew who they were cooking for . . .

It was all too maddening to contemplate. She need not be bothered by this. She was not Meritities.

Right. What would Sarah do in this situation? Masika stood and giggled. She had permission to call the Hill Fury by her rightful name. But what would she do? Tear the bars out of the wall and beat the guards unconscious with them? Create a wind to blow the roof off her imprisonment and simply climb out?

While these were all very likely scenarios given what she knew of Sarah, they didn't help Masika much. She did not have the kind of power that Sarah did. In fact, she did not have any powers at all. All she had was—well, she did have something.

The bracelet and ring glinted in the lantern's light. The guards never thought to take it from her, and neither the queen nor the baroness suggested they should. After the initial wave of dizziness passed, Masika's vision returned to normal, unless she found herself staring at something just beyond her vision, in which case that thing snapped into clear sight.

This was real magic.

The shadows shifted as Masika searched specifically for a key to her cell. Nothing appeared, but she could not help but feel as if Inlittan was trying to give her a hand. Just how specific did she need to be here?

"Not a key, then. Let's try anything that might open that locked cell door." The thought occurred to Masika that escape was the defense of the guilty, and perhaps she should wait for her papa and her sister, but she knew neither why she was here, the identity of her persecutor, nor the motivation. For all she was aware, she might be hung in the morning.

She had already been here the entire day, and it occurred to her now that waiting might not be the best defense after all.

This time, when the shift happened, her attention slid to the side of her mattress, beneath the sheet. She lifted the sheet and peered down between the mattress edge and the inside of the bedframe. There, poking into the mattress, was a thick splinter of wood, about three inches long.

After a bit of work, Masika pulled the splinter free, along with another four inches of wood that pulled out of the frame at an angle. A perfect handle.

Or rather, it would be if Masika knew the first thing about lock-picking.

The lock faced outward, into the hall. Masika poked her makeshift tool into it, unable to see what she was doing. The inner workings of dungeon locks were an alien science to her in any event. Still, she wished she could see into it.

Whoa.

Somehow her point of view shifted outside of her head and into the lock.

She froze. This was weird.

She turned her gaze within the lock. That was weirder.

The inside of the chamber was a small vertical cylinder, with a straight pin that ran through the top almost to the bottom. A pair of thin metal tabs ran back up from the bottom of the pin toward the top in a skinny V shape, preventing the pin from exiting the hole it poked down through. An inserted and turned key would press those tabs flat against the pin so that the door could be unlatched from outside, pulling the pin *and* the compressed tabs out of the top. When the door was latched again, the pin would descend and the tabs flare out, resetting the mechanism.

But with her wooden lockpick, Masika could only push against the front tab. How would she get to the one behind the pin?

With a thought, Masika returned her vision to normal. She pulled off a length of her wooden handle and bent it with a small crack. She inserted it and fiddled around before remembering to push her sight back into the lock. With a little adjustment, she twisted the bent end behind the pin, turned it, and pulled, pushing the back tab flat. With her other hand, she pushed the front tab.

Victory! Now all she had to do was lift the little bar latch in front. Her hands twisted into knots holding the lockpicks, and while she could touch the latch with a pinky, she lacked the strength to move it.

Failure.

No. Masika kicked off a shoe and wriggled, inching the slit in the side of her gold and red kaftan high enough for her to push a leg out to the knee, lift, turn, and grip the latch bar between her toes.

Victory again!

With the barred door unlatched, Masika put her shoe back on and pocketed the lockpicks. She would need to be utterly silent and surpassingly lucky, but she knew she could sneak past the inattentive dungeon guards and make her way out of the castle. Once done she would have to work out a way to contact Rainn and Heron, or maybe her papa and Meritities, but that could wait until she was free.

The door creaked open. There would likely be no more opportunities to stop for a drink on her way out. Masika returned to the desk and drank another goblet of mead, savoring the sweet honey taste, and ran into the hall. She went left, the way she had come in, and stopped at the banded door at the end. A tiny, barred window provided guards outside a way to see in. It was, of course, locked.

The picks came out and Masika smirked to herself thinking of Meritities's reaction when she discovered that Masika had escaped without any help from her after all. Even dour Rainn would have to be impressed and might even admit she was a worthy guide to him and Heron.

Voices through the tiny window startled Masika out of her self-congratulatory reverie. She spun around, but there was nowhere in the hall to hide.

A proper key entered the lock from the other side of the door. A man's voice grumbled.

The door opened.

Masika pushed the door closed and ran. Did it click shut? Would anyone notice she was no longer locked in? What would be done if they did?

Manacles? She hoped there would not be manacles.

"Ey, you done wif that?"

"Oh yes, thank you." Masika did her best to control her breathing and wiped sweat from her brow. She stood and picked the plate, goblet, and pitcher off the desk and walked across the cell toward the guard. Eyes closed so the guard could not see her relief, Masika gave thanks to Denari Clear Eyed that the cell door did not creak open on its own.

He took the items from her through the bars.

"Cook 'ad them dinner breads made up special for ya." The guard grinned at her. He was twice Masika's age, but sturdily built and rugged. His attitude was one of paternal care, not at all what she would have expected from a jailor.

"They fed you khef-tet? And you *ate* it?" Meritities's voice slunk out the hallway door an instant ahead of the woman herself. "I'd have starved. But then such things never really bothered you, did they?" She had changed clothes since Masika last saw her, and now wore a gown of subdued scarlet and a golden shawl around her otherwise bare shoulders. Even in a dungeon, Meritities shamed the heavens.

"They have plain bread with dinner in Greenshade." Masika's ears burned at Meritities's scolding. "Not all dinner breads are khef-tet." Why did Meritities always assume the worst? Even if it was, in this one case, true.

Meritities stared at Masika, a sly smile on her lips.

"Now, now, daughters." Tennat Oburn stepped through behind his eldest daughter. His typically smooth beard jutted out at unkempt angles, and puffy rings hung below his eyes. "There will be plenty of time to behave foolishly later. Unless I decide to sell one of you to the washerwomen's guild."

As close to a rebuke as she ever received, Masika swallowed her reply to Meritities's barb. Even so, a physical pain shivered its way into her gut at the sight of her papa. Her attempt at escape failed to prevent his seeing his youngest child in a Greenshade dungeon. What must he think?

Only then did Masika notice the way Merities fidgeted in the hall, her feet shifting and her hands fluttering here and there. The jab must have been to cover up her own discomfort. What had gotten her so spooked? On a normal day one might go from breakfast until dinner without ever knowing a true thought in her sister's head, but right now Merities was very obviously worried.

"I'll let you lot chat," the guard said with an unaffected—and unknowing—smile. "Give a shout when yer ready." With that he exited, shutting the door behind him.

Wary at Merities's discomfiture, Masika stood and watched her papa. Head lowered, he rubbed his temples and breathed. One hand shook.

"I have been too liberal in raising the two of you. I see that now." He lowered his hands and Masika realized the tremor was anger. A cold lump of dread settled in her belly.

"My affections are not a ball to be tossed back and forth or won in some nettlesome game of daggers between the two of you. You"—he pointed at Masika—"have an obligation to the two you released from the Fell Citadel. As a family, that means we all share that charge. And you"—he rounded on Merities, voice and shoulders tight—"will help to fulfill that obligation. That is assuming you wish to remain part of this family and can stop sabotaging the people you are supposed to love." He leaned in close to Merities's trembling face. "Are you entirely clear on your position? I will not go through this again. Whether you love your sister or not, you should know that *I* do, and that ought to be more than reason enough to behave like a decent human being."

Tennat put his hands on his hips, and his gaze flashed between his two daughters. "One more occasion such as this and I'll marry the both of you to a pair of shadow spiders. I can do it. I'm much closer to your uncle than either of you are."

Merities backed away from their papa, bumping against the wall behind. She nodded, though she never took her gaze off the floor.

What had Meritities done?

"Guard." Tennat stepped away from the door and sighed.

The guard reappeared.

"We're ready." Tennat stared into Masika's eyes, and she found she could not breathe. Whatever she had done to earn such wrath from her papa, she would never do it again.

The guard took his keys from his belt and approached the barred door. When he touched it, it swung open, neither locked nor pulled to.

"Heh," Masika said. "Open all the time. I should have left this morning and saved everyone the trouble."

CHAPTER

SIX

The Andoshi believe that the sun is a monstrous egg, laid by Khanah the god-chicken, set fire to by Hedra, and rolled across the sky every morning. This is one of the many ways the Darrish religion is revealed to be superior to the Andosh. Instead of a belief in such an obviously fabricated children's tale, the Darrish know that the sun is the exposed soul of Allz the Shining, who was chained to the Iron Wheel that spins above the Empire, when his belly was torn open by Matchi the Huntress's hounds in penance for his betrayal of Mother Love.

And don't even get me started on the Pavinn. They believe the sun is a portal to the Untamed Paradise that can only be traversed by a flying shark named Slago. As evidence of the ridiculousness of this claim, they plainly state that any shark could travel this gateway if it weren't so far up in the sky, necessitating the shark be able to fly.

But what about when the sun goes down and lands in the ocean?

As I said, ridiculous.

Volume Eight of *Thank Gods* by Kohmose Oburn

Masika and Rainn climbed the gangplank of the *River Krait* behind Tennat and Meritities, while Heron circled in the overcast morning sky above them. Captain Corin Ironmast showed them where to put their belongings, then stomped off to go yell at other people.

The ship was a two-masted caravel, typical of small merchant ships plying the Beacon Sea, with a shallow draft to allow for river travel. While not new, the *River Krait* was meticulously cared for and showed the temperament of her captain well.

"Do not tell anyone on this ship who Rainn and Heron truly are," Tennat whispered to the group. "There is no reason to distrust them, but there is also no reason to endanger ourselves in the event the information should spread to those who might seek to stand in our way."

Masika was impressed by her papa's ability to deliver the warning without even glancing at Meritities once.

"Have no fear on my account." Meritities's low voice came out in a purr. "The last thing I desire is to scandalize my family further by acknowledging our traveling companions."

"Be a shame if those clouds didn't squeeze out a little weather." Rainn stared up into the sky, a tight smile on his face. All morning long he jumped and ran about, as if he had eaten nervous energy for breakfast instead of half a sow's worth of bacon.

"I couldn't care less as long as we quit this dreadful village. Fish Hill indeed. It reeks." Meritities opened the door to the cabin hallway and paused, one graceful hand on the frame. "Papa, I'm going below to write our greetings to the queen and king of Kos. I am certain they would appreciate your attention as well."

"What's that?" Tennat stood straight-backed and stared south over the gray water, eyes distant and troubled. "Oh yes. Larustines and Odandria. Take care of that. I'll check your work when you're finished. We will not be repeating Treaty Hill's mistakes."

Masika winced as irritation flashed across Meritities's face, there and gone again. She needed to have a talk with her older sister, let her know she had put aside their childish rivalries, but their papa's pique threatened to derail her efforts before she had begun them.

To Masika, the road to equanimity lay paved with cobblestones of forgiveness. She and her brother Djephan were both athletic, invested, and competitive. They should have been natural rivals, and in some ways they were. But neither of them cared to bring that rivalry into their personal lives, as Masika and Meritities had. Djephan carried a ray of sunshine in his pocket just for Masika.

Could she create that kind of space for herself and her sister?

Perhaps. But what had Meritities done to upset their papa? It occurred to Masika that it might be something that should upset her too, especially after his cryptic remarks freeing her from the dungeon. He no longer yelled or acted angry, as was his way, but he obviously had not forgiven her either.

Sailors called to each other and cast lines above and around them. From the fore, Captain Ironmast's gravelly voice ground his displeasure against some poor sod's backside. The *River Krait* drifted away from the rickety dock, and a clean sea breeze lifted her sails, while the sun-bleached buildings of Fish Hill continued their gradual decay without acknowledging anyone's leaving.

Heron landed in the rigging near the top of the mainmast while Rainn wandered off in search of something to eat. Since his discovery of castle meals, his interest in human food had reversed itself. He wanted to try everything.

The aft deck harbored fewer shouting sailors than the rest of the ship, so Masika and Tennat headed there. They stood against the rearmost wales behind the helmsman and watched Fish Hill recede, a lighter gray collection of driftwood and ramshackle village between the slate gray sea and the darker frown of distant Treaty Hill. Aloof and vaguely ominous, the Forest Castle stared east, too important to spare a glance south to the small shipping town.

"Are you familiar with Mukahiit?" Tennat asked the question just loud enough to be heard, below the range of the helmsman.

"Fishing and farming town along the northern coast of Egren. I've never been, but Djephan likes it." Masika considered whether to ask her papa about whatever Meritities had done. Then again, the specifics hardly mattered. Masika only wished her papa wasn't also upset with her.

She did want to know, but she feared disappointing him by asking so soon after last night.

"Djephan, yes." Tennat gave a wry little smile to no one in particular. "Your brother has spent time there. We are interested in Mukahiit because it is the northernmost town in Egren, butted up against the southern slopes of the Little Gods Mountains, and is the closest port to Mount P'takkin. There is a small garrison of town guardsmen there, but they are not of the emperor's Saraph Jain and should not trouble us."

"Why would the emperor's soldiers want to stop us? Wouldn't the emperor want to help the Alir and have a favor of this magnitude to hold over the heads of all the Andosh nations?"

"They may not." Tennat opened his hands and shrugged. "Or the emperor may take your sister's view that this entire venture is a sacrilege." His face contorted, as if finding ground bitterbugs sprinkled over his morning fruit. "In that event we will want to evade notice."

"Nebet isn't going to evade notice."

Tennat's frown extended forward to the enormous bodyguard who had been part of their entourage from Egren. The man stood ramrod straight, golden armor glinting dully in the washed-out light. Currently the man's demeanor soured more than normal, given that his long spear and short swords rested, confiscated, in the ship's weapons locker. Only the captain might carry arms unless under attack.

Masika considered that Nebet had a face you would not want to hit with your favorite brick, for fear of breaking it.

The brick, not his face.

"Your sister picked him when I told her we needed more security on this trip. That was before, before . . ."

Again, Masika almost asked what happened that cast such a pall, but she did not. As yet, she had not even gathered the courage to thank her papa for releasing her from the Forest Castle's dungeons.

"In any event," Tennat went on, "we will have to stop in Kos and pay our respects to Queen Odandria and King Larustines. I had hoped to avoid it, but we made too much of a spectacle of ourselves in Treaty Hill. They will consider it a slight if we fail to drop in. After all, they are Darrish."

"I'm sorry I got arrested, Papa." This much was true, though Masika still did not understand why. "I apologize if I've hung this task around all our necks, and I'm sorry if I've made your job more difficult."

Tennat Oburn finally looked his daughter in the eye. When he did, his own gaze was not one of resentment, but sadness. "Our problems are not entirely of your making, daughter. Simply promise me that you will think before you act and that you will get along with your sister, and we will hear no more of it. Can I have that from you?"

A thousand replies rolled through Masika's thoughts. She had only discovered Rainn and Heron, not asked her family to be responsible for them. And it was Meritities who began every battle, not her. But even as she thought these things, she knew them for the half-truths they were. One did not need to ask family to share your burdens, and Masika often gave just as good as she got with her older sister, even if she were not often willing to admit it.

"Yes, Papa."

"Good girl." Tennat tousled Masika's thick black hair. "I suppose I should go check on Meritities before she writes anything too damning to the queen and king of Kos out of spite. Try not to fall in the ocean."

"No need, Papa." Meritities stepped up and handed Tennat a slip of paper. "I've brought it to you. I'll run back and give it to the orven keeper as soon as you . . ." She paused and her beautiful face wrinkled up. "As soon as you approve it."

Tennat took the message and held it out. His mouth traced silent words in the air before he stopped, his forehead folding in exactly the same way Meritities just had, only moreso.

It had more practice.

"Remove the word *baby* here. Masika is simply your sister, not an infant." He returned the paper to Meritities, who accepted it with a barely perceptible flash of irritation.

A quill appeared in Meritities's hand, and she unstoppered a tiny glass jar of ink. Laying the paper on the head of a water barrel, she scratched out the offending word, and returned her implements to her unseen pockets.

"I'll be back soon. Don't leave without me."

"We will not, my dear." Tennat did not look up at Meritities as he responded, so he missed her scowl given to Masika.

For her part, Masika would have been all too happy to leave Meritities in Greenshade.

Under the dungeons.

CHAPTER

SEVEN

Kohoc the Harvester's duties include ending the lives of the healthy and/or young who are destined to perish early. One such young man was Firven, a grain farmer in northern Egren. Kohoc did not appreciate the duty, and knew it was only passed to him because Mother Love did not want her worshippers to despise her for doing such things herself.

Firven, understandably, did not want to die, but Kohoc had little choice. Before the scythe fell, Firven revealed to Kohoc that the Darrish people understood. They did not hold Kohoc's duty against him, and secretly they all resented Mother Love, though none would ever say so out loud.

Kohoc killed the boy twice for his sacrilege, though he appreciated the sentiment.

Volume Four of *Thank Gods* by Kohmose Oburn

Early spring stretched out flat and relaxed on the surface of the Beacon Sea. While their speed flagged, Masika and the crew of the *River Krait* grinned and laughed at the boredom, preferable as it was to wind and storms. Even Captain Ironmast failed to scowl here and there.

Early in the morning of the second day Masika sat on the deck next to Heron in the bow of the ship and fed her strips of fish. Glowing blue runes peeked out from beneath the goddess's soft gray feathers, and her emerald eyes, intelligent and quick, unnerved the sailors and kept them at a distance.

"Oh, ah, I'll find someplace else to sit." Rainn backed away, mouth downturned and shaking his head.

"What? No. Please come back." Masika held out a hand to Rainn, realizing only an instant too late that it was covered in the blood and viscera of the three-stripe she'd cut up for Heron.

He grimaced but moved up into the high-waled bow and sat on a netted-down crate. "Sun's out." He said this as if explaining why the sea were on fire and they were sinking with five hundred barrels of whiskey on board.

"I'm sorry, Rainn. I know this isn't ideal for you." Masika gave Heron another strip of fish. The goddess took it, but her eyes never left Rainn.

"Guess there's no part of this that's ideal for anyone." Rainn sighed and picked white fluff from his dark blue vest. "Everyone else's shitty mood makes me feel a little better about how awful the food on this scow is."

"Rainn, do you know why Papa is so angry with Meritities? Did he say anything to you while I was in the dungeon?" She barely slept last night thinking about this. She could not ask her sister and would not ask her papa even if he would have answered, which Masika felt certain he would not.

A cool wind blew over her bare arms. There was no call for her fancy robe out here on the Beacon Sea.

"Nope." He stared south, where somewhere ahead lay the island kingdom of Kos.

Heron squawked at him.

Eyes cut sideways at the goddess, Rainn rearranged on the crate and resumed his stare.

"Nope you don't know, or nope you're not going to tell me?"

"Nope I'm not getting involved in family squabbles. Not human ones anyway." Rainn never shifted his gaze from the horizon. "There's enough of that crap back home. As I dimly recall."

A series of angry chirrups and squawks emanated from Heron, and she pecked Rainn on the leg.

"Well," he answered the irritated goddess, "you oughtta do that then. But I don't wanna listen to the bullshit from it. And don't peck at me."

"So you *do* know what happened." Masika placed her hands on her hips and tried to hold fast against her own anger. "Is this how the gods of the Andosh repay their debts? Allz's wounds, Rainn. Small wonder none of the other gods ever rescued you from Angrim. They probably left Heron there just to keep from having to deal with you again, and *she's* a delight."

With deliberate slowness, Rainn turned his head to look at Masika. "Your sister bargained with the headman of the textiles guild to get your pampered little ass thrown in the dungeon for a week. Some sort of political arrangement. That Baroness Roselle woman found out and ratted to your dad, who caught Meritities trying to run outta town for Egren. Dragged her back to the castle and made her cancel whatever deal she made with the textile guild." He opened his arms and smiled a cold smile.

"And here we are. How you didn't get any of that before now, I don't know."

An ambivalent coo came from Heron, and she hopped up on the wale.

"I am not." Rainn shifted again on his crate so he could better see Heron. "*You're* the monster here if anyone is. Bird monster."

She fixed him in place with one bright emerald eye and held him there.

A numbness settled over Masika. Was there a correct reaction to something like this? She was not angry nor sad nor any of the things she ought to be. She just felt—empty.

Past Rainn's knee Masika watched Meritities's bodyguard Nebet exit the passenger hallway and stretch on the main deck, his attention darting over the ship, on the lookout for danger. He wore his golden-hued breastplate and a honey-colored leather skirt with a pair of empty scabbards at his hips. Bulging shoulders rippled in the morning sun and turned the faces of a few of the Andosh sailors a bit paler than normal.

What must this man think of her? Nebet's imagination challenged that of a milk thistle in its sedentary range, and he hung on every word her sister said. So given his violent nature and Meritities's opinion of Masika, allowing Meritities to pick her own man as their guard might not have been the smartest—

Which was when Meritities stepped out behind him, in her sleeveless yellow gown.

Not realizing she was moving, Masika stood and walked out of the bow toward her sister. She didn't know her hand was raised until Nebet grabbed her by that arm and lifted her bodily from the deck. Unfortunately, this meant that instead of slapping the snot out of her sister's head, Meritities instead caught one of Masika's flailing feet in the stomach, prompting Nebet in turn to throw her to the boards.

Masika's skull collided with the mast.

Sailors cursed and rushed to get out of the way while Nebet drew a hidden dagger from his back and advanced on Masika, who shook her spinning head.

Somehow Rainn stood between Masika and the hulking brute; Masika never even saw him arrive.

"Settle down now, sunshine. I don't wanna . . ." There was a momentary pause. "No. I'm in a shit mood, and I *do* wanna take it out on someone. Might as well be you. Go ahead and make your last mistake."

Though she could hear perfectly, Masika's vision swam, and she kept bumping the back of her head on the coiled rope binding the main mast. People shouted everywhere. No. Rainn was going to get himself killed. He had not been allowed to keep Forbryttan on the deck.

She had to get up. She was embarrassing her papa again.

"None may touch Princess Meritities without punishment. Especially the wild sister." He scowled down at Rainn and spoke in broken

Andosh. "You are no god. You are a common liar who looks for gold in other people's pockets." He raised the dagger toward Rainn's face and lifted a fist over his own shoulder, prepared to dive in high and fast. "I will kill you now, and no one will be sad of your going."

Rainn's back was to Masika, but she heard the grin in his voice. "I would have expected someone in your line of work to be able to read a room better'n that."

"Read a . . . What?" Nebet's brows knit together as he worked out Rainn's comment.

"I mean I'd figured you'd be better at knowing when someone was sneaking up behind you with a sword. Ah. I see you've gotten the point."

"Drop the fuckin' blade," came a sinister growl from behind Nebet. Masika did not need to see him to recognize Captain Ironmast's voice, angrier than she had yet heard it.

The meaning carried through to Nebet, who dropped his dagger on the spot and kicked it away. One of the sailors ran in and spirited it off.

A boot to the back of the leg brought Nebet to his knees, and Masika pushed herself up against the wide mast. She saw Nebet's neutral face, Meritities's open-mouthed shock, and Captain Ironmast's stony anger.

She also saw Ironmast's short cutlass pushed into the back of Nebet's neck.

"None but the cap'n carries weapons on this ship unless it's time to fight and defend us all." The captain's voice grated across the waves, gravelly and clear as glass. "Don't do it again."

The blade rose and chopped down in a blur.

Nebet grunted, and Meritities shrieked. The huge bodyguard's ear landed beside him on the decking. The other sailors watched, but none made a sound.

The door to the passenger hallway opened a third time, and Tennat Oburn stepped out, blinking against the sunlight. "Good morning, everyone. Did I miss something?"

CHAPTER

EIGHT

The Darrish dinner custom of sitting to eat with a veil over the face at state dinners comes from the tale of Father Rain and the Mountain Boar. In the tale, Father Rain is hunting a wild mountain boar in another vain attempt to secure Mother Love's attention. There was to be a mighty feast that night, and Father Rain wished to provide the main course.

But Father Rain, being a sensitive sort, did not stab the boar through the eye, and the creature survived the hunt as well as its subsequent cooking. As the dinner began, the boar imitated the other gods' voices to insult Mother Love, resulting in a bloody end to the feast and the death of Beautiful Hemetre, favored princess of the P'tak. The boar escaped.

The veil is thought to reveal who is speaking by the motion of thin silk brought on by the breath of the wearer, but in truth this only works when no one else is breathing. I think I prefer the Andosh ritual of roasting the boar with an apple stuffed in its mouth. It removes any ambiguity and tastes better besides.

Volume Two of *Thank Gods* by Kohmose Oburn

Kos jutted defiantly from the Beacon Sea, an island of bright white cliff faces and vast expanses of green fields. Masika wanted to visit the westernmost island of Ippo, where the mighty colossus stood watch and provided a beacon to ward ships off the reef, but there was no time. Instead, they headed to Cyranes, the seat of Kosian power and home of the seven Royal Towers that dominated the top of the cliffs. Okkan, the largest of the three islands, held Cyranes in wide arms, protecting her smaller sister in a sheltered bay.

With a loud squawk, Heron flapped into the air to carry on whatever passed for conversation between dusk herons and hoop gulls.

"Wonder what the good of that is?" Rainn asked, observing platforms of barrels being lowered along the cliff face.

The *River Krait* put in against one of a series of lengthy stone quays at the base of the pale cliffs, and Ironmast ignored his passengers in favor of ensuring proper resupply with his crew.

A small town had been cut into the white stone where the quays met the cliffs, and Masika's eyes grew round at the unbelievable amount of work all of it must have taken, just as they did every time she visited here. A broad stair coiled around the outside of the cliff, six hundred feet high, upon which men and women carried crated goods both up and down. Massive stacks of barrels, bound tightly together with rope, descended a series of huge elevators, with men chanting in unison as they winched the cargo down.

"It's olive oil." Masika pointed to the barrels. The best is supposed to come from Cyranes, but they produce ten times as much on Okkan."

"For lamps?" Rainn squinted up at the elevators.

"For food." Masika smiled when she saw Rainn's brow go up. "You're going to like it here."

Tennat headed into the well-lit cave town and the private stair inside, with his daughters, the two gods, and one-eared Nebet trailing along behind. A trick of the wind ensured a steady breeze all the way up, and there were a half-dozen resting rooms that led from the stair for tired nobles to sit, drink, and have a quick snack before they resumed their climb. Masika waited impatiently for her papa to rest three times.

By the time everyone arrived and was settled in the Blue Tower, the bell rang out for them to change for their dinner with Queen Odandria and King Larustines.

The meal was to be served in the Crown Tower, the second tallest of the seven and the home of the king and queen. Broad open windows let in light and cool air along one curved wall.

Meritities glowed in her ivory and gold gown, her elegant veil transparent as breath, while Masika wore a borrowed dress the color of drying grass that fit her like a sack.

She pulled down again on her veil, dull and white with a tendency to ride up into her eyes.

"Thank you for the orven, Meri." Stately and ancient, Queen Odandria nodded to Meritities from the center of her side of the long table. She and the king sat together facing the windows, with all their guests arrayed across from them. "I must say I was a bit startled to discover that we would be playing host to a pair of Andosh deities. I'm not certain if I should be honored or running for the hills."

Tennat bristled to discover that Meritities had revealed the two Alir but smoothed it over instantly. "We have been nothing but honored ourselves, Your Majesty."

While he had checked Meritities's message, she apparently changed it before handing it over to the orven keeper in Treaty Hill. An orven once scratched Masika on the cheek as a child, and she never quite got over her fear of the big, raven-like messenger birds. Meritities loved them.

Probably for the same reason.

"Is there a purpose for your having failed to mention the *honor* in your own orven, Tennat?" The queen's voice sounded open and conversational, but Masika saw hidden teeth in it, ready to spring shut. She need not have worried though. This was what her papa did.

"I cannot be certain that some elements of Darrish culture, perhaps less sophisticated and far seeing than Your Majesties, will not take our mission to aid our northern neighbors as sacrilegious."

Tennat sounded the soul of parental reasonableness. "I did not wish to put your house at risk should the bird become waylaid. It seemed an irresponsible risk."

Face down, Meritities glared at the tablecloth and bunched her fists in her lap. Papa could not have been more damning.

"When's the food showing up?" Rainn asked.

"Well, he certainly talks like an Andosh." Queen Odandria leaned forward to peer at him. "Are your wrists glowing?"

"The Anger Under the Mountain captured him and Heron to experiment on." Masika instilled as much reverence for the queen and sympathy for Rainn into her voice as she could. "We were not able to return them to the Alir on our own, so we intend to ask the P'tak for aid." She could not help her feelings of distrust for the queen. Though speaking honestly as Papa asked, Masika saw no reason to reveal they intended to go to the actual top of the mountain where the P'tak lived. Let them assume they would entreat the gods from Mount P'takkin's base, as all other pilgrims did.

"Why would our gods help?" King Larustines, soft-voiced, bored, and half the queen's age, finally spoke up. "Aren't the Alir and the P'tak enemies?"

"What mortal knows the mind of a god?" Tennat said this with a chuckle. "My hope is that they will act to save others in their rather exclusive club, rather than squabble over political boundaries."

A servant placed a wide stone bowl lined with blue and white towels and filled with fluffy bread rolls on the table. Rainn grabbed two of them and shoved them in his mouth.

"It doesn't seem difficult to know the mind of *that* god." The queen leaned over to speak to the lead servant, a thin middle-aged man who watched the room more carefully than a score of sea hawks. "Ziryll, is Haphimenes making an appearance tonight or not? The old sorcerer may live forever, but the rest of us certainly won't."

"He is cleaning himself just outside." Ziryll bowed and indicated the door. "He has been in the fields."

"Oh, please tell me we are not going to have another dinner spoiled by the truly aggressive scents Haphimenes chose to roll in while he was out in some cattle yard?" Queen Odandria held out one hand in front of her and pushed her dark veil against her face with the other, as if some hero were about to burst in through the window and rescue her from their sorcerer's olfactory contributions to dinner if she only beseeched enough.

Masika decided she did not care for Queen Odandria. As for meeting Haphimenes, that thought bothered her more. Sarah wielded sorcerous powers and more, for good and as a hero. But the only actual sorcerer—no mere runecrafter like Romi or Catlia—Masika ever met in the flesh was Anan-jib, advisor to her uncle the Holy Emperor. That ancient stick of a man wielded his fearsome reputation to much more deadly effect than any soldier might use a sword.

The dining hall doors flew open, and a tall Darrish man stalked in, a huge and warm grin on his face. His hair and beard were short and shot through with gray, and a worn tunic covered his lanky frame. Before the door closed again Masika spotted Nebet standing tall just outside, his spear at the ready.

"Did I hear someone mention my name?"

This had to be Haphimenes the Elder.

The smell of open fields, grass, and fresh earth followed Haphimenes into the hall. Queen Odandria reacted as if physically attacked, recoiling from the air in front of her.

From her perch at one of the windows, Heron gave a bright croak, and Haphimenes stopped to laugh.

"Oh indeed." He turned the full force of his grin on Heron, who turned her head behind one wing in a coquettish motion. "Very entertaining observation. I take it I have been greatly in demand given no one has felt comfortable beginning their meal without me?"

Perhaps not the ogre Anan-jib was after all.

Another roll went pointedly into Rainn's mouth.

"As if it's not enough to have to worry about the staff gossiping over our every word, now we must contend with the birds." Queen Odandria waved to the thin servant. "Oh, let's do be about it and get this catastrophe started, before the crickets and field mice begin planning rebellion."

"Much too late there, my queen." Haphimenes took the empty chair opposite the royals and plopped down into it, with Tennat on his left and Rainn on his right. "Though I'd worry more about the tomato plants. They're the sneaky ones."

At the two ends of the less royal side of the table sat Masika and Meritities, the three men between them. When Masika leaned back to get a better look at Haphimenes, she noticed her sister sitting quiet and reserved, a perfectly well-behaved dinner guest.

Or a spider in wait.

Masika's stomach gurgled as the first course, an orange gourd and garlic soup, was presented. She grabbed Rainn's arm as he lifted his bowl and waggled her spoon at him. He blinked, nodded, set the bowl down and shoveled soup into his face with the spoon instead.

"Hmm," was all the queen said, accompanied by a flat glare.

"What do you require from us, Tennat old friend?" The king at least did not sound out of sorts to be here among guests. In fact, he was much more open and welcoming than the typical monarch Masika listened to. She decided she liked him much better than his crone of a wife.

"Your company and this fine meal are already overly generous, Sire," Tennat responded.

One brow rose on Queen Odandria's forehead. "And what exactly, pray tell, is your plan for when you get to Egren and everyone wants to kill you for heresy?" The end of the question came out of her with a chuckle, as if it were the most amusing thing she had heard tonight. "You can't expect anyone there to allow you to the foot of Mount P'takkin with a pair of Alir assassins in tow."

Why was the queen so openly hostile? Was she always this way? What was in the message Meritities sent ahead of them?

"Any more soup?" Rainn held his bowl out to the closest servant, who whisked it out of his hand. "Great. Also, not assassins. Just normal gods with their powers stripped by centuries and centuries of torture."

"Whether you're assassins or not will hardly matter after you've been killed for being assassins." The queen motioned to Ziryll, who ladled out a second bowl of soup and set it before Rainn. "Ziryll has a soft spot for pets. Even pet gods, apparently."

A low, irritated croak came from Heron, and Haphimenes raised an eyebrow at her.

No longer able to contain her pique, Masika asked, "If you're so worried about how Egren is going to respond, then why are you hosting us now?"

King Larustines raised a hand to speak, his mouth opening in a warm smile, when the queen cut him off.

"That is a question I have been asking myself since the moment the king suggested we do so. You clearly have no notion of what you're about, and that is likely to cause trouble for us all. Anyone with sense would simply turn you over to the Holy Emperor's Saraph Jais and be done with you." She sighed. "But as we collectively appear to lack even that much cleverness, you may stay the night and begone in the morning."

"Thank you, Your Majesty. I assure you no harm will befall you and yours because of our adventure." Tennat delivered this with utter earnestness. Masika found herself charmed by her papa's abilities.

Unfortunately, the queen did not share her view. "Assurances. I am too old and too battered by life to place any stock in promises concerning circumstances you have neither the foresight to anticipate nor the ability to affect."

Masika pulled the veil down again, out of her eyes. Glancing sidelong, she saw Meritities's lip curl upward in a tiny, secret smile.

Queen Odandria rested her elbow on the table and pointed a shaking finger at Masika's papa. "You're not stupid, Tennat. Are you telling me you have no real worries about how the Holy Emperor might react to this? How he might react toward *me*?"

A concerned frown settled over Masika's papa. He opened his mouth to speak . . .

"My worry, Papa, is how this course of action may affect our family." For the first time since sitting, Meritities spoke up. "I appreciate the possibility of a diplomatic coup, but I feel that you look at this through the lens of your job, and that's all you can see. These two gods have been buried for the entirety of our history, and no one has suffered for it. But your choices now have genuine repercussions for the people you love the most. I think . . ."

Meritities noticed both Papa and Queen Odandria staring at her with the same look of irritation, though doubtlessly for different reasons. She picked up her napkin and lowered her head.

The queen scowled at Tennat. "As I was about to say, return to me unkilled and in your capacity as Egren's diplomat and I'll know you are either forgiven or better yet, have abandoned these foolish plans. Anything else and I will assume you come bringing trouble to my islands, and I'll have you killed myself." She leaned back and lifted her soup spoon.

"I assure you."

CHAPTER

NINE

One specific form of religious play exists in Egren and nowhere else called the Noble Tragedy. In it, the main character arranges the downfall and demise of their loved ones, such that the doomed parties' plans, which would invariably result in their eternal damnation, cannot be enacted. They are murdered for their own good.

The instruction is that we should all be willing to sacrifice our own earthly happiness for the well-being of each other's souls.

These plays always end with the horrific death of the main character. Murder is still against Mother Love's law, after all.

Volume Eight of *Thank Gods* by Kohmose Oburn

King Larustines's waiting hall chilled Meritities's skin, sending gooseflesh up her bare arms. White marble floors, veined in gray and quarried here on the island, also stretched up the walls and made two rows of three columns each, all cold and sterile. Light from a pair of torches left the corners and ceiling draped in shadow.

This conversation necessitated darkness and secrecy. While at dinner, Masika obviously assumed that Queen Odandria was her enemy. Meritities knew better. The queen simply spoke her mind. She posed no threat to Masika's foolishness, even if she were intelligent enough to want to steer well clear of it.

The king, on the other hand . . .

Meritities felt certain even her papa failed to recognize the under-current of conversation between herself and King Larustines. He wanted to remove the threat of Masika's Alir as much as Meritities herself did but lacked the ability. A king in a matriarchy, this one at any rate, was little more than a figurehead, and if Larustines were caught out moving against an ally when Odandria dictated inaction, his punishment would be certain and severe.

So she would ensure that no one got caught.

Nebet snapped his spear to the ready, interrupting another shiver down Meritities's spine. Another person entered the lonely hall, padding soundlessly across the marble. She wore a long tunic, belted at the waist and black as her slippers, with her colors reserved for the rainbow hues dyed into her hair. Canny wariness showed in the ageless woman's eyes.

"Follow me, please." She continued past Meritities and Nebet, opened the ironbound door into the king's private audience chamber, and went inside.

Though lightless when the door opened, by the time Meritities made it into the room a quartet of oil lamps shone bright enough to make her squint. How had she lit them so quick? A marble chair at the far end and a long window overlooking the harbor below marked the only differences keeping this room from being a duplicate of the one before it.

"I was expecting an audience with His Majesty." Meritities stepped in front of Nebet to show both of them she felt unthreatened by the situation. A little confidence often relaxed a tense beginning in a conversation.

The pale skinned Andosh woman's face betrayed mild amusement. "I am aware. King Larustines is abed and determined to remain that way throughout the night. It would be bad form for word of his late-night associations with visiting princesses to reach the queen's ears. Thus you have me. I am Alexandra, and in this matter I speak for the king."

"For the king?" Surely this matter was too important to be farmed out to an underling. "Wait. Aren't you the woman that Haphimenes brought back from his travels in Arlea?" Merities knew very little about it, other than what she discussed with Papa, and that was mostly court gossip. When the old sorcerer returned from his wanderings he brought back an extra person, with little to no explanation. Merities assumed they were lovers.

When you were one of the world's most ancient powers who predated the nation in which you lived, you got a considerable amount of leeway in your personal affairs.

"The sorcerer helped me in Arlea, yes." Alexandra's cultured voice soothed the air between them. "I have resolved to aid him in return." Her face broke into a sunny smile. "For now that aid takes the form of plotting against your sister on behalf of the king. Is there anything more engrossing than someone else's family drama?"

While this statement displayed that Alexandra already knew roughly why Merities was here, it was also hard to find it reassuring. There remained little choice now though, other than to return empty handed, which she would not allow to happen.

Masika would not steal Merities's hopes of being empress the way she stole their papa's heart.

"If I am to help properly, you should tell me why we're doing this." Alexandra placed her hands on her hips. "Where is the harm in your sister getting ignored by the P'tak when she shows up at the foot of the mountain?"

"They don't intend to remain at the mountain's foot." Merities disliked being the one answering questions. "They intend to summit it, *with* the Alir." She neglected to include this information in the orven message she sneaked past Papa. Sensitivity necessitated obliqueness, and no messenger bird could be considered entirely secure.

Alexandra frowned. "That isn't very likely, is it? Mount P'takkin is supposed to be unclimbable. Wasn't that the whole point of it being where your gods built their house?"

"It will be considerably less likely if we stop them here," Meritities answered.

"All right, princess, what are your plans for this dastardly intrigue?" Alexandra's stiff coat of courtly rigidity fell away from her, the sudden lack of which left Meritities uncomfortable. "Murder? Kidnapping? Throw them all in the dungeon?" Her brow knitted and her mouth turned down in a false frown. "No, that last one certainly wouldn't work. We'd have to be idiots to try that."

"What aid has the king authorized you to provide?" Meritities strove to reassert control over the conversation.

"Any aid that will not reveal King Larustine's hidden hand." A small smile flitted across Alexandra's face. "The easiest thing to do would be to kill them all as they sleep and remove the bodies, scuttle their ship, and claim they slipped away in the night. Which would be sort of true. Would that fulfill your needs?"

"No. They must not be harmed." But Alexandra's idea did put a notion into Meritities's head.

Alexandra's gaze flicked to Nebet at Meritities's insistence that no one be hurt, but she held her tongue.

Meritities frowned in concentration at the cold marble floor. "I assume you have criminals in hand to enact any stratagems we devise here?" No way now but forward.

"Obviously." This time Alexandra's smile stayed. Her enjoyment nettled Meritities. "What did you have in mind?"

"Steal the *River Krait*. Send it to the ocean bottom. I'll take a Kosian vessel to Daynce. It's in Verran but there's always a few Egren naval ships there. I'll be back within a week to take my sister and her barbaric gods in hand with the emperor's Saraph Jais at my back, and King Larustines won't be implicated in the slightest. Can you make certain no one else gives my sister a ride out of Kos for that long?"

In answer, Alexandra raised an arm and snapped her fingers. A marble panel opened across the room and an older man, balding, nervous, and dressed in working clothes stepped out of a small corridor.

"Dockmaster? Thank you for waiting." Alexandra's smile grew feral. She was enjoying herself. "Can you ensure a few foreigners don't leave the island for the space of a week?"

"Aye, lady. I believe their paperworks just got lost. Whoever they are."

"My sister is resourceful." It bothered Meritities more than she thought it would to admit Masika's competency. "You will need contingency plans. No one means of shutting her down is likely to succeed."

"As you learned in Treaty Hill?" And now Alexandra's smile showed teeth. Who was this woman really? Why was she here, and why did she serve Haphimenes and King Larustines?

"It'll cost." The dockmaster straightened and scowled, though not enough to keep the eagerness from his voice.

"Lady Alexandra will be happy to see you paid," Meritities said with a nod and a softly upturned lip of her own.

Alexandra blew an errant fall of multihued hair out of her face and rolled her eyes. "Yes. I'll take care of it. Are you certain you wouldn't rather see them dead? It'd be easier, and probably cheaper to boot."

Meritities stared at Alexandra a moment before turning her attention to her one-eared bodyguard. "You will stay behind to ensure nothing untoward happens to my sister or to Papa. Do you understand?"

Nebet gave his mistress a quick bow. "Yes, Princess. Does your protection extend to the northerners?"

Unable to stop a derisive snort, Meritities shook her head. "It most certainly does not. But don't risk yourself either." She reached up and patted him on one bulging arm. "I will always need someone I can count on."

"Well, I suppose that handles that," Alexandra said in a voice that indicated she thought anything but. "I want you to know that I consider this an investment in your future. For such a time as you might better repay the debt."

Only a disciple of Tennat Oburn such as Meritities could have kept the gasp out of her voice and the white out of her eyes at such an observation. What did Alexandra think she knew about her? Surely she could have no idea of Meritities true ambitions here.

With calm graciousness, Meritities allowed the upturn of her lip to touch her eyes. "Perhaps such a day will come. In the interim, you have my gratitude."

CHAPTER

TEN

Contention exists over the origin of the Yellow Sea, the mighty desert between the marshes of Sedrios and the verdant farmlands of Egren. The Pavinn believe the desert was caused by Bukker, the gigantic seven-penised dog who played and destroyed the jungles originally there when their goddess Arlea was searching for a safe place to leave him.

The more likely Darrish version is that Father Rain's brief death created the Yellow Sea, as his tears no longer fell upon that land, and it withered under his forced inattention.

For completeness and no other reason, I include the Andosh theory that the Yellow Sea was always there, and the Alir gifted the territory to the Darrish peoples that they might have someplace to poop.

Volume Eight of *Thank Gods* by Kohmose Oburn

By the time Masika rose the next morning in her white stone room looking out over a brilliant blue sea, Merities had already left for Egren.

It was just as well, Masika reflected. Merities could brood all she wanted back at the family palace. Papa was much angrier than he let on, but even he had to see that her departure would surely make their task easier.

The only thing that bothered Masika about her sister leaving was that she left her bodyguard Nebet behind.

A long, low smudge darkened the horizon to the west as Masika stepped out of the cliff face town and onto the broad quay. Clean ocean air blew over her and rolled her curly hair to one side, whipping her gold robe against her skin. The calls of gulls and sailors alike carried her happy footsteps toward the *River Krait*.

She appreciated Queen Odandria's implied promise not to interfere with them, but the elder queen's vexation was sincere enough to make Masika doubt how long she might remain true to her word.

At the entrance to the westernmost prong of Cyranes's great stone quay, Masika ran into her papa, Nebet, and Captain Ironmast engaged in an intense conversation. Nebet stared mutely at the captain, his long-bladed spear ever ready.

Papa was speaking. "It's a Darrish country, Captain. We'll simply obtain a loan and make do. You'll be recompensed for any personal losses."

"'Scuse me, Lord Oburn." Up close, Masika realized that Ironmast was *seething*. "If I was to chop off your leg at the hip, d'you think you might make do if I bought ya a new boot?"

"No, but—"

Ironmast's weathered face, Andosh pale but tanned from years in the out of doors, turned red as a gutted cherry. "Then why're you offerin' a loan of an oversized bathtub and box of hard tack as payment for me *fuckin' ship gone missing?*"

Her papa said something in reply, but Masika did not hear it. The bottom fell out of her stomach, and she plopped down on the stone. The queen had made her move already. Masika would be trapped here for the rest of her life, along with Rainn and Heron who had stupidly trusted her, and she would never get to be the hero that the Hill Fury was. How could Masika disappoint so many people overnight?

Don't be stupid. Find another way. But how?

At least Meritities had gotten out in time. Would she be able to send help back for them? In this kind of international situation, would her uncle even allow it?

Heron landed on Masika's shoulder, and Rainn sat down beside her, cross-legged.

"What're we doing?" Rainn's conversational tone disarmed Masika. It was so far from his typical morose manner any time he was not discussing food. "Get tired on the stairs?"

"Why are you so happy?" Although Masika considered it rude to answer a question with a question, she could not help herself. Rainn's mood was unexplainable and misplaced.

In answer he pointed west at the smudge across the skyline, already bigger and darker than when Masika noticed it before. "Coming this way." He grinned and waggled his eyebrows. "Why're you so mopey?"

"Someone stole our ship."

"Huh." Rainn twisted around to meet Heron's gaze up on Masika's shoulder. "Hey, Heron. You spot our missing ride?"

A curious purr came from the goddess.

"You haven't been listening to a thing that's been going on, have you?" A croak in response. "No, it doesn't have a damn thing to do with fish or fishermen or that guy over there with the squid net. If you were hungry, you should have eaten eggs for breakfast with the rest of us." Rainn winced at the tirade of angry squawks Heron flung at him. "Bacon then. Whatever. Our boat's gone. Stolen. That means we don't go to Egren and we never get home. Is that what you want?"

Heron jerked upright, let out a squawk, and pushed herself up into the air. She chattered back a string of noises as she gained altitude and turned east.

"What did she say?" Masika asked Rainn.

"She said she wants to shit on my mother's head."

"I don't . . . What does that even mean?"

"It means two things." Rainn lifted up his knees and rested his elbows on them. "One, she'll help find the boat. I think she's gonna fly around the island coasts until she spots it."

"And the other thing?" Masika let Rainn's improved demeanor

relax her. If he was not worried, maybe she didn't have to be either.

"If we can't get her out of that bird form soon, I'm not sure we ever will."

So much for that.

THE WEATHER TURNED grim by the time the *River Krait* was finally tied off once again to the far western edge of the quay, right up against the cliff face. Heron located the ship within the first two hours, and the dockmaster reluctantly sent out a small rescue force into the oncoming storm.

It had been left floating a quarter of the way around Cyranes, below a broad expanse of undeveloped woodland, where no one would be likely to spy it unless they could fly.

The problem had resolved so fast, Masika barely had time to worry about who stole the vessel to begin with. At least its discovery quieted the voice in the back of her mind suggesting that Meritities had taken it back to Egren. Now the only thing to fret about was the storm. Should they push ahead and deal with the weather at sea, or tighten up here and strike out as soon as the weather abated?

"We have to get the fuck out of here now." Captain Ironmast, grim faced and dripping with rain, stepped into Masika's vision. "Except we can't. The eejit dockmaster set the *Krait* up on top of the rocks. Look at how she's heeling. Tide's pushed out ahead of the squall, but soon's it's back it'll come bash her to bits."

One hand on the grip of his cutlass, Ironmast cast a craggy glare at the dockmaster's house, and it took no imagination at all for Masika to picture his thoughts.

"I'll gut that rotted weasel."

That was pretty much what she imagined.

Behind her, Masika heard singing in Andoshi. Rainn danced through the downpour, shedding joy as the sky shed water. It was not only the happiest Masika had ever seen Rainn, but it may also have been the happiest she had ever seen anyone.

"Hang on," she said to Captain Ironmast and trotted over to Rainn. She grabbed his elbow, and he spun to see her, a madcap grin set in his face. The wet caused his gray shirt to cling to him, but she did not believe that alone could account for how much tighter it was against his muscles.

"Masika! This trip is finally turning up. We should find some tasks to perform out of doors before the cursed sun returns."

"I have just the thing." Masika pulled on Rainn's chin to return his roving gaze to her. "You told me you're stronger when the weather is poor, right?"

"Oh, *yes.*" Rainn bubbled laughter at this, deep and throaty. It reverberated in Masika's chest and pushed against the cold of the deluge.

"Follow me then."

Minutes later, Rainn was over the side of the *River Krait* with his back against the cliff face and his feet pushed flat on her broad hull. Waves splashed up over him prompting loud gales of mirth. Watching over the starboard wale, Masika and Ironmast strategized how this might go.

"Now we're untied, we only need to wait until a big enough wave hits to lift the ship so he can push it off the rocks." Masika bit her lower lip and watched the giggling Rainn beneath her. "If he's as strong as he thinks he is."

"I'm worried he may be." Ironmast drummed his thick fingers against the railing. "If the wave pushes her into him, he might kick a hole in her." He spun and barked orders at the sailors standing, wet and miserable, on the quay. In no time, they were braced starboard, with poles pushing into the white cliffside.

The waterline fell away.

"It's a'coming!" Ironmast roared.

With the rail gripped tight in her hand, Masika looked to port and saw a monster wave crashing toward them. This was either going to result in a crushed Andosh god or an Alir-sized hole in the hull. Choosing to take Rainn's word on his abilities, Masika dove amidships and returned with a plank about two feet wide and nine long.

Enough to spread the force of Rainn's push and prevent him from crunching through the hull, she hoped.

"Rainn! Catch this and put it under your feet!" She dropped it, trying to ignore the pounding sensation of the wave at her back.

Rainn lifted one foot to shove the plank in, when the wave struck and a gout of water flew up past him and pummeled Masika in the face.

"Heave!" shouted Captain Ironmast.

"Ho!" returned the crew.

The *River Krait* listed starboard toward the cliff and the mast dragged the wall above, dropping stones on the deck. Wrong way. All at once the ship lifted, scraping the side against the cliff. The sailors braced again and pushed, their screams competing with the groaning timbers.

Water shoved its way in a solid wall up between ship and cliff, and the *River Krait* lifted free of the rocks below. The ship rolled to port, and everyone on deck clutched at whatever they could find to prevent being swept off the opposite side.

Then they were free.

Masika raised her head to find Rainn sitting in the middle of the main deck, grinning like a loon.

"We should do that again."

"To port!" shouted Ironmast as he wrestled with a headsail. "Into the waves."

Grabbing a pole, Rainn sprinted to the bow and shoved the *River Krait's* nose away from land, while as many sailors as could get their feet under them pushed against the quay. The captain and three others maneuvered one of the headsails to catch just enough wind to pull them off the quay and into deeper water.

Not knowing what else to do, Masika ran to stern and took hold of the spinning ship's wheel. Ironmast spotted her and spun his arm to port, and Masika followed with the wheel.

Keeping just as tight a grip on her relief as she did on the wheel, Masika helped to guide the ship away from the rocks and into the weather. The effort exhausted her, but the joy of saving the vessel pressed a permanent grin, wide and toothy, onto her face.

In the end, the storm lasted no more than another half-hour, before Ironmast guided them back to a safer berth on the lengthy quays. Masika, spent and happy, lay spread eagled on the poop, her loose linens plastered against her body with all the wet. Miraculously, there were no cracks in the hull from either rocks or feet.

She leaned her head forward and flinched away from Heron, who was staring into her face.

"Oh, I'm glad you're all right." Masika smiled, and Heron hopped up on her stomach. "Listen, I think Queen Odandria had something to do with the *River Krait* being stolen and tied off over those rocks. Would you mind keeping an eye on her and making sure she doesn't try anything like that again before we leave?"

With a low chirrup, Heron flapped blue gray wings into the sky and up the cliff face. Masika hoped she realized just how important she had become to their success.

"That was a heroic bit of sailing." Rainn sat next to her, a tired smile on his face. The passing of the storm drained his energy and his exuberance. "Your father'll be glad to see you all not-dead."

Papa. He was in the entryway to the cliff town when the weather began in earnest. How much did he see?

Enough to realize how much like Sarah his daughter was becoming?

That thought lasted no longer than Masika finding her papa amongst all the other concerned faces, checking on loved ones and even more loved ships. His expression was drawn and gray-faced, as if his worry had been beating him with a chair leg the entire time Masika worked to rescue the *River Krait*.

"I am attempting to be understanding, and I know you take your responsibilities seriously." Tennat stepped out of the way as Masika bounced off the gangplank onto the quay. "I really am. But no one benefits by your throwing your life away to save a *boat*."

"Boat's saved. Everyone's fine." Masika walked past her papa, and he fell in to one side, Rainn on the other. It took all her will to stay upright and not fall to the floor. Her legs felt like overcooked noodles. "We didn't lose a man."

"That's not the point, Masika. You took a foolish risk. I'm *glad* you saved the ship and that no one was hurt, but I'm terrified you'll take this as some sort of justification to continue taking more and more foolish risks in the future. You could have died just now. Can you even imagine having this conversation with your mother?"

She truly could not. Masika's mother thought Kohmose's job as a scholar was overly perilous. The woman had taken to her bed for a week at Djephan's decision to become a member of their uncle's personal guard. Masika slowed, stopped, and turned to her papa.

"The hazard is over. Denari knows why you sanctioned my learning the sword and bow if you never intended me to get in any sort of danger, but here we are. There's no reason we should have to face that kind of peril again, and if we do, I shall run the other way." Masika took her papa's hand. "For now, I am cold, tired, and starved. Maybe we can save the rest of the lecture for after we have some food in front of us?"

"I like that plan," Rainn said. "There's a place just inside the cliff that's got roasted lemon and olive chicken. Everyone's talking about it."

Tennat squeezed his eyes shut and breathed. His hand remained tight around Masika's. "I need a promise from you."

"Promise for what?" What could Papa want of her that she was not already doing?

"Promise me you'll do as you say. If you find yourself in danger again, you will flee." Red rimmed Tennat's eyes and filled Masika with anxiety. She did not realize just how shaken up he was.

She took his hand in both of hers and squeezed as much as she could, which at the moment was not a lot. "I'll stay safe. If danger arrives, I'll show it the backs of my heels. If it follows, I'll throw Rainn at it and use him as a distraction to get away."

The brow went up on Rainn's forehead, but he said nothing.

Sarah never went on any adventures with her papa, did she? This was probably why.

CHAPTER

ELEVEN

In Darrish culture the heron is a sign of a good death. The birds are known to transport the souls of the faithful to the House of the Gods at the summit of Mount P'takkin, where they will join the armies of their fallen countrymen to do eternal battle against other Darrish nations, both past and present. This is because, even in death, the Darrish people are known to be superior enough to the Andosh and Pavinn that only their own are worthy of this perpetual combat.

The Andosh have a similar belief, although their dead battle other Andosh, trolls, and giants to prevent being annihilated by the Darrish.

The Pavinn dead are both stupid and lazy, spending their eternity laughing and having sex on the beaches of the Untamed Paradise.

Can you even imagine?

Volume Eight of *Thank Gods* by Kohmose Oburn

Masika, Tennat, Rainn, and improbably, Heron, all finished breaking their fast in the same tavern that served the roasted lemon and olive chicken the night before. The hard-boiled lemon and olive eggs tasted similar to last night's meal, which was good given the level of Rainn's insistence that they eat there.

They sent Nebet ahead. No one wanted to share table space with the dour bodyguard.

According to Heron, the queen behaved herself all night and morning, and reacted with concern instead of frustration at the news of the *River Krait's* recovery. Masika thought it was an act, though her papa was horrified to learn of her suspicions.

The quartet stepped out of the tavern into the wide, low-ceilinged chamber that served as the central square of the cliffside town. Businesses and homes were cut deeper into the rock in all directions, and everything was illuminated in oranges and yellows with regularly spaced fish oil lamps.

A minor argument broke out as a trio of sailors, two men and a thick-shouldered woman, ran into a chandler setting up her stall in the central market space, but they apologized and moved on, one even stopping to help pick up what he had knocked over. Beneath his colorless cloak, a crisp white shirtsleeve poked out. They were doubtless the servants of some important house in the towers above, here to buy groceries or other sundries.

The smells of a thousand spices walked with Masika toward the town exit onto the quay, where fresh salt air and the more acrid scent of bonfire mixed into the air. She closed her eyes to better appreciate the aromas and sounds. People shouted, haggled, and screamed as—

Masika's eyes popped back open. The *River Krait* sent a hundred-foot-high column of flame toward the heavens and stained the blue with a greasy pall of black smoke.

A hand gripped Masika's forearm. Tennat held her and prevented her from running to the flames to try and help. He leaned down to whisper in her ear.

"You promised."

Out on the quay, Captain Ironmast watched in stony silence as his home, his livelihood, and everything he owned roared in fiery fury. The dockmaster screamed at his porters to use poles to push the burning wreck off the quay and away from the other vessels. The *River*

Krait's lines, like most sailing ships, were covered in pine tar to keep them slippery and safer from rot, and the sails treated with an oil-based mix to strengthen them and protect them from sun and water.

It was an inferno.

"I'm starting to get the impression someone here doesn't wanna see us leave." Rainn fidgeted with the pommel of Forbryttan. "It's a little annoying."

"Heron." Something clicked in Masika's brain. A single puzzle piece fell into place and an avalanche followed.

The goddess landed on Rainn's shoulder and gave Masika her attention. Even still, her head twitched this way and that at the shouting and running people.

"On our way out, we passed three people. Two men and a strong woman, all wearing cloaks and nicer clothes underneath." Masika tried not to think about Rainn's insistence on stopping for breakfast and how close they came to getting back to the ship before any harm befell it. "They were headed for the stair. I thought they were shopping for their house, but none of them were carrying anything. Now I think they might have been our arsonists."

As one Tennat and Rainn turned to the cliff town. Heron gave a low, growl-like croak.

"Fly to the top of the stair and wait for them to leave it. Don't be seen. Follow them and watch who they report to. Follow *that* person too and keep doing it until we know who was behind this. We're coming up behind." It was a plan, but exactly what Masika would do when she finally confronted the queen with her behavior . . . She simply had no idea.

They followed up the wide stair, hugging the right wall to avoid the bulk of townspeople moving up and down. This time they went swiftly as they could, but they did not run, and they did not stop. Masika neither wished to catch up to their quarry and spook them nor get so far behind that they would take a chance on losing them in the towers.

Tennat was as gray as Rainn's shirt by the time they summited the climb, but he made it. "Where to now?"

That thought worried its way into Masika's brain during their ascent and sat there, throwing rocks at her plans.

"Rainn. Can you—feel Heron? Like the way you felt the imp? Can you take us to her?"

Frowning at Masika, Rainn nodded. "She's in the Crown Tower, close to Haphimenes. The sorcerer is strong. I can feel him anywhere."

THE OFFICIAL AUDIENCE chamber of the Crown Tower took up most of one of the upper-level floors, with huge open windows, floor to ceiling, wrapped around the curved wall. A pair of thrones dominated the far end, the larger reserved for Queen Odandria and the smaller for her husband King Larustines.

The audience chatted themselves up quite a froth.

Masika shoved her way through the nobility and masters in their white frocks and kaftans and ignored their indignant protests. They meant nothing to her. Ahead she could hear Heron's squawks and the queen's brittle complaints. An Andosh woman with jewel-toned hair nearly collided with her, as eager to leave the hall as Masika was to enter. She stopped and nodded to Masika with a knowing smile and exited behind her.

A large steel bird cage hovered in the air in front of the king and queen, who both frowned mightily into it. King Larustines nursed a bleeding hand, and Haphimenes spoke in a calming tone.

Heron, in the cage, was not interested in being calm.

"You." Queen Odandria pointed at Masika and two tower guards appeared out of nowhere to grab her. "You sent your creature to attack my husband. Are you trying to start a *war*?"

None of this was what Masika was hoping or expecting to find. How could she explain?

"Not her"—Rainn stepped out from behind Masika—"but him maybe." He pointed to King Larustines. "According to what Heron just said, he's the asshole who burned our ship out in the harbor. I'd bet he also stole it yesterday morning then paid the dockmaster to leave it where it'd be smashed to bits." Rainn waggled his finger. "Bad king."

Haphimenes said nothing but leaned on his gnarled olive wood staff and turned an amused smile on King Larustines.

The king sighed and raised his arms. He let them fall into his lap. "I had hoped not to involve the crown directly, but yes, I did scuttle their vessel." He looked over everyone's heads and spoke in a louder voice. "Not that anyone was supposed to know."

Old and gray brows creeped up the queen's forehead. She leaned away from her husband to better see him. "You did? Whatever for?"

"They admitted to trying to bring aid to our enemies, the Alir," the king said, his face reddening. "But they did not tell you everything. Young Meritities came to an associate of mine before she left. They intend to bring these Alir to the House of the Gods itself. That's why they are going to Mount P'takkin. Mother Love will not only kill them, but anyone who has given them aid. I won't have that fate brought down on anyone here who so much as refilled their wine-glasses."

"*You* won't have?" Queen Odandria asked.

"But why destroy our ship?" It made no sense to Masika that the king of Kos would care one whit for any of this.

"Indeed." The queen's scowl deepened. "You threatened every ship in our harbor with your reckless scheme. If the fire had spread—"

"I was not made aware of the specific plans." Larustines obviously felt as if this vindicated him, though Queen Odandria's expression indicated otherwise. "In any event, the *River Krait* was to have been sunk. I suspect one of the thieves intended to retrieve it later and sell it."

Anger and hurt swirled in Masika's mind. Just yesterday he seemed so kind and helpful.

"I have not received word from the Holy Emperor yet, but I will." King Larustines settled back in his throne, satisfied in his victory. "You will be kept here in Kos for the rest of your lives. As for why, look no further than Allz the Shining."

"Who?" asked Rainn.

"A god who betrayed Mother Love and opened the Undergates," Tennat answered Rainn in a whisper. "It didn't work out well for him."

"We haven't betrayed anyone." Masika struggled with the king's reasoning. "Least of all Mother Love. Or the Holy Emperor."

Anger spread over King Larustines's face. His scowl grew thunderous, and he showed his teeth. "Allz the Shining betrayed no one."

A gasp went up around the audience chamber.

"Allz traveled freely between the Undergates and Andos, just as Tennat confided in me you propose to do. His heart was pure and his motives beyond reproach." King Larustines's anger transformed into a dark smugness. "But he did not know the same thing you do not. Travel between the realms weakens the walls between them. Mother Love punished Allz the Shining for a crime he did not commit. None of the gods knew that his travel would eventually tear the barriers between Andos and the Undergates. Every morning the rising sun reminds us of Mother Love's unjust sentence."

The chamber went silent save for the wind that blew through it and the dark blue curtains that rustled beside the windows. Masika was no scholar, but the king's assertion sounded like sacrilege to her.

"How do you know alla this that the gods don't?" Rainn crossed his arms. "Don't get me wrong, sounds to me like you got your head stuffed up a cow's ass, but how d'you even *think* you know this?"

"I believe I may be of help there." Haphimenes gestured toward the cage and the steel fell away. With a series of angry squawks, Heron flapped out a window.

"There is a sect of heretics who believe as the king does. Shining Souls, I think they call themselves, yes?" Haphimenes cocked his head to one side and the king nodded. "They appear to feel that no god could ever be so imperfect as to unleash demons on the world. Sadly, their most basic premise is untrue. Travel between realms does not weaken the walls between, otherwise every death that sends us to the Undergates would do so, leaving them in tatters within moments."

"But—no!" King Larustines stood from his throne and drew his ornamental blade. "You're lying to protect them. Guards, take Haphimenes immediately."

No one moved.

Queen Odandria straightened in her chair and placed both of her hands in her lap. "Well. The king seems to have forgotten his place in the room. He has always been more useful for his beauty than his thoughts. I assume this scheme of yours originated with Meri? Boldness isn't really your style."

The king shrank in on himself. He nodded.

A red haze filled the edges of Masika's vision. Meritities, again. She found the perfect patsy in the king for her plots. And Masika had doubted the queen.

"This is what happens when foolish people are permitted to speak with anyone they want." The queen tutted and shook her head. "Dear Tennat. We shall endeavor to curtail the king's education to approved material and not allow him to reach his own conclusions in the future. I do hope that will be sufficient to satisfy the wrongs he has done you?"

"The wisdom of your justice is second only to Egren the Judge, Your Majesty." Tennat bowed as he said this, showing deference not only to the queen, but to the shamefaced king as well.

"Excuse me." Masika shook her arms out of the tower guards' grip. "Captain Ironmast has lost his ship and all his possessions besides. His only folly in all of this was agreeing to take us on as passengers. Surely there must be something we can do for him?"

The tiniest of smiles flitted across the queen's face. "It seems all the daughters of Tennat Oburn have inherited his persuasion. Very well. Your captain will be made whole too. Now is that all, or would you like me to offer cold winds and chopped herring to all the fish who were made uncomfortably warm by the burning of your ship?"

Tennat cleared his throat and stepped forward. "I'm certain that's all—"

"I could do with some lunch," Rainn said.

CHAPTER

TWELVE

The Andosh have a legend about a huge, silver-scaled fish named Sail Eater. This fish roamed the northern coasts of Andos feasting freely on any ship that caught its fancy. Thousands of sailors fell to its hunger.

One day Sail Eater decided it had outgrown human vessels and went after the sailing ships of the saltblood giants who lived nearby. After some struggle and a surprising turn, Sail Eater went home in a glass bowl as a present to the giant jarl's favorite daughter. It lived for a time on the stand next to her bed until one fateful day when the young princess determined that Sail Eater was thirsty and filled his bowl with whiskey, killing him dead.

The next day the jarl gave his daughter a puppy.

He did not put it in a bowl.

Volume Six of *Thank Gods* by Kohmose Oburn

The new ship went a long way toward relieving Masika's sense of guilt. A four masted carrack hastily rechristened the *Ocean Krait,* it was a huge step up from Captain Ironmast's lost caravel. Though big enough to preclude travel in all but the largest rivers, it nevertheless doubled the *River Krait's* speed and quadrupled her cargo. It even came with a hold full of olives and expensive woods bound for Egren—which Masika was fairly certain had been taken from the ship's previous owner by the queen. Reinforcing the notion that the ship had been taken with some haste, it was woefully undersupplied with food and fresh water, though Masika overheard that a barrel of gold coins had been left in the captain's quarters.

How had Masika been so wrong about the queen? Queen Odandria was an old woman who spoke plainly, and Masika had mistaken that candor for hostility. How stupid could she have been? She did not want to admit, even to herself, that she extended her trust to King Larustines in favor of his wife.

Some leader she turned out to be. Sarah never made that kind of blunder.

What did it mean that Masika might make so important a mistake? Would Rainn and Heron be better off without her? Was Meritities right? Was Masika going to ruin her family with this foolish adventure?

Just before they left, Masika's papa sent an orven home. She did not ask what the message said. She was too embarrassed over the possibilities.

Three nights later, the *Ocean Krait* arrived at Port Bibi, at the northern mouth of the Teawater. The broad river was big enough for them to trek south along the eastern edge of Sedrios beside the Little Gods Mountains, all the way to the open ocean south of Andos. From there they would sail east past the Yellow Sea and around the corner of Egren, eventually to Mukahiit and Mount P'takkin itself.

"I like this place." Rainn hopped off the wooden dock onto a dirt road that ran through the center of Port Bibi. The tiny town was dark and foggy, and the thick mist made them all cold and damp.

Heron shivered inside the cowl of Masika's cloak. According to Rainn, she did not care for the decreased visibility.

"How can you like it?" Masika peered into the murk. "You can't even see it."

"Just a good feeling." His teeth flashed in the lamplight from the *Ocean Krait*. "And you gotta love this weather."

"Be that as it may"—interjected Tennat as he stepped off the dock —"Port Bibi is not formally claimed by any nation. There are some town guards here, who may protect you unless anyone has paid them to do otherwise, but there are no soldiers and next to no law. Keep your heads down, don't get involved in anything that isn't your business, and we'll all be fine."

As Tennat spoke, Nebet moved up behind him and scanned the quiet town. A dark face in the even darker mist with only the bandage covering his missing ear visible, Masika could nevertheless see his cool disdain in her imagination. She did not trust Nebet, and the only way she might would be for him to prove himself in exactly the sort of situation she would never want to be in with a person she didn't trust.

"My business is finding a tavern. Think I can manage to ignore everything else." With that Rainn skipped off into the gloom. Masika even heard him giggle as the first wispy drops of cold rain fell from the sky.

"Everyone else stay close." Nebet's even voice was not loud, but the low tones carried easily. "We would not want to lose anyone important."

"I think I've had enough of your posturing, Nebet." Masika still could not make him out except for the edges where the lamplight hit him, but she turned her body to face that. "Rainn's a member of our expedition, and you are here to keep everyone safe, not just the people you like. Meritities left *you*, in case you hadn't noticed. Papa thinks we're safer with you here, but I'm not so sure. So just do your job and keep your comments about our two gods to yourself."

"They are not gods," came Nebet's immediate reply. "The Andosh worship monsters, not fools and birds."

"Then please protect them as if they were merely the friends of your employer." Tennat squared his shoulders and looked up at Nebet. "They are certainly that, whether you believe any more about them or not."

A tense moment passed, and Nebet shrugged.

"Hey, everyone." From the foggy dark ahead of them, Rainn's voice rang out, eerily loud. "Found the tavern, and it's open. Only place with a lantern at the door. See you inside."

In the distance, a door opened and shut.

They followed.

"WONDER if the owner knew how appropriate it was gonna be to name this place the Wishful Thinking when he opened it?" Pewter mug in both hands, Rainn cast his head to one side to take in the dimly lit interior. They sat at a small square table in a corner of the dirt-floored tavern. A pair of patrons took up all the space at the bar, while the owner cooked fish in a long-handled wire basket above a fire set in the far wall.

"Everything appears to be safe now." Tennat stood and smoothed his brown traveling robe, a match for Masika's own. "I find I am not as hungry as I am tired, so I'll be off to bed. Please don't kill each other over dinner."

Masika watched her papa climb the stair at the other corner. She never thought of him as an old man, and in most respects he was vital and energetic. But tonight he moved with a rickety shamble that worried her.

A curious coo from under Masika's bench accompanied the tavern owner's approach, four plates of fish and potatoes in his arms. He set them down, and Rainn immediately tucked in.

The owner looked over the table. "More beer?" he offered hopefully.

Rainn lifted his mug, face still down over his plate. Masika shook her head no.

"Water," said Nebet.

The owner smiled and nodded. To Masika the old Darrishman looked like someone's grandpapa, maybe even her own. Slightly stooped, with a thin neck and kind eyes, he took Rainn's empty mug and winked at Masika before heading back behind his bar.

For just a moment Masika decided this was a kind and decent man, whose empathy and compassion were an integral part of his job taking care of people. Then she thought of King Larustines and frowned, cursing her naïveté. She would not make that mistake again.

The dinner was fine, if plain. At the end of it, Masika relaxed and nursed the last of the beer in her mug. She fed Heron from the remains of her plate and thought about going upstairs. Tiredness pulled her toward the rented bed, but she did not want to leave Rainn and Nebet here alone. The other two customers at the bar were already gone.

The door slammed open, and a round man with greasy white hair strode in, an evil smirk on his stubbled face. A pair of dirty street toughs followed him in, leaving the door open. Instead of washing off the stink of them, the rain only intensified their smell.

The tavern owner went pale at the sight of them and pasted an anxious smile on his old face.

"Crestor. Can I get you anything?" The owner chuckled and wiped sweat from his forehead. "On the house."

"What's going on there?" Masika pulled at Rainn's shirtsleeve. "Those men have the owner terrified."

"Not our—" Nebet and Rainn said simultaneously and stopped. Rainn glared at the big bodyguard.

"Business," Rainn finished.

If you find yourself in danger again, you will flee. That's what she promised her papa. She wanted to find out what was happening, help out if she could. Maybe the tavern owner would tell stories about the brave Darrish girl who saved his life on a stormy night.

That's certainly what Sarah would do. That's why there were so many stories about her.

Crestor looked back over his soiled shoulder and eyed the three of them warily. Deciding they were of no consequence, he spat a foul-smelling gobbet of greenish brown on the floor and returned to the tavern owner.

"My man tells me you ain't been across the stream to Korris recently, Tomma. Says you *refused*." Crestor pointed and one of his thugs circled the tiny bar, walked behind Tomma the tavern owner, and pulled three beers from the wall mounted keg. "Jackleg Pete is feeling put out over the whole thing. You want that on your conscience?"

That name turned Masika's ear. Papa mentioned it once before: a criminal who ran a town close to Vastard. Dangerous.

Of course, Masika was not Sarah. For the first time, she considered that trying to act like her hero could result in everyone she was traveling with getting killed. That felt like a realization that was a little late in coming.

"I'm not falling into that trap again, Crestor." Tomma's eyes were huge, and his once warm and dark skin was clammy and gray. "It's too late now. We had a deal."

"Pete decides when the deal is final, and Pete's changed his mind." Crestor finished his beer in one go and slammed the mug down on the bar. The *bang* cracked through the dim tavern room, and Heron, well past her breaking point, exploded from beneath the table and flew out the open door.

The other thug burst into laughter. "I think ya sceered off t'morrow's supper, Crestor."

"Pete says you can stay if'n ya wanna, Tomma, but it'll hafta be in pieces." The expression Crestor made turned Masika's stomach, and not just from the half-mouthful of blackened teeth it displayed.

Rainn frowned and twisted in his seat. "I don't give a fuck who goes and who stays, but I'd sure appreciate some peace and quiet while I drink my damn beer."

A gasp came out of both Tomma and Masika when Crestor snatched the old man by the front of his threadbare shirt and yanked him around the bar. Tomma cried out as he was kicked across the floor and out the door. Crestor and one of the thugs followed him out, while the last of them pointed a long dagger at Masika's table.

"Go outside and we kill ya. Stay here and drink free. Your choice."

By way of reply, Rainn lifted his mug and finished it.

The thug walked out to the sound of rough laughter and smell of fresh rain.

"We have to help that man." Nervous energy flooded Masika. She squirmed in her seat. What should she do?

A scream came from outside, followed by more laughter.

Rainn's bench screeched on the floor as he pushed it away from the table. He picked up his mug and walked behind the bar.

"You." Masika locked onto Nebet's impassive face. "I'm ordering you to go help that man."

"No. That man is not my job. You are my job. I—stop!"

Desert blade in hand, Masika sprinted to the door and out into the muddy street.

"Then do your job and keep *me* alive!"

The light from the open doorway flooded into the rainy mud outside the tavern. Crestor, patchy gray eyebrows raised in surprise, drew a rusting knife from his bulging hip. Twenty men flanked him, each as hard and grimy as the two who had followed him into the Wishful Thinking. "Well, lads, looks like we'll be taking some extra entertainment home with us tonight."

Wicked chuckles surrounded Masika as the thugs splashed through the dirty water to encircle her.

Tomma lay bleeding in the mud.

"This was a mistake," Masika whispered to herself.

And then Rainn and Nebet were there, working their way around Masika from either side. Men shrieked and shouted and ran forward with all manner of blade and club brought to bear. They yelled instructions to each other which went ignored in the frantic combat.

Masika concentrated on defense, backing toward the tavern wall and pushing away with the point of her thin sword, pointed poniard in her other hand. To her right Nebet fought similarly, though he kept attackers off with one short sword and made occasional stabs with the other.

A silver flash shot by Masika's face from her left, accompanied by a ringing bang and a muffled scream. The flash, half of a thick-bladed sword, embedded itself in the wooden wall not six inches from her head.

Rainn, spattered in blood and actual rain, swung Forbryttan *through* the sword of another street thug and into the man's shoulder. The broken blade fell from his strengthless hand, and he tried to jump back.

This was as much as Masika could see before she was once again crowded with assailants. She ducked and a boar spear thudded into the wall behind her. If only there was more light for her to—and then there was.

Without knowing how she knew, Masika was aware there was not actually any more light in the street, but rather that Inlittan allowed her to see as if the misty night were a perfectly bright and sunny day.

A mischievous smile settled on Masika's face, and she ran under the spearman's arm to stab him in the back of the calf with her poinard.

What came next was a dance in the dark, as she swept beneath cudgels and baffled her attackers' senses with whispers and tiny taps on legs and arms. Carefully picking her targets, Masika disabled three more men before the fight ended. Her awareness extended all the way around herself, which confused her as soon as she thought about it, so she willed her perception to narrow back to normal. This bracelet/ring thing was amazing.

First, Masika saw Nebet, standing in the middle of three dead or dying men of his own. He bled from a few scratches, but nothing serious. His round-eyed face betrayed real terror, and he held both of his short swords in front of him as if they were protective talismans.

Opposite Nebet stood Rainn, who grinned with a mad shine and sliced the air with Forbryttan, sending water and blood in equal measure in wide arcs across the muddy street. More than a dozen of Crestor's thugs moaned, crawled, or just lay and held injured limbs about Rainn.

"This chops up folks better'n anything I've ever held. You tell your friend back in Greenshade she really knows her swords." One man pulled himself through the muck to get away from Rainn, but the god picked him up by the trouser leg and wiped Forbryttan off on him before sheathing the sword and tossing the man back in the street.

"It's true. He is Alir. He is a monster." Nebet circled away from Masika and Rainn, further into what was now becoming a downpour.

"Nebet, no one has ever lied to you," she said. The bodyguard shook, his razor-sharp blades trained on Rainn. Masika needed to calm him down before something truly stupid happened. "You knew you were traveling with gods. The Alir aren't monsters any more than the P'tak."

"It's a monster," Nebet screamed, his wide eyes never leaving Rainn's face. "It kills men so easily. They never had a chance against something like that."

Rainn rolled his eyes and frowned at Nebet, but he could not hold the dour expression. Masika could see the weather igniting Rainn's muscles and electrifying his brain, a divine body that ate foul weather and sweated death.

"He's not a monster; he's a person." Did she fully believe that herself? It was hard not to be at least a little scared of Rainn when he was like this. "Sure, he's scary when it rains, but lots of folks get aggravated when the weather's bad."

But Rainn showed no signs of aggravation. His grin, wild and blood-spattered, displayed the opposite, which made the spectacle of him all the worse.

Nebet turned to her, face searching for any sort of relief from his fear. But at that instant distant thunder rumbled and Rainn's eyes flashed lightning white.

"Everyone knows the Andosh worship monsters." Nebet spat the words. "I thought it was just a man trying to con you or something. But it's a beast. A real one. Meritities was right." One sword came up to point into the air while the other remained on Rainn.

"And I'll see it dead."

With that, Nebet turned and bolted away, sprinting up the water-soaked street and into a filth-strewn alley.

"I am not scary." Rainn opened his arms to indicate all the men surrounding him. "These idiots will all be just fine. With Forbryttan I can just smash their weapons and knock the shit out of them. No killing necessary. Nebet's being a big baby."

As it happened, Nebet had been the only one of the three of them to have killed anyone. Masika shook her head—what would Papa think about this?—and looked for Tomma. She found him curled into a tight ball and helped him to his feet. A blow to the head had torn skin. and he bled everywhere.

"Where's Crestor?" Tomma peered as best he could through the rain. "He can't die. Jackleg—Jackleg Pete'll burn down the whole town."

A short glance around revealed Crestor, lying on his prodigious stomach, head to one side, unconscious in the street. Other than a few missing fingers, he was intact.

Masika propped Tomma the tavern owner up against the wall of the Wishful Thinking and squelched over to Crestor's foul bulk. Breath held, she pulled the grease-slicked belt off his waist and tightened it around his wrist so the wound to his hand could not bleed him dry. In the rain, he had a sour odor that threatened to—

She threw up on him.

"It's all right." Rainn grinned at her. "Way he smells, he'll never notice it."

Soon they were all back in the warm tavern common room, Heron included, and Masika wrapped clean bandages around Tomma's forehead. They sat at a table she had dragged close to the fireplace to help them dry out.

"Not sure what I'll do tomorrow, but I appreciate you not lettin' me get killed tonight." Tomma winced as Masika cleaned his wound but held still regardless. He was a tough old bird.

What had Papa told her about Jackleg Pete? In the relative quiet, she concentrated and dredged up the memory. A smuggler who ran the town of Korris across the Teawater, Jackleg Pete's ruthlessness was legendary. Only the complicated network of bribes and payments he distributed and his high regard in the bandit nation of Vastard kept him safe, and had for decades. How would she and Rainn deal with someone like that before they moved on?

"What's he so pissed about?" Rainn sat on the other side of the table with three mugs of Tomma's beer. "They weren't asking for money. They wanted *you*."

"Jackleg is a devil." Tomma looked as if he were about to spit on the floor but reconsidered. "Last year he started squeezing me over some bad debts. He runs crooked Goldkeep tables over in Korris. I shoulda known better, but everyone's smarter lookin' over their shoulder, y'know?"

"This is going to hurt." Masika pressed the loose flap of skin down to Tomma's forehead and rapidly circled it with the bandage. Tomma squinted and hissed a quick intake of breath.

"No lie there." He gave her a weak smile. "Anyway, I didn't have the money. All I had was the tavern and a pretty wife who wouldn't shut the hell up. So I sold Jackleg my Lyssa in payment, clear and full."

"You what?" Masika's hands withdrew from Tomma, and she sat back in her chair.

"But Jackleg decided I swindled him, the cheap fuck. Like I said, Lyssa's never shut her damn mouth a moment of her life, and she's fuller of opinions than an owl is owl shit. So Jackleg says for me to come back and get her, and bring him his coin to boot, or he'll feed Lyssa to his dogs. But I already replaced her, right? Mousey little thing about your age, sorta plain"—he winked again at Masika, turning her stomach—"but she keeps her yap shut unless I put her on her knees, if you know what I mean."

The sick feeling crawling out of Masika's innards said she did, in fact, understand exactly what he meant. She was almost glad she had already thrown up.

"He could send a hundred bastards just as mean as the ones you put in the dirt soon's he hears about all the ruckus, but maybe he won't. Maybe he'll decide it ain't worth the trouble and he'll just knock Lyssa in the head until she—Ow!"

Tomma stared at Masika's poniard, pinning his hand to the table. His eyes goggled and his mouth worked, but no sound came out.

"You are going to go to Korris right now, and you are going to take Lyssa back from Jackleg Pete." Her voice stayed flat and even, all the more terrifying for the hot tide of rage that filled her. "You will give him the tavern to pay your debts, and you will leave. What's the mousey girl's name?"

"Pr-Prin," Tomma snuffled.

"You will leave Prin in charge to run the tavern for Jackleg Pete instead of you, *if* she wants it. Is all that entirely clear?"

Tomma stared at his hand and said nothing. Irritated, Masika flicked the poniard's pommel.

He screamed.

"Yes! Yes, I'll go now. Why do you even care? No. Please don't. It don't matter. I'm going. Take whatever you want. Just—AGH!"

The poniard jerked out of Tomma's hand and sent a beaded cord of blood in an arcing stream into his face.

Knifed hand gripped in the other, Tomma pushed himself to his feet and staggered through the door, dripping a trail of red on the dirt floor as he went.

"We have to get out of here tonight," Masika whispered to Rainn. "We can't take a chance on Jackleg Pete missing his goons early. I hope there's enough food here to get the *Ocean Krait* to Garpoint."

As soon as the door shut, Rainn burst into a gale of crackling laughter.

"What the hell are you so happy about?" Masika tasted bitter disappointment alongside her own bile. This evening had ended on a repulsive note. "This only makes things harder for us."

He quieted, snorted, and tried again. "I-I *told* you not to get involved."

"Oh, fuck off."

CHAPTER

THIRTEEN

The Pavinn construction of the Untamed Paradise puts them at adds with what scholars know to be true of gods in general. Gods reside in the real world, if in spaces set apart from their worshippers.

But what would our reaction be to a real god in our midst? Could our belief countenance an actual encounter with the divine, or, put in front of our very faces, would our "common sense" override the evidence of our eyes and deny the truth?

In my opinion, this is the true reason the gods live so far apart from their worshippers. Inaccessible mountain tops build fear, and fear encourages obedience.

No one in their right mind would want to be friends with a god.

Volume One of *Thank Gods* by Kohmose Oburn

The Teawater lived up to its name. A slow-moving river ambled below Masika's feet to twist between the Little Gods Mountains on the east, and the marshy jungles of Sedrios on the west. Tannins in the water dyed it dark as browl and made it acidic enough to discourage biting insects from hatching there.

Captain Ironmast traded the square sails for lateens to better navigate the snaking waterway in what little wind there was. The ship had been on half-rations due to their unexpectedly hurried departure from Port Bibi, and morale had not been great. Until, that was, the first lines and nets dipped over the side in search of river cats. They could not pull the soft-skinned fish in fast enough. Even with the extra sailors provided by Queen Odandria to operate the larger vessel, meat no longer proved a problem.

Given Nebet's reaction to witnessing Rainn's god magic, Masika did not want to tell the sailors about Heron's blessing. As the goddess of catching small creatures in still or slow-moving water, she could easily keep the crew fed.

Until they got tired of fish. And fresh water might soon become a problem. They needed to get to Garpoint soon, but there was so little wind.

Too bad neither of her gods could make breezes out of farts. Masika giggled at the thought.

"Something funny?" Tennat leaned against the bow railing and watched the jungle pass by. His displeasure at last night's events in Port Bibi were mitigated by Masika's keeping her word to run away when it looked as if things were getting dangerous.

She still owed Rainn some fried pirate candies for not telling him any different.

"No. Rainn is worried that we'll get all the way to the top of Mount P'takkin, and we'll find out why High King Oldam wouldn't let them into the Alireon."

Brow raised, Tennat lifted his head and stared down at his daughter in the watery afternoon sun. "Why is that a worry? Wouldn't that be the solution he's looking for?"

"Maybe." Masika watched her reflection ahead of the *Ocean Krait's* wake. Elbows on the rail, she leaned ahead of the slow sailing ship. "I think he's concerned it won't be a solution at all. What if he finds out the problem is something that the imp can't fix? What if it's something wrong with *them*? Something Angrim did to them that he can't undo?"

"Then he'll have his answer, and he can start looking for another life." He put his hand on his daughter's shoulder. It was the hand of a diplomat, warm and soft. "But he'll know that he did everything he could to find out, and he'll know he had good friends to help him."

Her papa almost made her feel better about it.

"That may not be enough. Rainn is also worried that if Heron doesn't change back into herself soon, she may become a bird in her mind as well as her body. She may never be herself again."

Tennat's hand fell away, and he leaned on the railing next to Masika. He pulled in a deep breath and let it out. "It's always hard to let go of the things we knew. But there are worse fates than to live your life as a beautiful heron."

That was true enough. Masika thought of Tomma and the women in his life whose bad fortune had put them in his orbit. She would rather be a bird than any of them.

But while this line of thought might make Masika feel better, telling Heron and Rainn that she had resigned herself to their fates was not helpful to anyone.

"Thanks, but that's not really an answer. I wish I had Kohmose's faith in the P'tak. Or even Djephan's." Masika stared into the water. Even Meritities's. *Especially* Meritities's. "I'm worried they will see to some truth we haven't guessed at yet and reveal our adventure to be folly. And where will that leave me? I promised the imp I would travel to the Undergates to retrieve his creator. What if I have to do it alone?"

It raised an interesting question. How many people could she disappoint all at one go?

He slid his warm hand across her shoulders, and his touch relaxed her, even if it did not dispel her fears. "Do not sell your friends short, Lahamila. I don't believe for an instant your Alir would abandon you so easily. And either way, you would have me. Surely you will need a negotiator in hell?"

"Of course, Papa."

Of course. What else was there to say? If she told him no, he would forbid her from proceeding and then no one would get what they wanted. But there was no way she would ever let that happen. As he just proved, Papa always looked for the best in people, which often times brought the best out of them—in staterooms and diplomatic councils. What little Masika knew of the Undergates leaned well away from refined courts of reasoned debate and more toward running, screaming, and fighting: absolutely none of which her papa would be any good at. His simple presence might well kill them all, if protecting him overrode their own survival.

Well, Masika's, at any rate.

She would be alert from here on out for ways to leave her papa, who loved her and only wanted the best for his daughter, behind.

He patted her on the back. "Think I'll go see if there's any fish left over from lunch."

As he walked away, Masika considered just what it was everyone did want here. Papa seemed to want nothing more than for his children to become happy adults with lives of meaning and purpose. Their mother constantly criticized him for allowing the kids to choose their own paths, and said he was a lazy parent. But it seemed to Masika that supporting his children whatever their choices was much more difficult—and brave—than making that support dependent on them choosing a life of safety and guaranteed success.

Her papa was kind of a hero that way.

Meritities, on the other hand, wanted to appear perfect in all ways and circumstances. This interpretation was less maddening to Masika than the thought that her sister simply was already perfect. Either way, Meritities had decided that Masika was *not* perfect to the degree that it made Meritities look bad, so she ensured that as few people knew Masika's name or saw her face as possible. While hurtful, it occasionally played to Masika's advantage, except when their parents were involved.

And why was Meritities so jealous of their papa's attention? He treated them both equally while their mother ignored Masika in favor of the more beautiful and elegant Meritities. Would her sister simply not be satisfied until Masika was pushed out of the family altogether? Is that what it would take?

At least she did not have to wonder what Rainn and Heron wanted: to get back home with as many good meals along the way as they could fit in.

Ild the imp wanted Glauth brought back from the dead so he could kill her again, and Romi and Catlia wanted to keep that from happening. That second part, anyway. If there was anything Masika could do to help the two runecrafters save Glauth's life on the other end of this, she would do it. After getting her into the Forest Castle in Treaty Hill and gifting her with runecrafted weapons, she owed them that much.

What then did Masika want?

When she rescued Heron and Rainn from the hole beneath the Fell Citadel, she had only wanted to be known as the person who found and returned them to their home. But things had gotten so much more complicated since then. She found what she wanted most of all was to go back to Egren and her old life, studying sword and bow with her uncle Mahu and his partner Sabni, laughing when Mahu complained about Sabni's religious parables, and drinking the fabulous concoctions their friend and ally Ameli made from exotic teas and flowers. Even that possibility fled her, now that Uncle Mahu decided to become a farmer and Sabni a priest.

Of everyone involved, Masika fit in here least of all.

A cheer went up as one of the new sailors, a short Andosh man named Roger with brown hair and beard as well as a quick smile, hit a green hare beside the river with an arrow. He pulled the animal through the water by a length of twine tied to the arrow. Heron's blessing worked for all manner of creatures in or at the water.

"Toldja," Roger shouted to his mates. "I can't miss."

A tall shadow stomped over to cover Roger, and the color drained from the sailor's face.

"I fuckin' *told* you no hunting near the shore. Did I not, crewman? Or mebbe yer needing yer ears cleaned out with the point of my cutlass?" Captain Ironmast's growl sliced through Roger's short-lived glee like a straight razor through steam.

"S-sorry, Cap'n." Shaking, Roger yanked his arrow free of the hare's green-tinted fur and dropped it over the side. Ironmast sighed, wiped his brow with one bony hand, and punched Roger in the face.

Movement in the tree line drew Masika's attention. Something large darted into cover on the western bank, and the sounds of movement followed from north and south.

"Armored lizards on the starboard side," shouted their lookout from the crow's nest. "Half a dozen at the least."

All of the sailors turned to see, but Masika noted they also ducked down behind wales, crates, and anything else that might break sight lines to the shore. She did the same.

"Why are we hiding?" Masika had heard of armored lizards before. While scary up close, a ship, especially one as large as the *Ocean Krait*, was beyond them. "They're just crocodiles that walk like people, right? They can't hurt us."

The sailor hiding behind an empty water barrel jerked around to stare at her. He was her age, barely dressed, and Pavinn. Masika had noticed him before but did not know his name.

He flashed her a grin.

"Aye, ma'am. Crocodiles what can walk and throw spears and talk at one another like any other folk, and we just snatched their dinner right out from under their noses. Likely as not they'll just be sore about it and watch us pass on by, but no sense in givin' 'em extra targets to toss their spears at while we do it."

"They can throw spears?" This was new information to Masika. Armored lizards did not range farther east than the Teawater. "If they're that smart, they'll stay away. We have far more arrows than six lizards can have spears."

The sailor's youthful grin spread. "That we do, ma'am. But the armored part of the name ain't fer show. They got metal in their scales. Arrows bounce right off."

This sounded like the sort of situation Masika should be scared of, but she was vastly more intrigued. She poked her head up over the wale to try and spot one of the lizards.

A pair of eyes situated on top of a broad head swiveled. The motion was the only thing that allowed Masika to see it, the creature being the same color as the jungle shadows.

Inlittan glimmered at her right hand, and Masika's vision cleared spectacularly.

The lizard was over seven feet tall and looked much like a thick-bodied crocodile with longer, powerful arms and legs, head and shoulders daubed with cracking yellow and blue paints. It carried a well-used spear with a long bone blade at the end. Before Masika popped up to look, it had been staring to one side, but her movement prompted its head to turn in her direction.

Though she could not have explained how she knew, Masika was aware of three further things. The creature was female, it was the leader of the seven lizards surrounding it, and it was burning with hatred toward the *Ocean Krait* and her crew.

"Woah." Masika turned and slid down, her back to the wale.

"Didja see one?" The young sailor had not lost any of his eager excitability. "I'm always too scared to look."

"I did." She spied Captain Ironmast in the aft castle. "'Scuse me."

Head down, Masika ran as fast as she could down the steps of the forecastle, across the main deck, and up to the wheelhouse where Captain Ironmast hunkered.

"You need ta get below." Ironmast's glare froze Masika and made her forget what she had come to tell him. "I'm not explainin' to yer pa why his pride and joy got herself filled up of bone spears."

"If you ever did, I wouldn't suggest putting it just that way." She searched Ironmast's face. "Should we be scared here?" Despite knowing how angry the reptilian matriarch appeared, Masika had no way of knowing if that meant the lizards were an actual threat. Could they harm the ship? Would the crew be safe if they just hunkered down until the *Ocean Krait* passed the lizards by?

"Normally, no." He kept an eye out just over the top of her head. "Lizards don't like pickin' fights unless they're certain to win. But while we were in Port Bibi, I talked to a captain just come outta here. Said he was part of a three-ship convoy. Number three spies a big mound onna bank and goes diggin' through it. They find hundreds of eggs and take the lot, over protest of the other two captains. There was a fight between the captains, and number three gets sore about it, so he sends sailors inna dingy out to smash every new egg mound they come across. Musta got a dozen before the lizards figured out what was what."

He tensed, eyes narrowing. "Guess lizards're shitty parents. Course the whole thing coulda been avoided if the third captain hadn't been such a colossal fuckwit."

Not seeing whatever he was looking for, Ironmast relaxed a fraction.

"The boys inna dingy died fast. Spears. But the lizards swarmed the sides of number three and killed those sailors slower. The first two boats fled to the sound of screamin'. When the captain I talked to made it out of the Teawater, his was the only ship left."

"And you knew this when we left last night?"

"I did. Course you was inna hurry of your own just then. Figured I'd rather take my chances that the lizards was satisfied eatin' two ships worth of sailors than ol' Jackleg suddenly growin' a heart with any forgiveness in it."

The captain's logic made sense to Masika.

"I saw a lizard . . . queen?" She had no idea if that was the right term. "A big female with yellow and blue paint on its head. Stared a hole right through me. I counted seven more besides her."

"Looks as through yer head may be good for something besides stopping arrows after all." Ironmast looked her over from top to bottom, as though seeing her for the first time. "Stay low and keep a sharp eye. You spot anything, shout it out. Yer lookin' for any increase in their numbers, anyone heftin' those spears, and most of all, anything inna water headin' towards us. You got that?"

A thrill ran through Masika's stomach. Had she just saved the crew of the *Ocean Krait*, or was she just about to? She nodded to the captain and ran back to the bow, bent nearly double. Sarah would be so proud of her.

CHAPTER

FOURTEEN

The single most defining characteristic of the Pavinn gods is their hunger. Whether they are eating unfortunate animals, the souls of the damned, or each other, the Untamed are always on the prowl.

One of the lesser-known myths of pirate hero Racha'o concerns a deal he made to keep the Stone People safe from being eaten by Mount Corosha, a nearby mountain peak that occasionally uncurled into an unimaginably sized granite lizard to devastate the land. In return for safe harbor and his choice of the stone people's three most beautiful daughters, Racha'o opened a salted rock shop that catered exclusively to mountain-sized rolling lizards.

The endeavor was so successful that the population of stone people exploded, which is the beginning of Racha'o's more well-known tale about capturing the stone clans and fastening them to lengths of chain for sale as the very first ships' anchors.

Volume Seven of *Thank Gods* by Kohmose Oburn

Over Tennat's strenuous objections, Masika took her new place as the *Ocean Krait's* primary lookout. She had to prove her superiority to the current lookout first, which was easy enough with Inlittan's help, but rather than the expected resentment, the crew were happy to carry a passenger who pulled her weight.

Since the first lizard sighting, she changed into her leathers—supple armor the color of honey with inset steel rivets and whorled flourishes. Masika had never worn it into combat before, so its protection was untested. But if the cost was any indication, she would be all but invulnerable.

She still would have felt better if everyone were allowed to carry their weapons, but it was not her ship.

The next two sightings of armored lizards showed increased numbers, but they backed off as soon as it became obvious the ship was alerted to them.

A week into their river journey, they had passed both vessels described in the lizard attack, derelict and haunted. The first ship leaned against the shore, a lonely old drunk who finally finished herself off and lay cooling in front of the tavern door.

The second floated freely in the middle of the river and spun slow rotations where some peculiarity in the riverbed caused a lazy vortex to hold it. The crew of the *Ocean Krait* were forced to push the ship out of the way with poles to get by, which felt rude to Masika. The poor ship could not even be allowed the dignity of dying in peace.

Above decks on the *Ocean Krait,* the ever-warming spring sun beat down on the boards, driving Tennat, Masika, and most of all Rainn into Tennat's larger compartment to plan their next moves. Masika felt guilty every moment she stepped away from the crow's nest, but she needed to be a part of any strategizing.

"I don't think it's a good idea to sail the whole damn coast of Egren to get to the place no one wants us to be." Rainn rubbed the tattooed skin of Heron's neck and head as he spoke, eliciting pleasant coos from the goddess. A single round hole with the shutter fastened open let in enough light for everyone sitting around Tennat's tiny table to see.

"That's precisely why we should do so," Tennat returned. "As of this moment, no one else knows what we're doing. The faster we get there, the safer we'll be. That means sailing right past the whole of Egren as if we had no worries at all."

"You know who's got no worries? Dead people." Under Rainn's tender fingertips, Heron stretched her neck and lifted her feathers. The glow from Angrim's desecration shone a dull blue. "You say no one knows we're here, but we don't really know that, do we? Meritities has been gone a while now. More'n long enough to tell everyone from here to the House of Gods we're coming."

"My daughter would never betray her own like that."

"Tennat Oburn, you got a hundred-and-fifteen-pound blind spot right in the middle of your fucking head, and it's gonna get all of us killed. Meritities is *exactly* the person to betray you. She's already done it twice."

It was hard to argue with Rainn, Masika having been the one thrown in the Forest Castle's dungeon, and then watching the *River Krait* burn to the waterline, but she still felt an obligation to come to her sister's defense.

"Meritities doesn't want us dead. She wants us to stop." In an effort to preserve the ship's water, Masika poured herself a small glass of wine while she talked. "She's embarrassed by us and what we're doing. She can't tell anyone else without everyone finding out, which even if she did want us dead, would prevent her from doing it. I think we're safe from my sister."

Tennat scowled. The result of Masika's assertion was what he wanted, but he clearly detested the way she got there.

"I'm more worried about what happens when we get to the mountain." She took a sip and stifled a yawn. The wine was sweet and yellow, and she had been up keeping watch the entire night before. "What if the P'tak and the Alir are too adversarial? The Darrish and the Andosh are getting along well enough for now, but that's not the norm, and who knows if the gods respect our politics anyway?"

"Can't say much about the last few thousand years," Rainn said, "but no one really paid much attention to what the humans were doing at all when I was in the Alireon."

A slow squawk added itself to the conversation.

"Sure, Hagrim and Magda did, but look where it got them." Rainn looked Heron in one bright emerald eye. "He gets named god of betrayal and chained to his forge, while she's forced to leave him for the Screaming Tower. Punishment forever just for being a little too interested in the affairs of humans. No wonder everyone ended up hating Angrim."

Angrim, the Anger Under the Mountain, was once an Alir himself, or so Masika understood the stories. He voluntarily left the Alireon to rule over humanity—or to destroy it? Something like that. She made it a point to find out about the Anger because of his famous rivalry with Sarah, but listening to Kohmose talk about him still knocked her unconscious.

"As I've already said, if the P'tak don't want to speak to us, we'll never make it to the top of the mountain." Tennat sounded as exhausted as Masika felt. "Our immediate concern should be getting resupplied at Garpoint. It was a shame we couldn't have stripped those two derelict craft for supplies without being attacked by lizards."

Rainn frowned at Tennat. "But you don't really know we won't make it to the top without permission, do you? You're not a god and you've never been to the House of the Gods. Maybe the real reason the legend says no one's ever made it there is because *everyone* has, but the damn Darrish gods eat them all. Or slit open their stomachs and wear them as shoes. You just don't know."

"Would you prefer we drop you off here and go home?"

There was a quiet pause as Rainn considered Tennat's question. "That's a fair point. Never mind."

An oversized spear slanted through the open porthole and splintered the tabletop with a long bone blade and a loud *crack*. Masika jumped in her seat, and Rainn went over backward, sending a flapping and squawking Heron to bounce off the walls of the small room.

"How bad is it?" Having regained his feet, Rainn leaned over Tennat, who grimaced with gray-faced pain.

"Papa!" Masika's hand flew to her mouth. After cracking the table, the spear blade entered her papa's leg a bit above the knee.

"No. Stay here. Let the crew fight—unh . . ." Tennat's command came out as more of a raspy husk, but his hands gripped Masika's forearm with strength. "I'll be fine here. Just going to sit and not move."

He fell unconscious.

Shock kept Masika fast in her seat. They were under attack? She had to take care of Papa. This would *never* have happened if she were keeping watch instead of relaxing below decks. She was not even wearing her armor.

Oh. Yes, she was.

"Come on." Rainn grabbed Masika's arm and dragged her out of the cabin. "If those lizards take the ship, your dad'll have bigger problems than his socks not matching."

"What?" She followed him through the narrow passenger corridor toward the deck.

"His socks don't match." Rainn heaved a sigh and shook his head as he climbed the short stair and grabbed the door handle. "Because one of his socks is dyed red now? With blood? You Darrish aren't a funny people."

Her fugue lasted until the sunlight hit her face on the *Ocean Krait's* deck and the world erupted into chaos and violence.

Sailors shouted and clubbed at the big lizards that tried to come over the side of the ship, their claws finding easy purchase on the outer hull. But the shouts were drowned in the air by the deep grumbling croaks of the armored lizards, whose war cries vibrated every inch of Masika's bones.

She should have been afraid. This was exactly the sort of situation her papa told her to be afraid of. But she was not. The cold-blooded creatures were merely an obstacle to getting back to him.

Damn Nebet for a coward, getting frightened of Rainn and running off back in Port Bibi. This was exactly the sort of situation he would be useful in.

The only situation, in truth.

Directly ahead a man went down as one of the lizards hefted itself over the bow railing and caught his head in its massive crocodilian mouth.

Masika pulled her bow from her back with one hand and nocked an arrow with the other.

The creature lifted the limp body of the sailor and shook it, teeth tearing into flesh. It was Roger. She pushed her shock and anger away and released her arrow.

The arrow flew . . . and bounced away from the glinting scales.

No. Look closer. Masika concentrated, allowing Inlittan to use her eyes. Time slowed.

Roger was dead. His final wind rattled out of his chest and his blood moved to the dictates of gravity instead of a beating heart. She pushed at her gaze, sliding it from his body to the creature who whipped him side to side.

Armored scales shimmered metallic hardness in the bright sun and pushed back against the light as much as Inlittan's probing vision. A strange calmness blanketed Masika's brain as the inevitability of the monster confronted her. They were going to die.

She was going to die. And she was not afraid.

A leap brought Rainn to the lizard's side, Forbryttan swinging down in a pointed arc. But before the tip of the runecrafted sword could make contact, the lizard swung its fist out in a savage backhand that caught the god in the jaw and sent him spinning to the deck. He collided with the wood and did not move.

For a single instant Masika wondered how Rainn managed to keep hold of Forbryttan before she nocked a second arrow.

The lizard leaned down over Rainn, its bloodied jaws opening toward his head.

She pulled the bowstring back.

In the shining light against the monster's scaled head, a black hole drew Masika's attention just behind its eye.

She loosed.

A deep roar that rattled the vertebrae in her spine pushed Masika back a step. She wanted to flee the crushing din. Instead, she ran to the starboard wales and took aim.

Another beast clambered aboard to the immediate right of her, and she spun and brought her bow up in line with that lizard's ear hole and released. Thankfully its death roar was cut short when it hit the water below.

"Aim for the ears!" Masika shouted. "The hole behind the eyes. It's the only place they're weak!"

Other sailors repeated Masika's cries and another two lizards fell. Captain Ironmast bellowed instructions from the aft castle, and the men pushed back against the reptiles, who lost their overwhelming aggression in the face of a newly organized and effective enemy.

A series of sharp bangs from shore caught the attention of another dozen swarming armored lizards. The queen snapped her powerful jaws in a loud staccato pattern, signaling the end of the assault. Or so Masika assumed from the other lizard's sudden retreat.

The instant the blue and yellow painted queen saw Masika she flung her huge spear, bone blade whistling, directly at Masika's chest.

Masika screamed in alarm, dropped, and increased the volume of her shriek when the spear glanced off the top of her head and yanked her hair on its way to the main mast.

Ow!

Instantly incensed at the pain, Masika jumped back to her feet and wrenched the spear free of the mast. With the weapon over her head, she turned to the queen and screamed again, at first incoherently, then with specific purpose.

"Fuck you, fucking lizard-lady! You wanna try and come over here and fucking kill me because some other asshole fucked your eggs up? I didn't have a fucking thing to do with that, but I'll be happy to put a fucking arrow in the head of every one of you fucks who tries to make it about me. You hear me, you hateful fuck? Come here and fight me yourself, you fucking fuck. Fuck!"

She got a little more incoherent again after that. She was not great with pain.

A final booming snap was the queen's only reply, and her glare, full of frustrated venom, her only attack. The lizards slithered up the shore and vanished into the brush until the queen was the only one left visible.

Masika dropped the spear and raised her bow one more time. The queen wanted this to be personal? That was fine with Masika.

A hand reached over her shoulder and grabbed the arrow shaft before she could let fly.

"That the only foul word you know?" Rainn turned the arrow up and removed it from Masika's fingers. "We're gonna have to teach you to do better'n that."

"Get out of the way." Her anger faded, red smoke blown into open sky. If she did not kill the queen now, she would not want to. "I can end this here and now before it goes any further."

"That's what I'm trying to do. No"—he pulled another arrow away from Masika and blood dripped from his face onto her shoulder— "lizard lady stopped the fight soon's she saw it wasn't going their way. Just like the captain said. You kill *her*, there's no one to stop them. We can't outrun them onna river, and who knows how many more they got hiding in the jungle."

The queen did draw her lizards back to prevent any more of their deaths. She might have misplaced her aggression onto the *Ocean Krait*, but she obviously cared for the well-being of her own kind.

"Maybe she doesn't understand Darrish." Masika lowered her bow.

"Safe bet." Rainn handed the two arrows back to her. "Since she's not climbing over the side of the ship to stick another spear in your head."

She stowed her bow and the two arrows and lifted the spear. The wood was dark and dense. Heavy. This weapon was for someone stronger than a normal person. Three feet of fired bone blade jutted aggressively, razor sharp and uncommonly hard.

"Papa."

Masika dropped the spear to the deck and ran to her papa's cabin, terrified. If he was dead because of her stupid adventure . . .

"Hey there. What are you looking so upset for? I just heard you single-handedly—Ow! Careful—um, *disobeyed me again* and single-handedly drove off the lizards." Tennat Oburn gritted his teeth in a reasonable approximation of a white-faced grin while the young Pavinn sailor from Masika's first conversation about armored lizards wrapped Tennat's leg in a series of tight linen bandages. The cabin stunk of the whiskey the boy used to sanitize the wound. "As your father, I disapprove of your risking your life, but as a person still drawing breath, I think you're amazing."

Chair legs scraped across the boards as Masika dragged the table aside, giving her papa and the young sailor more room. Fine. He was obviously fine. So why was she shaking now?

The sailor stood and grinned at Masika, his face bright beneath curly dark hair. "He needs lotsa water and rest. I'll check on him so the wound stays clean, and I got a tonic from the Paradisals that'll stop infection. Comes right from the Daughters themselves."

"Thank you." Masika touched his smooth brown shoulder. Young as he was, the Pavinn lad was obviously the ship's surgeon. "There are probably more people to worry about above."

She thought of Roger. The foolish sailor would still be alive if she had been on lookout, as she was supposed to be. Or would he? She had sat the crow's nest all night and was exhausted. What if she had fallen asleep up there?

The grin dissipated, and the boy nodded. "I gave him some herbs for pain and such. He'll likely be asleep any minute, so get him outta that chair and into the hammock. Don't worry none. I'll be back soon."

He left.

"Can't say you don't keep me on my toes." Tennat tried for a smile and ended up with a gray wince.

"That's your backside, Papa." She wiped clammy sweat from his brow. "Let's move you to the hammock." Lifting carefully and trying to ignore the sharp hisses of drawn-in breath from her papa, Masika helped Tennat off the blood-slicked chair and to the swaying bed.

"Why don't you try to get some sleep?" The water pitcher was empty, so she picked it up and moved to the door. "I'll get you some more water for when you wake up."

"Mm. Thanks. That's a good idea." So saying, Tennat closed his eyes and fell silent. As Masika watched and waited, his breathing deepened and his mouth fell slightly open.

His skin, normally a rich, dark brown, was ashen and waxy looking. That was the blood loss, right? He could just make more blood now, couldn't he? Curious, she let her vision slide into Inlittan and peered at her papa.

She could see the strain caused by the lack of blood on his heart, but also just how determined that heart was not to fail. She was certainly no surgeon, but he looked as if he would be all right to her.

With a small chirrup, Heron hopped onto Tennat, curled herself into a fluffy feathered ball in the pit of his stomach, and closed her eyes.

CHAPTER

FIFTEEN

Once the most controversial of all deific figures, now the most wholly forgotten, is Chamblin the Haunted, Hunter in the Night. What he is to have hunted is not clear as most accounts of Chamblin have been destroyed, but two facts are incontrovertible.

First, Chamblin was the god of fretting and indecision. Only happy when reading a book, any other activity was met with endless dithering and second-guessing.

Next, and the cause of all the trouble, is that Chamblin seemed neither to be Alir nor P'tak, but both at once. Though pale complected in the stories of the Andosh and jet skinned by Darrish accounts, all extant stories conclusively refer to the same godly individual. How this was possible and what it meant in the larger scheme of things is unknowable, though given the implicit weaknesses in Chamblin's character, he was almost certainly an Alir first and foremost.

Volume Eight of *Thank Gods* by Kohmose Oburn

121

U p in the *Ocean Krait's* crow's nest, Masika sat and stared into the slowly unfolding jungle and worried. Her papa traveled the world for the Holy Emperor and was no stranger to tense situations, but she was certain that had never included being attacked by spear-throwing, metal-scaled lizard people. He was no warrior and should not be here. How could Masika ever explain to her mother, an abrasively judgmental woman at the best of times, if she somehow got him killed before she could shuttle him off to safety?

"Hey, Mom, how've things been while I was gone? Me? Oh, fine. Hey, good news. One less plate to worry about on the dinner table tonight."

The joke fell flat to her own ears even with no one else to hear it. Below, Masika spotted another of the lizards watching them through the dense foliage. Invisible to everyone else, they practically glowed in Inlittan's sight. Keeping watch. Making certain the ship full of egg-stealing humans kept moving.

But Papa was hardly her only problem.

Masika's brother Kohmose loved to tell stories of grand battles between the brave and intelligent P'tak and the brutish and arrogant Alir pantheons of gods. There seemed to be little love lost between the two. She felt they might all soon climb Mount P'takkin to their deaths.

If they could scale the mountain in the first place. To her knowledge no one ever had before, and Masika had no reason to expect that she would be special in this regard. She had never climbed anything more challenging than a garden wall.

One of the sailors, weighted net in hand, turned to look up at Masika from below on the ship's deck. She peered into the water and pointed. With a nod, he flung the net in that direction and came back with enough fish to feed half the crew. At least this was one thing she could do.

Even without Heron.

"You know, Mom, now that I've killed Dad, I think I'm giving up on this whole royal family of Egren thing to become a sailor on a merchant ship. Thanks for the dance classes though."

She smiled. That one was funnier.

Of course, even if they did manage to get to the top of the mountain without being murdered by mortally offended gods for strolling up with yucky mortal dirt on their shoes, there was no guarantee that any of the P'tak would be able to help. Did they know how to bring a person back from the Undergates, and even if they did, would they entrust that knowledge to Masika? There were so many slender threads on which all of this depended, any one of which might send them all cascading onto distant rocks.

This was beginning to look like an extremely stupid plan.

Somehow Masika had been cast in the role of leader of this little group. Masika Oburn, sixteen years old, was leading a pair of gods *and her own papa* through the wilderness in search of an improbable answer at the top of an impossible destination. It was much more likely that she had hit her head, and this was all a ridiculous dream.

She hoped so, anyway.

A waving hand from the deck caught her attention. Rainn mimed climbing the ladder to join her, the question on his face. She nodded to him. Captain Ironmast had ordered quiet on board until the ship was well past the lizards' territory.

As Rainn climbed, Masika pondered her sister's role in all of this. Meritities stood solidly against them achieving their goals, most likely out of embarrassment for seeing a family member desecrate Mount P'takkin with Andosh gods. Would she stop at jailing Masika and having their ship burned?

Would she stop at anything?

"Your dad's doing fine." Rainn swung a leg over the top of the railing that surrounded the crow's nest and sat on it, his voice low. The blue glow from Angrim's tattoos faded to invisibility in the bright sun. "I've never seen any man be so polite when he orders people around. They don't even realize he's doing it."

"That sounds just like him." A strained smile stretched across

Masika's lips. "Are you here to reassure me that I'm not recklessly endangering his life?"

"Yup." He grinned at her, though it lasted only an instant. His lips pursed and eyes narrowed. "How'd you know that?"

"Was coming up here to check on me your idea?" Her smile became more genuine by degrees.

"Yeah . . ." One brow went up on Rainn's forehead. "That is, I was talking with Tennat, and he mentioned that you might be feeling . . . Khanah's damnable eggs!" He struck a closed fist onto the top of his leg and chuckled. "Did it to me too. Your dad's a menace."

"He is very persuasive."

Rainn pulled his other leg over and crossed them, leaning back against the rail. Masika stood to give him room but kept her eyes on the jungle.

"Anything interesting?"

An enormous jungle cat crouched under broad green leaves in the overgrowth alongside the river, watching the ship pass with a distrustful snarl on its face. Masika could see, though not hear, the vibrations its growl created along its glossy black flanks.

"Nope."

Silence passed between the two, cut only by the wild cries of birds and other less identifiable fauna. The jungle below felt steady and comforting now that nothing was trying to kill them.

"Rainn, what will you and Heron do if the P'tak know for sure there's no way to return you to the Alireon?" Would they still come with her to the Undergates? Was her papa's faith in the two Alir justified?

"I suppose we'll make miserable lives for ourselves among you humans." The hope behind her question was a dry branch, and Rainn snapped it over his knee. "You should do the same. You don't owe that imp anything, even if he does kill all those people from the tavern. They might think they're heroes, but it's not like they're gods or anything. Just . . ." He described a circular motion toward the dirt with one finger.

"People."

Why did she have to ask the question? Why could she not leave well enough alone?

In truth, it was difficult to justify asking for his help. Masika was just a mortal, and he and Heron had been locked away for so long. No matter what happened to her or her family, or any of the others, how could they compete with that? Denari clear the fog, what would she do if Rainn and Heron left?

"Have you asked Heron?"

"What? No." Rainn's brow creased in confusion. "Why would I need to? We're gods. You're a mortal. Our needs come first." His tone betrayed frustration. As if incapable of understanding why Masika might have trouble with any of this.

"Oh."

Why was she surprised?

She tried to be diplomatic, like her papa would. "I suppose that would make sense from your point of view." Masika struggled to find the right words. "But do you understand that we never would have helped you at all if that had been on the table?" Even as she said it Masika knew it for a lie. Her help had never been conditional, no matter how much she wished it reciprocated.

"Good thing it never came up then."

"Right." She crossed her arms in front of herself and turned away from him, staring at the jungle. Surprised at herself, she realized her rage only when she saw her arms shaking. "You should probably go. It's full sun right now, and I bet you're weak enough for me to throw you out of the nest. It's a long way down." Masika did not hear him move, so she twisted her neck to look him in the eye.

"Oh!" Rainn straightened. "You're serious. I, um . . ." He clambered back over the railing and went back down the way he'd come. "We'll talk later."

A trembling hand went to her forehead. She deserved this. She wanted to be special. To be better than Mer…ties, and to be mentioned in the same breath as the Hill Fury. What did she expect out of such preposterous hopes? Did she think that actual gods would consider her as an equal? At best she was a pet to them. A dog brought along to bark at things beneath its master's notice.

Her stomach clenched. A crow's nest was no place to be sick on a ship. In her search to distract herself from her anger, another thought surfaced.

Rainn led them to Ild the imp, that the painted creature might help him and Heron get home. That she found herself here in this position was entirely his fault, and that was not fair.

If you're looking for fair, you've already lost. Better to look for something to do about it instead. Fair isn't ever going to help.

Her brother Djephan said that to her once when Meritities threw Masika's favorite book in the mud and ruined it. She had not discovered the crime until the pages were trodden to filthy bits in the road by the hooves of a hundred horses. At the time she thought he meant for her to throw something of her sister's in the muddy road too, but that was not it.

Besides, Rainn did not own a pearl-encrusted formal gown.

CHAPTER

SIXTEEN

Something that seems obvious to adults yet requires endless explanation to children, is that the gods are not like us. A man must rely on other men to survive in a dangerous world. He cannot accomplish everything he must to live, and to thrive, without a web of connections amongst those who have spent their lives becoming experts in the things he is not.

But gods know no such shortcomings. They do not rely on their own kind as we rely on ours, and they rely on us for nothing.

This is why, even in the face of their all-encompassing mercy and compassion, most gods are dicks.

Volume One of *Thank Gods* by Kohmose Oburn

Meritities smoothed the yellow curl of paper on the table and read it again. *A hero to the empire.* Her. Risen in the eyes of her uncle the emperor.

Stay where you are. Sending support. Capture my brother and your sister and return them unharmed. You have been a hero to the empire and have risen much in our eyes.

—Holy Emperor Khasek V

She would have everything due her, and Masika be damned.

Gulls cried outside the open window, and Meritities swayed to the stone wall. Floated, really. The speedy little skiff from Kos carried her here, to Lord and Lady Parrex's keep just east of the western leg of the Little God's Mountains. The Parrexes presided over a trio of towns along the coast, only one of which was worthy of the name, and kept a small, centrally located villa to watch over them.

Importantly, they also kept an orven rookery, which allowed her to contact her uncle.

Though indifferent to Egren's court intrigue, Lord Parrex's obsession for what he considered to be fine art left him at Meritities's mercies. Within minutes she cracked open his vulnerability to her own family's art collection and made a deal.

Her mother might bemoan the loss of a few choice pieces, but she would rather pay that small price than see the family's reputation set ablaze by Masika's idiocy.

Fishing boats returned to shore under the bright midafternoon sun. All of the Parrex's windows faced south, toward the ocean, rather than north, toward the desert. The choice displayed a common behavior in the lesser nobility of the region, that by looking away from the harsh and toward the thing that made you money, one could ignore anything harmful and concentrate only on what made you money.

But Meritities knew the lie of this. Ignore your threats at your peril. Better to ally oneself with the desert *and* the ocean. That way you always held one to throw in front of the other in the event of unexpected strife.

A second slip of paper lay on the table behind her, from Nebet. Her bodyguard had been attacked and forced to flee by Masika's monstrous Alir and was even now on his way to her. Thank the hounds she had possessed the foresight to give him a place to meet her in case he should become separated from that wicked crew.

And her papa. He was bewitched by his evil baby daughter, not wicked.

Sunlight glittered off the ocean waves, and the sounds of the surf and the birds lulled Meritities. When she married her cousin and became the empress of Egren, she would have a holiday palace built here. She would have to annex the territory for Egren, as it belonged officially to no nation, but then there would be no one to contest it.

No one important, she amended, considering the Parrexes.

A dreamy smile came over her, and Meritities twirled slowly in place, letting the breeze from the window play with the skirts of her diaphanous borrowed gown.

You have risen in our eyes . . .

CHAPTER
SEVENTEEN

At many junctures the study of the religious myths of Andos butts up against very real and unexplainable phenomena. For instance, the area of Vincent's Folly, situated at the edge of where the eastern jungles of Sedrios turn into the Southern Grass Sea, is reputed to be cursed by either the Sea Witch, her first and most powerful sorceress daughter, or the goddess Matchi the Huntress, irritated over being stung on the thumb by a waxwood hornet.

Regardless of the reason, no one can argue that Vincent's Folly is one of the least hospitable, most inimical to human life, and altogether vexing stretches of territory anywhere in the Thirteen Kingdoms. Whatever Vincent did to earn his curse, it is a fair bet he should not have.

Also, there are seriously a lot of those hornets there.

Volume Seven of *Thank Gods* by Kohmose Oburn

Masika and Tennat rested in the starboard foredeck and listened to the sailors argue. Tennat sat with his leg bound and raised on a weathered crate in the dwindling sunlight and kept an eye out for the oversized waxwood hornets. Though repeatedly assured they never stung unless provoked, the first time he recognized one carrying a paralyzed rat in its chitinous claws was her papa's last moment of actual relaxation.

Heron stood next to him on the rail and eyed the water below with some suspicion. She had been attached to Masika's papa since his injury, and he seemed glad of the company.

The *Ocean Krait* left the jungles behind hours ago, and now sailed a slow path through the Southern Grass Sea, a low marsh that extended as far as the eye could see to the west and ended abruptly in the curving wall of the Little Gods Mountains to the east.

Her papa would have counseled Masika to abandon Rainn and Heron had she confided the last conversation to him, so she kept it to herself. But that did not stop her from worrying the problem.

"What would Sarah do?" It was far from the first time the question occurred to her. The Hill Fury was known not to be intimidated by the gods of the land, but *she* held their magic in her palm. What was there for her to be frightened of? Sarah would most likely have sliced the imp in half right there in the Jolly Chicken and not given the affair another thought.

Why had Masika not done that?

Neck extended, Heron peered into the dirty brown water. She turned her head side to side.

"I could not say, my Lahamila." Her papa spared her a nervous glance. "But perhaps rather than fret over the choices of a figment you have never met before and never can, you should instead ask yourself what your Uncle Mahu, who actually did train you, might advise. He would certainly know how to handle these hornets."

"Heh. Right." She had not intended to ask her question aloud but was relieved for her papa's misinterpretation. "He'd probably just pick them right out of the sky with that bow of his."

"Hush, child." Tennat's gaze roved feverishly over the darkening sky. "Don't anger them."

She patted her papa on the shoulder, grateful for an excuse to smile. "Do you still think we'll see Uncle Mahu and Sabni on our trip?"

"I don't know." Tennat grunted and shifted as he tried to see a commotion among the sailors behind him. "My orven may well not have reached either of them. I sent them our route, so we will simply have to hope for the best." He frowned over his shoulder. "Now what do you suppose they're on about?"

Following the pointing fingers and frightened gestures of the sailors, Masika stared west over the grassy marshes to a stone tower, black in the distance. A bright light shone out the top floor, but she did not require Inlittan's sight to know it was merely the setting sun showing through.

"Unless you squawking turds would rather wail than eat tonight, I'd be suggestin' you get yer asses back to work." Captain Ironmast grumped his way past the suddenly busy sailors and toward Tennat and Masika. "Vincent's Folly ain't any damned different than the last time we been this way, and it won't be any different the next."

A scowl followed the sailors' backsides as Ironmast paused to watch his crew hop to. He returned his attention to Tennat, prompting Heron to flutter a few feet away and fix the captain with one bright emerald eye.

"How's the leg?"

"Hurts like fire, but better than it was yesterday. Please express my gratitude to your young surgeon."

"Hmph," Ironmast replied. "Boy's got heart. Said he went explorin' in the jungles with a buncha treasure hunters and fell sick or summat. Woke up a week later in some shack of a tavern with a demon woman who taught him some healin' in trade fer work on the place. He's sure good enough fer us."

The captain inhaled and spit into the river. "Anyway, Garpoint's just past the mouth of the Teawater and about an hour west. We'll be picking up supplies there then head back east and north 'round Egren's Claw. The rock roams out a ways from there, so we'll be giving her a wide berth. I'm tellin' you now so's I ain't gotta explain it later. Ye ken?"

"Oh. Ah, of course. Thank you, Captain."

"Hmph." Ironmast went to return to his perch on the aft castle, but Masika interrupted him.

"Captain, why are the crew so concerned about Vincent's Folly?"

Ironmast rolled his eyes. "The lands between that old lookout tower," he pointed to the stone heap Masika spied earlier, "and that one up there." He pointed east to another, less obvious tower along the crest of the Little Gods. "Folks say it's cursed. Or haunted. Them'd be the happier tales. The bugs is bad and the fishing's for shit, so I'll be happy to put it behind me either way. Any other goddamn questions?"

"No." Masika flashed the captain a wide, toothy grin. "Thank you."

They watched the captain stalk back the length of his vessel, stopping occasionally to issue commands, or in one noteworthy case, encouragement, before returning their attention to each other. As he left, Heron resettled in Tennat's lap and closed her eyes.

Her papa shifted on his crate and winced, lifting his leg. He put a hand on the somewhat ruffled Heron and stroked her feathers. "So, Lahamila, do you think this marsh is haunted? If smell is anything to go by, I suspect we should be lifting ghosts out of the bilge by the bucketload."

Vision enhanced by Inlittan, Masika stared up at the tower nestled between two tall mountain peaks, stained red in the setting sunlight. She could not tell what it was, but something up there stared back at her.

"Do you think there will be a proper surgeon in Garpoint, Papa?"

"I have never been there, which should give you an idea to the size and capabilities of such a town."

She took his point. Her papa had been everywhere in the service of his older brother. If a place was not worth his visit, it was not worth much.

"However, in answer to your unspoken question, no, I will not stay behind there. I know you worry that your poor old father will be in danger, but I might point out that my value has never been in the strength of my arm or the speed"—he gave her a tight, quick grin—"of my leg. I can speak every bit as well as I ever have, and that is what you need. Would you have Rainn negotiate with our gods on your behalf?"

"Absolutely not!" Masika replied, a bit more forcefully than she intended. If things went the way she planned, Rainn would never speak to the P'tak. He may well not be allowed on the mountain at all, not being Darrish, and even if he were, his brusque Andosh manner would likely get him thrown bodily back off it.

A small chirp of agreement rose from the dozing goddess, though Masika doubted she would have appreciated the reasoning. Or maybe she would.

"Very well. Then let's not talk of it again."

Masika nodded, though she did not like it. Her papa was not safe out here, but there were some things she could not control, him being among them. "Do you think Meritities is done with us? She's always been so stubborn about her disdain for me and the way I've chosen to live. Even with that, I never thought she'd have me thrown in a foreign dungeon."

Glancing sidelong at his daughter, Tennat narrowed his eyes. "You and your sister are more alike than you realize, Lahamila."

"We are not."

"You are, and you will listen to me." A note of sternness crept into Tennat's voice. "Meritities is stubborn, as you say, but she is a retiring flower compared to *you*."

What could her papa mean? Meritities was a shark in the family pool. A wolf. A *monster*.

His gentle hand elicited a soft coo from Heron, but Tennat's eyes were serious. "Meritities has adopted the rules and customs of Egren royalty. She is hidebound to them, true, but even that is to be expected. You, on the other hand"—he leaned his head toward Masika —"have flown your own course since the day you were born, confident and headstrong and utterly convinced of the rightness of your own path. This is stubbornness of a sort Meritities would never be capable of."

"But—"

"You are my love and my pride, Lahamila. But Meritities is a reflection of your mother, and that is my *wife*. Do you understand? We need not agree with your sister to show her respect and harbor love for her in our hearts. I do not always agree with your mother, but neither do I speak ill of her behind her back. Meritities is family, and that is more important than any disagreement."

This discussion hurt. Tears welled behind Masika's eyes, though she could not place their source. Was she so invested in being Papa's favorite that she could not stand correction from him?

When she spoke, her voice was small and childlike. "Do you think Meritities believes that? That family is more important?"

Tennat scowled in concentration and the sun dropped fully behind distant grass. Heron raised her head to provide better access to his soft fingers along her neck. The blue glow of her scarring lifted between the feathers.

"To be honest, I don't know. Your sister values status more than I would like and escalates arguments faster than I believe is wise. But the kind of love I'm talking about doesn't live with her, it lives with you. Whether it is ever returned or not, you will make yourself far more miserable than you ever will her by hating her. Love for others is a gift you give to yourself."

"But how is that fair?" Masika could not grasp her papa's point. "She gets to be as horrible as she likes, and I have to love her for it?"

Masika's eyes went round when a waxwood hornet—a full handspan in length—landed on the bandages covering her papa's knee. Before he could spot it and begin screaming, Heron stretched lazily over and snapped it up with a loud crunch. Her papa looked down and seeing nothing, continued speaking, oblivious to his brush with the massive insect.

"Well, there is one thing that makes it easier." Tennat's paternal smile melted Masika "You never need tell her. Loving someone is not the same as letting them take advantage of you, nor do you need to profess that love in the face of bad behavior. It is more about not allowing your own negative feelings to pull *you* down. If you can find love for a sister who cuts at your heart, you will find that heart has become invulnerable to her attacks. Hurts might then go unanswered, and arguments may be forgotten. Eventually"—he winked at her— "you may even find yourself friends."

"It doesn't seem likely." Masika had certainly tried to make amends with Merities in the past. Hadn't she?

"If it were, it would not be worth as much." A long sigh escaped Tennat as he lay his head back against the gray wooden crate. "Do not worry about your sister. She may believe that our goal is sacrilegious, but now that she has tried to stop it and failed, I am certain she would prefer not to pull any additional attention to our activities. Additional failures will only make her look worse, and we both know how she feels about *that*."

That was true. Still, Masika wished she had her papa's surety.

Giving up was no more an aspect of Merities's personality than forgiveness was.

CHAPTER

EIGHTEEN

Supported by a hardwood crutch shoved into his armpit, Tennat Oburn stumped around his daughter and her godly charges to stand between them and the gangplank leading to Garpoint's listing dock. Three days had seen considerable improvement in his ability to get around, aided in no small part by the attentions of the *Ocean Krait's* young surgeon and the drafts he had procured from the Daughter's Coven out of Port Placid.

"I'll stay on board," Rainn said while eager sailors streamed past and onto the dock, causing it to lean even further away from the ship. "But only if someone's willing to go and get me some decent food. If I gotta eat one more bite of boiled fish and moldy carrot, I'll cook the man who serves it myself."

"Is that what gods do to humans who displease them?" The question popped out before Masika had time to pull it back in, but thankfully her papa did not seem to notice.

One brow rose on Rainn's face, but he said nothing.

"We can certainly get some dinners brought to us from the local public house." Tennat waved in the direction of the gloomy town as he spoke. The late afternoon sky hid behind drab gray clouds, perfectly mimicking the tone of Garpoint. "Beer as well. But considering the trouble we ran into back in Port Bibi, and in Kos before that, *and* in Treaty Hill before that, Masika and I are agreed that we would all be better off staying aboard the *Krait* while we're here."

Masika nodded. "Captain Ironmast says the people here aren't very friendly anyway." *Pinched shits* was the actual phrase the captain used. Farmers and fishermen, the populace had little use for sailors, visiting dignitaries, or itinerant gods. Even the home-grown merchant who ran the dock and resupply was viewed with suspicion merely for interacting with strangers.

"Fine." Rainn held out an arm to Heron, who hopped up from the rail. "Damn shame though. This is the first decent night we've had in a week." He gazed up at the bulging clouds, heavy with water and shook his head. Together he and the goddess went aft and sat, waiting for their meal.

Once Masika gave their request to the ship's mate and handed him some coins, she and her papa returned to their charges. She had no desire to visit with either of the gods, but she had less inclination to explain why she was avoiding them.

The four of them chatted and chirped while they passed the time waiting for their food. Soon enough the mate and another sailor returned with stacked plates and four mugs of ale. The crew was still not certain what to make of Heron, a bird with blue glowing runes under her feathers that people spoke to as if she were a human being. Masika heard whispers among them that she was some kind of holy creature to the P'tak, and that they would be blessed if they could get her to eat from their hands. While possibly problematic, Heron appreciated their misconception, and endeavored to bless as many of the sailors as wished it. Masika would have stopped it, but Tennat remained steadfast in his belief that the fewer people who knew of the two Alirs' true nature the better.

Covert laughter bubbled up behind Masika's lips when she saw the food: a hard black roll, some kind of orange root, scorched and pressed flat onto the pewter plate, with cubed and boiled fish unceremoniously spooned across it. Her amusement at Rainn's groan was almost more than she could hide.

Tennat took a bite and chewed—at length—before speaking. "Not the imperial kitchens, but I suppose we should be grateful, nonetheless. At least it is no longer moving."

Squawking and flapping, Heron leaped into the sky, frightened by a stranger's sudden appearance in their midst. Masika and Rainn both jumped to their feet.

"Can we help you?" Tennat asked.

The woman wore nondescript brown, her cloak up over her face, and stood on the main deck less than ten feet from Masika. How could she have moved so silently that even Heron had not noticed her until she was among them? Only her dark hands, clasped in front of her waist, revealed her as Darrish.

Oh.

Oh no. Someone knew. Someone knew and sent this woman to—what? To take them home? To kill them?

"Please. Do not let me interrupt ze dinners. I am here for talking, not fighting. No one is in any danger. Not yet."

"Alakeel?"

Masika's papa knew who this woman was? Did that mean they

were *not* all about to die? Palms suddenly wet, Masika set her plate down and faced the woman fully. Despite the gray light, she could make out very little. Very little beyond the pounding of her own heartbeat in her ears.

"You sure?" Rainn dropped his own plate and put a hand on the hilt of Forbryttan. "You caught me on a good day for fighting."

"Rainn." Tennat's voice stretched anxious and thin over his words. "Please sit. This woman is . . . She is a friend."

A deep frown settled on Rainn's features. "Your friend is a killer." He did not sit, but neither did he draw his weapon.

"And she would surely kill all of us if that were her purpose."

Even with Inlittan's help, Masika could see nothing special about the woman, other than she was fit and carried more than a few scars. A pair of dagger hilts protruded from her belt in front of her, partially hidden by her cloak.

"Thank you, Tennat. I asked for zis missions when I saw your name. I hoped to dissuade you from what you intend to do. Had any of my sisters been ahead of me, zere would have been no discussions."

Sisters? Masika gave a silent gasp. This woman was of the Khamsen. Masika had never even seen one of the Holy Emperor's assassins in the flesh before, and now she herself was a target.

She wasn't afraid, though, only fascinated. Wary to be sure, but not scared. Again, Masika wondered if her papa was right about her. Was she missing some crucial piece of self-preservation in her makeup that only allowed her to be scared when her life *was not* on the line? To be more fearful of disappointing others than an actual blade in her face?

"How did my brother find out what we were doing?" Though not relaxed, Tennat had regained much of his composure.

Alakeel the assassin brought a hand up to push back the worn hood. The hand was hard and strong, and the face it revealed was no less so, though it carried a strange sort of attraction as well. Like the beauty of the desert: vast, deep, and deadly.

"Merities has ze ear of her uncle ze Holy Emperor. She convinced him to kill ze two gods and bring you and Masika back to Plensa for his judgements. If you were not ze emperor's brother, you would already be dead."

"Alakeel, this is important." Voice gone quiet, as if he had no breath left, Tennat's face turned down. "We have taken charge of these two Alir from the Andosh. It would be a disaster to allow anything to happen to them. If our previous time together meant anything to you, you must let us go. Masika followed my instructions only. She is blameless."

"Zat is not for me to say."

Our previous time together? Masika stared closer at Alakeel. She gave no indication of being any more than ten years older than Masika herself. Assuming everyone survived this conversation, she would be asking her papa what that meant.

As Rainn's fingers crept around Forbryttan's pommel, a long and curving knife blade appeared in Alakeel's relaxed hand. Rainn studied that hand for a handful of seconds and moved both his own to his hips.

Heron flew into the rigging over their heads.

"But it matters little either way." As quietly as it appeared, the dagger vanished from Alakeel's limber fingers. "I am bound, by action or inaction, never to stand against ze wishes of the Holy Emperor. Ze Alir may go, but you and Masika will be coming with me. Zat is all I can do."

By offering to let the Alir go instead of killing them, Alakeel already displayed the true depth of her loyalty toward Masika's papa. She might claim their escape, a believable lie with gods in the mix. But there was no possibility of convincing the Holy Emperor that one of his most powerful assassins lost Masika and Tennat.

And the result was not all that different. Without a Darrish person to speak for them to the P'tak, Heron and Rainn's cause was finished, even if they could get to the top of the mountain.

"Can we at least take the *Ocean Krait* there?" Masika tried to inject as much reasonableness into her voice as she could. She envisioned the edges of a solution to two problems here, if she could only control this next turn. "It's already paid for, and it's certainly the most comfortable on the dock."

"Comfort is not important. We will go in ze skiff I arrived in. Ze sailors are discreet and efficient."

"Tennat Oburn is the brother of the Holy Emperor of Egren." A thrill ran through Masika's chest. The Khamsen were legends in Egren, and Masika needed to bluff the first one she ever met. "His comfort is far from unimportant. He is wounded, and that skiff"— Masika indicated the lean little vessel tied further up the zig-zagging dock—"is not remotely the equal of our ship. It is neither as safe nor as fast. Why would you want us on it?"

"Masika—" Tennat started.

"I demand that we continue on the *Krait*, and that you keep my father safe during our journey. Unless you consider yourself incapable of doing so?"

Never in her life had Masika sounded so much like a royal. Technically a princess, she spent most of her time ignoring the fact. Maybe she should have practiced more.

"Very well." A small sigh from Alakeel was her first, and only, sign of frustration. "But abandon any plans of escape. Your father will tell you of my capabilities. If zis is a ploy—"

Now to finish the deal.

"You forget yourself, assassin." Masika's own words faded against the singing of her blood in her ears. "We are the Holy Emperor's kin, and we have already agreed to your terms. Do not push your authority lest you find the foot you overstep with removed from you."

A nod was Alakeel's only reply. Silent as death, she stepped off the ship and returned to her skiff.

Laughter popped out of Masika when she saw her papa and Rainn staring open mouthed at her. Heat washed her cheeks.

"Where the hell did that come from?" Rainn asked. "You're scarier than you look."

"You sounded *just* like your mother." A wide smile shone through Tennat's black and gray beard. "It was almost as if she were here on the ship with us, yelling at assassins."

"*That* sounded like your wife?" Rainn's head moved side to side. "You've got more sand than I thought, old man." He lifted his arm. "Come on, Heron. End of the line for a while."

The goddess refused to come. Rainn scowled up at her.

"Wait a moment. Don't go anywhere just yet." With Inlittan's sight, Masika could see Alakeel in the shadows of the skiff, watching them and invisible to other eyes. "I've got another idea."

"NO. I ABSOLUTELY FORBID IT."

Masika and her papa stood on the main deck of the *Ocean Krait* and ignored the stares of the sailors, the captain, and the two Alir. The argument raged into its second hour and showed no signs of abating. Even the sailors loading a huge stack of cargo from the spindly dock paused to watch.

Hand pressed to her head to stave off the headache that already pounded behind her temples, Masika tried to recover some control. "There's nothing to forbid. We've been talking about this all night, and it's the only way this works." The strain in her chest from lack of sleep dragged on her and tinged all her words with frantic need. "Why are you being so difficult about this?"

"I am not being difficult; I am being your father. It is my place to prevent exactly this sort of stupidity in my children. I will not sit by and—"

"*Stupidity?*" Masika's voice jumped several octaves, and Heron circled around Rainn's shoulders, hiding behind his neck. "This from the man who trusted Meritities to keep her fucking mouth shut?"

"Oof." Rainn lifted a hand to cover Heron's ears. "She's not coming back from that any time soon. Heron, don't listen to that language. It's fucking horrible."

Face contorted with anger, Tennat slammed his walking stick down on the deck and shoved himself to his feet. "I am finished talking to you about this. If you are determined on this course of action, I am at least going to tell your uncle where you will be headed so he can arrange to have you taken into custody before you get there. I refuse to do nothing and watch you be killed over this exercise in your own vanity. At least Meritities is honest about her arrogance."

A flung stone, Masika's hand sailed of its own accord to strike her papa in the face. His head went sideways, then jerked back to glare at her, eyes bulging.

She stepped away, the offending hand now over her own mouth. Tears rolled down her face.

"I'm sorry—"

Without another word, Tennat clambered off the ship and stumped down the dock. As he passed Alakeel's skiff, she emerged and held up a hand.

"You must not go any—"

"Then murder me here, harridan." He did not pause to speak, only waved his stick threateningly in her direction. "I'm sending an orven to my brother. This is all your fault anyway."

As he thumped past her, Alakeel looked to Tennat, then to Masika. She studied the pile of crates being loaded onto the ship, did some calculations, and followed Masika's papa up into Garpoint.

Masika watched her go, breath held tight. Once the assassin was out of sight, she nodded to Captain Ironmast, who waved to the pair of sailors standing on the dock. They hopped aboard without comment, cargo left where it sat, and lifted long poles to push the ship away from the dock. Within moments they were away and unfurling great square sails meant for speed, not maneuverability.

"*That* was the plan?" Rainn grinned at Masika and behind them at Garpoint in equal measure. "I can't believe it. I was sure you two were gonna tear off each other's heads and dance in the blood."

Heron cooed into his ear.

"Oh yeah. I never did figure out what you were actually fighting about. I guess that shoulda been a clue."

Masika walked past Rainn and went to the aft railing behind the wheelman. She wept, breath hitching and mouth open. Their argument was never supposed to get that far. How could she have said such things to her papa? How could she have—her mind recoiled from the idea—struck him?

He looked so angry. So hurt.

Even with Inlittan's help, Masika never saw Alakeel return to the dock.

CHAPTER
NINETEEN

The Immortal Queen Nephret earned her place in the Darrish pantheon when she softened the heart of Egren the Judge. That's Egren the god, not the country. Were it not for her subtle and mysterious mind, the great Darrish Empire would never have been possible, and the nations of Egren and Verran would be little more than mud huts and wooden beads.

That is to say, Verran would be exactly as it stands today and Egren would be no better. Verran is awful.

But because Queen Nephret did, in fact, tempt the soul of the magnificent god, Egren the nation has become the greatest center of learning, power, and civilization this or any other world has ever known. Aside from Father Rain whose tears for humanity water the crops we eat and fill the rivers and oceans, no god has ever cared so much for their charges than Egren cares for us.

Of course, his judgements on humankind are ubiquitously negative and uniformly fatal, but no one wants their favorite god to look bad in front of his god friends and family, do they?

Volume Two of *Thank Gods* by Kohmose Oburn

Two problems solved in one stroke, Masika lay in her hammock and fretted over having done the right thing regarding her papa. She needed to get him to safety, but was that really with Alakeel? His part of the plan was to distract the assassin while the *Ocean Krait* sailed to the other side of the island, and then after Alakeel pursued toward Egren, he would travel overland to meet them. The ship sailing straight for Egren and leaving him behind would come as a bitter surprise that left a feeling of despair in the hollow place Masika's soul used to be.

She had made too many promises to too many people. Keeping her oath to the Alir meant disappointing her papa and breaking her own heart.

Their escape dwindled three days into the past, but her concern for her wounded papa loomed ever larger. If only there were some way to check up on him. But that was the sort of thing the real Sarah did, not teenaged wannabes.

When Masika offered the part of her plan to her papa—the part she wanted him to know—his reaction came loud and hot. But he admitted eventually that he held no better ideas himself.

Still, the violence of their fight caused Masika no end of worry. The things she'd said. The look in his eyes when she struck him. What was wrong with her? He was her *papa*.

But both pieces of the plan worked, and with every passing moment they sailed further away from both Garpoint and Alakeel, which could only be for the good.

With the vast desert of the Yellow Sea to the north of them, Egren rushed dangerously closer. Masika needed to find Captain Ironmast and negotiate some additional discretion on her and the two gods' behalf. Any merchant captain worth his salt would know how to avoid entanglements with Egren imperial ships.

"ABSOLUTELY NOT!"

The wind carried Captain Ironmast's bellow out to sea, to be crushed by gale-frenzied whitecaps. His great coat whipped dramatically in the gale, which added to his frightfulness, and the mist whipped up by the shrieking windstorm ran in rivulets down through his beard.

"But, Captain, we paid you good coin in advance—"

"And you can have it all back, lassie. How many sailors you think die under my watch onna normal haul? None. Any idea how many damn ships I lost before you in my whole damn career? None, that's how many." His craggy face reddened further as he shouted. "But I've lost both since we met, and that's not on me."

"But surely you—"

"Surely I can sail past the whole of Egren, avoiding one of the best trained navies in all the Thirteen fucking Kingdoms, to a place they already know to expect us? Are ye daft? The one thing we got outta all this is a fancy new ship, and I ain't looking to get her sunk too. So no thank ye very fucking much. You and yourn'll be stepping off first sign of sand we come across. No arguments about it."

"But—"

"Go!" His shout pushed Masika back a step. Rather than risk being bodily thrown to the waves, she fled belowdecks.

In the tiny hallway to the sleeping quarters, Masika paused to catch her breath. That could have gone better. Rather than coming up with a brilliant plan to secretly ferry them past the bulk of Egren to Mukahiit, Captain Ironmast reacted with quite understandable anger at being the object of a naval wolf hunt. Masika's geographical knowledge failed her here; she did not know where the closest sand might be, but the desert to the north seemed the most likely. And disastrous. If Ironmast dropped them in the Yellow Sea, their choices grew even more limited.

They could travel along the water's edge and be visible to passing ships and wandering patrols, or they could strike off to the north, further into the dunes, and become prey to bandits and thirst.

Or worse.

Alakeel's skiff no longer loomed as threatening as it once had.

Wind screamed into the narrow corridor as the *Ocean Krait's* first mate stepped inside. He pulled his vest tighter around his skinny middle and rubbed his bare arms. "Captain says getcher shit together. Yer getting off."

Masika stared at the man for a few moments before speaking. "Let me tell Rainn and Heron." The weather would have riled the god up, and she did not want any accidents.

The mate nodded and stepped back into the gale.

The desert it was then.

She stood in front of the gods' cabin for a full minute, considering what she might say. The worse the weather, the more volatile Rainn's personality became. He typically grew more boisterous and happy, but he was an Alir, and that happiness often seemed to express itself with steel. Also, and Masika could not believe she was thinking this about a *god*, but Rainn was not all that smart. He could not be relied upon to make the right judgement call for everyone's safety. She needed to lead him to it.

If he even listened to her to begin with: a mere human.

Every knock on their door rolled out sharp, gonglike notes in Masika's imagination, pealing booms to alert all the monsters of the desert where to find and eat her.

"Heya." Rainn yanked the door open and grinned at her, his breathing elevated and his skin flush. In this state he might easily kill everyone aboard. But who would operate the ship then?

"Can I come in?" Behind him, Masika spotted Heron balancing on a tiny tabletop. Only then did Masika realize just how much the *Krait* pitched in the high waves. The timbers creaked as the ship flexed with every huge swell that gathered beneath them.

He stepped aside and Masika entered, closing the door behind her.

"Great weather." The tight grin on Rainn's face never wavered. His eyes danced a manic jig in the candlelight.

"It's a peach." Masika put her back to the door, inhaled, held it, and let it go. "Captain wants to put us aground early. He's worried the assassin might have alerted Egren's navy to his ship. We can walk from there or try to flag down another vessel. It shouldn't be a problem."

"Ha!" Rainn stuck out his chest, muscles swollen from the squall. "Toldja we shoulda chopped off that bitch's head when we had the chance. That's fine. Walk or sail makes no never mind to me. Thunder and blood, but I feel good. You wouldn't think a bit of wind would get a fella all boned up like this, but there it is."

Behind Rainn, Heron gave a look that seemed to say, *See what I have to deal with?*

"Yeah, well, we're ready to go. So, anything you want to bring, just grab it and—"

"Already there." He strapped Forbryttan to his waist and picked up a blanket. "Let's get you all wrapped up, lady-god. Don't want those pretty feathers blowing off in alla that wind."

How Rainn kept hold of Forbryttan when everyone else's arms stayed shut in the weapons locker confused Masika, but somehow it felt like ill luck to ask about openly. Captain Ironmast hardly seemed the type to be intimidated on his own ship. As long as no one else said anything, She would keep her mouth shut too.

As Rainn encircled Heron in the blanket, Masika considered that even as drunk on the weather's power as he was, he never forgot the goddess or her needs. It would have been touching if Rainn had not already revealed himself as the ass he was.

No one spoke above decks as the trio entered a small rowboat and were taken away from the *Ocean Krait*. Instead of heading north to the shore and the desert, they went east, in the direction of a mountain island jutting out of the tumultuous sea. It was the Last Spike, the tail end of this leg of the Little Gods Mountains that extended into the ocean, and a legendarily dangerous place to be stranded. Masika had not seen it earlier in all the wind and spray and did not realize they had been so close to passing the mountain range.

"Well, that's shitty luck," she said to the wind.

The tiny boat climbed and fell across mountainous swells, with Rainn laughing and the sailors pulling as hard as they could on the oars. Icy torrents fell out of the sky and soaked them as thoroughly as if they traveled underwater.

A sailor thrust a bucket into Masika's hand, and irritated at herself for doing so, she lifted water out of the boat and cast it over the side. No good could come of sinking the small craft.

She hesitated. Could it?

No. She continued sloshing bucketloads of ocean and rainwater.

Minutes later the same sailor took the bucket back out of her hands and yelled over the squall into Masika's face. "Get out."

"What? Why?" The mountain loomed dark and huge against the lightning-lit sky, but they were still not aground. This made no sense.

"Rocks," shouted the sailor. "Don't wanna damage the boat."

"What about damaging us?" Masika could scarcely believe the man's lack of compassion. Did he think she was more worried about the boat than she was herself? But how did it help her if the oarsmen died out here too?

In the end they were forced to swim the final fifty yards to a small stretch of brown sand that appeared and vanished between the waves, Rainn booming laughter the whole way. At least someone was having fun. He held a sodden Heron in an even more sodden blanket above his head as he clambered ashore and made for the rocks. Masika scraped her leg against something hard and abrasive below the water, but it only bled a little. She lost both her shoes and her robe.

Meritities would have been mortified.

By the time they scrambled up the rocks and out of the way of the waves, a dense rain roared out of the sky, heavy drops hurled from clouds a mile above their heads. Masika and Heron shivered and watched Rainn joyously chop slick brown granite with Forbryttan into rough blocks and heft them, one-handed, into a semblance of a shelter just above the island beach. Three seven-foot walls with spaces between the top blocks for weaving tree branches and palm fronds later left the god inordinately pleased with himself.

While the topless shelter did little for the rain, it cut off most of the wind, and Masika and Heron were finally able to relax, though thoughts of her papa waiting, abandoned and alone, kept sleep at bay more than did the cold and wet.

THE NEXT MORNING Masika busied herself with the roof of their little island shelter while Heron caught fish and Rainn snored. He had been unable to settle during the storm and had only given in to sleep an hour ago. From past experience, Masika knew he would wake up feeling hungover.

Inlittan showed Masika the best limbs to pluck, the right places to cut them, and the most efficient ways to interweave them before inserting them into the holes along the top of their shelter's walls. She stopped more than once to examine the twin steel rings, fused together, that sat on the second and third fingers of her right hand. Surprisingly, the lightweight steel chain that connected the rings to the accompanying bracelet, also steel, showed no signs of wear or stress. Circles of runes traveled around the two main pieces, inlaid in copper and gold, some of which moved in crawling spirals.

Romi's gift humbled her.

Now she faced another problem. No vessel sailed to their rescue. No one out there even looked for them other than the entire Egren Navy, which Masika *certainly* did not count. Marooned here on the Last Spike instead of the mainland desert meant no further travel. Rainn's willingness to walk meant nothing.

The secret grew riper by the minute, and its spoiling smell thickened in the air. How long until the two Alir realized Masika held no plans in her empty hands? Before they figured out that their marooning was her fault?

If Rainn were the only concern, Masika might have more time, but Heron was smarter and more observant. She may already know and be waiting for Masika to come clean. What if Masika was disappointing the goddess even now?

Like she did her papa. For that matter, like she had her only sister.

No. Disappointing them further curdled in Masika's stomach. It occurred to her in that instant that she intended to prove Rainn's assumptions about humans wrong. His statement about the unimportance of humanity still set her hair ablaze, but that only stiffened her resolve.

She would not allow him to be right.

"Heron," Masika shouted down the small beach, now a golden brown in the morning sun. Twin walls of tumbled granite boulders spread into the sea to either side and sheltered the sandy alcove.

"Whazzat?" Rainn sat up inside the rough shelter, hauled himself to his feet, and stumbled his bleary way out into the sun. "Augh! Hard to believe such a fantastic night could end with something as ugly and offensive as that." He returned to the shelter and sat in the entryway, blinking red-rimmed eyes. His dark blue vest rested somewhere on the ocean floor, and rents in his soiled gray shirt showed glowing blue scars beneath.

Heron landed beside Masika and spat another fish onto the growing breakfast pile.

"Yesterday I told Captain Ironmast that the navy of Egren was looking for us and asked him if he could avoid their ships." Get it out all at once, then make explanations. "He—had other ideas. I thought I'd have time to talk to you and persuade the captain to let us off somewhere we could find another boat, but I didn't. That's why we're here on this island instead of still being at sea, or even set aground in the desert north of here."

A low croak vibrated from Heron, and Rainn coughed.

"So, you're telling us that we've been abandoned?" Rainn pushed the heels of his hands into his eye sockets and rubbed. "Traded one prison for another, because you couldn't keep your fucking mouth shut?"

The threat flaked off every word of Rainn's question. Was she in danger?

"Yes." Her voice cracked. "I only did it to protect Papa. Because of the assassin. Even if she never found us, she would have sent orvens to the navy, and Ironmast needed to know they'd be looking for us.

But there are woods here and game. We can survive until we build a strong enough boat to—"

"Get out."

The flatness of Rainn's order frightened Masika more than if he had screamed it. She took a step backward when Heron stalked over to stand beside Rainn. They were the gods, and they were obviously alone.

Why would they care about her papa's safety?

"We should talk first." Maybe a more thorough explanation would reverse Rainn's anger, perhaps even show him his own part in their predicament. His assertion of superiority convinced Masika she could *not* have talked to him on the ship without compromising her own safety. He had to see that, especially in light of his current reaction. "If you'll just look at it from . . ."

Rain stood and drew his sword.

Without consulting her brain, Masika's bare feet fled with the rest of her up into the wooded slopes of the Last Spike.

CHAPTER

TWENTY

The original little gods were the children and grandchildren of the P'tak and were many and powerful. But a mighty threat rose in the land of Ramlagha, which threatened the Darrish peoples even before Egren and Verran became countries. An army wielding weapons of shining silver fit to slay the gods poured forth, and none could stand against them.

Facing annihilation, Mother Love sacrificed her lesser progeny. She ordered them to stand, hand-in-hand, in a great circle around Ramlagha. There she transformed the little gods into an impenetrable wall of mountains that cut off the invaders, causing them to quickly starve to death.

Stories that the little gods who stood between Egren and Verran lost their way and were confused about where to stand are rubbish. Gods don't make mistakes.

Volume Two of *Thank Gods* by Kohmose Oburn

In the two days since the Alir cast Masika out of their camp, she had ranged over the northern face of the Last Spike, scouting, hunting, and exhausting herself. The more tired she was when she lay down to sleep, the less apt she was to stay up all night feeling abandoned and sorry for herself. In theory, anyway. The past two sleepless nights cast some doubt.

Below her, and for the entire five-mile stretch between the Spike and the shore, the ocean roiled in a constant state of white-capped fury. The mild day warmed Masika's shoulders in her sleeveless tunic, and the slight breeze cooled her legs, but no force could slow the crashing sea where the mountain's feet stretched below the waterline. The tide ebbed and flowed, but the west to east current ripped along those sunken foothills and dared her to step in.

Rafting to shore would be difficult. Swimming was impossible.

Captain Ironmast knew of this. He had to. The little beach they started at was at least partly protected, and on the southwest side, far away from these turbulent currents, which was why he chose it to land the small rowboat they were brought here on. Perhaps he even considered it a mercy, in that the mountain would prove more challenging for the Holy Emperor's hunters to land on.

She sighed. When had she started thinking of her uncle as the enemy? That was an easy one. When he let Meritities drip poison in his ear and sent an assassin that took her papa away, that was when.

Just another relationship lost to her mission.

Standing here helped no one. No vessels threatened to land anywhere on this half of the mountain, so if she wanted to keep watch, she needed to be on the opposite side. But she was so tired. If she lay here in the shade of this rock crest, maybe she could . . .

BRILLIANT STARS FLARED cold and white in the blue-black night sky. Thirst stuck her tongue to the roof of her mouth and hunger cramped her belly. She headed toward the small freshwater pond she made her own camp at, pushing aside thoughts of her papa and how her decisions eroded his status and his life.

What would her mother be saying about all this?

Heron's blessing, which allowed Masika to catch all manner of small animals in any slow or unmoving water, had become a sort of curse. She could not pull a drink of water out of her pond without drawing back leeches as well.

At least she could eat those.

Happily, Heron could not stop her from hunting the crested repents that dotted the slopes. The nearly three-foot-long variations of the gilded repents from the Yellow Sea were neither fast nor wary enough to avoid a woman with a bow and magical sight, and anything tasted better than leech. The past days imparted more information about Inlittan, as well. She taught herself to alter her perceptions from one manner of seeing to the next while looking at a thing. For instance, gazing at a path among the tall rocks she might desire to see which stones on the ground would cut her feet, then switch to any game she might hunt in the same area.

The runecrafted gift continued to surprise her with its unending utility.

Masika's path led her west, above the camp of the two Alir. Firelight winkled out between the fronds of the shelter's roof, and she envied them their warmth and their company.

No, she did not. Why would anyone want to be in the company of someone who considered her to be expendable? That was not friendship. Masika's hand gripped the leather pommel of her slender desert sword, grip stained with salt water. Now she understood why gods and humans did not interact with each other. Such interactions must inevitably end in heartbreak or death.

Not for the gods, of course. Only for the humans.

Masika pondered whether rescuing Heron and Rainn from Angrim's filthy lair was the right thing to do. If perhaps the world were better off with *all* the gods locked away in their hidden recesses. She stared down the mountain at the wavering orange light that escaped through the haphazardly built walls among the shadows.

Should the Last Spike serve as just another such hidden recess to hide a pair of gods? Another space secreted away from mankind for its own safety? In the dark she nodded to herself. Admitting this defeat was difficult for her, but it was time for honesty. She had been wrong to release the Alir in the first place, and wrong to try and bring them to Mount P'tak. Here they could learn to be happy with each other, even if Heron did eventually become a bird in mind as well as body, as Rainn feared.

Masika would find a way off the island mountain, or she would die here. Either way the two gods would stay, and no more lives would be ruined.

Saddened by her decision but no less resolute for it, Masika glanced up at the gently moving ocean's surface, glittering with starlight.

"Oh . . . fuck."

She ran down the mountain slope as fast as the grade would allow. Apparently Inlittan did not help you see things you were not looking at.

A ship of the Imperial Egren Navy lay anchored just offshore, black against the sparkling water. Closer, a long rowboat full of armed sailors closed in on the tiny brown beach.

Minutes away from Heron and Rainn.

"THEY'VE FOUND US. Douse the fire."

At Masika's breathless whisper, Heron took flight into the dark and Rainn kicked a heavy load of damp sand over the flames. She grabbed his arm and led him up and into the first scattered trees above the shelter. He followed without comment, though she did not need to see him to feel his irritation.

Men shouted in Darrish behind them for whoever was in the shelter to come out. Masika froze behind the trunk of a slender tree, and Rainn did the same. Neither was well concealed but perhaps the night might finish the job.

Three sailors with blades drawn closed on the shelter entrance while another dozen Saraph Jais in their sand-colored cloaks and red sashes covered their approach with short bows. The three entered the shelter and hurried conversation buzzed between the group. One burly soldier in ring armor stepped from behind and issued orders to the rest, prompting all but two to break into pairs and move off in search of their quarry. Three of those groups headed directly for Masika and Rainn. They were not sailors. These were the Saraph Jais, the army of Egren.

"We have to go," she whispered.

"We always do, thanks to you," Rainn replied under his breath.

The impulse to trip the arrogant god—loudly—and scarper off into the higher trees nearly ran ahead of Masika's sense of right and wrong. The torturous runes that Angrim carved into his body left him without his godly might except in foul weather, but they also left him able to withstand lethal amounts of punishment.

The Saraph Jais *probably* would not be able to kill him.

"Follow me closely," she whispered instead, and ran for the higher slope where the woods grew thicker.

"Look there. His skin glows blue!" So shouting, the soldiers pointed to Rainn in the darkness and gave immediate chase.

Inlittan showed her roots that tried to grab her bare toes, and which paths conspired to confound their pursuers. Looking back, she saw Saraph Jais spreading out in an attempt to get around Masika and Rainn. Would that be another problem, or would that make it easier to get around them? She knew the mountain island better than they did, but their numbers meant if they simply corralled her until daybreak when they could use their bows, her chances plummeted dramatically.

What would Sarah do? The thought prompted a memory of the last time she posed the question aloud in front of her papa. He told her not to worry about how the Hill Fury might handle a situation and think instead of what her uncle Mahu taught her to do.

Oh. Of course.

The Saraph Jais could not see to use their bows in the dark, but *she* could.

Masika stepped behind and rounded a tree, causing Rainn to stumble past. By the time she circled the other side, her bow was out and an arrow nocked. She drew as Inlittan pulled her attention to the soldiers' sandaled feet and let fly.

Two more arrows followed the first.

"Fuck it, girl." Rainn picked himself up and drew Forbryttan. Stars glinted off the perfect blade through the trees. "You trying to kill us?" He settled into a low fighting stance. "Khanah's damnable eggs, you know I can't see a thing out here."

Screams from behind launched woodland birds into the air, and Masika took advantage of the temporary cacophony to add two more Saraph Jais to the three she had already hobbled. It worked in Masika's favor that the soldiers initially headed off in different directions because it staggered their approach, but now *all* the groups ran toward the sounds of Masika's bow.

But the Saraph Jais could not see each other any more than they could see Masika, and the remaining five bore down in her direction to end the threat.

Thwip!

Thwip!

Thwip!

And the final two reached Masika's hiding spot.

She dropped her bow, pulled her desert blade and wheeled, pressing her back against the tree opposite the first soldier. As he jumped past, whirling on her, she pushed the point of her blade where Inlittan showed her, into the bed of the man's sword hand, just below his thumb.

He shouted and dropped his broadly curving scimitar, and Masika jumped forward, planted the edge of one foot into the side of his knee and kicked. He went down with a crunch and a scream.

To her left Rainn wrestled with a wounded Saraph Jais for his scimitar, Forbryttan on the ground beside them.

A hop carried Masika behind the soldier, and she reached out to run him through the shoulder, careful to avoid the major arteries there.

He gasped, dropped his blade, and fell to the ground beneath Rainn's furious blows.

Heavy breathing and groans of pain permeated the night. Downslope, still standing beside Rainn's shelter, Masika saw the Saraph Jais commander, scowling and squinting into the gloom.

"Stupid girl." Behind her, Rainn brushed himself off and groused. "That was foolish. What if you'd stabbed me?"

"Your people will live," Masika shouted down to the commander while she ignored Rainn. "You may collect them and leave—this time. Return and we will not be so easy with them."

"Oh yeah?" asked Rainn in a harsh whisper. "How many arrows do you have left?"

"Three. But they don't need to know that."

The commander cupped his hands around his mouth and shouted up at them. "We will be leaving, and I do thank you for not killing anyone. But you and I both know this won't finish it. When we come back, it'll be at first light, and we'll have enough so that you *can't* fight. Be ready to lay down arms and surrender so I need not kill you either."

"That bastard." Rainn gripped Forbryttan and growled. "He's not getting offa this rock."

"Shut up, Rainn." Masika struggled against her frustration with the god of doing things out-of-doors in poor weather. He and his attitudes were far more likely to get them killed than a little restraint on Masika's part. "This is human stuff. You're out of your depth."

She shouted back down the slope. "How long until you return?"

"You will have five days while I gather men. Meet us empty of hand on the small beach and I will see you to your uncle unharmed. Do we agree?"

"Unless I think of a better plan between now and then." By her honesty, she showed the Saraph Jais commander respect. He would expect nothing less. "I'm leaving to allow you the chance to collect your wounded, but I'll be watching."

"There is no other plan for you." The commander stepped into full view. "I will see you in five days."

Masika stalked past Rainn and up the mountain, toward her pond and tiny lean-to.

HERON PULLED YET another fish out of the little freshwater pond.

Masika shook her head. She would have sworn no fish even lived in that pond, unless you counted the never-ending supply of leeches.

Which she did not.

From beneath Masika's lean-to, Rainn grunted. "Now that you've trapped us on this mountain and fed the means to catch us to the enemy, I don't suppose you got any more grand ideas cooking, do you? Maybe you'd like to throw alla our clothes inna water and make new ones of brambles and thistles?"

"You're just angry for having to share the fate of the human who was stupid enough to want to help you," Masika threw back. The fire she labored over caught and flames licked the edges of dried branches, but none so hot as her temper. "I should have left you in the hole I found you in."

A surprised squawk escaped Heron, who jerked her head up to stare at Masika.

"I was thinking the same thing." Rainn propped himself up on an elbow and shouted. "And no, Heron, I don't think she's gone quite far enough. I wanna know exactly how she feels about us."

"How I feel about you?" Blinding anger threatened to steal Masika's speech, but she redirected it into the opportunity to finally cut loose. "You're an idiot, and I'm even worse for thinking you might be grateful for what I was trying to do for you. But you aren't, and you never have been. What if I die getting the two of you home? Who cares? I'm just a stupid human, right? Just like Papa, or any of the rest of us who put ourselves in harm's way for your sakes."

More squawking, this time directed at Rainn, erupted from the goddess.

He waved a hand to quiet her. "Humans aren't supposed to work for the gods for some kind of reward, you twit. You spend a few years being good little fuckwits and you get eternal happiness. How is that such a bad fucking deal? Thunder and blood, girl, how'd you find your way out of your momma's crack?"

"Eternal happiness?" Inlittan showed Masika only red. "*I don't worship the Alir!* Do you think they'll give me a place in their paradise?

Do you think the P'tak won't damn me for aiding you in the first place?" Tears wanted to burst from Masika's eyes and roll down her face, but she held them back. This was the truth she had hidden even from herself. "You've *ruined* me. You've taken everything from me when I only wanted to help you, and you don't even care."

Having left the water to make herself heard directly into Rainn's face, Heron screeched at him. She refused to relent, following his every movement to evade her.

"Get away. I can't hear myself scream at the human."

The screeching intensified.

"Fine! Yes, I told her we'd fuck off if we got the chance. Happy? I didn't know about the no-one-letting-her-into-paradise thing."

The cacophony halted, and Heron pecked Rainn in the forehead.

"Khanah's damn—Ow! What the fuck was that for? Ow! Stop it!"

Heron resumed her squawking, though faster paced and not as loud as before. Her scars glowed brighter through her soft gray feathers.

Whatever Heron told him, Masika could not help the smirk that stole over her, watching Rainn's abuse.

"I do too know what I'm doing." Rainn lowered his voice to a mere shout. "No, everything isn't perfect right now, but—Ow! I don't see you—Ow!"

This continued in a similar vein for a full minute, Rainn seemingly unable to block or dodge a single one of Heron's pecks. In the end they murmured to one another beneath Masika's hearing, with Rainn mostly nodding and Heron standing unyielding and aggressive. Finally, the goddess moved away from him and returned to the water.

"Your breath smells like fish." Rainn smiled as he said it but flinched away when Heron's head whipped up to stare at him. "I know. Sorry." He rolled out of Masika's lean-to and stood to one side, head hung and voice small.

"I'm, uh, I'm sorry, Masika."

Masika's mouth fell open, though she did not notice it. What had he just said? Surely, he did not just admit to being . . . *sorry*?

"You're right. You only ever tried to help us, and I acted like it meant squat. Even when you didn't tell everything, it was because I was being such a prick. We won't leave you *or* your family inna lurch."

Heron's next coo was draped over steel.

"Yeah." Rainn nodded to the goddess. "We won't leave until everything's set right. We're gonna make sure that there's a place set for you and yours in the afterlife somewhere. Somewhere good and sunny and happy, where everyone except your stupid sister can be content forever."

Another warning growled from Heron.

Rainn sighed. "And her too. If that's what you really want."

Emotion closed Masika's throat and left her unable to speak. She had suffered so much anxiety and tension since her and Rainn's conversation that day on the *Ocean Krait*, the relief was too much to process all at once. With an undignified *gawp*, she rushed forward and flung her arms around Rainn.

"Ah, all right." He patted her on the back with one hand and let the other hang at his side. "Course it may not mean a lot, but we'll do whatever we can. We owe you that much, don't we? But we'll have to survive the next week first before we can try and convince any gods of anything."

Masika's tears soaked into his dirty and torn shirt.

CHAPTER

TWENTY-ONE

Four days later the number of ships anchored in sight of the Last Spike had grown to three. Masika decided the Saraph Jais now possessed more than enough soldiers to compel a surrender, but that the commander felt honor-bound to his promise.

Capture would beach the island tomorrow morning.

"Hey Rainn, There's something I've been wanting to ask you about now we're off the ship." *And talking again,* Masika thought to herself. "Why did Captain Ironmast let you keep Forbryttan when everyone else had to put their swords and knives in the weapons locker?"

One side of Rainn's mouth quirked up and he gave a quiet snort of amusement. "I told him I was a captain of my own ship. It's a sorta mutual respect thing."

"I guess it's a good thing Nebet didn't know about that," Masika said.

"Oh, Ironmast told me if that three-hundred-pound cock tried anything else I could chop his damn head off." Rainn smiled at the recollection. "Except the exact words he used were, 'Bring me that big fucker's head and I'll pay ya for it in grog and cheap women.'"

His gaze wandered out to the Egren ships again and the near-moment of happiness evaporated in a dark frown. "If we could get more than ten minutes of shower every day, I'd swim out to those ships and slaughter the lot of them."

Rainn's frustration mounted daily. He no longer slouched in a depressive fugue whenever the sun struck his bare skin—in fact his arms browned, and his cheeks freckled in the brilliant tropical light—but he remained irritated nonetheless.

"No, you wouldn't." Masika smiled and patted him on the shoulder. He sat on the highest spot up the mountain they could easily reach, a grassy alp in miniature some hundred feet wide and a curving thousand feet long. She stood just behind him. From their vantage they could see a bit north, all the east facing, and most of the south. It was chillier up there, but the extra distance calmed Heron, who needed it the most. "You wouldn't kill any of them. You'd bonk them on the head with the flat of that sword and pile them safely away, then steal their ship."

Head forward and one brow raised, Rainn frowned at her. "What makes you say that? I love to kill people. I kill all the time. Want me to kill you?"

A squawk that sounded suspiciously like a laugh turned Rainn's head. "No one asked you," he told the goddess. She returned to stalking insects in the low grass.

"When we were attacked outside that pub in Port Bibi, you could have killed all those guys by yourself if you'd really wanted to." She sat down beside him. "But you didn't."

"Say what?" Rainn leaned away to stare down at Masika. "That doesn't mean anything. How do you know I didn't stab them all just enough so they'd die a long, horrible death?"

"Did you?"

Rainn shook his head violently as he scrunched around on his butt to face Masika fully. "No, but I will next time. Humans are awful, especially you. Always being dramatic or asking stupid questions about stuff. You can never leave well enough alone—"

A sharp screech from Heron caught his attention.

"Well, yeah." Rainn shrugged his shoulders. "Guess we'd still be chained to those stone tables under the citadel if you *could* leave well enough alone. So that's not totally terrible. But you're the only one I don't completely hate."

Masika flung her arms around Rainn and gripped him tight. He held himself rigid for a moment before relaxing into her grip with a small chuckle. He waved a hand in the direction of a pair of Egren ships.

"Still don't like any of *those* guys though."

THE NEXT MORNING Masika and Rainn stood on the narrow strip of golden-brown sand and watched the Saraph Jais row ashore. Heron observed from a nearby bush.

True to their words both Forbryttan and Masika's weapons lay on the sand in front of them. Unable to think of a way out, they chose the path of least violence, though Rainn had required some additional convincing.

Inlittan remained on the fingers and wrist of her right hand.

Four large rowboats with twenty Saraph Jais apiece approached, though only two at a time could land. They did so, and red-sashed soldiers poured out, circling the sand and the rocks above.

The third boat held the commander, who hopped out into the surf and helped pull the rowboat onto the beach, ring armor jingling.

How did he keep it from rusting? Oil?

The Saraph Jais commander approached the pair and nodded his head to Masika. "Princess Oburn, thank you for making this safe and easy on everyone. You will be taken to our camp on the mainland to discuss your transport with—"

"Hold it steady, you idiots!"

A monster of a man in a golden-hued breastplate clambered out of the final rowboat. Though still half-full of soldiers, the man's size and unfamiliarity with moving on a boat threatened to capsize it.

The commander lowered his face and held his forehead as he whispered a curse under his breath.

"Is that . . .?" asked Rainn, leaning over to mutter into Masika's ear.

"Oh." Masika stood up straighter, surprise pulling her gaze longingly toward the slender desert sword on the sand.

Nebet, Meritities's one-eared, hulking bodyguard sneered at Masika and Rainn both. Short swords strapped to his powerful thighs, he strutted much too close to Rainn and leaned down into the god's face.

"It is good to see you again, little god."

"Surprised you feel that way, Nebet." A hard smile spread itself across Rainn's features. That smile promised thunder and blood. "Based on the last time we saw you, I sorta figured you'd still be running awa—"

The big fist smashed into the side of Rainn's jaw, and he went down spinning.

"Now it is even better to see you." Nebet spat on Rainn's back and twisted his head to one side, so that all the startled Saraph Jais could see his smirk. "In the daylight, it is barely a man. Only the storm brings the monster. I will show you."

One gold-sandaled foot pulled back but stopped there. Masika stood between Rainn and Nebet. She winced ahead of the blow, but the kick never came. Apparently even Nebet balked in the face of assaulting an unresisting niece of the Holy Emperor.

When the foot did fall, it was only to shovel a face full of sand at Rainn, who spluttered loudly.

"Your sister is eager to see you too, Princess." With that, Nebet spun and lumbered back to the rowboats.

Sweat popped out on Masika's forehead, and she tried to control her breathing. If Nebet fell to kicking Rainn, he might not have stopped, and the rest of the Saraph Jais might have jumped in with him had the god attempted to defend himself.

She was not afraid for her own safety, but she harbored no desire to be responsible for Rainn's getting kicked to death.

Not anymore, anyway.

"Please accept my apologies. Princess Meritities sends her dog where she will." The commander extended a hand to Rainn, who took it and hauled himself to his feet. "She does indeed wait on the mainland. I do not know how she discovered we had found you, but she showed up two days ago and assumed command of our operation." He shrugged. "Perhaps you would prefer to ride back to the ships in my boat?"

Masika moved under Rainn's arm and helped guide him to the rowboat. His feet failed to make exactly the steps he intended, but together they made it there.

"Hey," Rainn whispered as they stumbled across the beach, "it's all good if I just kill that one guy, isn't it?"

"We'll make it a team project," Masika replied.

CHAPTER

TWENTY-TWO

Egren and Verran did not always harbor such animosity. In the infancy of the two nations, they worked together to protect each other from Andosh raiders and develop Darrish culture and civilization.

Whether the rift is attributable to Hamara and Shaitun or the failure of imperial expansion, as the nations matured, they continued to grow further and further apart, until they reached the state of wary detente they exist in today. Never quite able to find peace nor willing to commit fully to violence.

Obviously, this is the fault of Verran, as mere observation will demonstrate that no son or daughter of Egren would behave in such a manner toward their own kin.

Volume One of *Thank Gods* by Kohmose Oburn

Meritities smiled.

Open flaps at either end of her personal pavilion allowed ocean breezes to flow through and cool her skin. The huge tent, white canvas to better reflect the burning attentions of Allz the Shining, came furnished with dendro wood tables, chairs, and an oversized bed.

Just for her.

The Holy Emperor's favorite.

She curled her toes into the deep, tundra catskin rug, luxuriating in the silky feel while Seraph Jais laughed and joked outside around the central square of the extensive camp, where the crackle and thump of a bonfire kept the desert's evil spirits at bay. All five vessels returned from the Last Spike, a certain sign that her dangerously inconvenient sister and her barbaric gods came with them.

In retrospect, Meritities should be grateful to Masika for presenting such a problem. No one else provided such an opportunity for heroic action to impress an emperor. Would her uncle arrange her betrothal to the twelve-year-old Divine Prince Majada, or perhaps, if sufficiently smitten, would he have his carping empress killed and take Meritities for himself?

Either way, she would be empress of Egren, and from there, perhaps all the Thirteen Kingdoms.

"You look well pleased."

Who had spoken?

Craning her neck, Meritities searched for the source of the cultured woman's voice. "Where are you? Show yourself this instant." Though the soldiers just outside bristled with weaponry and awaited her word, Meritities still felt the sting of Nebet's absence. But she recognized that voice and felt no threat from it.

"Apologies, Princess. Just checking in on our little project."

As the woman spoke, some trick of the light revealed her to Meritities, standing where she always was, in the middle of the big pavilion. A sleeveless black tunic, belted at the waist, hung on her thin frame, and jewel toned hair ran in swirling rivulets over pale shoulders.

"Lady Alexandra?" Despite herself, Meritities goggled. The mysterious woman from the court of Queen Odandria and King Larustines bowed her head to Meritities, a knowing smile on her lips.

"How are you here?" Meritities asked. "How did you even know where to find me?"

"I was in the area," Lady Alexandra replied. "And being friends with a sorcerer does have benefits."

"Right." Merities regained her composure and narrowed her gaze. "So is this an errand for your superiors then? Did Haphimenes the Elder send you? Or are you still acting on King Larustines behalf?"

Lady Alexandra's smile erupted in a beautiful chime of laughter. "Oh no, my dear. As I said, Haphimenes is my friend, and the king is . . . well, he has his hands full at the moment. I rather suspect he wishes he'd never met you."

"Then why are you here?"

"Can't a woman simply check in on an acquaintance to see how she's doing? After all, you left things in a state back on Kos." Lady Alexandra slid long-fingered hands to her hips and glanced around at her surroundings. "And there is the matter of your debt."

"My debt?" At this Merities relaxed, though she kept the tension in her shoulders so as to not reveal her thoughts. Negotiations she could handle. "How do you imagine I owe you for anything? All your artifice gained me nothing. Masika escaped Kos with both her monsters in tow and is only in hand now because I took charge of her capture personally. At best you made my life more difficult, not less."

The wind reversed, and the smell of woodsmoke blew briefly through the pavilion.

"The payment is for my assistance, not what you make of it." Lady Alexandra purred the words over her smile. "If you buy an apple from the costermonger, do you demand your money back if you forget to eat it?"

"I certainly would if that apple were hiding a worm." Merities refused to yield the upper hand. "In point of fact, I am beginning to believe you owe me for your failure and for my inconvenience. If you had not inserted yourself between me and King Larustines, things would have turned out differently."

Lady Alexandra leaned in, an errant breeze from the open flap behind her blowing pink, yellow, and green strands of hair even as it carried in sounds of increased laughter from the Saraph Jais outside. "And do you believe that you could have done better?"

"I certainly do," Merities responded without hesitation.

At this, Lady Alexandra straightened, her smile now a feral grin.

"Then why didn't you?"

"Why didn't I what?" The question surprised Meritities. She didn't handle the affair with stealing, wrecking, and eventually burning Masika's vessel because she had arranged for this very woman to—

Ah. There was the trap.

With a subtle sigh, Meritities cast her gaze at the ground. She asked—practically demanded—Lady Alexandra's help, with the acknowledgement that she would return the favor, and then left. Things might very well have played out more to Meritities liking if she had stuck around to see it through herself, but she didn't. By choosing to walk away, she had accepted whatever result came to pass.

And now payment was due.

"Damn." Meritities met Lady Alexandra's amused gaze. "I hate losing. What do you want?"

"I'll be happy to tell you, but first there's the matter of a problem that you're about to have." Lady Alexandra pointed through the canvas wall toward the ocean. "You're going to lose your quarry."

Before Meritities could respond, a Saraph Jais runner appeared in the open square facing the fire.

"Princess," he said, "Your sister and her companion, an Andosh man, were just taken to their accommodations so they might make themselves presentable to meet with you."

Meritities chuckled. "And the bird?"

"It was spotted several times on the island and after we landed back at camp. It doesn't seem interested in going far."

"Thank you, soldier." Meritities poured two glasses of sweet palm wine and handed one to Lady Alexandra. The thought of Heron still flying free nettled Meritities, but her current happiness barred the thought.

The runner bowed and backed away.

"You were saying, Lady Alexandra?" Meritities discovered that she found this entire situation quite funny. In truth she should have captured Masika two days ago and would have if the Saraph Jais commander had not stupidly promised her sister they'd wait.

"I was saying that you are about to lose your sister and her two little gods unless you accept my help again." She took a sip of the wine. "Oh. That's delightful. But, of course, you'll owe me twice over."

Meritities laughed openly, a free, though refined, sound. "I think you've overplayed your hand here. The situation is well in hand. Just tell me what you want for Kos and you can be on your way."

More than half full still, Lady Alexandra set down her palm wine on the table, her finger absently tracing the huge dendro whorls in the polished wood. "Very well." She produced a small, lacquered box from behind her back, set it next to her wine glass, and opened it. "This is a present to the Holy Emperor, from you." She lifted a small steel ball attached to a neck chain from the box. "It is ancient and invaluable and will ingratiate you to him entirely."

A giggle escaped Meritities. "How is that a fit gift for an Emperor?"

Small frown lines flitted across Lady Alexandra's face. "You may try it on, but you must return it to the box and not take it out again until you are putting it in the Holy Emperor's hands." She handed the odd necklace over to Meritities.

With a snort, Meritities placed the necklace over her head and lifted the steel ball to get a better look at it. It glinted in the diffuse light of the tent and flashed. The steel became a dazzling diamond, clear and shot through with shining rainbows that beckoned to her. She felt her consciousness pulling forward into the object in her hand, clamoring for the unending happiness and peace it offered.

Her grip became iron around the object.

And it was gone, snatched effortlessly away by Lady Alexandra and returned to its box.

"Don't tell anyone else you gave it to him," Lady Alexandra said, her previous knowing smile back in place. "He will love and reward you for it, and then it will kill him. I trust that fits with your own desires as well? Payment doesn't have to hurt, you know."

Tears accompanied Meritities burbling laughter. The necklace was so *joyful*.

Lady Alexandra sniffed the air. "Time for me to run, dear. You'll wish you'd listened to me, but all the important matters have been settled. Best of luck, and don't take that back out. It's not for you. I'll know if you misuse it."

She walked out of the tent, thin hips swaying beneath her black dress, into the sunlight where Meritities lost sight of her.

Leave it in the box. Ingratiated completely. Lose her sister? The preposterousness of the encounter forced Meritities to throw her head back and guffaw, pausing only when she had no breath left to laugh again, joining the soldiers outside.

Another tendril of smoke entered the tent.

Was that cinnamon?

CHAPTER
TWENTY-THREE

The desire for flight is a recurring theme among Darrish heroes. From Aukashet who drifts over mountains on a line of silk, to Hamara who steals the wings of Shaitun only to lose them in a game of flix to Sahar-ka, soaring above the world as a bird might has always shown to be both an irresistible allure and a deadly trap. Consider the Fisherman and His Son, a parable every Egren child knows about a man who made wings of gull feathers and wax for himself and his boy.

The pair go flying, and the child, ignoring the warnings of his father, ascends too close to the Iron Wheel where Allz the Shining illuminates the world with his rent open body. Allz introduces the boy to drinking and decadence, and the fisherman is forced to watch his only child grow wealthy as he grows up owning an expansive and thriving tavern business.

A grim lesson indeed.

Volume Four of *Thank Gods* by Kohmose Oburn

S mall claws scratched along the roof of the big white tent the Saraph Jais parked Masika and Rainn in. Heron had followed the rowboats in the air and now kept watch from the tent's top.

Though uncomfortably warm inside, a pitcher of fresh water and a change of clothes had been provided, which Masika and Rainn both availed themselves of. Dressed in white linen trousers and long-sleeved tops, loose and lightweight, they sat on cushions stuffed to hardness and waited.

Sweat dripped off Rainn's chin, though they had been in the tent less than a half-hour.

"That commander guy said your sister wanted to invade the mountain and drag us back two days ago, alive or dead." He blew out his cheeks and drummed his fingertips against his ribs. "Guess she's not in a hurry anymore, now that we're already caught."

"In a hurry? No." How many times had Meritities done this exact same thing to Masika in the past. Dozens? Hundreds? "She's just trying to show us whose time is more important."

"Your sister is kind of a bitch."

"She takes after my mother."

"Oh." Rainn raised his hands in front of himself. "Sorry. Didn't mean anything by it."

"No, it's fine. My mother is kind of a bitch too."

A squawk sounded from above, and Rainn's chuckle was whipped away with the front tent flap. Two men in the sand-colored robes and red sashes of the Saraph Jais, hooded shawls covering their faces, entered and pulled the flap shut behind themselves. One loomed tall with a rangy economy of motion, while the second stood shorter but broader of shoulder. That one entered second, dragging a pair of unconscious Darrish men behind him, stripped to their smallclothes.

A shiver ran through Masika. She recognized the bow on the back of the shorter man, and that recognition stole her strength.

Seeing Masika's face, Rainn jumped up and readied himself to fight.

But before violence occurred, Masika shoved off her cushion and stumbled over to the shorter man to pull him to her in a grateful hug. "Uncle Mahu," she breathed. "I'm so sorry for the mess I've made. How did you find us? Is it safe for you to be here?"

Uncle Mahu held his niece out at arm's length and opened his mouth to speak.

"As safe as anywhere else, Featherwind." Sabni leaned over to put his broadly grinning face between them. His dark skin and black beard made his teeth glow in comparison. "We happened to be in the area and thought, oh my, look at all of those tents. I bet *someone* we know requires rescuing."

The scowl on Uncle Mahu's face put the lie to Sabni's claim. He pulled the satchel off his back and threw it to Rainn. "Later. Put this on. We must go now."

"Featherwind?" Rainn whispered.

Masika's finger whipped up between them, intensifying her scowl. "No. You don't get to call me that."

Rainn shrugged and lifted clothing out of Mahu's pack.

Stowing the rest of her questions, Masika pulled on her own robe, sash, and shawl, as did Rainn. Once finished, they stood close to the tent flap where Uncle Mahu and Sabni waited.

"Not yet." Uncle Mahu shook his head at Sabni and yanked the flap out of the taller man's hand.

"Of course." Sabni smiled and took a step backward. "She did say to wait for the screaming."

"What?" Rainn twisted to see around himself, though there was nothing to be seen other than the inside of the tent. "Screaming? I think maybe I'd rather wait outside."

"When we are well away from Meritities and her machinations," said Sabni with a warm nod for Rainn, "remind me to share *the Immortal Queen Nefret and the Fallow Orchard* with you. It teaches the ways in which even the mightiest of warriors may benefit from a little patience."

"Since when has anyone ever had to remind you to bore them with your endless stories?" Uncle Mahu's ever-present scowl fixated on Sabni, who returned a benign twinkle.

Masika laughed. "I've really missed you two."

Shouting quieted everyone in the tent and turned their faces to the flap.

"That, as Bahnesk says to his brother in the tale of *the Opal Woman*, is as likely a call as we will ever get."

Sparing only an instant to roll his eyes at Sabni, Uncle Mahu lifted the tent flap and rushed outside. Sabni followed, then Masika and Rainn.

"That's not screaming." Rainn craned his neck and tried to get a look at the cause of the commotion but could not see past the random scattering of tents, banners, and running soldiers.

The shouts of the Saraph Jais grew louder and more intense, but another noise swelled to overwhelm it. Masika's head canted to one side.

Laughter?

"Let's go." And Uncle Mahu stalked away, faster than Masika could follow without running.

They half-walked, half-ran into painfully bright sunlight, passing another dozen tents, a small corral of horses, a row of long wooden tables and benches set out in the sun, and an eight-foot-high wooden platform with some kind of scaffolding above it.

Tittering laughter and angry shouts pursued them, though the Saraph Jais themselves ran in purposeless circles, paying them no mind.

It was only when Masika spotted the hinged door in the bottom of the platform that she realized what it was. And Meritities controlled this operation? She intended to *hang* them?

In the far distance, visible only with Inlittan's help, Masika spotted Heron describing lazy circles in the sky. The goddess could keep an eye on them with her own superior sight while not revealing where they'd gone. Masika could only imagine Meritities's pique at not being able to capture Heron outright.

Good goddess.

Thoughts fluttered through Masika's mind, unable to find purchase there. Wouldn't it be wonderful to be able to fly? If she could transform herself as Heron did, Masika would never return to human. Who would even want to?

Dark images chased Masika's dreams of flight. Meritities could not possibly mean to hang her. Wait. What was it Alakeel the assassin said? The Holy Emperor ordered Masika's return and the death of the Alir. The gallows waited for Rainn.

Could he even be hung to death? How long would that take?

She spurted laughter at the idea.

Just as they reached the furthest edge of the camp, Masika caught a whiff of something sweet. It smelled like grain sugar and green nut, with just a hint of cinnamon. Something about the smell brought a wide grin to Masika's lips, and she paused to look at the Saraph Jais encampment behind her.

The camp spread out much larger than she had thought, now that she looked down the slope on it. Soldiers and sailors ran this way and that, a few bellowing angrily but the rest barely able to stand from their laughter. A ballista bolt flew above the camp and lodged in the side of one of the ships anchored just offshore to an uproar of hysterics, and even more anger from the sailors on the ship.

Masika giggled. Whatever was happening down there, it was *funny*.

Behind her, Rainn joined in, slapping his own chest in a vain attempt to rein in his own mirth. When one of the biggest tents exploded into flames, Masika and Rainn both lost their composure entirely, and together they stumble-stepped back in the direction of the camp.

"Where are they going?" Behind Masika, a high, girlish voice spoke in a soft Pavinn accent. "Did you forget to give them the flowers?"

Uncle Mahu appeared in front of Masika, his arms outstretched, and his brow drawn in worry. "Come along, Featherwind. Nothing for you back there." When Masika tried to evade his movements, he scooped her up and ran toward a curvy young woman with blue-gray desert robes and a wild headful of strawberry blonde curls.

Though she wanted to protest, Masika could not spare the breath when she saw Rainn bouncing up and down on Sabni's shoulder, snot flying from his nose as he chortled with glee.

"Can we give them the flower now?" Sabni asked the redheaded woman.

"Too late. It's only good beforehand, they'll have to let it wear off. Way to listen to instructions, dope. Let's go. I stashed the horses over that rise and between the foothills."

"I get a horse?" Rainn's voice bounced as his body did. "I never had a horse before. Wha'd I do if it doesn't like gods?"

"Walk fast," Mahu answered.

"Hey, you're Ameli." Masika grinned and sputtered laughter at the young woman. "You're a sorceress. Uncle Mahu told me all about you." She stopped talking to guffaw over what a funny name Ameli was. "You saved his-his-his life!"

Mirth turned Masika into a useless sack of beans around Uncle Mahu's neck, but not before she noticed the tightening around Ameli's lips and the wrinkle that appeared on her freckled forehead.

For the next hour Masika and Rainn rode with Uncle Mahu and Sabni while Ameli led their horses, and Heron watched them nervously from the sky.

CHAPTER
TWENTY-FOUR

Sorcery comes from Sahar-ka, first son of Mother Love and Father Rain. The holy majik was intended to protect the P'tak's people from the chaotic energies of the northern Andosh tribes, who received their evil gifts from demons.

Worst are the Pavinn, whose corrupted bloodlines stole majik from the Darrish and mixed it with the unholy wizardry of the Andosh to become something dark and wild. This includes the Arlean sorceress Olandrea who was turned to stone by her traitorous apprentice Deliah the Unbroken, the Old Man who lives in the swamps of Sedrios and feasts on the bodies of lost souls, and the Deep Witch of the Paradisals, a creature of such vile power that even righteous sailors of Egren feel compelled to offer her sacrifices.

Insidiously, the Deep Witch extends her power through her daughters, a coven of sorceresses born of the witch and sailors doomed to die at her hand, at the very instant of insemination.

Well, probably not her hand.

Volume Eight of *Thank Gods* by Kohmose Oburn

Exhaustion fell on Masika, a leaden blanket that made every movement a mountainous climb of its own. Uncontrollable glee drained a body. Still, she found herself happy and content as the five of them trekked northward along the Egren side of the mountains.

While this was technically the same mountain range they recently traveled south against, that end was the western leg of a curving range of peaks that encircled the Yellow Sea on every side but the south, which they recently sailed past. That western side abutted Sedrios, the eastern side, Egren, with the desert in the middle.

Far overhead, Heron wheeled in the cloudless blue sky. She watched, Masika knew, to make sure their new companions were not here to murder everyone before she got anywhere close.

This side of the peaks painted their broad lands in greens and yellows, with lush fields of food crops that fed the nation. The roads here ran straight and at right angles to one another, and the north road they traveled on was even paved with broad white stone.

The group of them wore standard traveling gear, which included the long shawls that hooded their heads and faces. Their sashes were put away and Ameli tied her red hair back so it would not be seen.

"I think it likes me." Since climbing on his mare's back, Rainn's face stretched wide in a huge grin. "Look, when I move the reins, it follows. Isn't that a bucket of tits? I guess horses are just more responsive when there's a god on board."

"I'm tired." Even breathing pulled more out of Masika than it gave back. She needed something to take her mind off her fatigue. "Sabni, tell us a story."

A groan escaped Uncle Mahu, and even Ameli shook her head.

"Which story would you most like to hear, Featherwind?" Sabni's happy baritone lifted the corners of Masika's mouth, a warm wind scattering seeds of joy everywhere. "Sahar-ka who gave majik to the Darrish at the behest of Mother Love? Ahmen and Dedi and their adventures among the kingdoms of the damned? Perhaps I will tell you of the time when Matchi the Huntress ran out of judged souls to feed her hounds and was forced to search all of creation to find another source?"

"No." Masika did not know those stories well, and she wanted something familiar. "Tell me about the human Queen Nefret and Egren."

A long arm reached out and Mahu steadied Rainn on his horse.

"Aha! That is a wonderful story. A very good choice for a beautiful day like today." Sabni rubbed at his chin, the perfectly cropped black beard framing his face in straight angles. "It begins on a day much as this, with Allz the Shining providing life to the crops, his treachery turned to light by Mother Love's wisdom."

AS THE SUN set over the Little Gods, Uncle Mahu turned their horses west to camp deeper between the foothills and away from prying eyes. Tired as she was, Masika found herself unable to settle down for the night.

Rainn collapsed on the grass immediately, not waiting for tents or bedrolls, while Uncle Mahu and Sabni bickered over where to place the campfire.

"We have you to thank for our escape from my sister's camp?" Masika asked, interrupting the discussion. "As much as I appreciate it, I don't fully understand it. You're both loyal servants of the Holy Emperor, and Sabni, I thought that being a priest would have put you on Merities's side of this fight."

The two exchanged a look. Sabni nodded and Mahu turned to speak.

"We serve the emperor when it suits us." The shattering admission came bluntly, as might an observation on the weather. "We have seen much of the world, Sabni and I. Enough to call your papa's brother's judgement into question."

At Masika's open-mouthed expression of shock, Sabni rushed over and pulled her tight into a protective embrace.

"That's not all," Sabni said, shooting Mahu an eyeroll. "You are our little Featherwind. You mean the world to us, and we could never stand by and allow you to come to harm, no matter the circumstance. We stand with you, behind you, in front of you, and beside you. That is not merely the creed of the Veiled Breath, it is the creed of family. Of us." He winked at her. "Especially when the cause is just and brave."

The words threatened to overwhelm Masika, and she buried her face in Sabni's arms until she felt more certain of her composure.

"Thank you. Both of you," Masika said, just a slight tremble to her words. "I-I thought I was alone. I'm happy I was wrong. Now get off of me before I start crying again."

Disentangling himself from Masika, Sabni stood and resumed his argument with Mahu over the fire, more in earnest now that his partner had taken advantage of Sabni's moment with Masika to begin putting it where *he* wanted it.

Masika crawled over and sat down on the ground next to Ameli, and watched the woman mix a dark paste into a bowl and rub it into her frizzy red hair. "How did you make everyone so happy?" Masika asked her. "Happy enough to not even notice our running away?"

"It was a good running away." Ameli paused, a wistful smile on her round face. "As good as any I've seen." She returned to her hair. "If Mahu told you who I am, I imagine he told you where I come from too."

"You're one of the Daughters' Coven. Your mother is the Deep Witch."

"You're right about my mother, but I got kinda kicked out of the Daughters' club. I killed one too many pirate royals."

"Oh." Masika's slow-witted brain thumped to a halt at that.

Ameli grinned up at her, her arms mushing paste into her hair up above her head. Don't worry. You're safe. They were all terrible people. I did it for the good of the country. Though I guess not everyone saw it that way." Her grin, toothy and reassuring, calmed Masika.

"And our escape?"

"Oh, yeah." Ameli worked a cord around her hair to bind it on top of her head and sluiced her hands into a second bowl filled with clean water. "My kicking out came before I was declared a full sorceress, but I still learned a lot of things. Especially about plants. That was my specialty. I worked up a couple of sachets that make this pinkish smoke when you toss them in a camp's firepits, like the boys over there did right before they found you. That smoke fucks you up pretty good. But I don't have to tell *you* that."

"I'm sorry." Masika looked into the fire to avoid her embarrassment at having breathed Ameli's smoke and making a disappointing nuisance of herself. "I didn't mean to be a burden."

"Hee. That wasn't your fault, honey." Ameli dried her hands and patted Masika on the knee. "If those two meatheads had remembered to give you the flowers when I told them, you wouldn't be feeling so shagged out right now."

Now that she considered it, Masika found herself growing heavier. "I think I'll go to sleep. If you see a tall gray bird around, tell her I said it's safe."

"What's her name?"

"Heron." Masika curled up on the bedroll she had been given and pulled a blanket over her legs. "Night."

Ameli shook her head. "A bird named Heron. Hope her mom was proud of coming up with that."

Sinking deeper, Masika wanted to say that all the birds were probably named after the goddess and not the other way around, but it was far too late for any more conversation.

THE IRON WHEEL slowly spun behind the polished blue sky, bearing Allz the Shining up into morning. His soul shone with brilliant heat on crops and travelers alike, and pulled the cool breath of the Little Gods down from the mountain tops.

It was a perfect moment, Masika decided. Her worries grew distant here in the Egren countryside, with her uncle and his companions alongside her. Green barley fields gave way to golden flax, trading food crops for textiles.

"Alakeel is a friend of ours," explained Sabni, riding straight-backed in his saddle. "We already knew Tennat was coming from his orvens, but she got word to us that she had taken him prisoner and was traveling by the slowest boat she could find to Plensa."

"Why would she do all that?" Despite the mild weather, Rainn's demeanor remained relaxed and upbeat. Was he finally getting used to being happy? Masika hoped so.

"The risk to her is minimal, and as I said, we are friends." Sabni shrugged and smiled. "Mahu and I were considering how exactly to free Masika's papa when Alakeel sent a second orven to tell us that you and the Alir were found and to be captured. The risk to you was *not* minimal, so here we are."

"So we have that assassin to thank for our rescue?" Rainn gave a rueful shake of his head and chuckled. "You Darrish play a deep game. Can't say I don't appreciate it, but I think I prefer problems you can swing a sword at."

"Probably a good thing these Darrish didn't think of you as that sort of problem." Ameli pitched her head sideways as she spoke and sent her wild mane over her shoulder. The earthy paste rendered her hair a less recognizable brown but left its golden shine.

Did Rainn just blush at the sorceress's playful rebuke? Masika watched, amazed, as red crept up the god's neck and into his cheeks.

The world never stopped proving to be an amazing and mysterious place.

"Niece." Uncle Mahu's soft voice, deep and calm, commanded attention. "What is your plan to scale the unscalable Mount P'tak? How may we assist?"

"Uh . . ." Masika looked at her hands. "I've never really been there. I just figured we'd take a look around and work something out."

Eyes on the horizon in front of him, Uncle Mahu grunted. "Hmph. That is not a workable plan."

"It wasn't before," Masika said, bright and hopeful, "but now I have my favorite uncle and his friends with me. I don't see how we can fail."

"Hey, Ameli, how long does your pink mist take to wear off? I think Masika's still stoned." Rainn spoke directly to the sorceress, as though they were the only two traveling the white stone road.

"I don't think you can blame this on me." Ameli ran her fingers through her horse's mane as she spoke, eliciting a happy snort. "That mix lasts an hour at most, and that's if you get a good snootful. She's just cheery."

Unprompted, Heron fluttered out of the blue and landed on Ameli's saddle. The sorceress scooted back to give the goddess a little extra room. "Well, hello there."

The goddess responded to Ameli with a small cluck and allowed herself to be stroked along the top of the head.

"Nice to meet you too, Heron. You have really pretty feathers."

Masika's eyes went wide. Jittery Heron never took to anyone that fast. And was Ameli actually talking to her?

"We will find a way to the top of the mountain, grumpy Mahu." Sabni swept an arm high above his head, as if reaching for the top of Mount P'tak. "My faith in all of us is as bottomless as the ocean, and just as broad."

Looking up from scratching beneath Heron's crest feathers, Ameli sighed and leaned back in her saddle. "The ocean's not bottomless, sweetie."

"It is not?"

"No. Mom lives there, remember? On the bottom."

"Ah." Sabni rubbed his chin and nodded sagely. "In that case, perhaps Father Rain's sadness does have a bottom as well, since it is his tears that fill the rivers and oceans."

"Rain isn't sad." Rainn chose his words with care, trying not to offend anyone for once. "Rain is joy. It's violence and laughter and getting hard and sex. Rain is life."

Uncle Mahu stared ahead, as if he could hear none of this. Sabni's eyes went round, and he pursed his lips.

"Rain brings life to the plants and animals." The comment sounded as if it were the closest Sabni could allow himself to come to an agreement with such an outlandish concept.

A rapid series of churrs and clicks came from Heron. Ameli followed along, nodding.

"Oh, sure. I can do that. Do you have the translations?" Ameli fell into a deep conversation about sorcery that flew well over Masika's head, and left Rainn with a quiet smile on his face.

Masika inched her mount closer to Rainn and spoke in a hush. "Did you vouch for Ameli with Heron?" Even Heron's calm acceptance of Masika's papa was not so instantaneous as this, and he calmed people by trade.

"No." Rainn contemplated the question for a moment. "Ameli has a—glow? There's something about her I can't quite . . ." he drifted off. "I can't look away. Maybe Heron feels the same."

Did Rainn look jealous?

"Something about her?" Masika grinned broadly. "Something like she's super-cute?"

"Please. She's human." Rainn rolled his eyes and then caught himself. "Not that there's anything wrong with that. I like humans. Ask anyone."

"You're really not that smart, are you?" Masika tapped a forefinger against her bottom lip. "Don't sit there looking like I stepped in your soup. It's part of your charm."

Heron chose that moment to erupt into that curiously laughing squawk, and she and a giggling Ameli threw less than surreptitious glances at Rainn.

"That was fast." The god scowled and urged his horse ahead of the group.

This time he was *definitely* blushing.

CHAPTER
TWENTY-FIVE

The Darrish god of cultivation and farmlands is Yeedi, Steward to the House of the Gods. Though worshipped by every Egren farmer with dirt on their hands, he is considered bland and uninteresting in the empire's cities and more civilized areas, who nevertheless depend on his blessings to fill their stomachs at every meal.

The appreciation of humans for the care their gods take watching over them is hardly as bottomless as the oceans.

Yeedi is reputed to have little concern, however, for it is this very quality of boring mildness that makes him such a perfect mate to Denari Clear-Eyed, first of Mother Love's children, and older sister to Sahar-ka. It is in Denari's nature to see straight into the heart of any matter, including the faults of her husband.

Happily, Yeedi isn't complicated enough to have any.

Volume One of *Thank Gods* by Kohmose Oburn

This is spectacular."

Rainn lay on his back in the grass, facing the Little Gods as the sun fell behind them. The slanting light caught towering spires of rock that jutted from the mountain peaks and sent flares of purple and yellow across the fields to the east.

"Those are the Flame Cliffs Featherwind mentioned yesterday." Sabni paused from assembling the tents to stare appreciatively at the mountains. "The colored lights they send down are known as the Lahamila."

"Hey"—Rainn pushed himself up on one elbow and looked at Masika—"that's the thing your dad calls you. Think he knows how much prettier this is?"

"You do know you're talking to a princess, right?" asked Ameli, who sat to one side in deep collusion with Heron.

"So? I'm a god and no one respects *me*." Rainn's horse gave a snort. "Except you." He leaned over to rub her neck. "You're the best horse ever."

"That's true." Ameli flashed him a mischievous smile and returned to her conversation. "About the respect. I'm sure she's a fine horse."

"So if that's a Lahamila, what's a featherwind?" Rainn rolled over onto his back again. "Some kind of bow thing?"

"In a manner of speaking." Sabni's face opened in a wide, happy grin.

"Don't you dare." Masika stood from the fire pit she was digging and put her hands on her hips. "I mean it."

This time Rainn sat up fully and spun around, his face eager.

"If you truly must know"—Sabni cast a sidelong glance at Masika and returned to Rainn—"Mahu began teaching Masika to fight and shoot when she was very small. What was she, three years old?"

"Four," Uncle Mahu answered.

"Four years. No taller than this." Sabni held a hand a couple inches above his knee.

Plans for revenge assembled themselves in Masika's mind.

"She was the most adorable thing." Eyes lost in happy remembrance, Sabni mimed pulling a bow. "She had her own tiny bow, which she was very proud of."

"Last chance."

"Let me tell my tales, Featherwind. The mighty god has demanded to know."

Masika folded her arms and stepped a few feet away, peering north.

"Now we may continue." Sabni resumed his stance. "You have never seen any child take so quickly to the art of archery. Even Queen Megan has never been her equal."

Masika thought back to the legends surrounding the queen of Greenshade and her considerable bow skills. Already a dead shot in a tournament, Sabni taught the then youthful woman how to bring those abilities to combat. He and Uncle Mahu really had seen a lot of the world.

"But there was one small complication. A tiny thing, really."

"It wasn't a tiny thing to me." Masika threw the comment over her shoulder, not turning around. Even so, she could hear the expanse of Sabni's grin in his answer.

"Every time she would pull on that bow, she would let out a bitty little toot."

Ameli and Rainn burst into laughter, and even Uncle Mahu turned away to hide his grin.

Her vengeance would be terrible to behold. Tales to scare children would be told of it. She turned back to frown mightily at Sabni.

"I'm sorry, sweetie." Ameli wiped at her eyes. "It's just so fucking cute."

"That was my opinion as well, but sadly her Uncle Mahu could not stop himself from giggling every time it happened." He pulled his brows together to scowl at Uncle Mahu, who had lifted his hand to his mouth. "The hand of Immortal Queen Nefret herself could not keep that man from laughing at this poor dear girl. She developed quite a preoccupation over it."

"Because I was a *baby*."

"Of course you were, honey." Ameli stood and walked to Masika's side, reaching a soft hand around her shoulders. "Your Uncle Mahu is a terrible man."

Uncle Mahu's shoulders shook with mirth.

"Eventually we decided to tell her that her toots were the magical *featherwind*, a signal that she was destined to become the greatest archer the Thirteen Kingdoms ever knew." At this, Sabni finally paused in his story to look at Masika.

"Oh, go ahead. The damage is already done."

"She was so proud of her special destiny, she told everyone." Uncle Mahu snorted into his palm as Sabni wrapped up the tale. "Apparently Featherwind was a huge hit with the Holy Emperor and his retinue, though I understand that both Meritities and Masika's mother found themselves unable to attend court for a month."

Masika stepped out of Ameli's embrace and extended her arms to either side. "Happy?"

"Oh." Rainn sniffed, and knuckled tears out of his eyes. "Oh, gods yes."

Featherwind. What a stupid name. Despite herself, Masika smiled thinking of those easier days when such things were the biggest complications life threw at her.

The vibration of trampling feet to the north brought out Uncle Mahu's bow, with Sabni's an instant behind. Inlittan flashed to life but was only fast enough to catch the back of something huge and dark as it vanished in the rocks.

Following her uncle and Sabni, Masika skirted wide around the boulders, alert and ready to loose an arrow at the first hint of danger. They found nothing.

From above Heron squawked.

"She can't see anything," Rainn translated. He stood, Forbryttan in hand, and scanned the jumbled terrain. His stance put him protectively between the rocks and Ameli, Masika noticed.

"There are no tracks." Uncle Mahu squatted over the path the thing had sprinted along.

Consciously switching Inlittan to find prints in the thin dirt, Masika came up with nothing. How was that possible? Had the creature flown? She glanced around at her companions. They had seen it. For that matter, it was the sound of its footfalls that first attracted their attention. What was it? The thing had been too big to hide like this.

A shriek came from the center of the barley field they crept behind, followed by wailing. Without pause, Masika ran toward it, thinking only to help.

"Wait!"

Behind her, Rainn held up his hand and trotted toward her. "This ain't our fight. We don't know what we're charging into or who they're gonna tell. You run up to help the wrong motherfuckers and we're all sucking sand."

She ran toward the sound of grief anyway. There was no time for dithering. Good people did not dither when others needed their help.

"Khanah's damnable eggs, girl, at least wait for me."

With Rainn at her side and Uncle Mahu and Sabni ranging out around her, Masika came upon a thin woman in her late thirties lying on her back and clutching a torn and faded green shawl to her chest. She rocked from side to side among the stalks, her miserable face wet and shining.

A flare from the cliffs drenched the scene in purple light, heightening the feeling of unreality that already took hold of Masika's imagination.

"What happened here?" Masika knelt next to the woman in her worn farm clothes and put a hand on her shoulder.

"It took my baby," she spluttered before losing herself to grief once again.

"What did she say?" Ameli's girlish voice betrayed her anxiety. Masika had not even heard her approach.

"What took your child?" If they were to help, seconds counted. They needed to know what they were after, fast.

"It was Sedja. My baby is dead!"

"Does this Sedja live in the mountains?" Masika stroked the woman's arm, not knowing what else to do. "Can you point to its home?" As she tried to calm the farmwoman's hysterics, Masika noticed a puncture wound on her leg. The bleeding was not bad, but the swelling was already considerable.

The woman nodded and pointed about halfway up the peak.

"I don't think we have the time for this." Rainn leaned over to catch Masika's eye and shrugged. He stood up straight. "Not that anyone cares what I think. We're sucking sand."

"Ameli, she's been bitten." Wide teeth marks on the underside of the leg showed that the top wound, which Masika took for a knife or spear stab, must be a single fang. The cloth covering the woman's leg stretched tight, so Masika cut it off with her boot dagger. "Something big, and I think it's poison."

The now brown-haired sorceress dropped to her knees and made flicking motions from the row of pouches on her belt to the woman, who fell quiet and lay suddenly still. Flows of earthy colors stained the air in the directions of her motions, as if she directed small gouts of exotic powders from her pouches into the woman's body.

For all Masika knew, she did.

"Is she all right?" Her hands on the woman's shoulders, Masika felt her breath, deep and steady. She was fast asleep.

"No." Ameli's answer came a bit fast and irritated. "She's been poisoned by a monster. I can make her comfortable and stop the spread, but I'll have to come back and fix her up after we go get her kid."

No hesitation. Just a need to help. That was what a good person did.

"Great. So now we're all going. I guess if we all die together no one's gotta listen to any toldja-sos."

"Please shut up, Rainn," Masika said. "I know you're in a hurry, but we can't walk past a person in need. That's not what humans do." The good ones, anyway. The Sarahs.

"That's not my experience with humans, but it's your show." Rainn's face darkened as the purple light faded to shadow.

Masika ignored him. "Ameli, do you know what a Sedja is?"

"He's not a what, exactly. He's a who. And yes. My-my older sister had a run-in with him a long time ago. She thought maybe she'd killed him, but I guess we just aren't that lucky." She stood and extended a hand to Masika. "We should go. There won't be much time if that kid isn't already . . ." Ameli did not finish her thought.

She did not have to.

ALTHOUGH NO TRACKS WERE VISIBLE, that was not exactly the same as there being no signs of Sedja's passing. Once Masika realized what she was looking for, the slightly worn trail became visible.

Just not very visible.

Rainn followed at a short distance to protect them should they be attacked from behind, while Uncle Mahu and Sabni worked their way up the slope about a hundred feet to either side, bows drawn. Heron circled overhead ready to cry out, though dusk was already upon them and the light dwindled fast.

Ameli and Masika walked together.

"So, who is Sedja?" Masika needed to do what she could for the woman left in the field behind them, but Rainn's worries infected her thoughts. "What's he want?"

Speaking just loud enough for the men to hear, Ameli responded. "According to my sister, Hettie, Sedja was a monster who rose up out of the sands on the other side of the mountains. He came over looking for victims. I don't know how he does it, but somehow he only kills them partway. That's what Hettie said, at any rate."

The idea sounded horrific to Masika. "Why? What's he get out of half dead people hanging around?"

"She said they were his slaves, so maybe they're easier to manipulate that way?" Ameli shook her head in disgust. "Hettie wouldn't say what he was forcing them to do. She said we weren't old enough to know. That always stuck with me, y'know? I mean, my mom's the Deep Witch. She fucks guys to death at the bottom of the ocean. What could've been so terrible our sister wouldn't even tell us?"

The question opened a very unwelcome line of thought in Masika's head.

"Why would he want a baby?" Masika very much hoped this and the question about half-dead people were unrelated to one another. "They can't do work."

Ameli did not answer. She merely climbed into the gathering gloom, silent and grim-faced.

Ten minutes later Rainn called out, just loud enough to be heard.

"Masika. Wait up."

She slowed but did not stop. Rainn frowned but followed at a faster pace.

"Heron smells something," he said. "There's rot and a serpent smell, but also bodies. Lots and lots of unwashed bodies."

"Those would be Sedja's slaves." Masika did pause now, putting her hands on her lower back and leaning backward in a much-needed stretch. "Ameli told me about them. They don't sound dangerous."

"I thought so too, but that's not all." Quiet followed as Rainn organized his thoughts. "There's power up here. Power like I felt in Treaty Hill when we were looking for Ild the imp. More'n enough to kill alla us three times over."

"You simply can't stop bringing me bad news, can you?" Despite herself, Masika smiled. Anger did not work with Rainn anyway. "You know, I appreciate you coming along despite your fears. It's hard to be brave when you know how scary things really are." Or was that the only time a person *could* be brave? When they knew better but acted anyway? Was Masika really being brave at all if she was not afraid?

What a stupid thought.

A matching smile lit Rainn's face for a fraction of an instant before an offended frown replaced it.

"I'm not scared. I'm just cautious. *Smart* people're cautious."

"That's how I know you're scared." Teasing him took her mind off what they might find at the end of their climb. "Can you point to where it is?"

The path rode up the rocks in an almost due western direction. Rainn pointed north of that.

"Let's get everyone together and decide which way to go. We might be able to surprise him if we leave the path."

Minutes later they worked their way up the mountain slope to the north of their earlier trajectory. The going was slower, but hopefully they would avoid any lookouts this way.

"I see something." Masika stopped at the crest of a big boulder. "There's a wall made of stones. It was behind this foothill before. Invisible from the ground."

"See any monsters?" Rainn asked.

"Nope. No half-dead farmers either." She gazed from one end of the wall to the other. Daylight fled fully, replaced by a scimitar of moon. "I don't think we're expected."

"That is very welcome news." Sabni, like Uncle Mahu, had stripped down to his honey-colored leathers, burnished plates of golden hued metal over the chest, forearms, and shins. "Always better to start the party when you arrive than to walk in on one already begun."

"What parties have you been to without me?" Uncle Mahu asked.

"None." Teeth flashed in the night in the shape of Sabni's big grin. "But I hear things."

Rainn climbed on top of Masika's boulder and hunkered down next to her. "Can we climb the wall?"

"I think so." She stared up the slope. "It's not mortared, just stacked stones. Should be plenty of handholds."

"Any doors? Can you tell where the front is?" Ameli's whisper made her sound even more girlish.

"Can't see from here." Masika scanned from one end to the other, about two hundred feet long in all. "I'd guess the south end since that's where the path was leading. But it's all wall from here."

"Then we will head to the north to make our entrance." Sabni's deep voice carried his confidence to the rest. "As Kohoc the Harvester tells the soldier in the Sermon of Swords, a keen blade may be the *right* tool to bring home your enemy's soul, but sneaking up behind him is still the easiest one."

"And there it is," muttered Uncle Mahu.

CHAPTER

TWENTY-SIX

Not all demons of creation landed in the Undergates. Some were too depraved even for that place and found holes within Andos itself to scuttle away into. Relics of the building of our universe, these creatures are pieces of the shattering of the Dead God, formed into nightmares by the undisciplined thoughts and dreams of humanity.

While it is tempting to believe that such monstrosities are nothing more than evidence of horror and hate, I prefer to think of them as proof of the magnificence and wonder of our making by the gods themselves. How else could we understand the innate superiority of the Darrish people if such remnants had not been gifted to us by our own mighty P'tak?

Not everyone finds these spirits of violence and darkness to be gifts, as such. But not all gifts are guaranteed not to try and murder you.

Volume Eight of *Thank Gods* by Kohmose Oburn

Up close the irregular wall loomed between twenty and thirty feet high and sat thick enough that even Inlittan revealed nothing through the gaps. There was simply more wall.

"I don't like this plan." Rainn's entire frame showed his pensive irritation. One foot tapped on the mountainside while he chewed a thumbnail. "I should go up there."

Masika lay one hand on the god's chest. "I'll be fine," she whispered. "I'm the quietest, I can see the best, and I'm not going to pick any fights up there." Even Heron could not see into the stygian black of the walled courtyard. "I'll be back in two winks."

Without replying, Rainn frowned further, but stepped back.

As carefully as possible, Masika crawled up the side of the structure, Uncle Mahu and Sabni covering her climb with nocked bows and Rainn standing beside Ameli, Forbryttan in his hand. Heron retreated from the ascent and flew circles below them over the fields.

An almost electrical charge filled the air as Masika neared the top of the wall, though she could not identify it precisely. Her nervousness came not for herself. She had bested every confrontation thus far, and she would best this one as well. But she did feel considerable fearfulness over the likelihood that she would soon have to tell the farmwoman in the field that her child was dead.

Her papa complained at her fearlessness in the face of physical danger, but he did not know just how scared she was of disappointing the people around her.

Even if she had just met them.

One hand reached the stone crest, and she pulled herself atop it. Ameli indicated that Sedja kept slaves. Why could she not hear them? Below the stench of rotten death, the smell of bodies, and a vast reptilian funk assaulted her nostrils, but the night was empty of sound other than the movement of the breeze.

From her new vantage, Masika saw the wall extend ten feet thick before dropping into a wide and dark hole. In all, the structure spanned at least two hundred feet long and a hundred fifty feet wide. No roof protected the silent occupants, and the wall rose and fell as if assembled whole and then ripped across in a jagged line. On the opposite side a twenty-foot-wide entryway had been left open, facing the direction Masika would have come had she continued up the path.

Inlittan showed Masika where to place her feet, and soundless as the dead, she crept across the wall. A thin smile came at the thought that this was *exactly* what Sarah the Hill Fury would have done.

She peeked over into the black and soundless courtyard.

Figures stood in the dark, not illuminated by Inlittan, though Masika saw them clearly regardless. No one moved, and no one spoke.

There were so *many*.

Dead bodies littered the ground among the living, as if they simply fell and died where they stood. Children lay among them, and even the breathing did not move. What was wrong with them? Masika pushed Inlittan to show her more. To show her what was wrong with—

All at once, Masika spun and thumped against a stone, breathing heavily. She willed herself to stand and return to her friends waiting for her below, and once there to flee to the north, leaving the woman dying in her field. But her legs were someone else's, unwilling to listen to her, and her arms only shook.

She was *terrified*.

How long did she sit there before Rainn reached her? How long did her terror whisper its dread obscenities into her mind, a cold communication that froze her will and left her a decoration atop an ancient pile of boulders?

"You hurt?" Rainn's whisper, barely audible, rang in her ears. Cacophony. Peals of doom to bring unbelievable horror down on their heads.

She grabbed at his shirt and pulled him to her. "Don't look," she breathed. "Don't look. Please don't look."

Rainn shook his head and pointed to his ear. He could not hear her. She could not make herself speak with sound.

He turned his head and leaned out over the side.

Eyes wide and shining with tears, Masika clapped both hands over her mouth to stifle her sob of fear.

When he shrugged, returning to her unaffected, shock momentarily dulled her fear. Until she realized Rainn did not have the benefit of—

She scrabbled at the jewelry on her wrist and fingers. Without

Inlittan the sight of what was inside this structure could never assault her eyes again. But would that matter? Its stain pressed firmly into her brain already. She would never be free of it.

Unable to yank the bracelet and rings from her hand for fear of making a sound, Masika shut her eyes, pushing the tears welling there down her cheeks.

Big hands, warm strong hands, lifted her and carefully carried her back the way she had come, toward the back of the eternal structure.

"Don't look. Don't look. Don't look."

By the time the pair returned to the ground at the base of the wall, Masika had recovered just enough of her faculties to run.

Uncle Mahu caught her before she leaped from the mountainside.

"She looks shook." Ameli's sweet voice threatened to crack Masika wide. "Sweetie, what did you see?"

"Is this what your sister described to you? The wall and the quiet and all? There was nothing but black inside, though the stink's a lot worse. Of course, I'm not wearing the vision-thingie." Rainn kept low and quiet, but Masika wanted to jump up and wrap her arms around his face to shut him up.

Instead, she sat with her fear and shivered.

"No," Ameli answered, "but she didn't say how long ago it was either. She didn't really say much more than it was icky."

Icky. Hysterical laughter tried to erupt from Masika, who bit her fingers to hold it down. What that monster was *doing* to those poor people . . .

"How old's your sister?" Rainn ran a hand along the edge of one of the boulders. "This thing looks ancient as the mountain."

The conversation flitted over Masika's head. She understood the words but could not concentrate on them enough to make sense of them all together. That thing, hulking in the shadows. Why was it even alive? What purpose could *that thing* possibly serve?

"She's pretty old." Concern creased Ameli's freckled features as she held Masika's wrist. "Poor thing. Your heart's running like a green hare in spring, and it's leaving you behind." She glanced down at the pouch of powders she kept on her waist. "I can take the fear away for a bit, if you want me to. You won't be drunk or anything, you'll just be less scared. How's that sound to you?"

Several beats went by before the meaning of Ameli's words sunk into Masika's consciousness. She nodded, gripped Ameli by the robe and mouthed, "Please."

Ameli inched backward and sat on her knees, putting a little space between herself and Masika. Her finger flicked out once, twice, and held, like a tiny viper waiting for its already bitten prey to drop.

But Masika did not drop. A strange sort of numbness formed in her middle and swirled there. It spread up and down her torso, rushing along her arms and legs to settle in her extremities. Last it rose over her face and crossed the top of her head to finish covering her body at the base of her skull.

That was when she realized it was not numbness, it was calm.

The motion of blinking her eyes snapped Masika out of her daze. "Oh. Wow. Thank you. That's-that's a lot better."

"Glad you like it." Ameli favored Masika with a worried smile. "It's way addictive, so don't get used to it. You'll have a headache when it wears off as it is." She leaned over and pulled the hair out of Masika's face. "But now that you're all super chill, why don't you tell us what you saw in there?"

"Hm." The images from within the wall continued to batter at Masika's mind, but she could no longer feel them. Their threat dissipated like smoke. "There are hundreds of people in there. Just standing around. Young, old, naked, clothed. All of them dirty. All quiet. So quiet."

Terror howled at the gateways of Masika's brain, clamoring to get inside and rend with ebon claws.

She ignored it.

"They are also wounded. Sedja is a . . ." Masika found no words for what Sedja was. So, she concentrated on what Inlittan had revealed. "He takes them and kills them? No, they're not dead. Not exactly. Not all the way."

"I don't like this. Not a bit," Rainn said. "You may just be a human, but you don't get rattled. Not like that. This fucking place is just wrong."

Masika responded to Rainn's extremely obvious comment with an eyeroll. "He was biting a child. Suckling from him, here." She indicated on herself where a monstrous mouth might bite down across the shoulder, teeth settling into the chest and back. "But not of him."

"What does that mean, Masika?" Sabni took a knee beside her.

"I know I'm not supposed to have favorites"—Masika reached up and patted Sabni on the jaw—"but I like you better than Uncle Mahu. He's so grumpy."

"Ah." Embarrassed, Sabni grinned sheepishly and scooted back. "That's the drugs. That's the drugs, right, Ameli? She does not mean that."

"Uh, she isn't apt to lie here, but she also isn't afraid of the consequences of anything she might say." Ameli added a sheepish grin of her own to Sabni's. "She'll be plenty embarrassed in the morning though."

"There is no harm." Uncle Mahu stood behind Ameli, thick arms crossed over his chest. "Everyone likes Sabni better."

"Sedja uses those it keeps as conduits." Masika stared at Inlittan. She never did get it off her. It had showed her much more than she'd bargained for, "It steals you, bites you. Its venom leaves you between life and—something else. Those people are aware of what's happening, but they can't do anything about it."

"Thunder and blood," whispered Rainn.

Masika flicked a glance up to him. "Whenever someone who loves you grieves for you, Sedja pulls that grief through you and—eats it? But that's a piece of that person's soul. The more Sedja eats, the more it weakens the griever."

"How does a baby have grief?" Sabni asked.

"No. That's not it." Masika thought about it, trying to find the best way to explain. "It takes the baby and pulls the mother's grief through her infant's body. It's not the victims' sadness it eats, but the sadness of everyone who would feel grief for them."

"Allz's wounds." Head shaking, Sabni looked down the darkened mountainside.

"Oh, honey. And when they weaken too much?" Ameli's tanned face paled.

"Sedja takes the rest. And once everyone who loves you dies, you're of no more use and Sedja finishes what it started with you too." Able to speak freely now of things that froze her breath only minutes ago, Ameli's herbs were a blessing to Masika.

A thought occurred to her. The reason why all of this bothered her so much. Why her terror was so complete. Papa hated that she was not frightened of getting hurt, and her mother claimed it meant something was broken inside her brain. If she did not handle this right, she could be killing thousands of people by literal disappointment. People who needed their loved ones back, but their grief at not getting them would lead to all their deaths.

Masika considered her earlier statement. "Sedja doesn't even eat the bodies. Just lets them rot. Hm. Don't you think that's odd?"

"Odd may not be quite the word for it." Rainn straightened up and loosened Forbryttan in its sheath. "Chopping Sedja's fucking head off sounds like a better word to me."

Rainn appeared to be little more than a man-sized hole in the starscape behind him. Inlittan would show her more if she asked, but the dark created a sort of intimacy to their little group that Masika found comforting.

"Discounting the Alir's definition of what a word is, I believe I agree." Sabni also took to his feet and gave Rainn a grim nod. "This is why Mother Love brought us to this place. We are to stamp out this blight on her people."

"Can you describe this Sedja to us, Masika?" Uncle Mahu's low voice carried caution, but also a steely purpose. He agreed with Sabni.

Looking down on the monster from above, even for an instant, stamped the image of the thing into Masika's brain for eternity. The very notion of forgetting it laughed in her face.

"His body is that of a spotted jungle cat, filthy and matted, but squat and much thicker. And tall as a horse. The neck is long, like a serpent, and the head is that of some enormous, frilled lizard, only much wider and with longer teeth and fangs."

"That's a remnant." A quiet hiss accompanied Rainn's slow draw of Forbryttan. He stood and stared at the blade. "A leftover piece of creation. How terrifying it'll be depends on how big a piece it was before it turned itself into—that."

The sword glinted in the starlight.

"Can we even kill something like that?" The pitch in Ameli's voice rose. She took a breath. "If it's part of the beginning of the universe, how do you take that down?"

"He's got a neck; I got a sword." Rainn's cold smile chilled the night air. "Seems to me the question answers itself."

"That's not what I saw." Masika pulled herself to her feet and extended a hand to Ameli, who took it. "Sedja has no weaknesses we can exploit, and I think he's been killed before by someone stronger than us. We need to think of something more permanent than just slaying the monster."

"Masika sweetie, when you looked in on our friends with your thingie, did you see blood from the wounds of the people standing around? You said they'd been bitten. Were getting bitten. Were they bleeding too?"

"Who told you about Inlittan?" Masika asked, pointedly not glaring at Rainn.

"Oh," Ameli said. "Heron did. She was only trying to be helpful."

Masika tried not to worry about how much information the smitten Rainn and Heron might be sharing with Ameli. The sorceress was an ally and had never done anything to make Masika doubt it.

"That's fine." Masika resolved to get over it. It hardly mattered now. "Yes, they bled, though not much. Some of the older people who still wore clothing had old blood stains. It's as if their blood doesn't flow as fast as it should anymore." Slowly, Inlittan fed her bits of what she had seen that escaped her notice at first. Masika marveled at the runecrafted jewel's capabilities. Did Romi understand everything it could do when she gave it away?

A gleam lit Ameli's gaze. "That's good news. *Very* good news. I think I've got the beginnings of a plan here. Maybe not a smart plan, but we'll work on it some. Did anyone see any quatha here? Short scrubby plant, likes hillsides."

"Do you mean khat?" Uncle Mahu frowned at Ameli. "The one that people chew when they have no money to eat food?"

"That's the one." Casting about as if she would spot the plant in the dark, Ameli flashed her happy grin. "It's a stimulant. Takes away the desire to eat when you're hungry. It should be all over the mountainside."

"Can you use khat to heal those people the way you did the infant's mother?" Masika asked.

"No." Ameli's brow furrowed in concentration. "She was just poisoned. Healing her only required knowing what herbs to use to counteract most kinds of reptile venom. Which was very informative, I might add." She smiled again. "This will require something a bit more disruptive."

"I see it." Masika stared into the night. "Tiny leaves. About two feet tall."

"Fantastic. Here's what we're gonna do."

THEY CREPT AWAY from the wall to get a few hours fitful sleep and spent the next day collecting and crushing the quatha plants. Masika, who *had* been embarrassed at her admission of liking Sabni better than her actual uncle, was glad for the buzz just getting the plant's juices on her skin provided.

The farmwoman was gone by the time they returned, so Ameli and Sabni went into the little village to the east to find and heal her.

Not a smart plan gave Ameli's initial idea too much credit, but throughout the day Uncle Mahu, Rainn, and Masika hammered, worked, and argued it into merely a stupid one. One unexpected blessing, which Rainn felt was more literal than Masika did, arrived in the form of distant marching clouds, dark and gravid-bellied, from the south.

"Can we be ready by the time that beautiful weather gets here?" Rainn asked Ameli.

She looked up and squinted into the distance. "If we hurry. Does it make that much difference?"

"Oh yes." He put his hands on his hips and grinned at the dimming horizon. "If we can time our party for when that thing hits, I might even put my own money on us winning."

"Won't the wet stop you from using your bows?" Masika asked her uncle, trying not to appear overly solicitous.

"Before we met Ameli, yes." Uncle Mahu opened the pouch he kept his bowstrings in and uncurled one in his fingers. "She has treated these so they will not soften in water. Here, have one of mine."

"Thank you, uncle. Sabni never offered me one of his bowstrings. You're much more considerate than he is."

"Shut up, niece."

Sabni and Ameli arrived back in the early afternoon, laden with salted meats and dark, hard bread from the farmwoman's family.

"Ameli here was the talk of the community." Sabni broke loaves and sliced meats for everyone. "We tried to get out before anyone took notice of her miraculous ability to heal poisoned farmwomen, but that proved more difficult to do than it is to say. I did not spy any Saraph Jais, however, so we may yet be safe."

"Hm," Uncle Mahu responded.

The soldiers that the group fled past on their way out of the camp may have been incapacitated with laughter, Masika considered, but they certainly had not been struck blind. The Saraph Jais would know exactly who they were looking for.

"You were right about what we would find in the village." Sadness covered Sabni as he spoke. "Many people wasting away from their grief being pulled out of them. Dying, without understanding why."

"We're gonna stomp that fucker out," Rainn said, putting a hand on Sabni's shoulder. "He's taken his last dinner outta these folks."

The supportive gesture from Rainn caught Masika off guard.

"How's the fire going?" Ameli wandered over to where Masika toasted the crushed quatha root in a shallow pan over a small fire pit.

"Faster than expected." In fact, the whole plan fell into place more easily than Masika anticipated, leaving her with an uneasy feeling. "We should have more than enough, assuming you're right about all this."

"Never second guess a sorceress." Ameli grinned and touched Masika on the shoulder. Her smile warmed the chill in Masika's heart. "We're doing the right thing here. We're saving lives."

Maybe Masika understood the Alir's ease around Ameli after all.

"I don't doubt that." The promised headache from Ameli's ministrations the night before finally gave up and let go of its hold behind Masika's eyes. "I only wonder—who's going to save us?"

"WHAT'S BUGGING YOU NOW? Still scared?" The wind picked up but only blew Rainn's words straight to Masika's ears. Did it always do that?

Despite the gloom caused by the laden clouds above them, the climb proved much easier at noon than in the true dark. At least for everyone without any runecrafted jewelry. Three hours in they spotted the wall, rising up behind the crest of the foothill.

"No. Maybe that's what's bothering me." Did the same wind whisk her words back to Rainn? "I can see Sedja in my head, feeding on the grief of that boy's relatives. Holding him in those giant jaws. The teeth went all the way through him, Rainn. But it's not upsetting anymore. Certainly not like it was before."

"Huh." One rock at a time, Rainn climbed the mountain, leaning forward on all fours, pushing and pulling. His muscles grew as the air, still dry though smelling of rain, whipped faster and faster. "That sounds typically human. Gotta be upset over something, so you're upset over not being upset." He flashed her a grin. "But for real, why *aren't* you still all shaky? You still drugged up? Ameli said that stuff was addictive."

"No more drugs." Masika raised a hand which the wind tried to push back down. "And I honestly don't know. Maybe . . ." She trailed off. Maybe what? She knew she cared. She knew she wanted to help, and not just because she worried about being a good person. That thing up there did not belong in this world. It was a mistake. One she intended to rectify.

But calm blew across her soul, a mountain wind born in a distant ocean. Anonymous as any other wind in the world.

Being honest with herself, she knew exactly why she no longer felt afraid. Because at the center of that calm, a cold anger blew in. She clung to that anger. Anger for the way she reacted and anger for what Sedja was, what it represented. What it took, even now, from the people on that mountainside.

Her anger shielded her, and she was grateful for it, despite what it might mean about her. The fear hid behind her wrath, and she was content to let it stay there.

Just over an hour later, they stood behind the huge stone structure once again. The scent of oncoming rain suppressed the unwashed smells, though the underlying stench of reptile shot through everything, as if soaked into the stones themselves.

A sidelong glance showed Rainn's shoulders growing, his step growing more lively and determined. Good. They would need that.

"Does everyone know what they're supposed to do?" They crowded in a circle, heads pressed together to hear Ameli's words. "There's no room for fuckups here, so ask questions if you got 'em. Everyone's depending on everyone else. Get yourself killed and we all go down." She smiled and winked at Masika. "No pressure though."

"How will we know if it is working?" The first fat drops of rain annihilated themselves against the stone mountainside as Mahu asked his question. Musty rock and sparse soil mixed with the smells rising off the ground.

Rainn snorted.

"If it works," Ameli said with a nervous glance at Rainn, "it'll be dramatic. If it doesn't," she let out a scared little chuckle, "it'll be less dramatic, but a lot hurtier."

"Mother Love provides for those who love her." Sabni's long arms, corded with ropy muscle, reached around them all. "And today, she provides miracles."

"That is not the correct quote." Uncle Mahu frowned up at Sabni.

"Is it not?"

"No." Uncle Mahu stood and stared at the stone wall. "Today she provides the miracle of death."

Confusion gave way to dawning light on Sabni's rain-spattered face. "Aha. You are correct. Thank you Mahu. I don't know how long I have been saying that wrong."

"I do," Uncle Mahu responded.

"But not our deaths, right?" Ameli darted her head closer to Mahu as the circle broke up. "Mother Love wants us to win. Doesn't she?"

Masika, Ameli, and Rainn—now bulging beneath his tight desert clothing while thunder played in the distance—crept along the outer face of the structure while Uncle Mahu and Sabni climbed the rear wall to take up effective sniping positions.

"Give them a few more moments." Hand outstretched, Masika held Rainn back, who steamed in the downpour, a teakettle red from the fire. Something occurred to her then that might loom important over what they were about to do.

"Ameli, is there any chance that the drugs you gave me are still affecting me? I need to know before we go around that corner and everyone is depending on me to keep us all straight."

"No." Ameli took the opportunity to wrap a cord around her sodden hair and tie it up on top of her head. "That's one reason it's so addictive. Passes out of your system pretty fast. Why?" Her eyes searched Masika's face, concern obvious. "Is something wrong? Do you feel sick?"

"No. Head hurts a little." Although this was the answer Masika expected, hearing it spoken aloud unsettled her. What if her terror of Sedja overcame her desire to see it killed when she finally faced it again?

"Oh, sweetie." Ameli reached out and hugged Masika, who gripped Rainn's wrist to keep him in place. "It's all right. The reason you were so scared in the first place was because you were running from your fears. But when the powders calmed you, you faced those fears. You got more out of a few hours under the influence than you would've with years of talking to someone about it. Be happy." She let go of Masika's shoulders but pulled her head, so their foreheads touched.

"You're brilliant. Sarah would've been proud."

Masika jerked back and looked away from Ameli's smiling eyes. Despite the sorceress's rosy assessment, Masika knew it for the lie it was.

Angry. Be angry.

"Are we ready to go murder some monsters now?" In the shadowy light, Rainn's form vibrated. He no longer appeared mere flesh and blood, but harder, stronger.

Implacable.

Masika's grim smile lent her courage. "Let's go."

They made the final corner and ran the last stretch to the wall's opening. Water rushed down the slope against their progress but could not stop them. They turned into the vast stony courtyard.

Lightning illuminated the scene in a stark white flash.

"Khanah's damnable eggs. Where *is* that fucker?"

Some two hundred ashen-skinned humans stood, sat, or lay within the broad and ancient edifice. Infants on their backs in deepening puddles, old men and women, arms thin as taut twine, stared at the stacked stone of the walls. Bodies of the dead rotted where they fell. The stink, up close and wet, was remarkable.

Of Sedja, no sign appeared.

Ameli moved in while Rainn roared his frustration. He needed something to channel his violence into—and soon.

Somewhere atop the far wall Sabni and Uncle Mahu settled into position. Masika concentrated on Inlittan, careful not to look into the bedraggled victims, and the rain evaporated from sight. Her uncle and his partner appeared obvious against the angry sky. Was Sedja behind them, creeping up to steal a piece of their lives too?

Would Masika's grief be the next to feed the monster?

Be angry.

The first of Sedja's victims found herself within range of Ameli, and the sorceress flicked a finger from a larger, waxed pouch on her hip at the skinny naked woman who stood and gaped at nothing.

A breathless pause that lasted for the next several years of Masika's life went by between raindrops, and the ashen woman threw her head back and screamed, bloody froth gouting from her mouth. She fell backward and jerked in the pooled rainwater.

That was certainly dramatic. Masika hoped Ameli knew what she was doing and had not just murdered one of Sedja's victims. A brief glance with Inlittan's sight showed Masika the woman drawing shallow breaths into her weakened lungs.

One less thing to worry about, thank Mother Love's fortune.

The sorceress pressed her wide lips together grimly and moved on, flicking her finger to more and more of the waiting victims.

As Masika did her best to ensure that no one cracked their heads falling to the stony ground, a long croaking roar, low and loud enough to rattle her eyeballs in their sockets, echoed in from every direction at once. Masika spun, trying to look everywhere, but seeing nothing. Nevertheless, she knew what that sound meant.

Sedja was on his way.

More men and women shrieked as Ameli worked her way through them. The compound that Ameli transported into their veins—mostly crushed quatha root—jolted their systems, pushing aside whatever toxins Sedja violated them with and violently restarting their brains. With no genuine evidence and more than a little hope, Ameli had reasoned that the "half dead" subdued state was essential to Sedja's ability to feed on these people, and if they could be awoken and taken away, the monster might have no more hold on them, and may even starve if they could injure it badly enough.

The only real thing they had on their side was Ameli's earlier success breaking the poison in the farmwoman back in her home.

A flash and a boom brought an evil chuckle from Rainn, which rumbled far too loud in Masika's ears. She spun and gasped.

The shadowed form of Sedja, enormous in the open entryway of the walled structure snarled a vast, eternal growl. Evil intelligence and horror from beyond this world tried to shut down Masika's brain. If it were not for Rainn's laughing shout of challenge, she might have collapsed on the spot.

But she did not. In her mind's eye, Masika saw the killing disappointment her death would cause her family, the grief that this beast would take from them, leaving them drained and weak to the point of their deaths. She saw the families of all those gathered here, disappointed in her for wasting the chance she had to rescue them all. But mostly she saw her own fear. She saw it for what it was, an instinct for survival that kept her sharp and lent her speed and cunning.

She pulled out her bow.

A huge, frilled head, like that of a gigantic lizard but thicker and filled with viper's fangs wheeled in the dim sky before crashing down toward Rainn, a stroke of malicious poison from the beginning of time. The god laughed, danced aside, and punched the thing in the scaled throat.

Sedja's voice cracked in surprise with a sound like the skin of the world torn asunder beneath them, and it leaped backward, two of Masika's arrows buried deep in the matted fur of its spotted chest.

The curving neck whipped forward, and Rainn batted at it with Forbryttan, slicing away a ridge above the monster's right eye.

A line of blood streaked down Rainn's sword arm, but he paid it no mind.

With the screams of Ameli's ministrations behind her, Masika almost missed the dark arrows that flew from the wall tops into the great beast. Uncle Mahu and Sabni had raced forward far enough along the wall to enter the fight, and made their presence felt.

Arrow after arrow punched through Sedja's hide, the massive creature's rapid movement insufficient to protect it from the two expert marksmen. And Rainn, dancing, laughing, and stabbing, carved slice after vile slice through fur and scale.

Masika's fear fell further and further away as her vengeance grew bright.

But Inlittan refused to allow Masika her victory. Through her runecrafted sight, she saw that none of the wounds dug deep enough to do more than madden the swift-moving creature. Indeed, as she saw into it, Sedja saw back into her.

And rushed for her, knocking Rainn into the water.

"Ameli!" Masika filled the ancient monster's eyes with arrows, but it did not care. The body was merely a vessel for the evil within. It would simply make another if this one became too damaged. Sedja was eternal. "Ameli, it's coming! Hit it with what you gave me! *All of it!*"

A clawed paw the size of a dinnerplate caught Masika in the arm and sent her spinning to the ground, blood spurting in a crimson gyre. Her vision faltered.

Ameli jumped in from Masika's right and rolled beneath the monster's stinking belly, flicking fistfuls of dark powders up into its body with the power of her sorcery. Powders that just last night cut Masika off from her own terror, and which now cut Sedja off from the source of its power: the grief of its victims.

The grinding shriek ruptured the clouds above, and Sedja stumbled backward. Bleeding, Ameli crawled out of the creature's reach, her darkly curled hair plastered to her back in the wet.

Then Rainn was atop the beast's back, Forbryttan driven to the hilt, roaring his own inarticulate rage into the storm and pounding Sedja's back with his free hand.

That serpent's neck whirled up and around, the hollow fangs extending, to sink deep into Rainn's torso, through his guts, his lungs, his heart.

A high-pitched screech followed as Heron attacked, stabbing at Sedja's already recovering eyes. It batted her out of the sky with Rainn's body, and Masika heard the bird's bones crack when she struck rock.

Sedja stood to its full height, grinding a limp Rainn in its teeth.

The monster stumbled to one side.

And the lightning came.

Bolt after cataclysmic bolt split the sky and hit Rainn, igniting blue and white fire over Masika's head. Roars from Sedja and from the wrathful sky battered her ringing ears, and Masika curled into a ball, her hands clamped to either side of her head.

But she could not stop watching.

The brilliance intensified as the lightning strikes increased, and blackened talons dug into the stone and split open, smoking.

At once everything stopped.

A deafening silence blanketed Masika, and she watched as Sedja fell to one side, soundless and headless. In front of the massive corpse stood Rainn, his clothes burned away, glowing a blinding white.

Sir God, indeed.

To one side Heron flew from an unmoving puddle of water, whole and restored, and though Masika could not hear her, she could see the goddess's beak opening and closing in a series of angry squawks.

Blood ran freely down Masika's arm, taking her balance with it. The last thing she remembered was the hands of her uncle lifting her from the ground.

CHAPTER

TWENTY-SEVEN

The tale of The Farmer and the Scorpion is a popular one with children and adults alike, and it teaches a simple moral about helping your fellow man and the good incurred from a life lived in humility and service. Though the grateful scorpion in the story is gifted with food and shelter—in return for assisting the farmer in building his house before the floods—most are unaware that the Old Darrish form of this story, with the scorpion complaining that the farmer is insufficiently gracious for the blessing of her assistance, as most of the old form tales do, ends quite differently.

Far from a homily about the benefits of aiding others, the moral of the older account translates roughly to "No doer of good deeds goes uncrushed by the feet of the gods, who doth not appreciate the competition."

In more common parlance, help out if you want to, but don't get a big head about it.

Volume Four of *Thank Gods* by Kohmose Oburn

217

ching muscles pulled Masika from slumber with greater strength than the bright morning sun. She lay on a pallet of woven mats beneath an open window in a one-room mud brick home. A round table with four sturdy chairs centered the space, with pantry shelves and a banked cookfire at one end and a single wide bed at the other. While empty of people other than herself, Masika heard laughter and conversation out the window, and smelled cooking food that made her belly rumble.

She stood, wincing more than once, and inspected herself. She wore clean but simple clothing, just a pair of wide and patched flaxen trousers and a sleeveless tunic. Someone had cleaned her and bandaged her wounds.

"She wakes!"

Warm light caressed Masika's skin, delighting her with its comforting touch even as she blinked against it. A nightmare receded into her past, pushed away by that hot glow. Before she opened her eyes to the new day, Masika held that nightmare in her mind and stared into it. Sedja was a monster, true, but the actual nightmare had been her own fears.

I beat you, remnant of creation. So go fuck yourself.

"How do you feel?" Sabni's grinning face occluded the bright farm village. "Ameli told us you would live, but Mahu could not help himself from assuming the worst regardless."

"I did not want to tell Tennat I watched his daughter die." Uncle Mahu lifted a wooden cup to Masika. "He is so emotional."

Masika laughed and bubbled cool water in the cup before her thirst took over and she drained it away. She handed it back to Uncle Mahu.

"More please."

A crying woman with an infant on her hip flung an arm around Masika and held her close, unable to speak. With a start, Masika realized she was the farmwoman Ameli had saved, and that the infant was her stolen, and recovered, baby.

The completeness of their victory struck home in that instant, and happy tears of her own welled in Masika's eyes. They really accomplished the impossible. They defeated a genuine monster and reunited families all over this province.

The woman pushed away from Masika and held her face in her other hand. "Thank you, Princess Masika Oburn, niece of our dear Holy Emperor. If it is no insult to you, anything I have is yours. Any task I might do for you is but an ask away. What do you wish of me?"

Though Masika's first notion was to tell the farmwoman that no, of course there was nothing she need do. Saving her infant was not only Masika's responsibility but her delight. But that was not what came out of her mouth.

"Do you have any food?"

Soon enough all of Masika's group were gathered at a small rectangular table heaped with mounds of khef-tet, dates, cheeses, and curls of cured and shaved meats. Masika noticed Uncle Mahu's eyebrows raise when she grabbed for the Egren dinner breads, but she also saw Sabni's eyes twinkle appreciatively. As she knew from her time in the dungeon below Treaty Hill's Forest Castle, the damn things were delicious. Regardless of their lowly status, Masika would not pass up the opportunity to eat them without Meritities's cool judgement.

Mouth stuffed full of food and brown ringlets tied against the back of her head, Ameli leaned forward on the table and pointed a rind of cheese at Masika. "I haffa ass, wha' maejoo fink ta hit tha' monser wif dribbenseed?"

Rainn snorted and turned his head as wine spurted out of his nose. "Ow. Tell a fella first when you're gonna do that. Did anyone understand what magic curl just said?"

"Happily, I speak jam-mouthed sorceress." Sabni lowered his own cup. "She wishes to know how, in the heat of the battle, our brilliant Masika thought to use the same medicine on Sedja that Ameli used on her the night before."

"Daf wha' I sed."

"The dose you gave me separated me from my emotions." Masika thought for a moment before continuing. "It gave me the space I needed to look at them without their being all over me? Like you said when we were about to go in up there. I'm not sure if this is making sense."

The cheese rind described a circular *keep talking* motion.

"Well, it occurred to me that if it did that to me, maybe it could separate Sedja from the emotions it was feeding on. Somehow weaken it."

"Hmph." With a dramatic swallow, Ameli took a long drink of her wine and belched. "Interesting thought. Except that's not what happened. Drivenseed does exactly what you're saying, in tiny doses and in humans. In ruminants like cows and sheep it just makes them sleepy. But in reptiles"—she paused for effect—"it makes them so horny they can't stand. The more you feed them, the worse it gets. If I'd realized that monster was a big furry lizard and not a big scaly jungle cat, I'd have warned you about the altered effects. As it was, I think we won because Masika gave Sedja the boner of his life and he didn't know what to do with it."

She took another bite of her cheese rind and smiled, while Rainn guffawed and Sabni and Uncle Mahu exchanged pointed looks. Even Heron gave her stuttery laughing squawk.

Ameli winked at Masika. "Remnants are a pain in the ass that way."

After a few seconds consideration, Masika joined in the laughter as well.

When she could breathe again, Masika asked, "Were all of those people Sedja captured from this village?" Everywhere she looked, underfed people, their skin still ashen but their faces smiling, ate, hugged, and chatted. A few simply sat beneath shadowed overhangs and stared out at the world around them, and one teenaged boy tried to eat but could not do so on his own. Another of the victims helped him by placing tiny bits of khef-tet in his mouth and miming chewing.

"From what I gather, yeah." Rainn followed Masika's gaze. "But some of them are really old for humans. Like a few hundred years or so. I overheard some of the villagers talking about a list of folks got snatched they'd been keeping as long as anyone knew how to write. Mosta these guys"—he hooked a thumb at the people they had rescued—"are on it. The ones that aren't mighta been grabbed even before that. I guess that thing kept pulling grief outta people until the last memories were gone. Maybe keeping that list wasn't such a good idea after all."

What an abhorrent thought. An eternal half-life, unable to speak, or love, or enjoy anything, while that monster slowly drained away anyone who ever loved you, one at a time. They had given these people back everything. And they had done it together.

"Allz's wounds!" Masika sat up straight on her bench, attracting several stares. "We were idiots. Our plan would never have worked at all if that storm hadn't come. There's no way we could've killed that monstrosity if Rainn hadn't been all lightninged up like that. We're only alive because of blind, stupid luck."

"But it did, and we took full advantage of it." Rainn favored her with a fierce grin. "That's not luck. That's brains."

Masika remained unconvinced. Yes, they did take advantage of the opportunity, and yes, such storms were not uncommon, but this seemed like . . . providence? Rainn grew more powerful in a storm but calling them lay outside his ability.

What other gods would possibly help them?

"Mother Love brought us to Sedja and provided us with the miracle of his death." Sabni grinned at Uncle Mahu, who rolled his eyes. "Our luck lies only in being her loving children."

Masika reached across the table and grabbed Rainn's hand. "And you. I *saw* you. You were a *god*."

"What were you expecting?" Rainn shrugged his shoulders. "I've always been a god."

"And Ameli knew Sarah." Masika's eyes went wide as she recalled even more astounding things about that night. "How did I not know that? Why wasn't that the first thing you said to me when we met?"

"They knew her too." Ameli pointed to Uncle Mahu and Sabni.

"*What?*"

"Was that important?" Sabni's face betrayed his confusion.

"I apologize, Featherwind." A deep sigh escaped Uncle Mahu as he spoke. "I was aware of your fixation with the Hill Fury, but I hoped it would pass."

"Why would it pass?" What was her uncle trying to say? "Why would you hope that? Sarah was amazing. She saved the world."

"She did." A brief nod slipped out beneath Uncle Mahu's frown. "But she is no fit role model for a young woman. The Hill Fury surrounded herself with a storm of violence. You could do better. Your own mother—"

"I am *not* having this conversation with you." The obvious pique in Masika's tone raised Uncle Mahu's brows, though not far. "If you're looking for a mother's daughter, you could've stopped with Merities. The one we escaped from at the shore? The one who's caused us no end of trouble? Who set fire to our ship and had me thrown in a dungeon?"

Looking at Sabni, Uncle Mahu shook his head. "This is why everyone likes you better."

"Sarah was always nice to me," Sabni said.

Her anger grew. They needed to get off this before she said something she did not mean.

"How long was I asleep?" Masika directed her question to Ameli, who leaned on one elbow and lazily picked at her teeth.

"Most of a day." Tipping her wine cup to reveal its lack of contents, Ameli frowned. "We got here yesterday evening, and it's just past noon now. You're young and strong. You could kill a remnant of creation every day and be just fine."

That brought up a different question in Masika's mind. "Did we kill him? Is Sedja going to stay dead?"

Ameli's gaze flicked up to Masika's and slid away. "I doubt it. He's not the sort of creature that just takes being dead lying down. But I've been talking to the village elders here. It might be that they can just send a few big guys with spears and axes up there every couple weeks or so and kill him again before he gets his legs under him. I don't know. It's a thought."

A dubious thought to Masika's ears, but she had nothing better. "Let's make sure we're ready to go in the morning. My *mother's* daughter may not know where we are yet, but we shouldn't make it easy for her."

Sabni grinned and punched Uncle Mahu in the shoulder.

CHAPTER

TWENTY-EIGHT

Most pray to Mother Love through intermediaries, making it easy to forget that the matriarch of the P'tak is also the goddess of self-knowledge. The most valuable trait possible

This is why the other gods rely on Mother Love to tell them who they are and what function they should serve, just as the priests of the Holy Emperor tell the people of Egren who to be to best serve their nation and each other. For the most part these decisions are obvious. The sons of farmers are of the most use as farmers, the daughters of weavers as weavers, and so on.

But occasionally a person is born of extraordinary capability and prom-ise, who might equally serve in any variety of roles. In these cases, the priests are called in and Mother Love's wisdom prayed for directly.

For some reason, these people are almost always deemed to be temple laborers for the priests consulted, bless Mother Love's fortune.

Volume One of *Thank Gods* by Kohmose Oburn

Masika squinted into the distance at the city of Baladh. Nestled between two of the Little Gods, it lazed in the cleft of a wide valley bordered north and south by long stretching foothills. The only regularly navigable pass into the Yellow Sea lay just to the west, and the now sprawling settlement had grown over the decades from a much smaller walled fortification assigned to guard it. While Baladh continued to serve this original function, it now held a place of prominence as the Jewel of the West, the sole thriving non-coastal metropolis of Egren.

"I didn't say it wasn't pretty." Masika glanced up at Sabni, who scratched at his perfectly trimmed black beard. "I said there were soldiers there. Lots of them."

"I agree with Sabni." Making a point to ignore Ameli's open-mouthed look of astonishment, Uncle Mahu pointed to the wide roads leading east out of the city. "Inside Baladh we have the cover of crowds, even if there are also more Saraph Jais. On the road we are more apt to be stopped and discovered. Look there." He pointed to the roads that bypassed the city. "Checkpoints at every intersection. Checkpoints we can avoid by going through instead of around. Like the parable of the Beetle in the Pasture."

Mahu grimaced. "The beetle was eaten by a horse and came out covered in dung."

"Yes," Sabni returned with a sunny grin. "But he avoided the spears of the Saraph Jais who waited for him outside the city."

"That's not the story." Mahu's grimace settled into a stern frown.

"A parable is only useful if you can adapt it to your situation." Sabni opened his hands toward the heavens. "This is why I am the priest and you are the farmer."

Slender towers with russet and blue stone domes dotted the broad expanse of the city. The Temple of the Holy Emperor rose over everything, a gigantic white edifice of huge stone blocks, shipped from northern Egren. A haze of dust and cooking fires hugged Baladh tight, promising warm nights and full bellies.

"Been a week since the village." Rainn leaned down to rub his horse on the neck. He had been showing the animal more and more affection over the past five or six days. "I could do with some food that wasn't dried out, wrinkled up, and better suited to fixing my shoes than chewing."

"That's four for Baladh, and two for taking our chances on the road where we'll certainly be caught and killed." At Heron's screech, Ameli stroked her feathers and leaned her head against the goddess's. Heron had rarely left Ameli's saddle over the past week. "I know, I know. You don't like crowds. I included you in the go-get-killed group."

"Baladh it is." The resolution did not help Masika feel any better. In fact, it only heightened her anxiety. She peered into the city with Inlittan, watching hawkers selling their wares and laborers hauling foodstuffs and wooden beams. Guards on the walls watched the streets and exchanged jokes and gossip with the vendors. An energy of humanity and commerce suffused the place, but it failed to reassure.

She had never been to Baladh herself, though her brother, Djephan, liked the place. It looked more wild and spirited than the carefully cleaned and manicured streets of Plensa, where she grew up. If it had not been a matter of sneaking past the Saraph Jais, she would have welcomed the opportunity to visit such a place. Now it seemed like an unnecessary risk.

Heron threw her head back and released a high trill.

"You and me both, goddess," Masika replied.

"BUT DIDN'T the other place have better food?" An empty pewter mug, recently drained, sat on the round wooden table in front of Rainn. He, as well as the rest of them, wore nondescript traveling clothes into town and sat in the common room of the Merchant's Pass, a busy tavern in the heart of the caravan district.

Above their heads, Heron kept nervous watch atop the three-story building.

"Yes." Masika's own mug made a small scraping sound as she pushed it back and forth between her hands.

"Then why are we here?" Rainn's lower lip protruded ever so slightly from his rugged face.

"I know you've gotten a taste for eating in royal castles, but places like that attract attention. Places like this"—Masika waved a hand at the room—"don't."

Loud conversations about trade routes, the best beers between here and Verran, and which municipalities could be convinced to neglect their tariffs in favor of some mild bribery filled the large candlelit hall. Masika's group would have been anonymous dancing naked on the table.

More beers arrived, carried by a stout Darrish woman with a sweating brow and no time to stop and chat.

Two of the mugs she left behind found their way in front of Rainn. "Beer has really come a long way in the last few thousand years. People used to make it out of yak's milk and blood."

"That's not true." Ameli searched the faces around the table. "Seriously. That isn't true. Is it?"

"I could not say." Ever cheerful, Sabni grinned into his cup. "Perhaps Darrish beer is better because we have never had yaks?"

"I think the milk and blood thing was Oldam's recipe." Rainn took another pull from his cup. "Just one more thing the old shit didn't know fuck-all about."

The talk of her friends faded in Masika's ears as she thought about that day, only two months ago, when she and the two Alir faced Oldam, High King of the northern gods. A statue of granite, at first indistinguishable from the stone mountain he knelt on, Oldam had refused Rainn and Heron passage further up the pass to the Alireon, their home. None of them knew why.

Was it possible that it was Masika's fault? Despite Rainn's warning, she had touched the mighty god on the knee. What if that transgression were sufficient to prevent her Alir friends from being allowed home? Could Oldam have expected Rainn to kill Masika for her sacrilege?

The thoughts swirled in her head until Masika noticed a man staring at her from the bar. The burly man with a smooth black beard and flashing, amused eyes lifted a wineglass to her in a familiar gesture. His yellow flaxen shirt strained against the bulging muscles of his arms and chest.

"Denari clear the fog." Masika shook her head, grinned happily, and rethinking her reaction, covered a gasp with both hands.

No, this was not good.

"What is the . . ." Twisting in his chair, Uncle Mahu spotted the younger man and slumped. "Oh."

The man stood and sauntered over to their table.

"Hello, Masika."

Unsure how to proceed, she fell back on manners.

"Prince Djephan, please meet Ameli and Rainn. Ameli and Rainn, this is my brother Prince Djephan."

Rainn extended a hand and a smile.

Eyes on the table, Masika finished the introduction. "He's a very highly placed member of the Holy Emperor's personal guard."

Both the hand and the smile withdrew.

"How did you find us so fast?" If they had been spotted by the Saraph Jais, their problems were so much worse than they appeared.

"I'm not without resources," he replied. "Uncle Mahu, Sabni." Djephan's easy demeanor concerned Masika. What did he know? Why was he even here?

"Djephan," Uncle Mahu responded.

Sabni eyed the exits for more soldiers.

Not a bad person exactly, Djephan's determined nature frequently put him at odds with Masika's own, even if it was typically a friendly competition. If Meritities had already gotten to him . . .

"Goodness. Everyone should relax, yeah?" Djephan set his glass down and swiped an empty chair from a neighboring table. "We're not enemies, you know. Not yet anyway. I'm only here to talk."

"I don't think you'd find me easy company to chat with." The threatening growl in Rainn's throat set a perfect counterpoint to the hand that slid for Forbryttan's hilt. "Not unless you're looking for a hole to nap in."

Masika caught Rainn's gaze and shook her head in a silent no.

Already nervous, it occurred to her that Rainn and Djephan were too similar. If they both decided they were defending her from the other, this could go wrong very fast.

"Good thing I'm not here to talk to *you* then." Djephan leaned back and hooked his thumbs in his belt where a pair of thin bladed daggers rested in their sheaths. "For you anyways, yeah? I see your dinners are coming. Masika, grab yours and follow me upstairs. I got a room up top for us to catch up in."

This time Rainn's hand did grasp the sword's grip and pulled it an inch from its scabbard. "She's going nowhere with you."

"Rainn, stop," Masika said. "He's my brother. He's not going to hurt me."

Sabni's larger hand covered Rainn's and pushed the sword back home. "All is well, friend Rainn. We will sit here and eat. Djephan will not harm his sister, and there is nowhere for them to go that does not lead through this room. This is not my first meal at the Merchant's Pass."

Her hand on Rainn's shoulder, Masika stood. "I'll be fine. But if you hear a scream, come running."

"As if all the demons of the Undergates rode to your rescue," Sabni said.

Pushing his chair away, Djephan rolled his eyes and rose smoothly to his feet. His every move declared him to be in absolute control of himself and everything he saw.

He had always been infuriating that way.

Together, they climbed the narrow stair leading to the private dining gallery. A partial second floor above the main hall, the gallery was open in the center, with carved railings all around. Behind the railings, large individual dining rooms, walled on the three sides not facing the center, stared down on the more active area below. Djephan led her to his room, and they entered, Masika with her laden pewter plate in hand.

They sat and stared at one another. In the corner of her eye, Masika could just make out Rainn's glower from down in the bigger hall.

"Seen our brother recently?" Djephan clasped his hands and set them on the table in front of him.

"Kohmose?" Small talk it was. "Not for over a year. I did see one of his books recently. In the royal castle at Greenshade."

"I'll have to tell him," Djephan said. "He'll be happy to hear."

Masika did not offer that she had seen it in the castle's dungeon.

"You're dressing down these days." His eyes betrayed no judgement, only curiosity. "Trying to avoid attention?"

Inside, Masika cringed at her dirty and road-stained tunic and pants, knowing what her mother and Meritities would make of it when Djephan shared his impressions of the sight of her. Outwardly she favored her brother with a strained smile.

"Just Meritities." While Masika hardly wished to explain anything she need not, she also did not want to get caught out in a lie.

"Yeah. Meritities." He blew out his cheeks and looked at the floor. This was the moment Masika dreaded. "She and I've been talking. You know she's spoken to the Holy Emperor about your plans to take those two Alir to the House of the Gods."

And there it was. No dodging the ox-dung on the dinnerplate now.

She pushed her cooling dinner away, no longer hungry. "I know."

He looked at her, eyes dark and handsome. Djephan had always been big and athletic, a natural ladies' man, even if he was not the smartest sibling in the brood. Competitive to a fault, his demeanor left him well-placed among the Saraph Jais, out of which he soon found himself promoted, as well befit a prince of Egren.

"The Holy Emperor asked me personally to bring you home and avoid any more embarrassment to the family. He knows I've got a lot to lose—personally—if he and I ever fell out of favor."

The sense of Masika's stomach falling hurt her physically. How would she manage this? Uncle Mahu and Sabni could be relied upon to stand down if she asked, and Ameli would follow their lead. But Rainn? After what she witnessed against Sedja the remnant, Masika doubted the god could be killed, but he could sure cause some damage on the way out the door if he were captured. And that could only complicate her life even more.

"I thought you didn't care for Meritities." Even if Masika could do nothing to influence her own fate here, she could at least understand it.

"I don't. She's a busybody who thinks she's better'n anyone who won't raise a pinky when they drink their tea." Djephan frowned. "And that's why I decided to let you make your case to me here. Now."

Eyes widening, Masika's head rose. Her stomach flip-flopped. Did she really have a chance to right the cart with Djephan? But she and Djephan were friends. Why was he putting her through this?

"Convince me you're in the right and our prig of a sister is wrong, and I'll set you free. Don't, and I got plenty of manacles to go around. And that includes the bird." He smiled and leaned back in his chair. Very little warmth shone through in that expression.

Her mind raced. What arguments surged ahead of the others in persuasiveness? What specifically appealed to Djephan? Wait. He said he had a lot to lose himself. Was he afraid of getting kicked out of the Holy Emperor's Guard? That suggested one possible tactic.

Hungry again, Masika pulled her plate closer and tore off a leg of the baked bird on her plate. "Restoring the northern gods to their rightful place is a big win for papa. If I can do it, he gains standing with all the Andosh countries, and he becomes more valuable to the Imperial Seat, not less. You'll be the son of a hero."

Face grim, Djephan shook his head. "Please don't insult me by pleading for the nation we just fought a war against. In any case, if the other Andosh nations find out Tyrrane's god took your two Alir captive, that's an embarrassment for Tyrrane and Dad suffers. They respect strength, not rescuing weaklings. If no one finds out, then Dad's reputation only goes up in Tyrrane, the nation that just lost the biggest war ever waged in the Thirteen Kingdoms. The political upside's less than nothing."

"That's not true." Far from righting the cart with her brother, Masika felt as if she were shoving it off a cliff. "I told Queen Megan of Greenshade about it myself. She wished us well and provided assistance. She wants to see the Alir restored."

"Damn." Clouds built behind Djephan's brow. "Too late to avoid the damage then—unless we take action against the perpetrators. Claim they're frauds and jail them forever?" His intense stare locked with Masika's frantic gaze.

"What? No. Rainn and Heron are victims, not perpetrators." Worse and worse. "They were captured and tortured by Tyrrane's Anger Under the Mountain for thousands of years. They *deserve* to go home. How could you—how could *any* of us stand in the way of that? What kind of people would that make us?"

"The kind who obey the will of the gods, ours and theirs." Djephan held out his hands in front of him and let out a sigh. "Isn't it the king of the northern gods who blocked the way for your two Alir? Your entire mission's at odds with what he wants. How does screwing up King Oldam's command put us in any better standing with the Andosh? And who're we to say what those two deserve when their own king exiled them? I'm sorry, Masika, you know I love you, but you got to do better than that."

Better than this? Masika felt numb.

"What if I told you it was important to me?" Not her best argument, but it was certainly honest. "I want to do something important. I want to help. I want to step out from Papa's shadow and from beneath our mother's skirts. Djephan, I *need* to do this."

"Masika." His voice grew soft. "You're a sixteen-year-old girl. You don't know *what* you want, and you got all your life to find out. Unless I let you pitch it all into the sea today and you suddenly find yourself without any family reputation to fall back on. And even if that *were* enough for you, how's that fair to the rest of us? To Kohmose? To me? To Dad? Even to Mom and Meri?"

"Fair?" Anger swelled in Masika's breast. "How many inconvenienced lives does it take to equal a few thousand years of torture? If Merities ended up a mere princess instead of a court favorite, would that be too much to ask to return a pair of gods to their home? If Mother had to work for her friends instead of having them fawn all over her every moment of every day? All Kohmose wants to do is study and no one needs know you and I ever spoke." She stood and went to her brother, kneeling on the wooden floor at his feet.

"Djephan, you have the chance to do something important here. You must believe you were spared in the war against Tyrrane for some reason."

Masika almost mentioned the imp in the tavern and all the lives it promised to end if she and Rainn and Heron failed to help it recover its creator from the Undergates. Bringing a woman back from the dead to be killed again by a disgruntled little monster hardly seemed a winning cause.

He took her hands in his own. "Masika. You're dear to me, but you're wrong. The lives of two Alir no one ever missed or even heard of aren't worth our family. They just aren't. And I know no one ever heard of them 'cause I asked Kohmose and he never did, so that means nobody knows them, yeah? Unless you got something better you're sitting on, I'm gonna have to take you back to the Imperial Seat."

She yanked her hands out of his, wiped her eyes, and leaped to her feet. "You never intended to leave me be. You want to see me fail. Why, Djephan? Why are you arguing Merities's cause so hard? You don't even like her."

"That's not—"

"She's always had it in for you and you know it." Masika's veneer of familial civility blew away, a parchment house in a hurricane. "Do you remember when you beat Anopsek in the Grain Games and he was declared Champion-for-the-Day anyway? Do you remember how that made you feel? That was because Merities convinced Elder Faul to honor Anopsek instead of you—because she was jealous you would become more popular with the Holy Emperor than she was."

"You don't—"

But Masika was not yet finished. Not by a league. "Or when your first assignment as the youngest Imperial Guard ever posted was to the Verran Pass? Where old Saraph Jais go to die? That was because she saw the Holy Emperor's son pretending to be you while he played soldier in the yard and she grew afraid he might ask you about her, and that you might tell the boy the truth. Or the day when you fought the northern assassin in the Holy Emperor's bath chamber and—"

"Stop." Djephan raised both his hands. "Please stop. I was going to let you go anyway, I just wanted you to feel like you'd earned it. I don't need you to parade every reason I have for hating Meri out in front of my face."

"You *what?*"

"What? It's so hard to believe I might want to see you dance a bit before I fold up and give you what you want?" A hint of a smile crept to the corners of Djephan's lips. "You weren't all that easy to live with either, littlest sister."

Masika punched her brother in the shoulder. It felt like punching a stone. "You asshole. I can't believe you made me go through all of that. I was trying to figure out how to keep Rainn from murdering you."

One muscular hand massaged Djephan's shoulder where Masika struck him. He grimaced. "I could handle one little god."

That brought a snort from Masika. "Sure. Unless it rains." She shook her head and smiled. "You really are an asshole, you know. How did you really find us?"

"Easy." He grinned at her, teeth even and bright in his handsome face. "I got an orven from a soldier in one of the villages. Seems you saved some farmers from a leopard or something nearby. I figured you'd have to slip through Baladh, so I sat on a wall and watched the roads. Once I spotted you, I just followed you here. The clothes might've thrown me off, but Sabni and Mahu are hard to disguise."

"And everyone calls you the stupid brother." Masika returned to her seat and took a bite of her bird. Would Heron be horrified at her choice of dinner? She resolved not to ask.

"Compared to Kohmose we're all the idiot siblings." Djephan frowned again and drummed his fingers on the tabletop. "We still got a problem with Meri. She won't give up just because I report you never came through here. And despite the empress kinda hating her, she's got the Holy Emperor's ear."

"Is there anything you can do to help?"

"Not much, though I might be able to throw them off a little." He leaned an elbow on the table and rested his chin in his hand. "I been thinking I might send an orven to the capital myself and say I been told you were sighted along the coast. That way it won't catch me if I'm wrong, I was just misinformed, yeah? Meri knows where you're headed, but if she thinks you're coming from the coastline, she might convince the Saraph Jais to protect the wrong side of Mount P'takkin. It's not much, but it's the best I can do."

He chuckled and waggled his eyebrows at her. "Too bad you're not really going to Mukahiit, yeah? I know a lot of people there. I could tell you where to go to have a seriously good time."

Masika finished her meal, walked around the table, and kissed her brother on the cheek. "Thank you, favorite brother. I barely hate you anymore at all."

CHAPTER

TWENTY-NINE

Souls sent to the afterlife in the Darrish custom serve in the armies and navies of the Darrish emperors and kings who preceded them. There are as many different military forces as there are deceased Darrish rulers, which is to say quite a lot. It is a permanent battlefield of ever-shifting loyalties, with epic victories and dramatic defeats. Of course, the Egren emperors lead the rest, and can only be defeated through acts of extreme treachery. While this happens often, of course, our *fallen emperors are typically much too canny to allow themselves to fall prey to it.*

The downside to this path to eternal glory lies in the fate of those who are killed (again) in combat. Those souls are typically fed to the demons who call the Undergates home, bringing some soldiers' eternity to an abrupt end.

Given that every soul must fight for eternity until they eventually lose and are killed, there does not appear to be much upside to the arrangement. Most religious scholars agree, however, that it is better than definitely *becoming food for demons.*

Volume One of *Thank Gods* by Kohmose Oburn

The early evening streets of Baladh glowed yellow and orange from tallow oil lamps set at the corners of most buildings. Masika and her friends followed Djephan through the throngs—who now sought food and pleasure rather than business—toward the city's north gate. Smoke from the lamps made a haze in the air that reflected the light and, while blotting out the stars, increased the illumination on the ground.

Sabni and Uncle Mahu followed separately and at a distance, being less easy to identify individually than together.

Music and smoke ran together with happy shouts and the whirl of human bodies, all of which got into Masika's head, distracting her and causing anxiety. She spotted far too many Saraph Jais in plain sight on the street, which worried her until she remembered that thanks to Inlittan she saw them in their red sashes far easier than they saw her.

She kept the hood of her shawl pulled tight around her face regardless.

As for Djephan, he eeled his way through the water of the crowds with grace and confidence. Despite his size Masika never noticed a single soul turn to look at him. She concentrated on emulating his movements and attitude.

At Djephan's insistence, they left the horses behind. The animals were both easier to spot and to track, which meant they would be on foot for the remainder of their journey. More time to be encircled and caught, but less chance of being spotted.

Having become attached to his animal, Rainn took this hardest of all.

Abruptly, they left the well-lit portion of town and entered a quieter, darker section where the older stone buildings sat empty and black on the bottom floors, used for commerce during the day, and hosted family dinners above. Masika's nerves calmed immediately.

"Don't relax just yet." Djephan held out an arm to slow Masika and Ameli. "There's less people moving through this neighborhood, so anyone who is'll stand out more. Stick close and let me talk if we get stopped, yeah?"

"Yeah," Rainn answered. Despite Djephan's assistance, Rainn refused to warm to Masika's brother. "Now that we're out of the populated part and we can't see where we're going and being led by the guy in charge of the people looking for us, there's absolutely no fucking way any of this is a trap."

"I can see." Masika waved a hand to Rainn, barely visible in the windowed candlelight.

"Can you?" One brow went up over Ameli's smiling face. At Masika's nod, she leaned in to whisper. "You know, the Hill Fury could see in the dark too. I can't, but it was one of her natural sorcerous abilities."

"C'mon." Djephan entered the narrow street and turned left. "And be quiet."

Feet hardly touching the packed dirt, Masika floated after her brother. She shared something with Sarah, and something surpassingly uncommon. In that moment, with all the doubt ahead of them and all the danger rushing up from behind, Masika felt certain that victory was not only possible, but assured.

"If you only came here because of your informant," Ameli asked Djephan, "why are we sneaking? The rest of the Saraph Jais don't even know to look for us."

"Just because I didn't tell them doesn't mean they don't know." Forced to cross a faintly lit portion of the street, Djephan did so with his back bent and a shuffle in his step, as though exhausted from a long day of labor. The others followed suit. "It would be stupid of us to assume that the Holy Emperor doesn't have his own people reporting to him. He's got the biggest network of intelligence of any nation in Andos, and I happen to know he's pretty ruthless about using it, yeah? For that matter, we should worry about who Meritities knows and is talking to. She's every bit as sneaky and mean as our Masika here is eager to impress."

Well, that spoiled Masika's brief euphoria. She was not trying to impress anyone. She was just trying to do the right thing. She'd given up all that wanting to impress people *weeks* ago.

At length, they came to the end of the neighborhood and to

Baladh's north gate. Smaller than the main entrance to the east, a pair of Saraph Jais patrolled the wall top, one to either side of the reinforced wooden exit.

"Huh." Djephan stopped at the corner of a shuttered freight warehouse with a guttering lamp set just above his head. "That's not supposed to be closed yet. And I don't know those two on the wall. That's not good."

"I'll take care of it." Forbryttan hissed out of its scabbard and into Rainn's hand. The god squinted into the dark. "How d'you get up there?"

"Just ask them to let down the ladder so you can climb up and chop their heads off, sweetie." A giggle accompanied Ameli's reply. "You should probably ask them to hold still for you too. It's a clear night and there's two of them."

Rainn's scowl melted at Ameli's clever grin. "What about Mahu and Sabni? Where are they? They can just shoot them right off the wall and out we go."

"Uncle Mahu's over there." Masika sighted along her finger to where Uncle Mahu hugged the shadows between a stack of crates and a stable. "And Sabni's under that wagon."

"We're not killing my brothers just to run away." The harshness of Djephan's voice showed his irritation. "We'll either come up with a better way or find someplace else to go over the wall."

"Well why didn't you say so, honey?" With that, Ameli patted Djephan on the cheek and stepped into the street. Broad and lit here in front of the gate, she moved in full view as she swayed her generous hips closer to the two soldiers. "Excuse me, but do either of you know where the Merchant's Pass is? I'm supposed to meet some girls there, and I'm *all* turned around."

"What the devil is she doing?" Djephan whispered.

Masika giggled at his discomfiture. "Just watch, big brother, and be amazed." She intended to watch too. Inlittan flared in Masika's eyes and went straight to Ameli's hands.

Although Masika had no idea how it happened, she saw Ameli's fingers curl in sorcerous patterns and pull a pale-yellow powder through the leather side of one of the many pouches on her hip. The powder swirled through the air, a sinuous snake of dust following Ameli's curling finger.

The older of the two soldiers grinned down. "You got friends right here, little girl." He reached down and came back up with a stoppered clay jug. "And our whisky's free."

That twisting finger straightened, and the powder shot up from where Ameli stood into the face of the soldier up on the wall.

He sneezed and stepped backward, and his younger companion laughed. "Don't drop the—*achoo!*"

The Saraph Jais sneezed and sneezed as Ameli returned to the anxious Djephan. She stepped up in front of him, raised an arm, and snapped her fingers.

Both soldiers stopped sneezing and dropped to the wall top.

"What did you do?" Djephan ran out to the wall. "Are they alive? I said no killing."

A pair of soft snores tumbled from the wall's height and Djephan relaxed.

"They're fine. Better than that, for sure." She came up behind Djephan and threw a soft arm over his shoulder. "I mixed a smidge of lover's tempest in with the pollydrop. They're having *real* good dreams."

A warm moan from above punctuated Ameli's statement.

Uncle Mahu and Sabni appeared as Djephan lifted the broad iron bar holding the gate closed and set it aside.

"Thank you, nephew," Uncle Mahu said.

"Mother Love smiles on you." Sabni reached out and hugged Djephan. "You always were a good boy."

Patting Djephan once more on the cheek, Ameli sauntered past. "It's always the ones with all the muscles. See ya round, big guy." As the sorceress exited the gate, Heron flew down to Ameli's shoulder.

An instant of envy flitted through Masika's mind, just as Heron flitted through the air. While part of their ultimate goal was to return Heron to a more human-seeming godly form, Masika could not help thinking about how amazing flight must be.

If it were her choice, would she even want to return to a human form?

Rainn walked past and out, without comment or acknowledgement.

As quietly as she could manage, Masika jumped up and threw her arms around Djephan's broad neck. "I love you, brother. Please don't get in trouble over us."

With a small laugh, Djephan lifted Masika off the ground and held her. "Ugh. When'd you get so heavy?" He set her down. "Be careful. Meritities isn't going to give up on this, yeah?"

Masika nodded. "When has she ever?"

She waved to Djephan as he reclosed the gate, then waved again to the two sleeping Saraph Jais atop the wall. The younger one already had his hand down the front of his pants.

"IT IS PERFECTLY easy to understand. If we can reach the Holy Kanista, we will already be halfway up the mountain and that much closer to our goal."

Once again explaining his thinking, Sabni tried to sound even more reasonable. It did not help.

"The temple guards will be at the Holy Kanista." Uncle Mahu's ever-present frown would have discouraged anyone but Sabni. "Even if we somehow avoid Meritities and the Saraph Jais and all the Holy Emperor's personal guard who do not happen to be related to us, they will clap us in irons the instant we set foot on that sacred spot, and then we will be thrown down the mountain."

"We will not be caught. Have faith, Mahu."

"I have faith that we should cross into Verran and make our ascent there, as would people who cannot fly when thrown off a cliff."

The argument went on beneath a glorious blue sky, with the vast plains of Northern Egren to their right and a scattering of trees before the Little Gods to their left. A temperate breeze offset the warm sun and ruffled the tops of the grasses.

Heron rode Ameli's arm and chatted with the sorceress as she had since leaving Baladh, though Masika had little notion of what they said. That left Rainn.

"How are you grumpy on a day like this?"

The flat look Rainn returned to Masika's question was all the answer she needed. While he had been irritable since leaving his mare behind, Masika suspected the perfect weather was truly at fault.

"Right. Forgot. Again. Sorry." She clasped her hands and smiled. "We had that really dreary overcast sky all day a couple days ago. That was nice."

He rolled his eyes and trudged on.

"I bet the weather's miserable somewhere," Masika said brightly. "It's always awful in Coldspine. Just imagine you're there."

"Sadness isn't something you can just imagine away, Masika. Besides, no matter how hard I pretend to be somewhere else, I can still hear your voice."

"Rude." She thought for a moment. "I thought you were learning to get past all that. You were acting happy even when it was pretty out."

"That's right. I *was* acting." He made a frustrated snort. "I had good food and a horse that loved me and some goddamn distance. But now I'm walking through sunny fucking meadows with chirping idiot birds and the stench of flowers in my nose and I have to *talk about it with you.*"

"Oh. I know what we can talk about, Sir God." Ignoring Rainn's groan, Masika plunged on. "When we fought Sedja. Well, when we tried to fight Sedja and you murdered him. That was amazing, by the way. I bet no one else could have exploded a monster's head the way you did."

"Thank you."

"But you don't actually control the weather do you? I mean if you did it'd always be gray out, right?"

"Yes, it would." The thought lit Rainn's face, if only a bit.

"So where did all the lightning come from?" The thought had been bugging Masika for days. "Who can do that? Could one of the Alir be helping you without High King Oldam's knowing? Is it even possible that one of the P'tak is trying to send assistance?"

The idea clearly stuck in Rainn's head. "I dunno." He frowned in concentration. "I don't know any of the Darrish gods, but there might be a few Alir who'd wanna help me out. Help Heron out, anyway."

"Oh yeah? Who?"

"Lorrianna's my mom. She and Heron were tight, but she couldn't do that sort of thing." He tapped his jaw as he talked. "Might've talked the damn monster away but no lightning. Her mother Hedra could've done it. Lori's one of her favorites, but I don't think Heron really knows her, and I certainly don't."

"Your mother wouldn't have helped you?" That sounded familiar to Masika.

"It's a complicated relationship. Fisantli's the only one besides Heron I really got on with, but everyone liked her. I wouldn't have been special. And no lightning anyway."

"I've never heard of Fisantli," Masika said. "What's she like?"

Rainn walked in silence for another twenty paces. "The Alir are raider gods. They're not all about farming and fishing and stuff like the P'tak."

"Sure. I know."

"A raider has certain kinds of . . . behavior . . . that's expected." Rainn's discomfort grew as he spoke, but that only heightened Masika's curiosity. "There's the raiding itself, obviously. The killing and the looting."

"Burning?" Masika asked. She had heard all about raiders burning villages to the ground.

"Sure, there's the burning too." Whatever had him so nervous to speak, it was not burning. "Anyway, Fisantli is sort of the goddess of rewarding the right kind of raider. Traditions and that sort of thing."

Masika's eyes went round. "You mean *raping*?" she hissed. She had a hard time even saying the word aloud.

Hands held out to encourage quiet, Rainn's gaze darted around at their friends. He slowed so the two of them fell behind the rest. "Different peoples have different standards. Northmen don't even see the raidees as human. So it's not wrong."

"Apparently they're human enough to have sex with." This grew more disgusting by the second. Was it too late to put Rainn back in the dungeon?

"Yes. Well, no." He looked at the mountains and then at his feet. "Fisantli inhabits the body of a woman being raped during a raid. So the raider isn't raping the woman who's there screaming and crying on the ground, but he's having sex with a willing goddess who wants to reward him for being a good member of his community."

Masika's brain rebelled at the idea of such a thing. "That's *barbaric*."

"I didn't invent it." Rainn's tone pitched defensively, and both Ameli and Heron turned to stare. "Yes, it's horrific. I've been away for a long time with no one but Heron to talk to, and my views have changed. Being victimized for a thousand years changes your point of view. I can't even imagine what you think about all this. But what are you gonna do?"

"Not rape people?" This answer seemed obvious.

Rainn raised his hands and let them drop, defeated.

Rage built up behind Masika's eyes. "Kohmose told me that the gods of the Andosh were monsters. And they are. You and Heron lay in Angrim's dungeon for a millennia, and they knew it, and no one came to help you. They didn't protect you."

She shoved the red-hot emotions down with both hands so that she might finish speaking without screaming.

"There's no excuse for that. But this . . ." She trailed off, grasping for words. "This is deliberate. A system created and used to perpetuate misery and violence. It's hateful, Rainn. They're not protecting any of us. They're *horrible*."

Speeding up, Masika left Rainn behind and pulled even with her uncle. She could not listen to him anymore. Was she being fair to Rainn? Sure, he wasn't a raider like the Andosh, or hadn't been in thousands of years at any rate, but why would he want to go back to a family like that? A sudden thought struck her.

Had King Oldam refused Rainn and Heron entry because they were too good for the Alir now? Kohmose told Masika endless bedtime stories about what horrors the Alir were, and how the clever and resourceful Darrish heroes defeated them again and again. After first meeting Heron and Rainn, she had decided that was all they were, just stories.

But after really getting to know them, she was no longer so certain.

"The eastern slope is the only possible ascent." Sabni's exasperation shoved aside his reasonable-sounding voice. "We would never make it through the Verran Pass."

Masika sighed.

CHAPTER

THIRTY

Not every story about the Darrish pantheon is about the gods themselves. Take Hamara, for instance, a demigod of uncertain parentage who over and over again serves Mother Love through her guile, charm, and strength of arm. Although Hamara is half-divine, her tales are universally about the triumph of the human spirit in service to the gods.

Later retellings of Hamara's exploits have included a cautionary element, often punishing the brash explorer for successfully completing feats reserved for the P'tak alone, even when those deeds are in the name of doing good.

Doing what appears as good from an earthly perspective and serving Mother Love are not always the same thing, as these stories teach us. The lesson here is that when choosing the greatest good in any given situation, humans simply aren't qualified.

Honestly, any historian could have told you that.

Volume Two of *Thank Gods* by Kohmose Oburn

What are you two on about?" Masika asked. The overcast spring day put Rainn in better spirits, although the looming turn in the Little Gods, now in front of them as well as to their left, acted as a sort of enormous stone deadline. "Even I don't understand what you're saying, and I speak bird."

The terrain to the west of them had reverted to farmland, though long fallowed. While they saw no one there, Mahu led them up and down the foothills to the east to stay well away from any possible encounters with people.

"That's because we're talking magic stuff, not bird stuff." The constant interaction between Ameli and Heron relaxed both of them, and the goddess had never exhibited less apprehension. "Heron is trying to explain to me how she turns herself into a bird and back. I'm hoping I can help her get control again. She's so pretty and sweet, it seems like the least I could do." Ameli carefully lifted the feathers behind Heron's head and scratched there, much to the goddess's obvious delight.

A small blue glow flashed from underneath those feathers.

Since before Baladh, Heron had ridden on Ameli's saddle, then when they left their horses behind, either her shoulder or as now, her arm. Masika felt a twinge of jealousy at how well the goddess had taken to the sorceress, but if Rainn acted like it did not bother him, she decided that she would act as if it did not bother her either.

Of course, Rainn treated Ameli much the same, so perhaps it was not a fair comparison.

"Why don't the farmers tend these fields?" For the past three days Masika had seen no person nor tillable crop anywhere. Just field after field of overgrown weed and brush.

"Too many men and women were taken for Greenshade's war against Tyrrane and Norrik." Sabni swept an arm to the north "There were not enough people left to till all the land. Many were consolidated into nearby farms, leaving their own fallow."

"All those people wasted. What a shame." Ameli paused to listen to Heron and nodded in response. "I suppose. But just because

Angrim would have killed everyone doesn't mean war's the best way to stop it."

"What would you have mortal men choose to do?" Sabni asked. "The most powerful of rulers have only the lives of others as their tools. I do not advocate for war under any circumstance, but it is understandable."

"Even the sorcerers of Andos gave way to the Anger," Mahu agreed.

Ameli shivered. "I know. I was there, remember?"

"Rabbit." As she said it, Masika pulled her bow from her back, strung it, nocked an arrow, and loosed into a stand of grass a hundred and fifty feet away.

"That's four." Rainn craned his neck to see the rodent in the grass. "I thought we said three was enough, what with all the berries and roots and other stuff you found. We planning on company for dinner?"

"No." Masika unstrung her bow and returned it to its sheath. "I just got excited. We'll save the foraged stuff for breakfast. I don't want the rabbits to feel like they're being wasted too."

IN THE DISTANCE and under the cover of night, Masika watched a man creep out of the foothills to the west and lose himself among the unpopulated town northeast of them. He moved with grace and confidence, and he carried a curved sword on his hip and a large carved bow behind him. His desert clothes, colored patterns faded by the sun, proclaimed no particular origin.

"Mercenary," Rainn announced on Masika's description. "Here to pick the bones of whatever the poor folks who ran off might've left behind."

"You've been under a rock for what, two thousand years? Three?" The idea of Rainn's expertise in the modern era brought a smile to Masika's lips. "How would you know what a mercenary looks like these days?"

"Some things never change," he replied.

"There's no one in that town." Inlittan showed Masika nothing but abandonment. "Whatever he can find, I'd suggest he's more than welcome to it." Her gaze narrowed. "Wait."

The mercenary approached one of the run-down buildings and unslung the bag from his back, moving as if it were heavy. He reached into it and withdrew a large portion of what Inlittan showed to be salted meat wrapped in burlap and hung it from a hook set into the door. He repeated the action with a cloth bag filled with loaves of bread, and finally with an oversized bottle of wine, wrapped in rope for safe transport. He knocked on the door and ran back the way he had come.

"Well, that's surprising behavior for a mercenary." Masika's brow drew down as the door opened cautiously, and an elderly woman peeked out. She and an even older man recovered the goods from their door and shut it tight once more.

"Not all mercenaries are bad you know." Ameli punctuated her statement by blowing a brown curl out of her face. "Some of them are taking time out of their busy days to help a princess on her *very* questionable mission to save an ungrateful god."

Heron squawked in Ameli's face.

"And his beautiful bird companion," Ameli finished with a huge smile.

Whoops. Masika forgot that Ameli, Uncle Mahu, and Sabni had all served as mercenaries in the past. She grinned sheepishly.

"What is the devil in question doing?" Sabni asked.

"Ah, right." Masika peered again into the black. "He's headed back into the foothills. I guess that means he's from Vastard?" The bandit kingdom, populated by criminals and mercenaries alike. "But he's feeding the people who were too old to relocate. That's what it looks like to me, anyway." The unexpected kindness caught Masika off guard. If a villain such as a fighter from Vastard could set aside his own self-interest to help those in need, perhaps their quest need not languish in hopelessness after all.

Perhaps not all the world sought to thwart them.

"Masika, can I talk to you for a minute?" Rainn stepped away from the group. In the dark only Masika saw the pensive expression on his face.

"Of course."

They walked a short distance from the others, and Rainn turned to face her.

"I just wanted to say . . ." He stopped, uncomfortable with his words. "I mean, I wanted to tell you thanks."

Masika struggled against her surprise until she realized that Rainn could not see it anyway.

"Thanks?"

"Yeah." He fidgeted, playing with Forbryttan's hilt. "I'm not always an easy person to be around. I can be an asshole sometimes."

"Mm-hm." Masika did not trust herself to open her mouth.

"Anyway, you've been good to me and Heron." He dragged his foot back and forth as he spoke, like a five-year-old caught stealing candy. "Even when we didn't—when *I* didn't—deserve it. You shoulda left us a long time ago, but you didn't."

He stared away into the night.

"I meant to say this before, but there was always some fuckery going on and maybe I was a little scared to tell you anyway. But that guy. That mercenary." Rugged face set in a frown, Rainn's jaw worked to get the rest of his speech out into the open air. "If some stupid shit like that can go out of his way to care for some old fucks he doesn't even know, I guess I can spare a little wind to say how much you mean to Heron and me. To me."

For all Masika knew the elderly couple were the mercenary's parents, but she refused to spoil the mood.

"So, thanks."

And with that, Rainn spun on his heel and stalked back to their dark campsite.

Masika grinned into the night.

"You're welcome."

IN THE MORNING the group continued their trek north toward the looming Mount P'takkin. The holy mountain loomed above the rest of the Little Gods and stared down with favor over Egren. From her brother Kohmose, Masika knew that the mountain's northern face glared with disdain across the nation of Verran, filled as it were with fools and indolents. He told her once that the Verranese believed all the world to be laid out on an enormous coin that flew through the heavens, tossed by the thumb of Mother Love. Good deeds ensured that the coin landed, when it eventually did so, human-side up. Evil tilted the coin humans down and would result in the deaths of everyone everywhere.

Preposterous.

Excitement warred with anxiety in her heart. On the sunny hand, the end of their journey lay just ahead. The first leg of it, at least.

On the sanded hand, every step they took moved them closer to the one place Meritities and the Holy Emperor knew they journeyed for, and they still had no idea how . . .

Wait.

"Ameli, Heron said you and she had been working on a plan to get us up the mountain." Excitement kicked anxiety to the dirt and stomped on its face. "Is that true? What've you thought of?"

"Oh. Right." Ameli exchanged a glance with the soft gray bird on her arm. "Well, we haven't been able to work out how to turn Heron back into a person yet. She's still locked, and I don't know how to jolt her out of it."

This was not the promising start Masika hoped for.

"But," Ameli went on, "I might have figured a way to turn the rest of us into birds. Just for a little while, and I'm not sure if I can do us all at the same time, but it's a starting point."

"Unless the Saraph Jais have bows."

Uncle Mahu's grim observation floated well beneath Masika's high-flying exhilaration. To be a bird! Gaining the peak of Mount P'takkin would be thrilling enough in its own right, but to get there as a bird, flying under her own power? The notion sent a shudder through her body.

More than that, it meant that they really were doing good. A thing such as this could not be accomplished without the favor of the gods, and such favor would never be extended to evildoers.

"That's a big grin for a girl that don't know the first thing about flying," Rainn observed.

"You're right." Masika could not keep a jitter out of her step. "I need to practice!"

"Oh, uh." Ameli looked to Heron again, who fluffed her feathers in a sort of shrug. "I mean I *guess* we could do that. I'm not . . . I don't know if . . ." She settled herself and made the decision. "You're right. I need to practice too. What good would it do us if we got all the way there and I couldn't figure out the spell?"

"Yay!" Masika shrieked. "Can we do it right now?"

"Um, I suppose." While Ameli's words failed to inspire confidence, her tone failed more. "Don't fly anywhere though. I don't know how long I can hold your form, and I've already killed enough royals."

"Killed enough—?"

Masika's question was cut off by a swirl of thought and color. Abruptly she found herself staring up at the world from within the tall grass.

But what grass!

The sandy ground ran dark and blue, while the grass shone in vibrant yellows and teals. Uncle Mahu and Sabni's normally rich brown skin carried hints of sapphire and violet reflections, and Heron! The goddess *glowed* with bright green patterning across her shoulders, while her beak and chest glittered metallic golds and blues. Only her emerald eyes remained unchanged.

Unable to stand it, Masika opened her tiny wings and launched herself into the air.

Shouting rose from below when Ameli fell to the ground, and Masika—herself once again—fell as well. With a shout and a grunt, Uncle Mahu leaped forward and caught his niece, rolling across the grass with her in his arms.

Laughter flew as free and uncontrolled out of Masika as her short flight had propelled her through the air. The brief experience opened her eyes and her mind in ways she never could have imagined. She hugged her uncle tight, her entire being made of joy.

In the midst of a worried Rainn and fretful Sabni, Ameli sat up out of the grass, her frizzy dark curls, lightening a bit back toward their original red, splayed about her head with abandon. "I said don't fly."

Masika only grinned.

"That was foolish, Featherwind." Uncle Mahu untangled himself from his niece and stood, bits of grass sticking to his skin. "Please do not try to fly yourself to death again."

"Figures she'd be some chirpy damn sparrow." Rainn pulled Ameli to her feet. "You did pretty good though. Think you'll be able to get us to the top by the time we make the mountain?"

"Whoof." Ameli held onto Rainn's arm, steadying herself. "I dunno. Turning birdbrained people into birds really takes it out of you." She cut a glance at Heron. "It's a lot easier than turning people-brained birds into people though."

"Next time," Rainn offered, "let's practice that inna burlap sack. Sacks don't fly and they're easier to catch."

CHAPTER

THIRTY-ONE

In the Hero Hamara's most popular tale, she seeks to prove to Mother Love that Allz has betrayed the gods by releasing evil into the world. But Mother Love takes the word of Allz over that of Hamara and refuses to listen. Finally, Hamara changes tactics and gifts Allz with a shirt stained red in the Blood of All-North, which she stole from the bed of the Alir.

Allz puts on the shirt, unaware that Matchi's hounds, who despise the Alir with a slavering passion, are nearby. The hounds rend Allz, releasing the light of his soul.

Making the best of a questionable situation, Mother Love announces that Hamara has passed her test, thanks the demigoddess for her efforts, and hangs Allz, now Allz the Shining, on the great iron wheel that he may bathe the world in his radiance.

While easy to criticize someone for not admitting their mistakes, if it results in sunlight and crops enough to feed the world, who are we to judge?

Volume Two of *Thank Gods* by Kohmose Oburn

The *Silver Spray* stayed just out of the tiny bay, watching over Meritities and Nebet as sailors tied off their pinnace against a small, but sturdy dock. The name of the tidy fishing village was . . . Hakmayt? Named after the P'tak goddess of fishes. Perhaps this village enjoyed a particular blessing from the P'tak.

The very gods showed their support for Meritities's mission to stop her sister.

One of the big boat's crew, a mate of some variety, failed to finish his knotwork before Nebet grew tired of waiting, and found himself flying over the big rowboat's bow, to land in the water on the other side. The bodyguard's increasingly irritated behavior entertained Meritities. The poor man only wanted to kill the two Alir, whom he blamed for the reprehensible Captain Ironmast cutting off his right ear.

It was almost time.

Placing her graceful hand in his huge one, Meritities allowed Nebet to help her from the calmly rocking pinnace. She did not wait for her things; the sailors knew where to take them. As the daughter of Egren's premier diplomat, only one accommodation in Hakmayt could do: the estate compound of the noble merchant, Tahir Nav.

The visit provided an excellent opportunity for Meritities to obtain information on the Imperial Court, as Tahir Nav counted himself among the aging Empress Khadiga's favorites. Infamous at court, the noble merchant's force of personality drove many a hopeful courtesan scurrying back to their farms. His reputation included arrogance, volatility, and cruelty.

In short, putty in the hands of one such as she.

Hakmayt itself impressed Meritities, who had witnessed hundreds of similar little fishing towns from the deck of a ship ferrying her and her papa past, on the way to some important destination or other. This place—it really was more of a town than a village—boasted straight, cobbled streets, well-maintained docks and homes, and most difficult to credit, smelled more of baking bread and ocean breezes than it did of rotting fish.

Astounding, really.

Tall sandstone walls surrounded Tahir Nav's estate, though disciplined and courteous servants saw her inside readily enough. Merities soon found herself in a well-appointed and airy room inside the manse, gazing out the open window while white cotton drapery blew back over her bed. It all felt very theatrical.

A polite knock came at the door. Nebet glided over and opened it, received something from a servant, and closed the door.

"They got an orven for you this morning, Princess." Nebet extended three yellow slips of paper to her. "Also, you're invited to dine with Tahir Nav. His meal's in an hour."

Merities slid the papers from Nebet's hand. That hand could crush a man's head. She watched it happen once, protecting her from a possible thief on the streets of Agran-ti.

Protecting *her*.

The orven messages, transcribed by Tahir Nav's orvenkeeper, bore the Imperial stamp at the top of each one. Merities only just left the Holy Palace two days ago. A thrill ran through her wondering what her uncle might have to say to her so soon. His happiness at her visit on the way to Mount P'takkin had been obvious, a fact the empress noticed as well.

Pulling the paper taught between her slender hands, she read:

Darling Niece,

The Imperial Throne has received word from our trusted personal guard and your brother, Djephan Oburn, that your wayward sister has been spotted traveling by ship up the Egren coast. As Hakmayt is the logical debarkation point on the way to Mount P'takkin, you are already perfectly positioned to capture Masika and bring her home.

Merities slipped the first paper behind and read the second.

Stay where you are, enlist whatever additional help you require from the Saraph Jais stationed in Hakmayt. Tahir Nav is a blowhard and an ass, but he remains yet a true citizen of Egren, and enjoys our trust. You may rely on him for your needs, and he is to deal with you as if dealing with the Imperial Seat itself.

She pulled the third and final piece of the message to the front. The Holy Emperor sent *three* orvens to carry his message. That's how important it was for him to talk to her.

Thank you for the unexpected and delightful gift. I find myself entirely taken with it, much to the consternation of the empress. My aches are diminished, and my joy is abundant. (So fuck her.) I believe it may soon be time for a change in court, and I find myself eager to see your face here more permanently.

Your uncle, the Holy Emperor Khasek V

No expression reflected in Nebet's face to Meritities's loony smile, nor in the way she bonelessly drifted about the room. She needed a bath and a change of clothes, but the reason why fled her mind. Something to do with the merchant whose house she stood in.

Oh. Right.

Masika. Very soon Meritities would have her foolish sister in hand, the monster gods would be dead, and Meritities would be rewarded with the highest position of power in the world.

She rang for a maid.

AS IN THE rest of the manse, the dining hall's high ceilings drifted airily above its inhabitants, encouraging cool breezes and cosseting the calls of gulls from the nearby shoreline. Shadows grew in the higher reaches while Allz the Shining's place on the Iron Wheel dipped below the horizon.

Thus far the meal had passed with only the barest minimum of polite conversation. While telling in its own right, Meritities intended to provoke a more rounded response. "I have spent too long in the wilds, Tahir Nav. Your chef is a revelation."

The noble merchant's brow rose. "My chef would be excellent no matter where you most recently hailed from, *Princess*. I have him as a personal gift from the empress herself."

Tahir Nav's nasal drawl leaked irritation across the lengthy, white-linened table. He sat at one end, while Meritities, Nebet standing against the wall behind her, sat in the midst of the table's length, a choice intended to show disrespect. A pair of house guards stood at attention behind him, trying unsuccessfully not to appear intimidated by the hulking Nebet.

No one else sat at the table at all.

"Keep a firm hold on him, Merchant." Mer.ities allowed the rumble of a purr to enter her voice, as if she were being playful and unaware of the insult she toyed with. "I can see myself stealing him away from you."

Rather than increasing his ire, the comment calmed Tahir Nav, even bringing a nasty smile to his overly generous lips. "Heh. No. I don't think that you will."

The man thought he knew something Meritities did not. Time to find out what that might be.

"Even the best servants will only follow a falling star so far." She batted her eyelashes winningly. Tahir Nav's appetite for young women was well known. "What if fortunes at court changed? Don't you think you'd be best served giving an up and coming niece of the imperial family anything she wanted?"

"In other times." Tahir Nav set his spoon beside his untouched cold melon soup. "But immodest young women are always more apt to find the back of a man's hand than be rewarded for pridefulness."

There it was.

Not only did he display no fear of Meritities and her station, he also showed her open contempt. That meant he felt the protection of the empress, which in turn meant the empress knew whatever it was he planned to do here.

So what was he planning?

"So tense." Meritities followed suit, placing her spoon beside her bowl. A shame. She loved the chilled dessert soup. "There's nothing for you to be worried about. Do as I say and you support not only me, but your Holy Emperor as well. I will collect my criminals and return to the capital for my reward." She smiled at him. "Which, should I decide it does, might very well include your cook."

The black beard bristled around Tahir Nav's rounded face. "I'd see him dead first." He ground out the words as if they were cut stone. "Not that it'll be necessary. I have been instructed to give you the empress's warning about overreaching your station, and a threat about what such things will mean to you and your family. But I've just decided that when I delivered her words to you, you displayed such scorn for the empire and its rulers that I had no choice but to have you executed immediately for treason."

He returned Merities's smile, laced with venom.

"Sure you don't want to finish your soup first?" he asked.

At the question, four more house guards ran in from the double doors opposite Merities, loaded flatbows in their hands.

Before the first guard let fly, Nebet sprang from the wall and yanked Merities over backward. He caught her chair with her head barely an inch from the floor. At the same time, he flipped the long table forward onto its side and ducked.

Bolts thunked into the table, razored heads protruding from underside.

Without waiting, Nebet dropped Merities the final inch to the floor and leaped over the table.

"Ow."

Screams and crashes followed from the other side of the table. On her back and amused, Merities turned to see Tahir Nav, face as pale as his linens, as he sat and watched the carnage she could not see. A clammy sweat broke out on his face and neck, and he flinched from a sudden cracking noise and the piteous howl of a guard.

The two men behind him shook off their shock and ran out of sight, spears raised. A spray of blood flew back the way they'd come and slapped Tahir Nav in the face.

Merities grinned at the noble merchant. "You should tell me now if your cook has any other specialties he's particularly good at making." A wash of disemboweled house guard floated through the air, challenging the high ceilings. "Before it's too late, that is."

Both Merities and Tahir Nav realized that he still sat with his knife in his hand at the same time. She struggled to roll out of the chair while he bellowed his indignation and charged for her, the weapon held above his head.

She rose into a crouch, knowing she could not get up and out of his way before that knife fell.

And then Tahir Nav lifted from the ground, a surprised *yarp* on his lips. He stabbed at Nebet's arm, but he may as well have been attacking an oak tree with a spoon. The blade poked into Nebet's massive forearm just before the bodyguard's other fist crunched into Tahir Nav's soft face. Still holding a short sword, Nebet's return swing plunged into the throat of a house guard trying to sneak up behind him with a broken spear haft.

The body hit the floor, and the room fell silent.

Nebet raised an eyebrow and shook Tahir Nav's unconscious form.

"I believe the noble merchant Tahir Nav displayed such scorn for the empire and its rulers that I had no choice but to have him executed immediately for treason." Meritities watched Nebet chop at Tahir Nav's neck one-handed and decided she could not possibly reveal to the man's chef—now *her* chef—that no one had eaten his melon soup. That would not be the way to begin a promising new relationship.

A NAPKIN HANGING FROM A WINDOWSILL, held in place by a crystal wine glass, was all the communication necessary to bring Meritities's squad of two-dozen Saraph Jais from the *Silver Spray* to Tahir Nav's estate. She called the staff and the bulk of the house guard together and explained to them that Tahir Nav's traitorous behavior finally caught up with him, and that for the brief future, she held sway over the house.

As Meritities expected, no one mourned Tahir Nav's passing, though a few quailed when told of the deaths of the house guards in the dining room. Surrounded by Saraph Jais and facing a blood relative of the Holy Emperor, they quickly recovered themselves.

The estate came with a tidy little town and a prestigious title. Whom would she give it to once her own fortunes were settled?

"Come, Nebet." Meritities cast a beatific smile across her new staff. A cool wind blew in through the open roof of the estate courtyard, bringing salt and ocean mist with it. "I would like to look over the gardens. I hear they are spectacular."

Tahir Nav's gardens impressed Meritities and made no appreciable impact on her bodyguard. Trees, bushes, and a bewildering array of flowering plants festooned the walled grounds behind the house. Their perfumes competed fiercely with their bright beauty to quite take her breath away.

A tall-backed chair with swooping arms rested beside a small round table on a clipped expanse of lawn. Just in front of the chair, water cascaded from a ten-foot drop into a pool where red and silver-backed fish swirled and cavorted.

None of this seemed Tahir Nav's personality to Meritities. Whose was it? She knew his wife died a dozen years ago, perhaps living in her mausoleum contributed to his disposition? Had Tahir Nav been boning the empress? Is *that* what happened to his wife? Killed to clear the way for an imperial mistress?

Meritities added the idea to her list of the man's posthumous crimes. If true, the emperor likely already knew and had no issue with the arrangement. But whether he knew or not, as soon as rumors of the affair began to circulate, drastic action would follow.

Everything was falling into Meritities's lap.

Except this one. She knew for a fact that her brother Djephan's warning to the emperor concerning Masika's whereabouts was a lie. While word traveling to Djephan first and *then* to the emperor sounded unusual, it was certainly possible. Especially if it came from a private acquaintance and not a military source.

No, what set off bells in Meritities's head was Djephan himself. The big, competitive oaf loved Masika. They played against one another since Masika was old enough to stand, and both of them valued that relationship more than even they likely knew. Masika asked Meritities for her silence, and she would have asked him too.

And Djephan would have given it to her.

The very fact that Djephan claimed Masika traveled by sea meant, for a certainty to Meritities's thinking, that her younger sister came by land, likely as close to the western range of the Little Gods as she could. That was a fair distance from here, but it also meant that Meritities was in the lead.

Her papa's unwelcome voice chose that exact moment to enter Merities's head. "Masika is more like you than you realize, Meri," he had said. "All your fighting holds you back. Look at everything you have accomplished and imagine how much greater your successes might be if you not only stopped wasting energy fighting with one another but took the time to actually help. I have never met any two people in the empire as strong-willed and driven as the pair of you. Together you would be unstoppable. And you would be *family*."

Family. Was Masika truly that to her? Was family meant to be an eternal obstacle to overcome again and again? A stone in your path that only grew as it learned your habits and strengths?

Yes. That was how Masika made Meritities stronger and why Meritities would never allow her sister to be killed.

She owed her so much.

The emperor ordered her to stay in Hakmayt, but he would forgive her disobedience when she returned with Masika and the corpses of the two Alir. And once Meritities whispered the right words about the empress in the right ears, he would do more than forgive.

All in her lap.

"Nebet, did you happen to see the livery? We need to see how many wagons our dear Tahir Nav has at the ready. We have a lot of soldiers to transport."

CHAPTER

THIRTY-TWO

When Allz the Shining sent his monstrous son, Shaitun, to direct Verran against Egren and teach foul majiks to their generals, Hamara stepped in to lead Egren's armies in battle.

Shaitun and his forces traversed the length of the Bond of Empire, the wide pass carved into the Little Gods that leads between Egren and Verran, freely. But Hamara treated with the P'tak to place hooks into the wounds of Allz the Shining as he rode across the sky on the Iron Wheel, causing his burning soul to beat down upon the Verranese army with blazing intensity. When Shaitun and his forces reached Egren, they set upon the first town they saw for water and food.

But Hamara had poisoned water, grain, and beast, leaving the Verranese sickened and weak. Shaitun was thus no match for Hamara, daughter to the gods, and lost his head to Cutting Wind, her questionably named scimitar.

This battle, the culmination of the Great Darrish War, is also the source of the well-known Egren proclivity for passing gas when unwanted guests come to call.

Volume Two of *Thank Gods* by Kohmose Oburn

Beside Masika, Rainn peered north, trying to make out the contingent of Saraph Jais between them and Mount P'takkin. "How many you see?"

"A hundred at least." Masika peered north and south along the mountain's base. "But they only appear to be stationed between those foothills. There's nothing immediately north or south. What d'you think that means?"

"Do they know which way we're coming from?" Ameli's question, asked in her girlish voice, sent a shiver through Masika's belly. "Shouldn't these guys be way south of here? Between the mountain and the ocean where they thought we were coming from?"

"They are likely there as well." With the end of his scarf, Uncle Mahu wiped the dust from his face. "There is no reason not to have a dozen such contingents around the mountain."

The five of them wore the sand and red uniforms of the Saraph Jais now, but Masika had no illusions that their disguises would hold up once they came against the real thing. "That's not very reassuring."

"It was not intended to be," Uncle Mahu answered.

"This is a problem," Ameli said. "There's no way I can turn us all into birds yet. I can barely hold Masika for a full five minutes, and she's little."

"Meritities is not foolish," Sabni said with a shrug. "She knows your original plan was to sail to Mukahiit and assay the peak from there. You might have found another ship once you escaped her camp, which we did not do, or you might have traveled north along the mountains, which we did. Our only advantage was Djephan's willing-ness to lie for us."

Not reassuring. Djephan's honesty notwithstanding, Meritities rarely believed anyone completely.

"We haven't exactly been quiet about it either, honey," Ameli said. "Any number of people might have told on us, without even meaning to."

Sour faced, Rainn hooded his eyes with one hand and stared into a crystal blue sky. "We could always wait for bad weather. I could kill a hundred men in a good storm, no problem."

Horrified expressions fell across Masika, Sabni, and Uncle Mahu, while Ameli looked contemplative.

"*Rainn.*" Masika's hiss startled him. "Those are my people. They believe they are there for the good of all Darrish. They don't deserve to die for that. Shame on you."

"Sorry." He lowered his head. "It's just this shitty weather. Got me all crabby."

Ameli touched Masika softly on the shoulder. "You said they're between the foothills?"

"Yes." Masika looked as far as she could see to either side. "There's no one else in sight. And that's a long way."

A bright smile appeared on Sabni's face.

"No." Uncle Mahu glared at Sabni and shook his head. "I told you already that is unwise. The monks may not be well armed, but we do not know how many live there."

"The monks need never see us, and they have no contact with anyone below regardless." As he spoke, Sabni bounced his lanky form from side to side. "We would be the first to see the Holy Kanista and return."

"What's a holy cannister?" Rainn asked.

"It's a temple partway up the mountain." Masika sat on the grass as she answered. "Only the holiest of monks live there, and they have to renounce every bit of the world that exists below them, which is pretty much everything but the House of the Gods." And how would they react to invaders from below in their sacred home?

"The Holy Kanista is at least a quarter of the way up." With every passing second, Sabni's shining grin grew. "That could be enough for young Ameli's spells to carry us the remainder of the way."

"Ugh," Ameli answered. "After all our practice, we haven't had that much luck. Or did you forget when you thought Rainn here had broken his neck in his last fall?"

"*And,*" Sabni continued as if Ameli had not spoken, "there is said to be a narrow stair hidden in the north side of the mountain, well away from those Saraph Jais who are so politely waiting for us. No need to harm anyone."

"Really?" Masika had never heard that. This could change everything.

"Indeed. This may surprise you, but there was a time when I wished to become one of the Holy Kanista monks." Sabni sat next to Masika. "I learned everything I could about them from the library in the Veiled Breath."

"I do not believe that surprises anyone," Uncle Mahu offered. "You have been a priest for the past three years."

"I'm not surprised," Rainn agreed.

"Nope," Ameli said.

"*Squawk.*"

Masika put a hand on Sabni's forearm. "It's very sweet though."

ONCE NIGHT FELL, traveling past the foothills out of the Saraph Jais's field of vision proved embarrassingly simple. Inlittan's sight showed no one waiting ahead to the north, and even found the stair up the mountain with ease.

If you could call it that.

"I do not care for this."

While Masika sympathized with her uncle's complaint, she also did not know what to do about it. The "stair" was in truth a series of uncut stones that jutted from the mountain at intervals just close enough to climb, at widths anywhere between three feet and six inches. Invisible to the unaugmented eye from below, it required endurance, will, and more than a little faith to traverse. Small wonder the Holy Kanista monks utilized it as a test of worthiness for their supplicants.

Sabni was in heaven.

"Mother Love has never blessed any of her children as much as she blesses us today. I feel like the scorpion who helps the farmer rebuild his home and is gifted with one of his own. Thank you, Featherwind, for gifting *me* with this experience."

Though she wanted to respond, Masika required all her attention at that moment to prevent herself from falling off the mountain.

"Should we survive," Uncle Mahu responded in Masika's stead, "I shall feel grateful. For now, I merely feel imperiled."

Bringing up the rear, Rainn snorted. "I can't believe what babies alla you are. It's a mountain, not a sunny day. And look." He pointed up toward the mountain's peak. "Clouds. Been there the whole time. I'm feeling better with every step."

"Can we please shut the fuck up so I can climb and fall and die in peace?" White-faced, Ameli clung to the rock wall at her back, her terror apparent. "At least if I go splat, my mom'll be pissed she didn't get to kill me. That's a relief."

Masika hoped she would get to ask Ameli about the story behind that, but for now, more important concerns arose. "Hey, Ameli's right guys. Shut up. I see the temple. We're almost there."

In silence, they gained the last hundred steps to the Holy Kanista.

They need not have bothered.

"You gotta be shitting me." At the end of the climb, Rainn's head finally rose above the wide expanse of the Holy Kanista where Masika and the rest already stood, surrounded by two dozen Saraph Jais, the enormous, one-eared Nebet, and his singular charge, Princess Meritities.

"Hi, Meri." Masika forced a smile, though she doubted its persuasiveness. "Hope you weren't waiting long."

"Not too long. How was your trip?" Slapping dust from her thighs, Meritities gave Masika her full attention, a thing she rarely did. "You are quite the heretic, coming here. It was no great leap to assume you would defy the sanctity of this place in your vain quest."

"Such a shame you beat me to that." Masika stood straight and unbowed. "The defying thing, I mean."

How did Meritities still manage to look so poised, so perfect? She wore baggy yellow pants and a red shirt, both coated with dust from her own trek up the mountain, yet she held herself as if she commanded the Holy Emperor's court. "Yes, well the monks aren't all that accommodating to visitors, no matter your blood. We had to promise them we wouldn't tarry."

A wave of exhaustion overcame Masika. She was so tired of this relationship with her sister. Merities was so beautiful, and so loved by the emperor, why was it so important to her to hold Masika back at every turn? She sighed.

Behind Merities and her soldiers, a series of tower and monastic façades glowered, carved by long labor into the cliff. Within, the face of the occasional monk glowered out as well, unhappy at the intrusion yet obviously unwilling to step out against Merities's Saraph Jais.

"I assume we'll be heading back down the mountain now?"

Merities smiled. It was a face that melted hearts and bent minds to her will. Even Masika wanted to believe it was genuine, though she knew better.

"We can't be rude to our hosts. Hand over your weapons and we'll be on our way."

"Meri." Masika forced the words out. "Do we have to do this? Papa would be so disappointed in us. Can't we find a way out of this that gives everyone what they want?"

"And just what is it that you think I want?" Merities asked, a plaintive edge to her voice. "How do you propose to bring monsters home to our very gods and not ruin our family? Not ruin me?"

The question surprised Masika in its earnestness. If she could come up with a good enough answer, could she end this struggle right here?

"Maybe." Masika considered it. "Explain to me how returning the Alir to their own home ruins our family. If I understood your reasoning better, I'm sure the two of us could figure a way out of this mess."

"There are no ways out." Merities's smile pasted over obvious hurt. "Papa was right. We really *are* too much alike. Neither of us can ever set aside what we believe is right, and neither of us can ever be happy living in a world made by the other. So, the only important question is whether we value our own family more," she paused and glanced to Rainn and Heron, "or someone else's."

Masika's throat clenched, clamping back an angry reply. What had Papa said about this? *Meritities is family, and that is more important than any disagreement.* And there was more. *Whether it is ever returned or not, you will make yourself far more miserable than you ever will her by hating her. Love for others is a gift you give to yourself.*

A sob threatened to break free.

If you can find love for a sister who cuts at your heart, you will find that heart has become invulnerable to her attacks. Hurts might then go unanswered, and arguments may be forgotten. Eventually you may even find yourself friends.

Friends.

As much as Masika might desire it, she knew she and Meritities would never be friends, and at long last she understood why. Though they wanted dramatically different things, they wanted them exactly the same way. In that they *were* too much alike.

"Your silence answers my question louder than all your lies, Masika."

But where they diverged was in Meri's embrace of tradition and ambition that Masika simply never could. Not only was it not in her to value those things, it was against all she did believe in. No rule was more valuable than happiness and freedom. The two of them would never find peace.

Papa was wrong.

"Princess." Nebet leaned down to speak to his mistress.

"Yes? Have I forgotten something?"

"You promised I could kill the god before we left."

Meritities's eyes widened, and she turned to her huge bodyguard. "So I did. I'm sorry, Nebet. Of course you can. Pitch him over the side when you're done so we don't have to carry him down." She backed between the Saraph Jais to watch from a safer distance.

Tiny patch of cloud at the mountain's summit notwithstanding, the sky rang as clear as a bell. Rainn's strength equaled little more than any man's, and Uncle Mahu and Sabni would be hampered by their unwillingness to seriously hurt anyone. Meritities had over twenty trained soldiers, plus the murderous, dangerous Nebet.

Masika looked at the hilt of her slender desert sword. That could not be the answer.

"*Please* come and try it." Forbryttan hissed out of its sheath, and Rainn lowered himself into a combat ready pose.

Out of options at last. As much as it galled her, Masika had to admit Meritities had outmaneuvered her again. But perhaps she could at least negotiate for Rainn and Heron's lives. That must be worth something.

"Meri?"

At once, Uncle Mahu and Sabni pulled their shields from their backs and dived forward into Nebet and the soldiers, who, too late, tried to raise their spears.

"Ameli, now!" Uncle Mahu shouted.

And Masika's world once again exploded into color.

From below, she heard Sabni's bellowing laughter and Nebet's enraged shout. From above, Heron's triumphant squawk. Masika looked back to see Rainn, now a large crow with drooping feathers of iridescent blue and green, and farther down the Saraph Jais struggling with her uncle and Sabni. Ameli lay on her back on the stone and waved, while Meritities screamed her frustration.

Sympathy for her sister rose in Masika's tiny breast, though whizzing arrows lent vigor to her wings. Masika understood the pain behind that wail.

Uncle Mahu was the brother to Masika's mother, and Sabni was his partner and battlemate, and both were once Veiled Breath. Meritities likely would not even bother bringing them back to the capital. Hopefully that protection would extend to Ameli as well. There was little Masika could do about it now either way.

Higher in the whirling sky, Heron pumped her beautiful multicolored wings toward the cool clouds at the top of Mount P'takkin, within which lay the House of the Gods.

CHAPTER

THIRTY-THREE

The House of the Gods sits atop Mount P'takkin and is the residence of all one hundred and four members of the P'tak family. Refuge and reward, no more sacred place exists anywhere on the continent of Andos.

Constructed by Sahar-ka, firstborn son of Mother Love, the house is said to be a place of incredible beauty and unspeakable grace, as befits the home of the gods. Any mortal setting foot there would be instantly blasted from existence, erased in full from all of creation. In theory. It has certainly never happened before.

Narratively the House of the Gods serves as the ending to many tales of the P'tak, as they either return or are carried home after any number of trials and adventures. It is thus considered bad luck to try and spot it upon the mountain crest for fear the mere sight of the divine home should bring the end of the viewer's tale as well. Much safer that we simple humans keep our eyes on our own ground and seas and books.

Who needs that kind of trouble?

Volume Two of *Thank Gods* by Kohmose Oburn

Masika flew through the damp cloud, the chill drawing beads of moisture to the surfaces of her small wings that pulled against her efforts. She flew truly blind through the rainbow shafted mist; even Inlittan's sight was defeated by the protective fog of the P'tak.

Although wind buffeted her and pushed in random directions, it also brought her the sounds of Heron and Rainn, who croaked and squawked around her, and she joined in with a string of chirps to keep them all together.

But her true worry was for Ameli.

How long could the sorceress hold them aloft? This was already longer than Ameli had been able to keep Masika alone in the form of a bird, and now she must be straining to do the same for both Masika and Rainn. The idea that she flew straight to her death battered at her, just as the unpredictable winds battered her wings and stole her strength.

She flew and she climbed and she struggled against the wind and the wet. Searing pain replaced the chill in her shoulders. She had managed so little practice with this, and there was no opportunity to rest now.

Chirps turned to cries of pain. She could not lift her wings one more time.

And then she was through.

Just above her a wall of perfectly fitted stone blocks rose a hundred feet into the sky, parapets of brown towers the same color as the mountain just visible over its lip. But she knew she would never crest it. Though physically exhausted, the confrontation with Meritities truly sapped her will. They could never be family. They could never have peace.

Papa would be so disappointed.

She had nothing left. Masika folded her tired wings and fell back into the clouds.

The mist glittered in sharp jewel tones; refracted sunlight cast through a million-million shining droplets. Masika considered as she plummeted that many of the colors she watched were not colors she could name, so different was the eyesight of a bird. Brilliant. Beautiful.

This was not the worst way to die.

Clawed feet, cold, leathery, and strong, caught Masika and arrested her fall. Once again, she lifted up and up through the glowing clouds.

Disappointment evaporated. A strange thrill ran through Masika's tiny body. They were going to make it, not because Masika was here to save her friends, but because they were here to save her. Happy warmth filled her feathered chest.

They cared. Heron and Rainn had her. They would not let her fall.

Spontaneously, Masika sang.

She broke into the sunlight, a vault of liquid blue and lavender above her, the wall of square cut stone set into the mountain to one side, and the broad multicolored wings of Heron beating powerfully toward heaven.

Please let us not be too late to save you, Heron. Please do not be caught in the shape of a bird forever. If nothing else, she wished this for Heron, even if the rest of it were for naught.

It occurred to Masika that she would turn back into a human one way or the other, as soon as Ameli grew too exhausted to maintain the spell any longer. She also hoped *that* might not happen until they all landed on the other side of that wall.

Heron topped the wall and dove for a shimmering crystal lawn, much too fast for Masika's comfort. She squirmed in the goddess's grip, but to no avail.

They landed beside Rainn, prostrate on the flat grassy courtyard, his drooping feathers spread out around him as if splattered that way on impact.

Musical chirps erupted from Masika's breast in a warbling torrent as she tried to thank Heron and check on Rainn at the same time. Separating concepts in her mind exhausted her further. All her thoughts slipped sideways when she clutched at them, somehow both fuzzy and slick at the same time.

The goddess cocked her head to one side, and Rainn let out an irritated caw.

"We made it!" Masika felt her suddenly human face with her suddenly human hands. "Ameli did it. She really did it. I thought we were all going to die, but she actually got us up here in one piece. She's an amazing sorceress."

"Hang on." Rainn rolled over, sat up in the faded grass, and rubbed his shoulders. "That whole time you thought we were gonna die and you let her do that to us anyway?"

"Don't be crabby, Sir God. You were obviously in good hands. And it wasn't my decision anyway. I thought it was all over. I was trying to come up with a way to talk Meri out of killing you."

Masika grinned and flopped back on the grass. "I was only saying look how much better Ameli did than she ever has before. She held that spell for both of us three times as long as she ever did for either one of us alone. Isn't that incredible?"

Not answering, Rainn shook his head and stood. He rolled his shoulders and grunted. His gaze dropped briefly to his hip. "This fucking sword won't shut up. I'm beginning to wonder if it's worth it to carry the damnable thing around."

"What's it saying?" Unable to hear Forbryttan herself, she typically forgot that it could speak into Rainn's mind.

"Mostly it wants me to run around and look at stuff. It's like a baby that's never seen a damn thing. Makes sense, I suppose." He glanced around him. "I gotta say I was expecting a little—more?"

"Huh." The thought struck Masika as sacrilegious, but she agreed. Astounding architecture stretched into the sky, stone fit perfectly into stone, but the whole of it lay drab and lifeless, any color or spark faded away into the years. The rectangular courtyard, much longer than it was wide, sat occluded from Allz's shining light, its last breath long past. Dry, stiff grass poked at her, and she too pushed herself to her feet.

One of the short ends of the yard contained a series of brownish towers, while a single gigantic building stretched across the long side opposite the outer wall, its stone doors shut tight. The furthest end, narrower than the one with the towers, terminated in a palace made of swirling walls and twisting steeples. It struck Masika as reminiscent of the grand palace of Oulan in Agran-ti, with its lack of any straight angles and its beautiful gardens.

Except there was no beauty here, only dry stasis.

"Should we knock on a door?" Everything here looked like solid stone, heavy and inviolate. Although Masika doubted her ability to create an audible sound with her human knuckles against the dead rock, she also lacked a better idea.

Hang on.

Inlittan sprang to life in her vision, and she stared at her surroundings. But either there was nothing to see, or she looked for the wrong thing. No way out of the courtyard presented itself.

"Whoops." Masika spun and caught the small silver table she hit with her hip as she turned, carefully righting it before any of its contents could fall to the grass. "Where did you come from?"

With a squawk and a flutter, Heron beat her way back into the air.

Forbryttan in hand, Rainn spun and searched for invisible attackers. "Who put that there? I'm not in the mood for getting fucked with here." He swung the heavy blade experimentally, in case any unseen bodies carrying additional silver furniture happened by.

"I don't think we're in much danger from the table." She scrutinized the curling silver strands that made it, as if formed of a tiny whirlwind frozen in metal. "It's not very big."

"What's that on it?" Rainn lowered his sword, but his body stayed tense. "I'm not drinking that. It's probably poison."

From the top of the outer wall, Heron added her own disapproving squawk.

Two stoppered crystal vials and a deep crystal bowl held blue-tinted water on the table, glinting in the shadowed light. Inlittan revealed nothing about the contents one way or the other, but Masika had not traveled across the whole of the Thirteen Kingdoms to be stymied by a sip of water.

"Suit yourself, but you're going to feel silly when it's god-water that grants wishes and you missed your chance." Masika picked up a vial, plucked out the crystal stopper and drank. The liquid ran cool and slightly sweet down her throat, and invigorated her muscles, burning through her tiredness and leaving her springy and refreshed.

"Wow. That's better." Her eyes went wide, and her mouth opened in a silent O. "Denari clear the fog. It's . . . Rainn, drink it."

Rainn reached over and removed the second vial from the tabletop. He frowned at it, pulled the stopper, and slugged it down. A slow grin stole across his face. "C'mon, Heron. I think the bowl's for you."

As Heron fluttered down and sipped suspiciously from the small bowl, Masika stared in amazement at the grandeur surrounding her. Every drab surface now glittered in eye wateringly beautiful colors, and every stone block shone, shot through with blue-green glass and gold, swirled into impossibly intricate patterns.

Entirely unidentifiable scents of warmth and joy, somehow combining hearths and hugs and chocolate, but so very much deeper, as if she smelled them with her very soul.

And the music! The thrilling ecstasy of the notes surrounded her, lifted her, and threatened to carry her bodily away. Masika's cheeks ached with the strain of her smile, though she found herself unable to banish it. Nor did she want to.

"The goddess Denari will see you now."

An unassuming young man in a simple white tunic with blue trim spoke, his voice even and unthreatening. Rainn just smiled, and even Heron failed to react any more than a small churring sound.

"As you know," the young man went on, "Denari is gifted by Mother Love to see straight into the heart of any matter." He eyed Rainn. "Any matter at all. It is important that you not lie. It is not unheard of for a human to make it this far, though none have survived to return to the mortal world. Hosting an Alir, much less two, is fairly novel ground." He took a few steps and cast a glance back over his shoulder.

"Well come along. This is what you are here for."

They caught up with the—was he a servant?—young man, and he led them across the fiercely green courtyard toward the palace at the far end, now full of life, color, and motion. Butterflies the colors of rubies, emeralds, and sapphires flashed in the blue above towers that twisted slowly against the sky. A tall arched doorway opened for them as they approached.

Within, the grand surroundings took on a cozier feel, more a home than a palace, though Masika turned her head from the simplest of fixtures and decorations lest they overwhelm her with feeling.

Heron lit on Masika's shoulder and murmured in her ear. Though unintelligible, the soft sounds helped to settle Masika's racing emotions.

Still a goddess. Not a bird.

They continued up a grand stair that curved into a wide landing, set with a pair of stools and a wooden perch, all facing a tall chair in front of a wall sized stained-glass window that stretched deeply into the distance of the universe. Stars glowed in its overwhelming patterns, and Masika felt as if she looked at every story creation had ever known.

Lowering her gaze, Masika inadvertently caught the eye of the unbearably beautiful woman in the chair, and gasped.

"Thank you, Yeedi. Return to your painting if you wish. I will call if I require your services."

"Denari Clear Eyed." Masika dropped to one knee and stared at the floor. And the unassuming young man had been Yeedi, steward to the House of the Gods and paramour of Denari.

"Rise, Masika Oburn, daughter to Tennat Oburn, Sarach of the Divine Grainlands and niece to the Holy Emperor of Egren. You have already desecrated our home with the barbaric feet of the Alir. There seems little sense in standing on formality now."

"I, um . . ." For once, Masika found nothing to say. Were she standing on the floor, Denari would have reached at least ten feet. Seated in her towering chair with its white stone stairs, she was twelve. Masika didn't notice what the goddess wore, so entranced was she by her mesmerizing eyes.

"Indeed," Denari said. "And you are?" She directed the question toward Rainn and Heron, though her tone indicated she knew full well the answer.

"I am Rainn of the Alir." He spoke with all the enthusiasm of a man reporting to his own execution. "I am the god of Doing Things Out of Doors in Poor Weather. And this is Heron, goddess of Catching Small Animals in Still or Slow-Moving Water."

"We're here for a boon." A small but loud voice in the back of Masika's mind shouted that if she did not state her intended purpose soon, it might easily become too late. How far could a goddess's patience for an unwanted mortal possibly stretch? "We're searching for a way into the Undergates, to retrieve a soul for a magical imp who has promised to return Rainn and Heron to the Alireon, where they belong. Will you help us?"

If Denari felt any irritation, it hid far from her perfect face. "The Alir and the P'tak are enemies, as the very nature of creation has eternally dictated. The wrongs done by the animalistic gods of the north are infinite in both number and consequence."

Masika's heart crumpled. As she stood here, in the very place she worked so hard to achieve, she saw her every hope crushed before her. There would be nothing to show for all her sacrifice, everything she had put her papa and her family through. Any relationship she held with Meritities was destroyed, Rainn would be cast from the mountain, and Heron would live as a bird forever. She had disappointed everyone.

Even herself.

"Oh, don't be a baby about it." Denari rolled eyes the color of a spring morning toward the vaulted ceiling. "Your father was not incorrect. Helping these two godlings would certainly be a thorn in the side of their 'High King' Oldam, and thus worth doing. I shall help you."

"Really?" Masika could barely believe her ears. After such a devastating blow, success sat in her hand, ready for her to simply accept it. This was a lesson. A lesson not to accept defeat, even at the hand of the mighty P'tak.

That sounded sacrilegious.

Denari ignored the question and raised an eyebrow toward Rainn. "Your blade is certainly chatty."

His glance flickered over Forbryttan's hilt. "You learn to ignore it."

"That magic doesn't belong to you, you know."

A storm cloud passed over Rainn's features. "Would you like to come over here and take it?"

The smile Denari shot at Rainn left Masika weak in the knees. "That won't be necessary. What were we talking about now? Oh yes. Me helping you, my invaders, to travel across the realms to the Undergates." That smile did not change, but it moved to Masika, who felt it as a sinister regard. "Your fears, Masika Oburn, are well founded. I do know why King Oldam refused these two passage home, and yes, I could simply address it now."

Again, Masika felt the floor of her stomach drop away. It somehow never occurred to her that the P'tak might simply send Rainn and Heron away, dooming her own quest for the imp. Treating with gods took more constitution than she expected. She steeled herself and prepared to defend her right to be here.

"But I won't." Was Denari smirking? "Taking the route you have planned will prove so much more entertaining. For me, anyway."

Despite the passive aggression, Masika could not help a small thrill of elation at the news. She would not have to travel to the Undergates alone. Denari played with her as a cat toyed with a string. In that regard she was little different than Meritities. Masika would not submit to such treatment as easily from a goddess as she had her own sister.

They had never been family.

"Do not mistake me, Masika Oburn. My aid is not kindness. I seek only the vexation of King Oldam, who will not take the return of these two with happiness or with grace. Not after having formally expelled them from the kingdom of the Alir."

"Then why would you tell us all this?" It made no sense to Masika. If they played on a board not of their own making, Denari's admission only invited some attempt to thwart the game. Why say any of it?

The laughter of Denari Clear-Eyed rang silver notes in the grand chamber. Behind her, the stained-glass universe shuddered in delight. "Because, my dear, despite my disclosure, and in spite of whatever consequences you know will be in store, you will not relent. You will continue blindly, in the vain hope that you may yet avert your fates.

Which I might add will not be pleasant. Oldam is a brutal tyrant of a king and will not accept the frustration of his desires."

This goddess must be wrong. Masika knew it in her soul. Just because no one knew the solution to obtaining High King Oldam's good graces yet, did not mean it could not be done.

And Masika would do it.

She tried not to think about the fact she was even now proving Denari right.

Denari's eyes narrowed, and her smile grew ever more ominous.

Fluttering from Masika's shoulder to the perch stand, Heron gave a low, sad call, and Rainn's brows knit together in anger.

"Even if you won't do anything about it, how does it fuck your fun to tell Heron and me why King Oldam won't let us go home?" Rainn's growl covered something else. Not anger, not even his typical tired depression.

He was just sad.

"Oh, it would not." Denari's delight at the question alarmed Masika. The goddess was not at all as she had expected.

"I would be happy to share. The Anger Under the Mountain has corrupted the two of you past all reason. You have been rendered into something much less than gods, and you no longer belong among them. Even with such peasant divinity as the Alir."

Angrim spent millennia deforming Rainn and Heron. The runes he carved into their flesh that reduced them to their current state went past their bones into their essences. Rainn told tales of Angrim removing limbs from them down in his dismal chambers, which regrew with runes intact. They could never be removed.

"So Angrim's work can't be unfucked?"

At Rainn's question Denari's ominous smile widened into a truly disturbing grin. The expression changed the beautiful goddess into an object of terror. "Of course it can. That corruption can absolutely be removed. In fact, both your problems, retrieving Glauth for the imp and cleansing yourselves have the selfsame answer."

"The Undergates?" Masika held her breath waiting for the answer.

"Yes."

"Then observe your promise and send us there." She tried to remember the stories of the hereafter her brother Kohmose told her. Would there be a grand galley full of skeletal oarsmen? Or perhaps some hole in the back of the mountain with a million steps leading down to the afterlife? "I'm ready to go. Now. How do we do it?"

"Well," Denari said, "it *is* the afterlife. All you have to do is die."

"Excuse me?" The continual whipsawing nature of this conversation left Masika dizzy. Denari's answer promised a distinct lack of flying skeletal galleys.

Squawk!

"This is fucking useless. I'm going back down and getting murdered by your idiot sister, Masika. At least she's got the balls to stab me straight to my face."

"The real trick of the Undergates will be the return trip." Denari tapped her chin with a gracefully tapered finger. "But I'm sure three individuals as resourceful as you will be able to find some aid on that score. After all, you managed to obtain my assistance to get you down there."

"Forget it." Rainn stepped forward, his hand on Forbryttan's grip. "None of this shit is happening. We'll take our chances with the mountain and the goddamn Saraph Jais once we fall to the bottom of it. You can kindly go fuck yourself. Goodbye."

"The Alir have no standing in my house to refuse my aid, godling." Denari, entirely at ease, leaned back in her chair and rested her chin against thumb and forefinger. "The decision was already made by the one devout Darrishwoman among you."

"What?" At every turn Masika felt left behind. Out of her depth. This was such a mistake. She needed to reassert control. How would she handle Meri in this situation? "I never made a decision. When did I make a decision?"

"Do not forget who you treat with, daughter of Tennat." At last, Denari displayed a hint of pique. "I see into your heart. I know what motivates you. The true reasons you arrived here. And the decision was made the instant you drank the blue poison I provided in the courtyard. The same draft that allowed you to see the House of the Gods as it truly is."

"I fucking *knew* it!" Rainn shouted—and dropped to the stone floor. "Ugh. I knew it."

"Keep your sword in your hand," Denari instructed Rainn. "I'd imagine you'll be needing it soon."

The world canted left, and Masika stumbled sideways. Heron already lay at the foot of her perch and beat one wing on the stones weakly.

Masika fell to her knees.

"Stay together," Denari said, her words penetrating the increasing fog in Masika's mind. "You are not people where you go now, you are currency. Make what allies you can."

A haze covered Masika's perceptions, blanketing all her senses.

"And good luck."

EPILOGUE

One problem inevitably arises for any scholar of religion, whether Darrish, Pavinn, or even Andosh. Gods fight, create, love, and destroy, and ultimately, we all find ourselves entirely at their mercy. It is the basic structure of the universe, unfair as it might be. All our struggles and goals are as irrelevant to the gods as the gathering of leaf snippets by an Arlean ant to a farmer in Coldspine.

So, what then, is the point? Why struggle against the turning of the world? Why make goals we might never reach? What drives humanity to reach so far above ourselves as to try and affect the destiny of the very cosmos? What are we, stupid?

I would suggest our existence as proof that it is the struggle, the goal itself that is important, rather than the attainment. Our stories are of a thousand unfulfilled labors for each that finds success, yet that is somehow enough. We lift each other by our potential, not our victories. We are an inspirational people, even in moments of the most venal greed and jealousy. Wanting what we cannot have is what makes us great. Which is probably a good thing, given that, yes, we are *pretty stupid.*

Volume Eight of *Thank Gods* by Kohmose Oburn

Denari Clear-Eyed, first daughter of Mother Love, sat in her tall chair and watched her guests die on her floor. They would need more than luck where they were headed, but who knew? The Darrish girl showed remarkable resilience in getting them this far, a feat that should have been all but impossible, so perhaps the odds were not so stacked against them as all that.

Curious, the perfect goddess stood and gazed into the Long Window behind her chair. She saw where the trio awoke, saw the forces arraying against them, and saw a darkness rising in that place to smash them and their goals.

No, she had been right the first time. They were fucked.

After another minute staring into the window, Denari turned her head to one side and spoke. "Was that more or less what you were after?"

"Yeah," came the reply. "I think that'll do it."

Denari faced her visitor. Tall for a human woman and broad shouldered like a man, the visitor shook loose her dark wavy hair and pulled out a worn leather sleeve. She wrapped it around the hair in a practiced series of motions and inserted a wooden pin to keep it all in place.

"Any chance that was enough for you to tell me where the twins are?"

"That's just god-stuff," the visitor said with a crooked half-smile. "Not really important enough for me to bother with. You keep swinging though. You're bound to hit something eventually."

"I sent the lightning to kill Sedja for . . . Ah. You're already gone."

The visitor faded from view and Denari sighed. Sarah the Hill Fury might be an improvement on the other cosmic forces the formerly human woman had clawed her way over to get where she was, but that did not make her any less of a pain in the ass.

ACKNOWLEDGMENTS

It's kinda funny, but as I go I find that rather than "standing on my own two feet" and becoming self-sufficient as a writer, the truth is that there are ever more people to thank for my success. These acknowledgements are to you, but they're for me. I love that I have a place to tell you thanks.

Always first is Lena. I can scarcely comprehend the lengths to which you go to be there for me in this grand, time-consuming project. It has become my life's work just to be worthy of your love and affection. You are amazing, and I am so much more than I'd ever have been without you.

Second are the Colbys, Kelly and Kevin, the owners of Cursed Dragon Ship Publishing. (Publications? I dunno.) Kelly found me, published me, pushed me, and created my career out of whole cloth. And just when I thought the stories of the Thirteen Kingdoms were done, she invited in five more embarrassingly talented authors to push out the corners of my world and create so much more from the small start I had.

And Kevin was there too. (Kidding aside, Kevin has been a constant presence of assistance and enthusiasm since the beginning. I see you, buddy, and I appreciate everything you bring to the table.)

I must also acknowledge those five aforementioned authors. Jen Bair, Jessica Raney, William Galaini, C.M. McGuire, and Ethan Cooper. (Listed in order of appearance.) These folks have done something I frankly never thought could possibly happen; they have volunteered to lend their incredible talents to Misplaced Adventures. I am flattered, humbled, and eternally grateful to you all. One book is hard, and you are each writing entire series for this world, which is now every bit as much yours as it is mine.

Well, as much as is spelled out by the contracts.

You have all taken your bolt of Misplaced cloth, twisted it around your fist, and run with it to places I'd never thought to go. Each of you makes that world not only bigger, but better. I will never have enough thanks.

In the end, and at the end, I would like to give my most important acknowledgement, that being to you, the person holding this very book in your hands. (Or Kindle in your feet. Or computer monitor on a string. You know, however you want to read it. You do you. I'm not gonna tell you how to live your life.) You are the person all of this is for, and you are the literal reason all of us do what we do. The writers, editors, artists, publishers, and printers. It's all for you, and you have our thanks.

So, like, thanks. What are you still doing reading this? This is the boring part. There's a whole world to read here. Go! Have fun!

ABOUT THE AUTHOR

Kevin Pettway hails from Jacksonville Florida and is the author of the Misplaced Mercenaries books, a funny adult fantasy series that was awarded by the NYC Big Book Club, a finalist in the 2022 Imadjinn Awards, and has received several professional write-ups in Kirkus Magazine for which the author did not even have to pay. He has published a modest number of short stories, both within and without the Mercenaries world, with more on the way. Most excitingly, Kevin's publisher, Cursed Dragon Ship Publishing, has threatened encouraged him to open his world to other authors, creating the Misplaced Adventures Shared Universe. There are currently six authors toiling away to bring even more humor, fun, and backstabbing murder into the world, with plans to add even more in the next few years.

Although the old stereotype about writers just wanting to be locked away in a darkened room with a typewriter is as true of Kevin as it is anyone else, the other thing he enjoys tremendously is going to conventions and meeting new people. (In writing, two opposing motivations in the same person are often used to create tension and conflict and engage reader interest. Now that you know his conflicting motivations you understand just how deep and fascinating Kevin is!)

He regularly attends a large number of popular culture conventions, selling books and telling stories to people who haven't heard them before while his wife Lena tries to ignore him. Feel free to walk up and say hi. Nothing makes him happier. (You might also express condolences to Lena, who has heard all the stories.)

River and Book, Kevin and Lena's two dogs, also love meeting people, but hotels rarely love meeting dogs, so they stay behind at the puppy resort. Canine fan-mail will be accepted and forwarded to the appropriate addressee.

Kevin thinks Strange New Worlds is the best Trek series, nudging The Orville off that top spot, and is enjoying the Tolkeinesque comedy The Rings of Power more than he thought he would. His favorite new author is Tamsyn Muir, and his favorite old author is Roger Zelazny. (He may be dead, but he's still selling!) He is also developing an obsession for kayaking, having discovered it late in life and is unable to get enough.

Despite being from Florida, Kevin still has all his own teeth and has never had a restraining order placed against him.

Make sure to join Kevin's newsletter from his website: https://kevinpettway.com.

CHECK OUT THE ANTHOLOGY FEATURING CHARACTERS FROM EACH MA SERIES

A card cursed with self-awareness seeks a hero to retrieve his creator from the afterlife. Nothing could possibly go wrong.

CHECK OUT THE SERIES THAT STARTED IT ALL

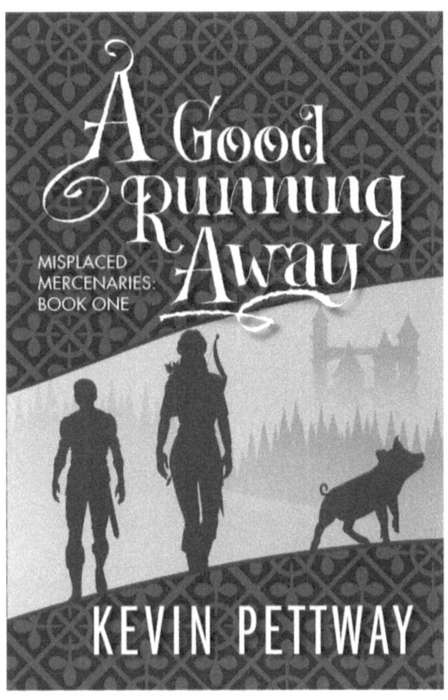

Stealing the cash box of your mercenary unit as you run away probably isn't wise, but it sure is funny.

JOIN THE CURSED DRAGON SHIP NEWSLETTER

Love what you just read? Want more just like it? Sign up for our newsletter so you don't miss out on the adventure. You'll get:

- A free book for signing up
- Advanced notice of new releases
- First word of books on sale
- Opportunities for free books
- Most up-to-date information on author appearances.

We're busy and know you are too. We won't send more than one newsletter a month.

Register below.